ex chattered lightheartedly as she and her friends
ched the dressing rooms once the show was finished.
us to get on a plane back to LA, she pushed through the
models gathered around the doorway and made her way
her dressing table.

alting just steps away from her reserved station, Alex
d in horror at the vandalism awaiting her arrival. The
hat had once held the beautiful arrangement of yellow
vas now on its side. The sound of water spilling onto the
ent a chill down her spine. The roses had been crushed
ewn everywhere. A saturated note lay across the entire
e.

*ou're next."

Oh, my God!" Star shrieked, clutching Alex's arm.

he brilliance of the light in the room seemed to sudden-
. "No!"

er scream was full of terror. She didn't realize it had
rom her own throat until Desi protectively collected her
er arms.

# Indigo Love Storie

An imprint Genesis Press Publishing

Genesis Press, Inc.
315 Third Avenue North
Columbus, MS 39701

ISBN: 1-58571-097-0
Manufactured in the United States of America

First Edition

Visit us at www.genesis-press.com
or call at 1-888-Indigo-1

# Fragment In The Sand

By
Annetta P. Lee

# Genesis Press, Inc.

*To Stephanie Salyer, who sacrificed time and concentration in the middle of her own turbulent storms to assist me in finishing this project.*

*To Larry Gleason with the Oklahoma City Police Department, who was very obliging in giving insightful guidelines helpful in creating procedural methods.*

*And to my husband, Kenneth, whose gentle support has been my main source of encouragement.*

# FRAGMENT IN THE SAND

## Prologue

### October 1980

Little Alex jolted up in bed and sluggishly rubbed her eyes. Her pink flannel gown was so twisted from all the tossing she had done in her sleep that she could hardly move. The storm was much louder than usual, she thought, groggily. Maybe Daddy and Zeke had come back from their camping trip already.

She anxiously patted around the empty place beside her in bed in search of her doll. She'd gotten it last month for her sixth birthday. Once she had the rag doll in her hands, she clutched it to her lovingly and drew the covers around her shoulders.

She'd always liked the sound of rain at the windows. "It's God's way of rinsing away all kinds of uninvited things," her mamma had said. "If you look real close, you can get a glimpse of your guardian angel...but only if you believed they were there."

All at once, a flicker of lightening brightened the room, followed by a loud, thunder roll. It made the whole house shake, and Alex clutched her doll even closer. "It's nothing to be afraid of, Dolly," she whispered. "It's just a storm. It'll be over in the morning."

The trees outside dipped and swayed in the wind, casting waltzing images against her window blinds. She lay back on her pillow and envisioned her guardian angel dancing while her heavy eyelids slowly closed.

"Daddy, I'm not ready to get up?" she whimpered, resting her head against his shoulder. "Can't I sleep a little while longer?"

"Yes, little one. The storm is starting up again. It'll be safer if you sleep in the cellar tonight."

"Where's Mama?"

"She's still asleep," he whispered. "Shhhhh...we don't want to wake her before its time."

"Can Zeke come down to the cellar with me?"

"He'll be down after a while. You go back to sleep now."

# CHAPTER 1

## *Threats*

March 1999

Alex Webb stared without flinching into the lighted mirror on her dressing table. The caramel brown face peering back at her didn't even blink as she shoved the card that had come with the flowers into her bag.

The media had labeled her "The Regal Nubian," but that aspect wasn't very apparent now. She wondered why all of a sudden her stomach was twisted in knots. She felt as if at any moment she would be sick.

"Ooh, how pretty," Desi said, slipping up behind her with Star. "Robbie?"

"No," Alex said, clearing her throat.

"Then, who?" Star asked, brushing past her to get a whiff of the yellow rose arrangement. Alex forced a smile toward her roommates, grateful to have them in New York with her this time. She had never liked the New York scene, but it came with the territory. Desiree Sparks and Staria Muse were also models, but unlike Alex, they couldn't get enough of the "Big Apple."

"I don't know," Alex answered, trying to sound indifferent.

She was just nervous, she decided. Her mind seemed to labor for clarification of what might be causing the alarm she felt. It couldn't be this assignment. She had made hundreds of runway strolls and this one would be no different.

She glanced again at the beautiful yellow roses that had arrived for her backstage and pondered who could have sent them. They were her favorites.

That was it! The choice of flowers had been too familiar for comfort, especially arriving with such a menacing card. Why had she forgotten that?

# Fragment In The Sand

A wave of fear swept over her. The card had intentionally been left unsigned and had one simple sentence scrawled on it. *I'll be waiting for you in the dark, sweet Tabitha.* Using her first name with subtle undertones was unmistakably threatening. Who besides her family and roommates would know she had a phobia of the dark? She shuddered as her dread intensified, leaving her feeling suddenly skeptical of her surroundings and everyone she encountered.

Desi moved alongside Star to breathe in the soft scent of the roses, and turned curious eyes on Alex. "Honey, you look a little strange. Are you ill?"

Alex fidgeted with a stray wisp of hair at the nape of her neck. "I'm fine. I just wish I knew who sent the roses."

"You get fan mail and gifts all the time," Star said, casually stroking the air with her hand. "What's the big deal?"

"Yeah, but they always go through Uncle Lou. This time, it just feels…sort of…invasive." Alex tossed her bag beneath the table and tried to convince herself that her misgivings were unreasonable. Maybe the small amount of sleep she'd gotten over the past several weeks was responsible for her irrational notions. Insomnia was so prevailing that she'd been forced to get another prescription from her doctor.

Taking another look at the roses, Alex attempted a smile but it was no use. She couldn't feel the cheer that flowers were supposed to convey. And based on the words on the accompanying card, they weren't meant to.

She took a deep cleansing breath and hoped she was just being overly sensitive. But she couldn't get past the impression that something wasn't right. Despite living the American girl's dream, she almost wished she could leave the fashion industry altogether. The prestige and affluence, not to mention the countless perks that came with such distinction, meant very little to her. It didn't satisfy the deep ache she felt growing inside of her, and this puzzled her.

Desi had dubbed Alex a religious nut because she endeavored to maintain scrupulous morals, refusing to get caught up in certain aspects of their trade. Not that such remarks bothered her. In fact, they actually strengthened her faith. Presently, she hoped it was strong enough to see her through the rest of this day.

So what if a fan got a little too close for comfort? She couldn't allow the intrusion to get to her—not now. It would show all over the runway. She had to focus on the job at hand. She could do it. She was good at that.

"Don't be so suspicious," Desi said, swiping her red hair behind her ears disdainfully. "I wish somebody had sent me roses. And I wouldn't care if they'd gone through proper channels. Personally, I think Lou should stick to running the modeling agency, and let us deal with our own fans."

"Five minutes, ladies."

Alex glanced up to see the stage manager gazing at them through the throng of other models. "Coming," she called, slipping on her heels.

Mentally taking a precursory inventory, she fixed her smile in place and waited behind the curtain for her entrance. She could still hear the words of one of her Paris instructors ringing in her ears.

"Breathe," Madame Dumelle would say. "Smile…posture…grace…now float."

Then she stepped easily onto the platform. So many flashbulbs. Lord, please get me through this. She cautiously allowed her eyes to sweep over the audience as she advanced to center stage. Everything was fine, she told herself. She was just being paranoid. By the time she started down the runway, she had regained the familiar poise. Focus…Swallow…Smile. She moved fluidly down the landing, having successfully blocked out the crowd.

Alex chattered lightheartedly as she and her friends approached the dressing rooms once the show was finished. Anxious to get on a plane back to LA, she pushed through the other models gathered around the doorway and made her way toward her dressing table.

Halting just steps away from her reserved station, Alex recoiled in horror at the vandalism awaiting her arrival. The vase that had once held the beautiful arrangement of yellow roses was now on its side. The sound of water spilling onto the floor sent a chill down her spine. The roses had been crushed and strewn everywhere. A saturated note lay across the entire

## Fragment In The Sand

muddle.

*"You're next."*

"Oh, my God!" Star shrieked, clutching Alex's arm.

The brilliance of the light in the room seemed to suddenly dull. "No!"

Her scream was full of terror. She didn't realize it had come from her own throat until Desi protectively collected her into her arms.


Alex babbled on without end in an effort to convince her uncle that she wasn't taking the threat she'd received in New York to heart. She finally succeeded in persuading him that she was okay when she began to turn on the charm and tease him as was common for her. The most difficult challenge had been convincing him not to mention the incident to her brother, Zeke.

Zeke was such a worrywart when it came to her. She grimaced as she thought of what her brother's reaction would be if he knew. The two men worried about her nonstop, but she was growing weary of being treated like a fragile child. It went without saying, however, that Lou and Zeke were just trying to protect her from lapsing back into the severe catatonic ordeal she'd suffered as a little girl. Despite the fact that it was a concern that plagued her as well, she had to prove to them that she was stable and quite capable of taking care of herself. At least she hoped she was.

***

Ezekiel Webb sat alone in the courtroom, reflecting on his most recent case. It had been a difficult one, but as was his custom, he never closed a case without thanking God for His guidance and offering a prayer for everyone involved.

Inwardly thankful, Zeke stood at to leave. He grimaced as a familiar hefty voice growled out his name.

"Webb?"

Zeke turned to see the angry glower of Curtis Tyson, the man who had just been sentenced to die. The barrel-chested captive attempted to break free from the officer's restraints and move towards him.

4

"Payback comes in ways you least expect, Mr. Big Shot Detective. You watch your back. You haven't heard the last of me."

Zeke understood, even expected Tyson to hold a grudge against him. He had been instrumental in his capture. Yet, even though he was used to irate threats, there was something in Tyson's voice that set his nerves on edge.

Tyson had maintained his reputation as nothing more than a petty swindler for years, always in and out of trouble. To Zeke's knowledge, this was the first time that a victim had been killed. Tyson had spent his childhood subjected to abuse until he ran away from home at fifteen. Zeke's eyes narrowed in reflection as he remembered *his* own flight from the authority at that age.

Ambling down the steps of the Oklahoma City courthouse, he felt the gloom draining the remnants of his strength. He never delighted in the death of another human, not even a monster like Tyson. It always unsettled him. But he *did* have confidence in the justice system. If he didn't, he wouldn't have chosen the career he had.

After climbing into his car, Zeke laid his head back on the seat and closed his eyes. Something else was troubling him besides the Tyson case. Something he couldn't quite put his finger on. The world seemed to be spinning out of control with hatred and depravity. And he felt helpless to prevent any of it.

Recalling all the grand ideals he'd had just after graduating the police academy made him feel all the more incompetent. He had always hoped he would make a difference, and knew that every day he walked in the light of God's goodness was a day that bore witness against the darkness. Yet he couldn't help wondering what real effect it was having on the world as a whole.

He was just glad that he at least didn't have to listen to any more of Tyson's trial, and prayed that God would send someone to minister to him before it was too late. Zeke had been compelled to closely follow the trial, concerned that Tyson might somehow get off through some legal loophole. He had tried unsuccessfully to shake the gruesome scene of the dead girl from his mind's eye. His heart ached as he remembered

**5**

# Fragment In The Sand

how devastated the young murder victim's parents had been—hardly able to answer any questions for authorities.

His mind turned to his own daughter, Tracee. Though she was only three, it was at times like these that he desperately wanted to shield her from the realities of a cruel world. But he knew that all he could do was pray for the wisdom to teach her how to walk through it. He found himself responding to most of his cases with Tracee in mind, even though logic and training told him that this probably wasn't healthy.

Zeke didn't know how long he sat in the parking lot outside the courthouse, but when he started the engine he knew he would spend the rest of the day with his own family. Tracee and his wife, Peg, would be glad to see him home early.

He had worked in homicide for eleven years now—the past two as an inspector. If all went according to plan, it was a pretty sure deal that he would be next in line for the lieutenant's spot once promotions were granted. The department needed conscientious black men to keep rising into leadership positions and he intended to do just that. He knew the murder of his own mother eighteen years ago had played a significant role in his decision to become a cop—that and Ike Oliver. But he questioned whether he'd been wise in choosing to be a part of the homicide division.

At last he smiled contentedly to himself as he pulled into his driveway, surveying the freshly tilled ground that bordered his home. Peg was good with that kind of thing, he thought. She had probably already planted her flowers, too.

Zeke braked and got out of the car to move his daughter's tricycle from the driveway. Gazing down at the miniature pedal-powered toy, his thoughts turned to his younger sister. He recalled the initial panic Alex had shown in riding her own tricycle. It was hard for him not to still think of her as a kid. Although a grown woman now, it didn't stop him from worrying himself sick over her.

He would be a lot less anxious after she and Robbie were married. Especially after reading the recent newspaper article about her assignment in New York. Maybe it was the cop in him, but he felt that her profession kept her too much in the public view and was much too stressful for her temperament.

He had been clever in hiding his disapproval from her.

Besides, Lou was there. Even though Zeke didn't like it much, Lou had been quite effective in keeping her safe and managing her business affairs. As long as she was happy and safe, that's all that mattered. Yet he still felt guilty for leaving her in California when he'd run away. He had done exactly what their father had done, and he could never forget that.

The intensity of pain and anger at his father's abandonment was just as fresh as it had been eighteen years ago. Despite having learned of his death, Zeke's stomach still lurched whenever he thought of him. Charles Webb had turned out to be the opposite of the kind of person he had taught his children to be.

Slamming his open palm over the dash, Zeke laid his head against the steering wheel. Why had he let Tyson's comments bring out so many ghosts? He supposed every cop had them, but *his* seemed to get weightier with the years.

Zeke quietly slipped into the house and headed for the bedroom. After changing clothes and locking away his gun, he sauntered into the kitchen to find Peg busy at the sink. The room was a perfect setting for her—bright walls, tidy counters and the aroma of good country cooking. He noticed she had scooped her hair up. She probably thought the twist at the back of her head was practical—and perhaps it was, he mused. But the loose slivers that escaped the clip and fanned around her neck made her seem more alluring than practical. He moved behind her and wrapped his arms around her waist. She immediately rested the back of her head against his shoulder as he lowered his own to nuzzle the curve of her neck.

"Hello, beautiful," he whispered.

"Hi," she said, turning around to give him a proper kiss. "Aren't you home a little early today?" Her brow was etched with worry lines as she gazed up speculatively into his face.

"Yeah. I wanted to see my favorite two girls," he said. "Where's Tracee?"

"In her room, making her daddy a masterpiece picture. You sure that's all it is?"

Instinctively, Zeke averted his eyes and immediately

regretted the tell-all sign that her suspicions were accurate. "Of course I am." He released his wife and strolled to the table and sat to stare out the large paned window, looking at nothing in particular.

"I noticed that Max-Stem has been in the news a lot lately. Why haven't you mentioned it?"

Zeke cringed and stared incredulously up at his wife. Before that moment, he hadn't realized that the news about his father's former employer had helped to prompt his emotional journey. He had assumed that it had simply been due to the tension he'd experienced at the courthouse.

"Peg, that has nothing to do with my day," Zeke said, uncertainty thick in his tone. "I'm a little distracted, that's all."

He hoped she would drop it, but after five years of marriage, he knew her well enough to know that she wouldn't. Usually when Peg got her mind set on something, she'd peck at it until it unraveled right in front of her. Despite the irritation of her practice, he also found it worthwhile. He could always count on her to prudently shine light on things he avoided.

Peg's baking emitted a pleasant aroma throughout the kitchen that made Zeke's mouth water. She moved back to the counter across the room and resumed her dinner preparations. Picking up a large bowl, she mixed the contents with a wooden spoon, smiling deliberately at her husband. "Ezekiel Webb, I know you."

Zeke searched his mind for something that he could use to change the subject. "That was a long time ago, Peg. What's that smell tugging at my palate?"

"Peach cobbler," she said absently. "I'm baking one for Casey, too. Is he in town?"

Casey Oliver was as close to a brother as Zeke could have. Zeke had gone to live with him and his father as a teenager. "I think that he's due back tonight," he muttered. "I need to drop something else by his apartment, anyway. I'll go right after dinner. Looks like you've been busy today."

"Yeah," she said, brightening. "But I like it. By the way, Alex called to see if you had been listening to the news lately. She almost sounded scattered. Probably all the excitement of being in the lime light."

"Frightened?"

"No, more baffled than anything. And why should she be frightened? You still expecting a relapse after all this time?"

"I certainly hope not," Zeke answered, deciding against telling Peg about the article. "But we can't be too careful. What did you tell her?"

"I told her you'd probably heard about Max-Stem on the news, but hadn't mentioned anything to me about it. Then she started asking me some things about your dad. I told her I knew very little. She also asked for a snapshot if we had any."

Peg turned and placed the bowl back on the counter and hurried to open the oven door. The steam escaping disbursed the aroma of baked spices even further into the house.

"Why would I have snapshots?" Zeke asked, speaking more with declaration than inquiry. His face grew haggard as he tried to squelch the anxiety dancing around in his gut.

"I can't imagine not remembering my dad's face," Peg continued. "I guess that's all a part of the trauma she went through, though."

Zeke's eyes grew wide and reflective as he pondered how it must feel to his sister not to remember her father's face. "They call it retrograde amnesia. Although Alex was six, the effect of everything wiped his face from her memory."

"I wonder why?"

"Why what?" Zeke asked.

"Why it was *his* face that she can't remember, and not your mother's."

"Her therapist said it had something to do with the subsequent pain of grief. His abandonment added insult to the injury of losing her mother."

"Thank God she's all right, now. Is that when she stopped talking?"

"Nah. It wasn't until *I* left her with Aunt Sarah and Lou. We could have lost her, Peg. She stayed like that for months. I failed her. Like father, like son I guess."

The empty acid chuckle and sting in Zeke's words revealed the depth of his bitterness. Peg had heard him tell the story before and had always been patient and willing to listen to it again, but she always cautioned him when it went too far.

"Zeke, you stop that, now. You were just a boy. And you don't know what all your father was dealing with back then," she said softly. "At least he sent the two of you to his sister. You said yourself that your parents were very close. He must have been torn half out of his mind to come home and find your mother dead. Think about how you would feel if, God forbid, you lost me like that. You've just got to let go of all that anger you feel."

"It's not just Dad, Peg. I failed Alex, too. I should have known better. She was curled in a ball with her hands over her ears when I found her in that cellar. How could I have left her after seeing that?"

"You were instrumental in bringing her back, Zeke. Don't forget that," Peg said abruptly. "You need to forgive your dad—yourself, too. Not being able to forgive has eaten away some of your insides. You know as well as I do that it will destroy everything worth anything in your life if you don't do something about it." Peg turned her back to Zeke and moved purposefully to the refrigerator. "I just don't understand how you can give everything else in your life to God—except this. I'd hate to see you let it go on much longer."

Shaken by her curt words, Zeke glanced up at her in surprise. "I don't want to feel like this, Peg. I just can't understand how any man could walk out on his kids two weeks after they've lost their mother. Especially when Alex was so traumatized by it."

"Alex wasn't the only one traumatized," she said, handing him a glass of lemonade. "You and your daddy were, too. You best not forget that."

Zeke gazed absently at the glass, then gulped its contents and continued his verbal reverie. "Dad and I had gone on a camping trip. We always had a great time together," he said, gazing absently into the glass. "A bad thunderstorm came up that night, so we headed back home. That's when we found—"

"Zeke, don't keep putting yourself through this, honey." He glanced up at her, then continued talking as if he hadn't heard her.

"Mom and Alex were at the house alone. The police said that the intruder obviously came in while they were both sleeping. He killed mom, ransacked the place, then took Alex to the cellar and locked her in. She still has problems with the dark because of that. There were never even any suspects."

Peg gently reached across the table and patted her husband's hand. "Zeke, come back to me."

"I'm here," he said, realizing he'd allowed himself to drift too close to the edge of the past. I never should have left her with Lou and Aunt Sarah, Peg. She would have been a lot better off with me."

"No, she wouldn't have. You were a kid, Zeke. How could you have made a life for either of you?"

Zeke lightly chuckled under his breath. "Alex took to Lou the moment we arrived. I couldn't stay there and watch him play daddy to my sister, so I left"

"Didn't you tell me Lou's first wife and daughter were killed in a car accident?"

"Yeah. Alex and his daughter would have been about the same age."

Peg shook her head reflectively. "Well, it's a good thing Ike Oliver understood troubled young boys. He and Casey were a perfect family for you to plug into. The very idea of you robbing a store…"

"God has been good to me," Zeke said, affectionately imagining the face of Casey's father.

"Now, all you have to do is get rid of that baggage. Go get your daughter, daddy. Dinner's just about ready."

\*\*\*

Casey pushed the empty dish aside and took a gulp of hot coffee. Peg really had a way with peach cobbler, he thought absently, leafing through the paper that Zeke had left on his counter.

Zeke's note had said that he'd gotten the newspaper from a friend who lived in New York. Wondering why Zeke would think that he wanted to see the New York Times was beyond him. Casey shook his head doubtfully and tossed the paper aside. Yawning absently he stood to head for the shower.

# Fragment In The Sand

His attention was immediately seized when the paper fell open against the fold, exposing a bold caption beneath a familiar image. Casey carefully picked it back up and read the caption. "REGAL NUBIAN THREATENED IN BIG APPLE."

His back stiffened as he sat back down on the edge of his sofa to read the article in its entirety. Zeke had to be worried half out of his mind, he thought.

Casey studied the picture intently. He didn't know Alex well—only what Zeke had told him. But he assumed that she was a spoiled prima donna that snubbed all the little people of the world—like him. A dubious expression settled on his face as he reflected on all the photographs that Zeke had proudly shown him. Proud, despite his extreme dislike of her career choice. She was indeed endowed with a beauty beyond words, he thought. But he had never liked arrogant, self-absorbed women, which she undoubtedly was. Her innocent looking photographs probably conveyed a bogus impression to her audience. It couldn't be genuine—he was sure of it.

He reflected on the fact that the Regal Nubian found very little time to visit her family in Oklahoma, yet Zeke would toss reason to the wind and fly across the country at her whimper. It was understandable that he would worry about her after all she's been through, but she was, after all, an adult now.

Casey stared at the panic-stricken image in the photograph and wondered what Miss Webb was really all about. He certainly had no interest in finding out for himself, but knew that his friend was probably on edge.

His gaze landed on the cordless phone. He'd better call him. He was probably still awake. Casey hit the speed dial and breathed a sigh of relief when Zeke picked up on the first ring.

"Hey, Case, I expected you back yesterday," Zeke called out.

"It took a little longer to get back into the country," Casey said, moving toward the bedroom. "Are you all right?"

"I take it you've read the article. What do you make of it?"

"I don't know. She probably has to deal with this type of thing all the time. What did she say?"

12

"Nothing. She hasn't even told me about it. She called and talked to Peg, but she asked about other things. I think she was trying to figure out if I knew about this incident. I *did* call Lou, though. He said she didn't want to worry me."

"I've gotta' admit, you're taking it well," Casey said. "I half expected you to be in LA by now."

"That paper came to my office. I didn't want to leave it around the house for Peg to see. No sense in getting her all worried," Zeke said. "Besides, Lou assured me that she was all right. He tries to keep the girls from having to see this kind of stuff. Their addresses aren't published. The only one that the public can get to, supposedly, is his."

"Good. I'm glad that it's nothing to worry about. You let me know if there's anything I can do for you, man."

"You still coming by for dinner this Friday?"

"Yep," Casey said, getting back to his feet. "I'll be there with bells on. How's my little buddy?"

"As cute as a cricket," Zeke said, his smile emanating in his voice. "Don't forget to bring Brenda."

# CHAPTER 2

## *Hope Valley*

Alex glanced up from the magazine she was scanning through when the front door opened with a whine. Star stumbled in with two overstuffed grocery bags and slammed the door shut with her foot.

"Why didn't you phone me from the car to come help?" Alex queried, quickly jumping to her feet.

"That's okay. A man standing out front gave me a hand as far as the door," Star said breathlessly. "He was kinda cute, too. Wore his hair back in a ponytail."

"Probably some radical."

"I guess he must have recently moved in, 'cause I hadn't seen him around before."

"You're too trusting, Star," Alex said, shaking her head. "He could well be an axe murderer. And you've got enough stuff here to feed an army. You must have gone to the store hungry."

After grasping one of the bags from Star's arms, she was taken off guard when Star abruptly pressed the other bag as well into her arms.

"Stop naggin', Gram," Star said, brushing her hands together. "There. I've done my part."

Without warning, she made a mad dash toward her bedroom. Alex placed the bags on the floor and gave chase, reaching Star's door just as she slammed it shut and locked it.

"Open this door," Alex demanded, bubbling with laughter, "or I'll blow it down."

"Not by the hair of your skinny, trim chin," Star retorted, giggling excitedly.

After several unsuccessful moments of trying to persuade Star to come from behind her locked door, Alex gave up and commenced to put away the groceries and start dinner. She

**14**

was busy chopping onions when Star wandered back in.

"Where's Desi?" Star asked, sniffing under the lid of the pan.

"She called to say she'd be late."

"Hmm. Chops and potatoes!" Star said. "You put onions in that?"

"Yes, ma'am, I certainly do," Alex said, gently steering Star toward the small kitchen table on the other side of the counter.

"Wonder what she's off doing today?"

"I don't know. I wish she wasn't so angry all the time. And the way she's so turned off to God, it's getting harder trying to pick and choose words around her."

"What's that all about, anyway?" Star asked, glancing up curiously. "I thought her dad was a preacher."

"He is. I think it has something to do with her and her brother growing up so poor," Alex said with a shrug. "I'm not sure, though. I just know she has issues."

"It's not issues—it's that mouth of hers. She's going to wind up in trouble if she's not more careful with it."

Despite Desi's bodacious manner, Alex found that she really loved and cared about her. She recalled how Desi had brought her to tears when she explained that she disliked anything that remotely reminded her of her poverty-stricken childhood. She and her younger brother had endured a lot of cruel teasing from other children, especially when they went to church.

"I know—she's harmless—a big bag of love bones," Star said, loudly snickering. "She's almost as wonderful as I am." Star licked the salt she'd sprinkled from her fingers. "I grew up poor, too, you know. You don't see me flicking my nose in God's face like she does."

"I guess I worry about how unstable her moods are sometimes. But that's how she carries her anger."

"She'll be all right," Star said, with a grunt. "She's just like a cat—always lands on her feet. But I didn't realize she had issues, I just thought she was nuts."

"Oh, be quiet. Underneath all your sarcasm, you know you're just as concerned about her as I am."

## Fragment In The Sand

"She never mentions her brother. I wonder why? You don't think something's wrong with him, do you?" Star asked, totally unaffected by Alex's reprimand.

"Don't get started, Miss Thang, and stop licking on that salt like that."

"Well hurry up and feed me," Star said, giving Alex a quirky look.

"It's just about ready—don't eat your fingers off," she said, tossing a tea towel over her left shoulder.

Alex moved to the stove with an insipid grin and spooned a portion onto a plate, added salad and bread and sat it at her usual spot at the table. With a wide smirk on her face, she eyed Star cautiously while she poured herself a glass of lemonade.

"Do you actually expect to partake without my repaying you for your cute little prank?" Alex said, sitting across from her wide-eyed friend.

"Oh, come on, Alex," Star whined, fattening her lower lip. "I don't have a birthright or anything to give up. How about I spring for a lunch on the cruise that you and Robbie are taking for your honeymoon?"

"It's already paid for," Alex quipped. "I'll just take your first born son."

"I only plan to have little girls."

"I'll take her," Alex said, a broad smile spreading across her face, "and I'll name her Horachio."

"But, Alex, you love me," Star whined, dramatically batting her eyes. "And I'm so hungry."

"We'll see how hungry you are," Alex said, sliding her plate closer to Star. She snickered fiendishly as she fanned over it, attempting to disperse the fragrant steam.

"Okay," Star surrendered, throwing her hands into the air. "You've got me. I'll make up your bed for a whole week—starting next week."

"Deal." Alex paused, tightening her gaze on Star. "Wait a minute. I'm out of town next week."

"I know," Star said standing to her feet.

Without warning, Alex pulled the towel from her shoulder and snapped it at the seat of Star's pants. She hit her mark, then squealed in dismay as Star turned and grabbed her weapon away from her.

"Okay…okay," Alex said, chuckling and holding up her hands in surrender. "You can have some dinner."

\*\*\*

"Look at those eyes," Terri raved, her own beginning to dissolve into huge drops. "Here I go again," she said, scrambling in her bag. "I get so emotional when it comes to kids. I don't know how I can stand to work around the ones who are hurting."

Alex shifted uncomfortably in the vinyl chair, watching the nurse feverishly try to dab away her slip of emotion with a tissue.

Her schedule as a volunteer was left flexible due to her modeling career. The head nurse was simply glad to have an extra pair of hands to help distract the children from their woes. While Alex did very little, she enjoyed being with them. She read, played games and sometimes just held them until they fell asleep. Children were always eager for attention. So the moment she recognized the way the camera seemed to strip away their inhibitions, she started keeping a photo journal of her patients. Like Terri, it broke her heart to see so many of them in agony. Giving them a moment of distraction was the least she could do.

"Are you and Scott ever planning to have any of your own?"

"We've been trying for over a year," Terri answered, glancing up at Alex who had already opened her mouth to respond. "And before you ask…yes ma'am, we have prayed about it. The Lord is probably tired of me coming before his throne begging to get pregnant." She chuckled absently as she continued to gaze fondly through Alex's collection of photographs.

"I'm sure it'll happen," Alex said. "Just be patient and don't close yourself off to other options."

"Adoption?"

Alex nodded her head, studying Terri intently. "I've even heard of couples getting pregnant on their own once they've given up and adopted."

# Fragment In The Sand

"Yeah, but I wouldn't want *that* to be a motivation for me making a decision like that, Alex."

"No, of course not," Alex said, her eyes widening incredulously. "I didn't mean to imply…"

"I know," Terri said, tossing the tissue into a nearby trash can. "So what about you?"

Alex scrunched down and laid her head back on the chair. She and Terri seldom got to see each other outside of Hope Valley Children's Hospital. Short little visits in the nurses' lounge were about all the time afforded them. She propped her feet comfortably atop the small table and glanced back at the nurse whom she'd befriended two years earlier. She enjoyed the easy way they could share their faith with one another, and looked forward to the days when her schedule would permit her to do more volunteer work with the children.

"I don't know if I've reached that far in my planning yet," Alex said, her eyes crinkling with mirth. "Robbie wants children and I have to admit, I'd like to get pregnant right away after we're married. But we'll have to see."

"I meant about these pictures," Terri said, gesturing vaguely toward the photographs in her hand. "You obviously aren't aware of how good you are. God might be showing you something."

"That's just a pastime I picked up several years ago. God could probably care less about my minor obsessions."

"Would you say that if you weren't so wrapped up in your modeling career?"

"What gives you the impression that I'm wrapped up?"

"Because you haven't done anything about this. It's obvious that you get a great deal of fulfillment with your photography. It's so clear in these photos. And I think you're wrong about God not caring. In fact, when you get to heaven, He'll probably ask why you wasted so much time being unfulfilled. Doesn't Covington Elete Fashions have a magazine?"

"Yeah, but what would that matter?"

"Well, maybe someone down there can give you some pointers on this pastime of yours. Or direct you to someone who can. Maybe it would be a way to tie both your worlds together."

"Girl, if CEF got wind that I might be pursuing something other than modeling, they'd keep me so busy I wouldn't even have time to come up here. Not to mention what Uncle Lou would do."

"Oh, that's right. He's your agent, isn't he?" Terri asked, assuming a judicial expression. "Have you ever thought about sending these out to one of the other magazines?"

"Not really." Alex answered, beginning to regard Terri's inquiry with more scrutiny. "Do you really think they're that good?"

"Yes, indeed. If you don't mind, I'd like to borrow a couple of these to show my brother-in-law. He enjoys playing with the camera, too. He's even sold a few here and there."

"Sure," Alex said. "Take as many as you like."

"Look at this one," Terri said, pointing to a shot Alex had taken of two children on the playground. "You've managed to capture the very essence of these children with a single flash. See how the energy in this one's eyes dulls, then in the next frame it brightens? Your timing is flawless. You snapped it just before it completely disappeared."

Alex watched in stunned silence as Terri went back and forth through the pictures of the two children. She had never given any serious thought to photography as a profession, but couldn't deny the leap of excitement she'd felt the moment Terri implied such a possibility. She wondered if she was really any good—at least good enough to thrust herself into a competitive business.

It was as if Terri had found a hidden place deep within her where she kept her true passions. But this was one that she'd never really considered. But it was very apparent that she was becoming disenchanted with it. And the incident in New York only confirmed how she had been feeling for some time. She and Robbie had already casually discussed her leaving it all behind, once they were married.

"Actually, Terri, I guess I have given some thought to making some changes. But I can't say that I considered photography as an option. I have to admit...I do love the camera. Every thing about it—even the zoom sound it makes after I snap the shutter."

# Fragment In The Sand

"Girl, are you kidding?" Terri asked surprised. "Would you *really* consider leaving modeling?"

"Maybe," Alex said. "After all, life's too short to live like a puppet, doing things that don't really matter. One of the residents at the nursing home where I go to shoot sometimes told me that he'd worked all his life in a job he didn't like, only to get sick before he had a chance to enjoy his retirement. I guess it started me thinking."

"It sure makes sense. You and Robbie will be married in June, right?

"Yeah."

"Well, now would be the time to start doing your homework. That way, you won't have the pressure of uncertainty pushing your buttons when you decide to make the move. That is, unless you're too in love with the money."

"It's not the money, Terri. You know that," Alex said shrugging. "Change isn't easy for me."

"I'm surprised we haven't talked about this sooner, Alex," Terri said, placing some of the photographs in her bag, "the way you come up here loaded down with your camera equipment and all."

"Me...a real professional photographer," Alex said reflectively. "It's such a risky notion—changing my whole career focus."

"You can make it in anything if God gives you the urge," Terri said, glancing at her sideways. "Don't back pedal on me now; especially with those stars lighting up in your eyes like that. Take a leap of faith."

"But how would I know if this is God directing me?"

"If the desire is pure and your heart is to please Him," Terri said, "It's Him."

"I do want to please Him. But I also want to be happy and fulfilled."

"Well, there is nothing more fulfilling than pleasing Him. And remember, He placed the desire in your heart. So I would say that it's up to you to make the next move."

"I would love to give it a try. But my uncle would be so disappointed if I backed out of my contract without a good reason. He's invested so much into my career."

"With good reason," Terri said. "He's getting a great return."

"I'm sure it's nothing like that," Alex said, waving her hand in a dismissive gesture. "But my contract *does* come up for renewal in a few months."

"Why is it that I get the impression that you're too busy trying to please other people?" Terri leaned forward and gently touched Alex's knee. "Listen to God, girlfriend."

"You'll have me chasing all kinds of fantasies if I'm not careful," Alex said, her thoughts already stirring."

Terri stroked the air with her hand and gazed pointedly at Alex. "I've seen you with that camera and these children. Anybody with eyes can see that your heart's not in modeling."

Her words seemed to pierce through some invisible layer of Alex's subconscious and dance a little jig in her stomach. For two years, she had enjoyed lugging her camera gear up to the hospital, but she never dreamed that she should look into photography as a career.

Before their break ended, Alex agreed to leave the whole batch of photographs with Terri. "Thanks for the encouragement," she said, jumping to her feet to head out the door. "I'll give it some more thought."

***

Rosell's smile was hard as he stood back into the shadows and watched Alex rush through the sliding doors with her camera bag. She walked fast, almost raced to get to her car. "We have to beat the sun home," he snarled in malicious delight. "We're afraid of the dark."

He tossed his cigarette to the ground and flipped open his digital phone. Dialing the familiar number, he waited for the indignant woman on the other end to pick up. It was ridiculous that he hadn't yet met his boss eye to eye, but he was being paid a handsome fee to scare this pretty little doll—he shouldn't complain. He wasn't even sure if the boss was a man or a woman—probably a jealous boyfriend, considering some of his instructions. The closest he'd gotten was the answering service, which served only as a relay station for messages and instructions.

# Fragment In The Sand

The moment he knew his assignment concerned the beautiful Tabitha Alexis Webb, he had offered to woo her into his confidence. For some reason, she had always intrigued him. His plan had been to get close enough to her to already be in place when the command was given. But to his great disappointment, his offer was rejected. His boss had other plans, but promised he could have her once the job was finished—if she was still worth having by then.

"She just drove off," he said gruffly to the woman that answered the phone. She always sounded so formal—sterile—as if this was an ordinary business transaction. "Should I follow her?"

"No, not right now. Your next instructions are to hire the person named in the envelope you were sent last week. She's a lady of the evening and is waiting for your call. The money for the transaction has already been placed in your post office box."

"Are you sure you're not ready for me to just grab her?"

"Your instructions are very explicit," the woman snapped. "You are not to go outside of them or the deal is off."

Over-cautious cowards, Rosell thought, contemptuously. He didn't generally do business this way, but the money was so good that he couldn't pass it up. Still he didn't like taking orders from someone he couldn't put a face with.

"Are we clear on that?" the voice demanded.

"Yeah. I got it," he said, abruptly disconnecting the call.

Why were they hesitating instead of letting him do his job? Everything could be clean and simple. All they had to do was figure out what effect they wanted to make and let him know. He'd do the rest. But they were straddling the fence, and he wondered why.

It was after seven when he strolled to his car. He would call the hooker tonight, but right now, he wanted to take another look at Miss Webb's fire escape.

# CHAPTER 3

## *Appointed Corrections*

It was after midnight when Alex arrived at the security gate of her apartment complex. Biting into her lip to hold back the tears, she entered the code, drove through and swung her Mercedes into the parking space. After shoving the gearshift into park, she staggered from the car and climbed the outer stairs to her apartment.

Shuddering in the crisp April breeze, she wiped her eyes to determine which key to use to unlock the door. She should have come straight home from the airport, but she had wanted to tell Robbie about the correspondence photography course she'd checked into.

Her hands were trembling. She made a fist around the keys and glanced out towards the parking lot. The wind seemed to whisper out to her in the dark—taunting her. *"You can't leave modeling now. You're trapped. You're trapped."*

Alex slammed the door to her apartment and leaned heavily against the frame, closing her eyes in an attempt to shut out the image that was still vivid in her mind. Abruptly, she opened them again, realizing with some indignation that her roommates were in the living room.

The girls looked back at her with startled eyes, and Alex quickly straightened and tried to gain some composure. Clearing her throat, she managed to quell the rising emotion enough to head for her bedroom without making a scene.

"The wedding is off," she announced firmly. The wedding is off. The impact of her own words seemed to dawn on Alex all over again, and she felt a rush of heat rise to her face.

She hoped to avoid the inevitable interrogation, but she knew she'd have to face them eventually. Flinging herself onto the bed, she succumbed to the agony that pressed in around her and let the tears flow freely.

After a few moments, she sat up. She had to get a hold of

herself. Though the pain was real, she couldn't allow this set-back to trip her up. Years of therapy had taught her that she'd have to focus on something other than what had caused fear or pain. She could do this. Maybe the new photography course would give her a new point of convergence.

What had Terri said? Something about God having been the one who'd placed the desire in her heart. Maybe it was her way of escape. She wondered if this truth applied even when a person such as herself hadn't been aware of it. Did He really deal with such insignificant things?

Unable to make sense of anything at the moment, she wiped her eyes and grabbed her Bible from the top drawer of her nightstand. Turning to the thirty-seventh Psalm, she began to read the passage that Terri had alluded to. Maybe it would somehow keep her hope from dwindling completely away.

*Delight yourself in the Lord and he will give you the desires of your heart. Commit your way to the Lord; trust in Him and He will do this. He will make your righteousness shine like the dawn, the justice of your cause like the noonday sun. Be still before the Lord and wait patiently for Him; do not fret when men succeed in their ways, when they carry out their wicked schemes. Refrain from anger and turn from wrath; do not fret—it leads only to evil.*

She would have to trust and wait on the Lord. But how could she do that in the middle of such a mess? She wondered if she had the faith to believe that He would fix it all. She'd always fought to keep doubt at bay, especially after remembering elements about the night her mother died. She wanted so desperately to believe that God would indeed take care of her. But her mother had trusted Him, too. What if? No. She couldn't allow her mind to go there. She wouldn't.

She glanced at the passage again and the words began to penetrate her anguish, like a laser beam. She had the oddest sensation that she had been prepared for this blow simply by having that conversation with Terri. She wondered if God hadn't been preparing her for a long time for what she'd seen tonight in Robbie. She closed the Bible and wept anew as tension slowly ebbed.

Alex could almost see her pastor pointing his finger at her

and repeating the words that he found opportunity to preach at least four times a year. *"You've gotta cast your cares. Cast all of them on Him."*

She smiled, remembering his caution to avoid allowing the disposition of others influence her walk in the Spirit. That was the time she had approached him about Desi's hostility toward God.

Glancing over at the antique hourglass sitting on her nightstand, Alex instinctively flipped it over. And breathing a heavy sigh, she watched the small granules of white sand dimple and trickle through the slender middle with fluid-like rhythm. Watching it somehow made her feel like she was connected somehow—maybe because it had been in the Webb family for so many years. But tonight, the usual comfort it gave her wasn't apparent. Her mind kept recalling the scene of Robbie with another woman, which sent feelings of rejection and anger racing through her. Massaging her temples, she tried to rub away the migraine she felt coming on.

Without warning, her door sprang open and Desi barreled into the room. Her eyes were wide with questions, but Alex could tell that she was suppressing the urge to dive into them. The tall, slender, gray-eyed woman had been her friend for three years. From the instant they met, Desi had behaved like an over-protective sister towards her. However, there were times when her acid remarks were more than she could bear. More times than not, Desi seemed to be absorbed in her own world and walked around with a big chip on her shoulder. But when she or Star were troubled by one of life's hiccups, Desi had never hesitated to storm out of her self and come to their aid. She had a nurturing side, it seemed, that very few people got a chance to see.

Ever since the time Desi had dumped her salad onto a waiter for simply forgetting to omit olives, she knew there was something to the cliché about the nature of redheads—at least this one.

"Honey, what is it?" Desi asked. "Last minute wedding jitters?"

She calmly eased onto the foot of Alex's bed. Her mouth was set firmly and a wrinkle was on her brow. It made her look

# Fragment In The Sand

much older than her thirty years.

"Goodness, Desi, I can't believe you're drilling her *now*," Star exclaimed, strolling through the open door with her hands firmly at her waist. "At least give her a chance to calm down. Can't you see she's upset?"

"I've given her plenty of time. And who are *you* supposed to be all of a sudden," Desi snapped, half turning to meet Star's reproachful stance, "her mother?"

Star, a petite twenty-two year old blonde, had stumbled into the fashion world less than a year ago. She was bright, kind and still had the bubbly personality of a teenager that appealed to many designers. Though Alex loved and cherished the friendship of both her roommates, she found that she especially enjoyed the playful relationship she shared with Star.

Alex lifted her head from the headboard just in time to see Star wince from the sudden harshness of Desi's remark. "I'll be okay, you two," she murmured, still stroking her temples. "Don't start in on each other."

Through trembling lips, she managed to convey the torment of pulling up to her fiancé's apartment to find him in the arms of another woman. Star gasped in horror and rushed to the side of the bed to draw Alex into an embrace.

"I'm so sorry," she said, her face contorted with sadness. "You're really catching it from all sides aren't you? I can't believe he'd do this to you."

"I'm sorry, too, honey," Desi said, moving toward Alex. "But good riddance to bad rubbish."

"Desi!" Star shrieked. "You need to do something about that nasty tongue of yours. How could you?"

"Maybe she's right, Star," Alex said, trying to still the hitch in her voice. "I was so looking forward to a new life, but maybe it's an appointed correction."

Ripping another tissue from the box on her nightstand, Alex blew her nose. Desi moved to the dresser mirror to view her reflection. Mirrors had that effect on her. She rarely entered a room with one without being drawn into a series of self-admiring rites.

"I'm sorry that I suggested that you stop by there, but you were so excited about the course." Desi suddenly stopped primping and turned from the mirror to face Alex. "You sound more upset about losing your new life than you do about losing Robbie. Maybe deep down, you knew what a scamp he was."

"I've seen stranger things happen," Star said, her eyes as round as goggles. "I saw a movie the other night where this woman had a sort of intense insight about things like that—almost as if she was able to see the future."

"Oh, Star. Give us a break!" Desi demanded, touching the bristles of Alex's hairbrush to her nose. "Sometimes I feel like I live in the same cave with Moses *and* Cinderella."

"What are you doing?" Alex asked, gazing quizzically at Desi.

"I was making sure this brush was clean," Desi said, gently stroking her red curls. "Black people seem to have a thing for oil."

"Well, I don't want your stringy red strands in my brush anyway, Miss Thang, so get your own!"

"Alex, what did you mean about *appointed correction*?" Star asked, easing onto the bed beside her.

"Well, I believe that agreeing to marry Robbie was a big mistake. I guess that's obvious," Alex said, taking a moment to blow her nose. "He's not the person I fell in love with. I don't know. Maybe I had my head in the clouds."

"But what does that have to do with correction?"

"It means God is looking out for me. If this was meant to be—"

"Oh, knock it off, p l e a s e," Desi snapped, tossing the brush aside. "Robbie is a man with obvious needs. You were too squeaky clean to have sex, so he found somebody who would."

The words were biting, despite the fact that the thought had already occurred to Alex. She sat stunned, staring wide-eyed at Desi's detached gaze.

She *had* noticed that when things got a little steamy between the two of them, it took all she had to pull herself away before things went too far. Lately, Robbie had gotten so annoyed with her for putting on the brakes that she was forced to endure a sour attitude for the remainder of the evening.

**27**

# Fragment In The Sand

Although she'd tried to overlook his behavior, it felt like betrayal and had deeply hurt.

"Robbie always said he understood my position on pre-marital sex, Desi," Alex said with some degree of uncertainty. "Why does everything have to center around sex with you?"

"Evidently, Robbie lied about how he felt," Desi said, studying her teeth in the mirror.

"Evidently," Alex conceded, looking away in disgust. "I can't believe how wrong I was about him."

"I don't think you should have to change who you are because of some lustful moron," Star squawked. "All men aren't so undisciplined in that area."

"How would *you* know?" Desi asked, turning a critical eye on Star. "You're just as fanciful as Alex—wishing on a *Star* for that house in the country, a couple of kids and a white picket fence."

"What's wrong with that?" Star asked.

"Nothing, if that's your cup of tea. It's not mine. I want to be self-sufficient. And I'm not one to tiptoe around life because I'm afraid to enjoy it. You two really crack me up."

"What Alex said makes a lot of sense. This just *wasn't* meant to be." Star turned sympathetic eyes to Alex and patted her hand like a consoling grandmother. "So tell me more about appointed correction?"

With a noticeably impatient sigh, Desi uttered an explanation. "It's simply the way God offers a way out of all the trouble we get ourselves into."

Alex's mouth dropped open in astonishment. The two women gawked at the redhead in doubtful confusion. She had gone out of her way to show them she had no interest in God or His word, yet she seemed to grasp a basic principal that had escaped many Christians.

The look Desi shot the two of them was sharp and filled with disdain. "Don't look at me like that. I'm not an idiot."

"We were just—" Star began.

"I know what you were thinking," Desi interrupted. "I know I'm a little strong willed sometimes, but it doesn't mean I'm an atheist."

"Good," Alex said, tossing the balled up tissue into the

wastebasket. "How about coming to church with me on Sunday?"

"Don't go there," Desi snapped, giving her a warning glare. "I grew up sitting on the front pew. Remember? All that organized religion makes me ill. And if you keep going around trying to fix everybody to suit your standards of right— making them feel as if God couldn't love them like he does you—you're going to be chopped off at the knees at every turn."

"I do no such thing," Alex countered, questioning if Desi's indictment had any truth in it. "I believe that my walk with the Lord is the single most important thing in my life. I know you think I'm fanatical, but I have to be."

"Why?" Star asked, intrigued.

"I guess…I'm just afraid I'll slip into rejecting God at the least little problem…like so many other people. I don't want to miss heaven just because I don't understand why some things are the way they are. My way of dealing with the urge to question Him is to draw even closer."

"What do you want to question Him about? Robbie?" Star asked, her eyes glassy with intrigue.

"It doesn't matter now," Alex said, somberly. "Someday, maybe I'll get married and have a family. But I have to trust God to send me a husband that loves Him as much as I do."

"Don't hold your breath," Desi said. "Look at you—so quick to talk the faith, but anyone can see you're miserable."

"Of course she is—for now," Star retorted protectively. "Don't worry Alex. Just remember what Pastor Frank said— that God won't allow us to go through anything we can't handle, with His help. You just be patient."

"I would venture to say that there are probably twice as many women going to that church than men," Desi said, with a catty chuckle. "And they're all hoping and believing for the same man."

"There are plenty of men there," Star said defensively. "What does that have to do with anything?"

"They're probably all married," Desi said. "Their wives probably drag them in every Sunday. Most men don't go in for the church scene."

# Fragment In The Sand

"Real men do," Alex said. "But right now, that's the last thing I need to be thinking about. Especially if they expect me to step beyond who I am. For the time being, I'll just start spending more time at the hospital and focus on this career."

Alex turned to see Desi's left brow rise in contempt. "Where did that come from? *This career,* my dear, gives you a pretty good life. You sound like you'd rather spend all your time wiping on snot-nosed kids than making good money."

"Desi, be quiet and stop trying to be so hard," Alex said, scowling. "I really don't need that right now. At least I'm doing something worth while."

"Sounds to me like you've forgotten how to be grateful, Miss Christian. Some people would kill to have the life we live."

"This isn't life, Desi," Alex muttered. "*Life* is that special, all encompassing thing that the Lord died to give us."

"Yada, yada, yada," Desi muttered, pulling her hair back behind her ears. "You know I love you, honey, but I still think that your sanctimonious attitude will keep a lot of good prospects away. And that includes those that God sends. You need to start appreciating what you've been given…and that, my dear one, means enjoying your God-given right to have sex."

"Auugh!" Star gnarled in frustration as she threw a small pillow toward Desi and stormed from the room. Desi followed suit, leaving Alex alone to ponder the accusations. She wondered if her dissatisfaction could possibly be an indication that she was ungrateful for all that she had. Had she taken everything for granted?

Alex realized with a sense of sadness that she had placed entirely too much hope in her relationship with Robbie. She did in fact want to wait on God for the right man, but she couldn't help wondering if all men were as deceptive as Robbie had been. It could be something in the genes. Why should she be so surprised? Maybe she should just throw herself into studying and forget about romance altogether.

She glanced longingly at the phone. For a moment—one weak moment, she considered calling Robbie to retract her cancellation of their plans. She quickly shook her head in an

**30**

attempt to clear her thoughts. She was hurt and confused, but she wasn't stupid. She couldn't allow those feelings to make her a mindless victim. Notwithstanding, she hoped that she hadn't destroyed the only chance she would have of having her own family.

Despite the glamour, Alex felt trapped in a vocation that she was quite good at. She loved and appreciated her uncle, but had often wished that she had gone to live with Zeke after her aunt died. She was sure that he would have encouraged her to pursue the things that were important to her.

When her uncle had introduced her to his accountant, she had fallen in love with him almost immediately. Robbie romantically proposed at Christmas, and sure that it was the answer to her prayers, she accepted. She recalled thinking that she wouldn't have to flagrantly disappoint her brother or uncle by making an abrupt change in her life, like quitting and becoming a secretary somewhere. Each time she spoke with Zeke, she could hear how proud he was of her. It made her feel all the more guilty for her hidden restlessness.

Her uncle, on the other hand, saw her as his ready and willing protégé without seeming to give much regard for her aspirations. He still thought of her as a child, incapable of making good decisions—but then, so did Zeke. Lou counted on her more than he did the other models. It felt a little like he was clipping her wings so that she had to stay close to the nest. At least she had her friends, and for that, she was very thankful. While her roommates sang a different tune than hers, they were still very supportive of her.

After wrestling with many confusing thoughts, Alex washed the day away in a warm, soothing shower. She seemed to realize that though she was hurt, there was a hint of relief in this turn of events.

Before closing her eyes, she gave a final glance around the room. The warm glow of several nightlights gave her a sense of stillness. They illuminated her bedroom and adjoining bath with soft assurance that everything would be all right. Satisfied that she had turned them all on, she snuggled beneath the covers and closed her eyes.

Alex's eyes sprang open with a twinge of panic, having

been jarred back to alertness at the sound of movement. Her eyes met Desi's worried gaze as she padded through the door in her pajamas.

"You *will* be all right, won't you, honey?" she whispered. Alex wasn't at all shocked to see the tender side of her friend, but it always caught her off guard when it came.

"I think so," she replied with a gapping yawn.

"You know, sometimes I wish I had your kind of faith, Alex. I would like to think that God loved me enough to direct a divine correction my way, but it would take a gigantic one." She almost sounded apologetic, but then let out a frivolous laugh. "I got off on the wrong track a long time ago."

"Of course He loves you, Desi."

Desi paused, obviously struggling to hold back the tears that were filling her eyes. "Do you think God can use bad people to accomplish something good?"

"Yes. I guess I do."

"I really don't mean to sound the way I do—so sacrilegious," Desi said. "Maybe one day, I'll talk to you about the things that bother me about God."

"Anytime," Alex said, stunned by the admission her friend had just made. She wished that she could get through to her and show her how much God really loves her, but Desi wouldn't stand still for much more than what she'd already said.

\*\*\*

The anticipation of spending time with the children at the hospital was enough to infuse Alex with a sense of purpose. She hurriedly dressed, thinking how wonderful it was to have one more thing to distract her from her own problems. Just as she was about to rush out, the bell rang. She opened the door to find Lou Ramsey leaning against the doorjamb.

"Uncle Lou," she said in surprise. "I was just on my way to the hospital."

Lou was a brawny, short man with striking blue eyes and ash gray hair. "Hello, little one," he said, engaging in his usual greeting of squeezing her cheek between his fingers. She liked it when he called her that. Though she remembered nothing about her father, it somehow reminded her of him. "Doesn't my favorite niece have fifteen minutes to spare?"

"I'm your *only* niece," she said, leaning into his embrace. Lou strolled into the living room casually, steering Alex toward the sofa. She didn't want to rush him, but she really wasn't in the mood for his gentle prying. Obviously, the girls had told him about Robbie.

"I wanted to come over and check on you—see if maybe you were free for lunch."

"Well," she said hesitantly. "They're expecting me at the hospital."

Lou sat next to her, his mustache wrapping gently around a half smile—his dark brows furrowed. "I know it must have been a shock for Robbie to behave like that. I didn't realize that he was that kind of man." Lou lowered his head, absently intertwining his fingers. "What do you plan to do about him?"

Alex looked into the soft eyes of her surrogate father and sank comfortably into the cradle of his arms. The sadness in his expression revealed a guilt that she didn't want him to feel. At that moment, she wished for his sake more than hers that she had never met Robbie.

She loved Lou. He had stepped out years before it was acceptable and married a black woman. Her Aunt Sarah had been her father's older sister. They had kindly opened their home to Alex and her brother, Zeke eighteen years ago.

Her uncle and Zeke were pretty much her only remaining family since her aunt had died eight years ago. Lou and Sarah had never had children together and eagerly doted on her the instant she arrived in California. She recalled how her aunt's Christian values had been a source of irritation for Lou. In many ways, he reminded her a little of Desi. Owning a casino in Las Vegas didn't help matters any. As long as she could remember, he had been very involved in the entertainment and recreational industry. At least that's what he called it. Her aunt had called it *the devil's canvas*.

"Frankly, I don't plan to do anything," Alex answered, struggling to swallow past the lump in her throat. "I'll just move on with my life." Alex averted her eyes as she withdrew from her uncle. She hoped that his attempt at comfort would-

# Fragment In The Sand

n't prompt the very emotion she was trying so hard to subdue.

"I'm glad to hear that," he said. "I only wish that I hadn't introduced him into your life." He paused and lifted her chin, gazing intently into her eyes as if he'd find gold if he went deep enough. Then he patted her on the back of her hand in a gesture of support and leaned forward on the sofa.

"It's not your fault, Uncle Lou. You had no way of seeing into Robbie's heart."

"I've been working with him for quite some time—I should have known something. I'm just glad you're not going to let this push you back."

"Don't you think I'm a little old now for you to worry about me withdrawing from life? Besides, I think God had already prepared me for something like this."

"I know, but you can't take shock and strain too lightly, Alex."

"No, I can't," she said with conviction. "But the longer I'm *outside*, the stronger I am. I certainly don't want anyone feeling sorry for me." She cocked her head and glanced over at him pointedly.

"No one's trying to feel sorry for you. We're just concerned," Lou said. "You still have to deal with things that you know may be affecting you negatively. So I've made you an appointment to talk to Dr. Gleason tomorrow morning."

"Do you really think I need to talk to a shrink at this stage of the game, Uncle Lou?"

"Alex, you're important to me. I just want to make sure…"

"I know, and I'll be fine," she said, surprised that he would use almost the exact words that Zeke had used when she phoned him. "Don't worry, I'll go."

Alex had been frustrated having to stand on the sidelines as undeclared hostility elevated between her brother and uncle. It was a dark issue that neither would discuss. In many ways, she knew Lou better than she knew Zeke, but nothing took the place of her relationship with her brother. His voice had once been her only link between reality and the trap of illusion. He had called into her therapy sessions weekly to help pull her back from a land that was still tucked away in her subconscious and she would forever be grateful.

Zeke had always been a sort of icon that represented who she really was—a connection to something that both intrigued and haunted her—much like the hourglass. He was her most devoted fan and sometimes even her best friend. The years and miles between them could never change how she felt about him.

"I know you'll be fine. Thank God that you have your career." Lou paused and glanced into the distance, his reassuring smile having suddenly turned somber. "You know what your aunt would be saying right now?"

"Yeah," Alex said, nodding her head. "She'd remind me, in no uncertain terms, to put my trust in the Lord."

Lou snickered, his eyes glistening with delight. "What was that funny saying she always used?"

"*A steady rock won't sink or slide,*" Alex said, smiling as she envisioned her aunt's face. She hadn't thought of that little expression in a long time. "I always thought she said that when she couldn't think of anything else."

"Yeah, me, too." Lou chuckled under his breath. "Did you ever figure out what it meant?"

"Not a clue. You?"

"No idea," he said, shaking his head. "You're so much like her, you know?"

"By the way, did you ever get all the repairs done at the casino?"

"Yeah, thank God, it's all repaired," he said. "That fire nearly wiped me out."

"Is the insurance company still holding out?"

"Yeah, but don't you worry your pretty little head about it."

\*\*\*

From the moment she stepped into the quiet elevator, Alex felt a strange, sinking feeling in the pit of her stomach. The bell rang as it came to a smooth halt and opened its doors. She stepped off and headed for the nurse's station to get her assignment from Mrs. Waters, the most ill humored being on the planet. She always looked like an over-stuffed teacher who glared at everyone over the rim of her glasses.

The hushed blue walls were easy on the eyes, but did very little for one's disposition, Alex thought, moving down the corridor. Behind the counter at the nurse's station, Terri was directing a visitor to a patient's room. She looked at Alex and smiled. Nodding back with a smile, Alex proceeded to the office just behind the station.

"Hello, Mrs. Waters," she said, breezing through the open door.

"Good afternoon, Alex," she said, peering over her glasses. Though she attempted a smile, her lips were stiff and her gaze steady. "I'm glad you're here. I wanted to have a word with you before you got started."

"Sure."

"There's a four-year-old little boy in the burn unit. I want you to spend as much time as you can spare with him. His name is Brian and he's not responding very well to treatment."

"Certainly," Alex said, a frown beginning to crease her brow. Although Mrs. Waters could be quite intimidating, Alex was aware of her complete devotion to her patients.

"The doctors suggest that his emotional state is very important to his recovery. We were hoping you could try to get close to him. We've seen how good you are with the children and quite frankly, you're our last hope. He's had no family to visit him at all."

Apart from the critical nature of her discourse, Alex was floored by the woman's attempt at being pleasant—even to the extent of a near compliment. But her heart went out to the child—just a baby, really—who'd had no visitors from family. "I'll do the best I can," Alex said as she hurried out.

Brian had been burned over seventy-five percent of his body. Bandages, ointment and tubes seemed to swallow him up. The smell was like nothing she'd ever experienced. His weakened, disfigured body lay limp on the hospital bed, his arms suspended over his head. Since he was burned down to his third layer of skin, cultured tissue—the newly grafted skin was very fragile and couldn't be rubbed against the bed. He was heavily sedated, but it was still pure agony to listen to his moans. It was almost more than she could bear.

The day finally arrived when Brian could open his eyes. Alex was thrilled for the progress, but astounded by the mournful dullness that lay within them. She later learned from Terri that he hadn't spoken a word since he'd been brought in.

It greatly troubled her that he might be scared. She knew what it was like to be scared when so young. She recalled her own trauma and how her aunt and uncle had refused to send her to an institution.

Taking an extra couple of weeks at the hospital exclusively with Brian, Alex filled his room with bright balloons and pictures. She even took a cassette recorder and music, which seemed to lift his disposition.

To her relief, she hadn't thought much at all about Robbie except to listen to the messages he left on their answering machine. Her resolve to put the ordeal behind her was working and she couldn't have been happier about that.

She recalled listening one evening while Desi read Robbie the riot act on the phone. She swore that if he didn't stop calling, she wouldn't be responsible for what she did. At that instant, Alex felt very sorry for him while at the same time, incredibly moved by Desi's protective stance.

# CHAPTER 4

## *Changes*

Bone weary, Casey Oliver removed his jacket and ran his palm over his scalp before ringing the doorbell at Brenda's apartment. Following a grueling day of debriefing and paper-work, he would much rather have gone home, but thought he would at least drop in to see her.

"Hi, handsome," she said, beaming up at him. "How was your day?"

"Same—o, same—o," he mumbled, brushing his lips gently against her cheek. He moved stiffly into the small but stylish living room and plopped down on the couch with a sigh. Instinctively, he reached for the remote on the coffee table while Brenda disappeared into the kitchen. She chatted on busily as he stared blankly at the television screen. "How was your day?" he called.

"Pretty good. I think I might be getting that promotion I was telling you about, she said, dropping ice cubes into a glass. "I'm waiting on the call now. I'm glad you're here."

The frosty sizzle of the ice as liquid contacted it produced a thirst in Casey that hadn't been there a moment earlier. "That's great," he said inertly.

A few moments passed with the television displaying images of a basketball tournament that he wasn't paying much attention to. He looked up just as Brenda approached with two glasses of tea.

"Thanks." He smiled and took one of the glasses from her hand. "You look nice today."

"Thank you, kind sir," she said, playfully. "I bought this for my interview this morning."

"How do you think it came out?" Casey asked, eyeing her eager expression.

"It went well. I'm very hopeful."

He'd been seeing Brenda for only six months. Initially he was looking for someone to accompany him to public gatherings and spend a little time with to pull his mind off what he thought were problems. He recalled that one of the first things he'd noticed about her was her calculating drive and ambition. He often felt like an old man around her, and feared they had very little in common.

At least he had been totally honest with her from the start. He was very much aware that Brenda wasn't the one he wanted to spend the rest of his life with, and wondered if there *was* such a creature. If his experience had taught him anything, it was that he should probably remain single.

His dad had warned him that a lawman's life wasn't an easy one, especially if a lot of travel was involved. It could be a curse, an incredibly lonely existence with the wrong woman at his side. Ignoring his father's admonition, he had married Angie after only five months of courtship. She'd gotten enough after only a year and walked out on him. Maybe if he had taken more time and gotten to know her better, he wouldn't have made a mistake that had hurt them both. He recalled how she used to say that their marriage was like living on constant alert.

After the divorce, both his dad and Zeke had been very supportive. He didn't think either knew how much he still hurt behind the calamity. He thought the world of his dad. He'd been nine when his mother died of a massive heart attack. Even at that early age, he was aware that his dad was blaming himself for her death.

"You haven't forgotten that we're invited over to Zeke and Peg's on Friday, have you?"

"No, I remember. In fact, I'm looking forward to it." Brenda sat next to Casey and began to massage his neck. "Boy, you're tight."

"I'll be okay after I get home and take a hot shower," he said, leaning forward.

"Why don't you move to the floor and let me try to get this kink out?"

Reluctantly, Casey slid to the floor directly in front of her. And with robust vigor, she massaged his shoulders while he

# Fragment In The Sand

made funny little grunting noises. His mind moved to his best friend's family. Apart from his job and church, the three of them were his only solid bond in Oklahoma City. Despite his pleasure at being in their company, he sometimes felt a little awkward—sort of like a crippled relative. He knew they didn't think of him as such, and his opinions were probably based on his critical views of himself.

He privately longed for a family of his own, but didn't see how it was possible with his commitment to law enforcement. He often wished for a considerably more stationary situation and had already talked with his supervisor about getting off the road. As of yet, there had been nothing else that intrigued him. He loved his job with the Marshal Service and had decided a long time ago to stick with it.

When the phone rang, Brenda rushed to the kitchen to answer it. She talked for several long minutes and returned to the living room exhilarated.

"I got the promotion!" she shrieked. "That was my supervisor."

"Great," Casey said, reaching up to tap his glass to hers. "Congratulations."

"Thanks," she said with a noticeable hint of disappointment. "I've really worked hard for this."

"I know you have." Casey was too sodden with the lingering sensation of disorder in his life to notice Brenda's need for shared excitement.

"You *could* act like you were really excited for me," Brenda said, a pained look in her eyes.

"I *am* excited for you," he stammered. "I'm sorry. I guess I'm a little distracted this evening. I don't mean to put a damper on your news. I really am proud of your accomplishment."

"Casey, you need a vacation. Why don't you take one? It'd probably do you good."

"I don't know that a vacation would help," Casey said, perplexed. "I've been thinking about making some changes."

"What kind of changes?"

"I don't really know," he said, absently. "Maybe I'm experiencing a mid-life crises." They both chuckled.

**40**

"Then a vacation in a quiet place would probably help you focus. Why don't you give it some serious thought?"

"You may be right. I could go down to Gregory Falls to see Dad—maybe stay in that old cottage in the woods and do some fishing."

"Y'all have a cottage?"

"Nothing fancy. It's just an old shack that used to belong to my grandparents. It still doesn't have electricity or running water," Casey said chuckling. "Zeke and I fixed it up back when we were in high school. Dad even let us move out there for a while." He snorted, remembering how excited the two of them had been at making all kinds of boyish plans.

"No electricity or running water?" Brenda asked. "Why in the world would you want to move out—" She broke off when she saw Casey's sly grin. "So, how many girls did you take out there?"

"None, but not because we didn't try. Dad kept such a sharp eye peeled that we were more restricted than had we stayed in the main house." Casey paused with a pensive expression on his face. "I think I will. A vacation *does* sound good now that I think about it. Maybe I'll talk Zeke into joining me."

"You think a lot of Zeke and his family, don't you?"

"Yeah, I do. He's been my best friend since the day Dad brought him home. He was a confused and angry fellow back then." Casey's grin widened as he thought of Zeke's former disposition.

"That's hard to believe," Brenda said. "He seems so gentle and easy going."

"That's what life with Peg and Tracee has done for him. Zeke doesn't have much family left—except a younger sister out in Los Angeles."

"How sad," she said. "Do you really think you can pull him away to sit around on the bank of a pond?"

"Maybe. I know he could stand to get away, too, though. I'll get my dad on him. Zeke will listen to *him*."

"What's his sister like?"

"I don't know her well…haven't seen her since she was a little kid. She's a fashion model now—quite successful, I understand." Casey leaned back against the sofa and shut his eyes. "One of those pampered princess types, I suspect."

"She must be gorgeous."

"I guess," Casey said, indifferently. "They call her the 'Regal Nubian.' I've only seen pictures of her lately."

"Oh, my God!" Brenda squealed. "*That's* Zeke's sister?"

"You know of her?" he asked, glancing back surprised. "Zeke says she's really rather reserved. But then, my friend has a blind spot when it comes to his sister."

Hoping that she would return to her kneading, Casey worked himself into a more comfortable position while still on the floor. He was just about to glance at the score of the game when he caught a glimpse of something peeking from beneath the sofa. He instinctively pulled it out for a closer look. It was a credential case, much like the one he carried his badge in. As the two continued to pass small talk, he slyly opened it and was jolted by the identification inside. The familiar signature of a deputy U.S. Marshal's badge boldly glared up at him, evoking a strong sense of betrayal.

Closing his hand over the case, he glanced up at Brenda, who was totally absorbed in the game by now. More relieved than hurt, Casey placed the case into his shirt pocket and leaned back again, unsure exactly why the discovery wasn't much of a surprise.

He recalled the party at Earl's, his boss's home. He had taken Brenda and introduced her to everyone that had come. He smirked inwardly. He thought she was making herself a little too comfortable with Sanger.

Casey exhaled a long blast of air and turned his eyes back toward the television. He was certain now where he should start making changes. He hadn't been completely honest with himself, much less any woman he had kept company with. He would simply pick a moment to end the relationship. Obviously, there was no need to concern himself with hurting her.

He toyed absently with the credential case in his pocket, envisioning the tall, blue-eyed deputy to whom it belonged. Casey smiled, determining to return the badge to Sanger tomorrow morning. He wasn't into playing tag with a fellow deputy who at some point may have to watch his back.

***

The days passed with consistent monotony. By Friday, Casey was ready to end his relationship with Brenda. But wasn't sure how to go about it.

Pacing impatiently around his living room, Casey waited for her to arrive so they could head over to Zeke's for dinner. He was deep in thought when the doorbell startled him.

He fumbled miserably with the lock, spurred mostly by the urgent rapping and another repeated ringing of the doorbell. It kindled an anguish that made him jerk the door open with a snap. Glancing down into Brenda's angry face, he realized that she was in no mood for the reprimand he was tempted to give her.

Her eyes emitted dagger sharp rays aimed directly for his heart. She sashayed past him into the living room, dropped onto the sofa, and crossed her legs. "I understand that you found something in my apartment belonging to Sanger," she said defiantly. "Why didn't you mention it to me before you tossed it back in his face?"

She was bold, but he also detected a trace of embarrassment, maybe at being caught. Casey traced Brenda's steps, unable to veil his amusement at her impudence. Easing down into the chair opposite her, she continued with her railing without giving him a chance to answer.

"I'm sorry, Casey, but you obviously wont be ready for a serious relationship for some time," she began, lowering her eyes. "I need more. Between your job and issues concerning your ex, I don't see much hope for us."

Casey knew that Brenda had probably been shocked to learn that he knew about Sanger. She wanted to confront him with a trumped up complaint in an effort to avoid rejection. He decided to grant her the easy exit. It would, after all, accomplish what had to be.

"Maybe you're right, Brenda. I'm sorry if my behavior caused you any anguish." He couldn't help throwing her one final jab. "I wish you and Sanger the very best."

Her eyes widened then tightened into slits just before she

opened her mouth to deny the implication. "Sanger and I aren't seeing each other like you assume. I simply entertained him one evening when you were out of town."

Brenda stood and moved to the door, then paused with her hand on the knob. "I—I'm sorry," she said without turning.

Casey stepped forward and gently embraced her from behind, lightly kissing her on the cheek. "It just wasn't meant to be. I hope that you find what it is you're looking for."

"I wish you the same, Case," she whispered. Brenda slipped through the door without even looking him in the eye.

Zeke and his exuberant three-year-old greeted him at the front door. To Casey's delight, Tracee thought of him as family.

"Hi, Uncle Case," she squealed, raising her arms over her head to be lifted. Casey complied, lifting her overhead and swinging her around until she became a squirming ball of giggles. Zeke stood back and smiled as he watched his friend and daughter's greeting ritual.

The charming tot had stolen Casey's heart the moment she'd opened her eyes. He smiled, remembering how often she'd fallen asleep in his arms—one hand on his head, the other in her mouth with her head lying comfortably on his shoulder. It almost pulled tears of joy and surrender from his eyes to see her so free and filled with glee. And the high-pitched giggles and shrieks were infectious, and spread through the house like perfume. To have that fanciful way of spilling delight over the adults in her life was a blessing he'd always be grateful for.

The moment he set Tracee back on her feet, she was pulling him toward the kitchen to show him her new puppy. The kitchen was filled with the aroma of home cooking while Peg moved around comfortably, checking the oven temperature and stirring pots.

"Hey, Case," Peg greeted cheerfully. "Brenda with you?"

"Couldn't make it," he said, trying to keep Tracee from dragging him through the back door. "By the way, that peach cobbler was great."

"I'm glad you enjoyed it," she said genuinely. "Dinner

should be ready in half an hour."

"I can hardly wait," Casey said, clumsily planting a kiss on her cheek as Tracee tugged at his legs. "Smells great."

"Making yourself at home doesn't include kissing my wife and mesmerizing my daughter," Zeke teased, standing in the door behind him.

"Oh, but I enjoy it," Peg quipped, grinning up at her husband and playfully wiggling her brows.

"Me, too, Daddy," Tracee chimed in, still holding onto Casey's hand.

After they all recovered from the resounding burst of laughter, Casey had no choice but to give in to Tracee's insistence. He allowed her to pull him through the door leading into the back yard to meet the new puppy, Chuck. After the brief introduction, he strolled over to the other side of the yard and sat in a lawn chair and watched as Zeke placed chicken on the grill. Tracee had become preoccupied with Chuck and didn't even notice that he had left her side.

Casually picking up the newspaper that Zeke had left lying on the ground, Casey scanned through the financial section. He could tell that something was bothering his friend by the tight set of his jaw. "How was your day?" he asked, glancing up over the paper.

"Just fine," Zeke answered without turning around. "Spent most of it catching up on paperwork."

"Good day in the sun!" Casey blurted out, looking intently at something in the paper. "Boy, I'd like to have a piece of that."

"What?" Zeke said, turning to look at Casey.

"Max-Stem Technologies," Casey said. "Their stock has split two to one eleven times in the last five years. That's remarkable."

"Yeah, I saw that," Zeke said impassively, turning back to the chicken.

"It's based right here in Oklahoma," Casey said, continuing to read. "I didn't know that. Didn't your dad work for them"

"Yeah. But it was pretty small back then."

"Don't they make health machines or something?" Casey

**45**

asked, closing the paper and placing it back on the ground. He watched as Zeke's lips tightened into a smile. His eyes had shadows beneath them. Whatever was bothering him, he wasn't willing to discuss it.

"Something like that," Zeke said absently. "All kinds of diagnostic and hospital equipment."

"If your dad had bought stock in the company back then, you'd be a rich man now."

"If my dad had done a number of things back then, I would simply be satisfied now," Zeke countered.

"What's going on, Zeke?" Casey asked abruptly. "You seem a little...distracted."

Zeke turned around and flashed him a grin. "You worried about me? I'm touched."

"Nah. I just don't want to look at that ugly mug of yours all evening."

"I guess I let something Tyson said the other day start me thinking about things," Zeke said. "And all this ado about Max-Stem—"

"Tyson threatened ya, huh?"

"Yeah. How did you know?"

"A couple of deputies were in the courtroom, remember?" Casey asked. "Threats come with the job, Zeke. They've never spooked you before. What's so different about this one?"

"I can't say it spooked me as much as started me thinking about some of my old cases."

"Wade Sparkman," Casey guessed. "Don't tell me you still let that one haunt you?" Casey was aware that Zeke had never gotten over having to kill the young man who'd attempted a robbery on a little corner store. He looked hard at his friend. He had always thought that particular case spooked Zeke because it reminded him a little of himself.

"He was only a kid, Case. I guess I never quite let it all go. What if Ike had shot me?"

"Zeke, there are a lot of differences. For one, you were only fifteen and as the arresting officer, Dad saw your youth and pain. Wade was nineteen years old and had a loaded gun in the mouth of a fellow officer. You had no real choice in the matter."

"He was just a kid high on crack," Zeke said. "I wasn't on drugs, but just as desperate to get money and…"

"I know. So you could get back to your sister."

Casey had heard it all before and always felt compelled to try to console him somehow. It concerned him that Zeke couldn't seem to let that part of his life fade into the folds of his past. "Sparkman unquestionably would have killed your partner, Zeke. You know the story, man. Let it go."

"I will," Zeke said reluctantly. "I'm carrying way too much baggage around in my head right now. Don't say anything in front of Peg. She doesn't know that I still think about Sparkman. I don't want her to think I'm beginning to let the past spook me out there."

"Don't even worry about that," Casey said. "By the way, I was thinking about going down to Gregory Falls—just to get away and do a little fishing. Wanna join me?"

"Nah, not right now. I have a desk full of paperwork and not a lot of vacation left. Peg has her heart set on visiting her parents for Labor Day this year."

"Your sister will be having a birthday around then, won't she?" Casey asked, wondering if something about Alex was bothering him.

"Yeah. September ninth. She'll be twenty-five," Zeke said, already becoming more animated. "By the way, what's up with you and Brenda? I thought she would be joining us tonight."

"That, my friend, is a thing of the past."

"You okay with that?"

"Absolutely," Casey said, smiling up at him. Although he knew he couldn't prevent it, he didn't want Zeke adding him to his worry load. Just then, his cell phone began to ring. When he hung up, he looked at Zeke and shook his head. "Just as well. Got an assignment in a couple of weeks."

"Will you be gone long?"

"Maybe a week. Flying out to the west coast with a transport." Casey carefully shoved the phone back into his pocket. "Well, so much for that vacation."

"Maybe by the time you're actually ready to go, I'll be

**47**

able to join you," Zeke said. "Hey, if you get near Los Angeles, why don't you..."

"I'm already ahead of you," Casey said. "I haven't seen Alex in years. If she weren't splattered over every magazine in the country, I probably wouldn't be able to recognize her. I'll just need her number and address. Do you think she'll mind?"

"Alex? Nah, of course not. I've been kinda worried about her since that New York incident."

"I thought Lou said everything was fine?"

"He did, but something's not right. She's been withdrawn since she called off her wedding—a little too cool. She usually sends me email pretty regularly, but she hasn't been her usual chatty self. I think this may be bothering her more than she's willing to admit."

"Weddings are a big thing for women, Zeke. I can imagine what she's going through."

"Actually, her focus is different. She believes it was a divine correction. I'm really proud of the way she's holding to her faith," Zeke said with a broad smile. "But there's something...I don't know...something is haunting her. If you can get close enough, see if you can pull it out of her."

"Tall order, Bro. But I'll see what I can do."

# CHAPTER 5

## *Harassed*

When Desi received the news of her father's death, she was unbelievably poised. Although Alex could tell that she was upset, she seemed very deliberate in handling her grief calmly. Flying out immediately, she convinced Alex to take her place on a weeklong photo shoot in Cradleview, Arizona.

Cradleview was a little ghost town just south of Phoenix that CEF used occasionally to shoot their autumn line. Reluctantly, Alex agreed and drove her own car, anticipating the road time as a good opportunity to clear her head.

The chain of events over the past weeks had started her thinking more about taking some serious time off. She felt as if she was on a merry-go-round that had spun out of control and for the first time that she could remember, she didn't welcome her uncle's interference. She wouldn't think of hurting him, but she had to find a way to stabilize herself. Maybe a place deep in a secluded little town—someplace she could be alone and think.

Zeke had been right. She had allowed both him and Uncle Lou to manage her entire life, and she wasn't at all contented. She didn't even see a way at the present to move in a fulfilling direction. She accepted her new perspective as a sure sign that she was earnest about listening to God for her direction—not what someone else thought that she should do.

Between her dissatisfaction and growing commitment to Brian, the little boy she'd met in the hospital, Alex was, indeed, at a crossroad—a junction that would require insight to navigate. She knew now more than at any other time that she wanted children in her life. And she wanted the freedom to photograph real people and places of beauty that spoke of the goodness of God. She'd pray for wisdom. And hoped she would recognize it when it came.

# Fragment In The Sand

It excited her to think that whatever was hidden in her heart, God had put it there. Surely He would guide her through all the twists and turns that life seemed to be throwing at her. Yet she felt that her passions were insignificant in light of the aspirations of others. She supposed their simplicity was due to her continual yearning for the restoration of her family—a childhood fantasy she'd never quite outgrown. She knew, of course that it was quite impossible for her family to be restored to her. According to her uncle, her father had died not long after sending her and Zeke to California. And Zeke now had a family of his own.

She'd never really gotten a chance to know her parents—she'd been too young. Not like Zeke. Maybe that's why he had taken their father's disappearance so hard.

She wished she could remember his face. She could close her eyes and see her mother's, but she always drew a blank when she tried to conjure up her father's. She didn't know if he was tall, short, fat, dark or bright. By the time she'd started to wonder, her uncle told her that he was dead and then her aunt had died. Although they provided wonderfully for her, she'd never felt as if she really belonged.

Her uncle had often stressed to her that her career was her only way toward finding herself. She somehow knew that this couldn't be true. At the time, however, she had concluded that her only chance at fulfillment or even obtaining a portion of her dream was marriage. And right now, that too, was unrealistic. She wanted very little to do with men.

Photography was another story. She had briefly mentioned her thoughts on God placing certain desires in our hearts to her pastor who, as always, had a ready reply. "Though it's a sound concept, you must remember that the timing of God is also involved."

It had sounded more like a warning than encouragement and had, in fact, daunted her a little. But she would take his advice and start journalizing the fragments of her life when she felt the Lord was involved in it. He had assured her that after an adequate span of time, she could put them together like a puzzle and ascertain the direction that God is giving.

Despite her eager anxiety over anticipated changes in her

life, she could also detect a hint of apprehension. She felt as if she were chomping at the bit for something without a shape— without a name.

Alex's thoughts roamed during the drive to Arizona. She rolled down the window and seemed to detect dampness in the air. At certain stretches, she almost felt completely alone in the world. And for the time being, it didn't feel too bad.

She reluctantly pondered Desi's allegation that she had lost Robbie to another woman because she wouldn't have pre-marital sex. After seeing him with the woman, she supposed it was true. Feelings of betrayal and anger welled up in her all over again. It was painfully obvious that the woman she'd seen was indeed offering him something that she herself had-n't been willing to.

She had to find a way out of her present life. "Help me, Lord," she whispered into the darkness surrounding her. She knew that her hesitance to leave modeling had more to do with fear and uncertainty than anything else. Whatever security it seemed to offer, she didn't want to make a mistake that would cause her embarrassment in the long run.

It was quite evident that God had blessed her in her present career. Would He do that if she weren't where she was supposed to be in her life? And if this was where she was supposed to be, why was she feeling so disconnected—so confused?

She purposely turned her thoughts then to little Brian and immediately her eyes brimmed with tears. The hurt little boy had stolen her heart completely. The doctors didn't have much hope at all for his recovery, and she had done everything in her power to make sure he knew that someone cared about him. She wanted him to know that he wasn't alone—that she was there, she cared, and she loved him.

Though her presence was thought to be good medicine for him, Mrs. Waters urged her to avoid becoming too attached— to let a few days slip by here and there without visiting. The woman didn't realize that her advice had come much too late.

Her heart had skidded to a halt the first time he had smiled and squeezed her fingers. In fact, it seemed that she was the only one he had responded to in a positive way. It made her feel good that the young boy would accept her, especially when he probably remembered that his own mother, high on drugs, had doused him with gasoline and ignited him. Alex felt the warm tears running down her face. She angrily swiped them away, feeling overwhelmed with the ugliness in the world.

She had panicked when she learned that the state would be placing Brian into foster care if he were released from the hospital. On impulse, she had discreetly checked into her chances of adopting him. She had been very disappointed when her pursuit was discouraged. The fact that she was single, inexperienced and very busy in her profession presented certain obstacles Brian shouldn't be asked to deal with. It would be difficult enough to endure the ongoing dilemma of his recovery, not only physically, but emotionally as well.

She realized it had been an impulsive move and had no choice but to drop her pursuit. In fact, she even felt a little embarrassed for her thoughtless crusade. Nevertheless, they had commended her for the kindhearted efforts of embracing the child's well being. Deep down, however, she knew her motive had a degree of selfishness in it. She had acted on emotion and her own desperate need to have someone in her life to love.

Regardless, her heart had already swelled with anticipation when she went before the authorities with her inquiry. Thank goodness she had mentioned this to no one, maybe because deep down, she knew her mission would be futile. Even though it felt as if she was abandoning him somehow, all she could do was leave Brian in the Lord's hands. She had to believe that He would do what was best for him.

Alex drove on, her throat constricting as her heart ached. All at once, her mind drifted back to the bright grassy field that went on forever in her subconscious. It was a safe place for her—one she'd clung to as a child in an attempt to find refuge from traumatic events. Dr. Gleason had warned her sternly about engaging in this kind of deliberating. But the memory was so pleasant compared to what was going on around her that she had to force herself to let go.

Dr. Gleason had resorted to prescribing stronger sleep aids

when she'd admitted to feeling a slight compulsion to return. He encouraged her to call him if she started to have the same dreams she'd experienced as a child. They had been extremely frightening. She would literally fight to wake herself. It was always dark and stormy in the dream. The safe place was just beyond her and she couldn't find a way to get there. They always ended with her being trapped in a grave beside her mother.

Despite the temptation to stay connected to that safe place, she knew the danger of returning. She doubted seriously whether she would be strong enough to escape its grip again.

\*\*\*

In spite of the long drive, Alex arrived in Cradleview refreshed and ready to work. She was elated when the photo shoots ended a couple of days earlier than scheduled. Armed with a six-pack of caffeine packed soda, she set out for the drive home with hopes of driving straight through. Although the rest of the exhausted crew returned to their hotel in Phoenix, she was anxious to get on the road home. Desperately needing to see Brian, she left at midnight.

After a grueling week of working with Omar Stevens, one of the most sought after photographers in the industry, she was emotionally worn out. She had hoped to speak to him about her options as a photographer, but she never got the chance. He was serious about his work and extremely demanding of the models. Nonetheless, when the sessions ended each day, he turned into a tenacious lothario that she had successfully managed to keep at bay.

Despite what she thought was tactful evasion Omar had apparently taken offense. Towards the end of the shoot, he had begun to treat her with unmistakable animosity. Even the other models had commented on his hostile discourtesies. After her breakup with Robbie, putting up with a hotheaded rogue accustomed to getting his own way was a biting indignity. And she'd had quite enough of little boys in the bodies of men and the games they played.

"God, if I ever become involved with another man—not that I aim to—but if I did, I'd definitely want him to be a man of God. And I won't just take his word for it either."

With having said that, Alex realized that she would never be able to determine that prerequisite without God's help. Robbie had told her that he was a Christian and she had simply taken him at his word, assuming they both shared the same morals and convictions. How naïve she had been. Obviously, being a Christian meant something different to different people. She had to find a way to be sure that she didn't miss God's direction in her life.

The darkness of night had been unsettling to Alex for as long as she could remember. Many years earlier, she had been assured that her nyctophobia would likely dissipate with time, but it had instead intensified. Maybe she should've waited until morning to leave. What was she thinking?

Nervously pulling her Mercedes onto I-10, Alex hoped the black Pontiac trailing so closely behind her didn't mean trouble. She had noticed it pull out behind her back at the gas station, but she also knew that lately she was inclined to be overly suspicious—ever since the incident in New York.

She followed the dark highway, recalling how recent thoughts of being watched were beginning to dominate her mind. Just last week at the grocery store, she'd felt a pair of eyes boring into the small of her back. Even in her own bedroom, she felt the same sensation. She couldn't put her finger on it, and had considered mentioning it to her uncle, but decided at the last minute against it, dismissing the sensation as nervous imagination.

Her anxiety quickly turned to panic when after speeding up, the Pontiac instantly matched her, slowing down only when she did. Alex anxiously began talking out loud to the Lord in an effort to keep her mind from drawing inward. Without doubt, she could sense the pull. Not sure what she was going to do with it, she reached across the console for her camera.

"This man could very easily be someone on his way home," she said, aloud. "Maybe I happened to be taking the same route. After all, I'm not the only one out past midnight." She chose confirming words to convince herself that there was really nothing to worry about. Scanning the relatively paltry traffic, she quickly returned her glance to the rearview. The car was customized with bright amber fog lights. It wouldn't be difficult to keep it in her sights.

After several minutes of gazing at the car, she watched worriedly as the Pontiac pulled up beside her. Panic stricken, she attempted a glimpse of the driver out of the corner of her eye, hoping that she didn't appear as frightened as she felt. Fearful recollections of recent news stories took over, allowing her imagination to peak. She could feel the perspiration sting her underarm. What if this were going to be like that movie Star had brought home where a woman was abducted after her tire had blown on the highway?

When the car dashed in front of her, Alex grabbed her camera and snapped. The car quickly shot back behind her, and she fumbled nervously for her phone. Dialing her uncle's number, Alex hoped the driver would assume she was calling the police and pull off. Her mind imagined all sorts of frightening scenarios and wondered if he was attempting to rob her.

"Alex, calm down," Lou said, "and tell me what he looks like."

"I think he's white—maybe biracial…in his thirties with long dark hair pulled back into a ponytail. I can't see much more…it's so dark…I think he's wearing a dark shirt."

"Can you tell what kind of car he's driving?" Lou asked.

"It's a black Pontiac Firebird. I'm not sure of the year."

"Get to the next city, honey. Stop at a hotel and call me back. In the meantime, I'll notify the authorities."

Again, the driver pulled up next to her. Though it was dark, she was sure he'd gestured an obscenity. Who was this guy? Her mind frantically tried to make some sense of this absurdity while she tried to control her trembling. She wondered if perhaps Omar might have sent him out to frighten her, but that didn't make sense. Omar might be intense, but surely his ego could withstand being snubbed.

Slowly, the man began to force her closer to the edge of the highway. Alex screamed when she lost control on loose gravel that flung her car into the guardrail. Sitting stunned for several moments, she noticed the man pull in behind her. A sigh of relief escaped her lips when she saw the patrol car approaching from behind with his lights on. The driver shot back out into traffic and sped away.

The patrol car stayed with her for several miles then took an exit just before she reached the Buckeye city limits. She chose however, to keep moving towards Los Angeles rather than stop at a hotel.

By the time Alex arrived, she was a nervous wreck and drove directly to her uncle's condo. After a few grueling questions by the LAPD, which included a sketch drawn with the few details she was able to give them, she went to bed at her uncle's as opposed to going home.

She awakened a few hours later in a cold sweat, trembling uncontrollably. With a pungent stab, she realized the dreaded nightmare had come.

# CHAPTER 6

## *A Prince*

"I scared her pretty good," Rosell said into his cell phone. "For a minute there, her eyes looked like they were gonna' pop out of her head."

"Did you get rid of the car?" the woman asked frigidly. "You don't want to keep a stolen vehicle too long."

"Yeah. I got rid of that before she made it into LA." He laughed and anxiously glanced around his room. "Is there something else? I can't stay in this dead motel room too much longer without going stir crazy."

"That's enough for the night. You can start with the calls in a couple of days."

"All right." He hung up and grinned. Little did they know he was spending quite a bit of time watching the lovely Miss Webb from her fire escape. She was a fresh young thing—didn't go in for all of the glitzy parading like most of the women in her line of work did. He hadn't missed the legs, long wavy hair, glistening eyes and that knockout figure, either. It was nice to see someone with her looks spurn the usual attractions—not at all like his mother. It had been all money, men and liquor with her. He sneered recalling the constant thrashings he'd endured at her hands—that is, until he chopped them off.

He laughed out loud and turned to glance at an enlarged picture of the "Regal Nubian." She certainly was that, he thought, and more. He knew that he was beginning to feel quite a fondness for the unsullied little beauty. He usually didn't mix business with pleasure. But with this one he was willing to make exceptions.

It was amazing how naïve she was to assume that just because she was on the third floor, she was safe from harm. She slept with her bedroom window slightly ajar—probably liked the feel that she wasn't locked up in a small little room. He used to be like that. He liked the fact that when she finally got to sleep she slept so soundly. He had even gotten the nerve a couple of times to venture into her room.

He couldn't wait to make her acquaintance face to face— but he would have to. The boss owed him a couple more payments. Right now, he would simply enjoy being near her— watching her.

\*\*\*

"You guys go ahead," Alex said to her roommates. "I'm going to sit here by the pond for a while." The girls had decided to go for a morning run in the neighborhood park. Despite the emotional cloud that hung over her head, the bright May morning was perfect for some clean fresh air. The sun was bright over the clear pond, and the singing of birds was very distinct.

She hadn't yet been able to shake the despair that was gradually mounting. After getting over the initial shock of the highway incident, she had learned that Brian had taken a turn for the worse. They wouldn't even let her in to see him. Taking a huge risk, she had stolen into his room the night before, just to be with him. There was little else she could do for him but pray and sing.

Amid her anguish, she had fought to find something else to focus on, and had been surprised to see a Max-Stem emblem attached to several of the machines in Brian's room. Her thoughts had quickly turned to her deceased father as she once again tried to conjure up an image of his face. It was always so frustrating. The description that Uncle Lou had given her was imprecise and left many questions unanswered, but she knew that he didn't really like talking about her father for some reason.

Alex felt like she was weaving about in a haze of confusion trying to grab hold of something solid—something that would keep her in the sphere of reality. She had to focus on the Lord when she felt herself slipping, but generally, the allure was so sudden that she didn't have time to refocus. It was all quite spontaneous—frightening and unconstrained.

**58**

*A steady rock won't sink or slide.* Her aunt's frequent expression floated into her mind as if it had been beckoned. She was jolted from her reverie when she heard Desi's concerned voice.

"You okay, honey?" Alex impulsively lifted the camera that hung on a cord around her neck and snapped Desi's priceless expression into the archives of her collection of faces.

"I'm fine," she said, lightly waving off the worry as needless. "I'm just a little winded. I'll sit this one out and enjoy the pond for a few minutes."

"It doesn't look like you intended to do much running anyway," Desi said, lifting her left brow. "Not with that thing flopping around your neck."

Alex glanced absently at her camera and shrugged. She hoped her restrained comments would prompt her roommates to continue on their run, and mechanically stooped to retie her right running shoe. Turning her eyes out toward the small pond, she watched the lazy waves move inward—mesmerizing her.

The words to her aunt's favorite hymn came to her mind just then. It was as clear as crystal and she began to hum them. *On Christ the solid rock I stand.* Her aunt had often sung it around the house and it always made Alex feel safe. She could almost see her swaying back and forth to the melody.

Hearing the sound of movement, Alex turned startled eyes to see her roommates still beside her, jogging in place.

"Will you two *please* get going!"

"Well, if you're sure," Star said, gazing at her impishly. "But we'll be glad to send a wheelchair back for you." Alex rolled her eyes and glanced up just as Star winked at Desi and turned to trot down the path with Desi close in pursuit. She glanced after them, gratified that they had left her alone with her thoughts. Aware that her friends were trying to keep an eye on her by staying close, Alex felt a little guilty for cherishing her solitude. With everything that had happened to her lately, she knew that their concerns weren't unwarranted.

Although Desi was more of a pleasure seeker, hitting the lively spots every chance she got, Star could be just as reserved as Alex could. Even though she often accompanied Desi, she

# Fragment In The Sand

looked notably out of place. It was obvious that she still felt awkward going along with her. Alex had never understood Star's compulsion to do so. She snickered in spite of her self, thinking how like a lost child she was. Maybe all three of them were. She certainly had no room to cast stones. She, of course, had her own issues—many of them never spoken of to her roommates. Her past psychosis wasn't a thing she thought would make for pleasant conversation. Only her brother and uncle were aware of her dread. They, of course, tended to smother her with intense protection—something she had to find a way to stop.

She had been coddled and protected by others all her life, and now was the time that she had to start depending on her self. She perceived a growing expectancy with regard to her relationship with God, but didn't know how to go about preparing for it.

Why couldn't she just be happy with the life she had? She recalled how her aunt had swept her off to church every chance she got, strolling down the center aisle, exhibiting one of her many colorful hats. Had it somehow warped her perspective?

While Desi often teased her about being a religious nut, Alex knew she didn't mean it maliciously. And she had been pleasantly surprised that Star had frequently attended Sunday services with her.

Alex absently began to focus and snap several photos, singing as the words gently rolled into her mind.

*"My hope is built on nothing less than Jesus' blood and righteousness.*

*I dare not trust the sweetest frame, but wholly lean on Jesus' name.*

*On Christ the solid Rock I stand – All other ground is sinking sand.*

*All other ground is sinking sand."*

She smiled to herself, thinking how easily the words to the song had come back to her mind even though she hadn't heard them in a long time. Her church seldom sang any of the old hymns, yet the words seemed to flow into her mind as easy as the ripples blew across the pond.

She probably just needed to get away and relax, she decided. She really would like to go visit Zeke, but it would have to wait until after the awards banquet. Several big name designers were hosting the event and though New York wasn't her cup of tea, she was looking forward to going with everyone. Even her uncle had planned on attending this time.

Alex jolted when a large black and tan shepherd cantered over and sniffed at her feet. Although he looked quite intimidating, there was something about him that made her unafraid. She'd seen him before in the park walking with an older distinguished looking black man. She'd noticed him because his gait had a soulful bounce that invariably compelled her to smile.

The dog wagged his tail steadily, appearing good-natured. When he playfully looked up into her face, she cautiously bent down to give him a gentle rub behind his ears. Panting heavily, he almost looked as if he was smiling.

"Hello, pretty boy," she said.

The dog abruptly leaped up and took a couple of wet swipes of her cheek, triggering an eruption of laughter. Gently grasping his head between her palms, she embraced him as impulsively as a child. "What a friendly puppy you are!"

"I'm afraid his puppy days are over," said the gentleman, approaching from behind. Alex abruptly turned toward the dog's owner.

"Hello," she said, trying to maintain the smile that was fading in spite of the delight she found in her new canine friend.

"I'm sorry about Gangster," he said, attaching the dog's leash. "I'm afraid he got away from me this morning." The stranger's smile was warm and sincere, instantly putting her at ease.

"That's okay," Alex said, stroking Gangster gently down his neck.

"Hello. My name is Calvin Prince and this feisty fellow here is Gangster. Any friend of his is a friend of mine. He obviously likes you." Calvin flashed another bright smile as he extended his hand. He was tall with an impressive build and wore a black lightweight pullover, neatly tucked into khaki trousers. The gray that sprinkled his temples completed a look

**61**

# Fragment In The Sand

of distinction. His short hair crested a caramel complexion, emphasizing eyes that sparkled with the same genuine warmth of his smile.

Though she retained a few subtle misgivings, there was something in his comfortable manner that made her instantly like him. Her smile involuntarily broadened as she shook his hand.

"Pleased to meet both of you, Mr. Prince. I'm Alex Webb."

"Tabitha Alexis Webb, to be exact," he corrected. "Please—call me Calvin."

Her eyes widened in alarm at the mention of her full name by a stranger. Visions of the card that had come with the yellow roses instantly leapt to her mind. "How—"

"I read the rags," he interrupted, obviously knowing what she was about to ask. "In fact, I work for one." She raised a brow and abruptly retrieved her hand, fully aware that he was referring to the small weekly tabloids that exploited the private lives of entertainers and the like.

Her uncle had vehemently warned them all about talking to reporters or giving interviews of any kind without checking with him. As if reading her mind, Calvin suddenly held up his hands in a posture of surrender.

"Don't worry, I wouldn't think of invading your privacy, Miss Webb. Besides, I'm not a reporter—just a copy editor."

"Oh," she said, immediately breathing a sigh of relief. "I'm glad to hear that. A girl can't be too careful, you know." She didn't know why she so wholly accepted his explanation, but she did and suddenly realized that she wanted to trust him.

"You're right," he said. "The paper I work for isn't into tale bearing like some of the others. They mostly report on community affairs and family related issues. Would you care to join Gangster and me on our walk this morning?"

Remarkably, she felt no sense of threat with the stranger and surprised herself by accepting his invitation, completely ignoring her uncle's warnings. Hesitating only slightly, she reached for the arm he gallantly extended and strolled back out into the sunlight, her camera rapping against her chest in harmony with their stride.

She wasn't exactly sure when her misgivings ceased or why exactly she decided to keep her new friend hidden from her uncle. But after introducing Calvin to Desi and Star, she'd made them promise not to mention him—but not before they questioned and teased her mercilessly about him.

"It's nothing like that," she'd assured them. "He's just a nice older gentleman whom I simply enjoy being around. There's something intriguing about him. Besides, I think he's just lonely and enjoys being around younger people."

"Why?" Desi asked. "You said he worked for the paper. Doesn't he have friends of his own?"

"I don't know," Alex answered honestly. "I've never seen him with anyone but Gangster."

"I don't understand why you don't want Lou to know about him," Star muttered, her eyes narrowed with suspicion. "Is there something you're not telling us?"

"Uncle Lou worries about me too much already," Alex said with a shrug. "I love him dearly, but I'm beginning to agree with Zeke and see myself as a child on his short leash. Ever since I was little, he's been there to pick me up when I fall, but I think I need to start picking myself up."

"Why?" Star asked. "I've always sort of envied your relationship with Lou—I mean, it's sort of like having your dad right there to keep you safe. What girl wouldn't like that?"

"I need a change," Alex said, a little frustrated. "I need to meet people outside of Uncle Lou's safety net."

"I'm sure he's just trying to protect you, Alex," Desi said. "And I hope you're not blaming him for Robbie's behavior."

"No, of course not."

"I *am* proud of you for recognizing that you need to grow up, though," Desi added. "Lou does pamper you a lot."

"I didn't know you felt that way, too," Alex said. "Why didn't you tell me?"

"If Lou caught wind of my opinions, he'd have my head," Desi quipped. "Besides, I didn't wanna' interfere with family."

"Since when?" Star blurted out, her eyes widening in disbelief. Then she turned and studied Alex. "What's wrong with

## Fragment In The Sand

you, Alex? You've been acting kinda' distant lately."

"Just have a lot on my mind," Alex admitted. "I'm not satisfied anymore. I want more out of life than this."

"With all that's been happening, I almost expected you to feel this way," Star said. "But what else could you want?"

"I'm not sure. I just hope I recognize it when it comes along."

"You know, Lou is going to figure out you're hiding something," Star suggested.

"Maybe so. I'll tell him eventually," Alex said with a shrug. "But I don't want him running any kind of checks. That's so embarrassing when he does that. Calvin is just a nice man who wants to be my friend. In a strange way, he almost reminds me of Zeke, but he's funnier—not so serious. And I don't have to bite my tongue so much."

"You'd better bite your tongue," Star warned. "Have you forgotten he works for a newspaper? They have a way of twisting words to say just the opposite of what you meant. And what could the two of you have to talk about anyway?"

"Everything and nothing," Alex replied smiling. "We spend a lot of time just enjoying each other's company. We talk mostly about his boyhood days. That's why it's so nice—so undemanding. He never asks me about me." Alex suddenly started to giggle, causing her roommates to look at each other skeptically. "I noticed this Christmas tree shaped scar on his shoulder the other day. He told me he had gotten it when he and a friend went fishing. When his friend fell in the pond, he jumped in after him like some hero." After another chuckle, Alex continued. "His friend ended up having to pull *him* out. Even though he laughs and has a good time, there's a sadness behind his eyes."

"Uh-uh, here we go," Desi said, rolling her eyes. "Saint Alex to the rescue."

It soon became routine for Alex to meet up with Calvin and Gangster on the walking trail in the park. Although she often carried along a camera, he would never allow her to take pictures of him. It strangely intrigued her.

When she wasn't working out of town or at the hospital,

she and Calvin would spend time walking and visiting coffee-houses where they laughed and talked for hours. Alex learned that he did most of his work for the paper from his home, leaving plenty of time for these excursions. He showed up regularly to fix things around their apartment and stayed for dinner much of the time. He had even asked a trusted photographer at his paper to talk to her.

To her delight, Desi and Star liked Calvin from the start. She had giggled under her breath when she saw his eyes light up after persuading the three of them to attend services with *him* one Sunday. It baffled her that he was able to convince Desi to do something that *she* hadn't been able to before. She watched him strut down the aisle with a triumphant grin on his face.

"Do you have any family, Calvin?" Star asked one evening after dinner.

He had grown noticeably quiet, as if looking off into the distant past. Alex thought for a moment that she saw tears pool in his eyes, but wasn't sure after he suddenly snapped out of his reverie. "Nah," he said. "I lost my family a long time ago."

She made a mental note that talking about his family, or lack thereof, was a topic not up for discussion. She would make sure to clue in the other two so no one made him feel uncomfortable in the future.

While visiting during a thunderstorm, Calvin helped Alex move her computer into the living room one evening. When the lights began to flicker off and on, it evoked such apprehension in Alex that she thought she would be sick. Star and Desi were both out for the evening and she found herself hoping that Calvin wouldn't leave right away.

"Alex, why are you so fidgety?" Calvin asked. "You look like you could tear out of here."

"I don't like the dark," she answered anxiously. "I just don't want the lights to go out."

"There's nothin' in the dark that light can't find," he said kindly. She lowered her head, slightly embarrassed. "I'm sorry, Alex, I hope I didn't say anything to make you feel bad."

She knew that his comments concerned the light of Christ

# Fragment In The Sand

in her heart. The two of them had already enjoyed countless conversations about the Lord. Despite being labeled a religious nut, she felt extremely naive about the deeper things of God.

"No, it's not you. You're right. It's just a childhood fear I've yet to conquer. I hope I don't sound like a silly goose?"

"Not at all," Calvin said soberly. "But if there's any way I can help, you be sure to let me know. Oh…by the way, I've met someone. I need some help with my wardrobe; it's kind of outdated. I have a date tomorrow night and I don't want her to think I can't keep up with the times." Alex giggled at her friend's boyish challenge and was more than willing to oblige.

It was only a couple of weeks after Calvin started seeing his new lady friend that he arranged for an introduction between her and Alex. Vivian Cox was a chatterbox indeed— and not the least resistant to speak her mind when she felt the need. She was tall and agile, wearing jeans, a sweatshirt and tennis shoes. Her brown eyes behind wire-rimmed glasses reflected the same warmth as Calvin's.

In spite of her objections, they began to include Alex on some of their outings. Their persistence resulted in their quite often being a threesome. She could tell that Calvin was quite smitten by the spunky woman, and seemed happier than she had seen him in the short time she'd known him.

\*\*\*

Casey drained the rest of his coffee from the mug and finished shoving the rest of his belongings into his satchel. Maybe he should call his dad. He always did before he went out of town.

The housekeeper sounded winded when she answered the phone. "Hi, Sylvia. This is Case. You all right?"

"Hi, Case," she said. "Yeah, I'm fine. One of the horses got out and I was helping Ike get him back in. You wanna talk to him?"

After a few moments, his father came on the line. He spoke with a clear, confident tone. At that moment, it was easy for Casey to feel like a kid again. Since his mother's death, the

**66**

two of them had taken on the unspoken challenge of taking care of one another and being strong for each other.

He recalled his father's tear filled eyes as he knotted his only son's tie just before his mother's funeral. It had been the first time he'd ever seen his father cry. It had frightened him a little and caused him to want to protect him. His father's emotion and unsuccessful attempt to quell it had been so intense that Casey had decided then and there that he wouldn't cry himself. He would be a rock and stay strong for his father's sake.

"Hi, Sonny."

"Hey, Dad," Casey said. "You're not working Sylvia too hard, are you? You don't want her going back home to her daughter too exhausted."

"Nah. You on your way out?"

"Yep. Thought I'd just check on you before I left."

"I'm doing fine," he said. "But this housekeeper you forced on me is cooking up everything in sight. I had to trick her into going up to the café with me the other night just to save food."

Casey chuckled at his father's perpetual complaint. Sylvia had taken care of the house for years and he still grumbled about having her under foot.

"Dad, I was thinking about coming down to fish sometime soon. Is the old cottage in any kind of condition that I could stay in it?"

"Needing some think time?"

"Yeah, maybe so," Casey answered.

"I can have it ready. Just been storing a few things out there. Is Zeke doing all right—he coming, too?"

"He's doing great, Dad. I don't exactly know when I'm coming, but it'll be soon. Maybe by the time I'm ready, Zeke will be able to get away, too."

"It'll be ready when you are, Sonny," Ike Oliver said. As if reading his son's mind, he added, "I don't believe you were meant to spend your life alone, Casey. You're not made that way. Trust the Lord."

\*\*\*

# Fragment In The Sand

One evening during a casual dinner with Calvin and Vivian, Alex found herself sharing detail after detail about Brian. Much to her surprise, she found them both easy to talk to. She even surprised herself by showing them several of the photographs she'd taken of him. Vivian, a nurse herself, was so moved by his story that she started to cry. By this time, Alex felt secure enough to mention something she hadn't told anyone else—her thwarted plans of adopting Brian.

"Adopt?" Calvin blurted out. "Alex, why would you want to take on such a demanding responsibility as a sick four-year-old?"

"I don't know," she said, shrugging. "I hate to see him suffer all alone."

"You're just a child yourself," Vivian said, dabbing her eyes with a handkerchief. "What could you know about that kind of suffering?"

"A child?" Alex protested, putting away the photographs.

"Honey, compared to me, you're still a babe in diapers," Vivian said.

"When you were my age, I'll bet most women were married with lots of babies by now."

"I can't argue with you about that," Vivian returned, lightly chuckling. "But honey, you can't be going around dallying about in other people's lives like that. You've gotta seek God to fill that void you seem to be feeling."

"I agree with Vivian," Calvin chimed in. "I've seen a lot of people try to put their own idea of happiness in a spot that only God can fill. They're never quite satisfied. You have an exciting career, Alex."

"It's okay, but not all it's chalked up to being," she said, scrunching up her nose. "I've been sort of in the business since I was ten. I've never understood what all the ado was about. It's just a job."

"Does your uncle know how you feel about it?" Vivian asked.

"I've tried telling him, but I don't think he really understands. He probably thinks I'm being emotional because of my cancelled marriage plans."

"I'm sure your uncle wouldn't want you doing something

only to please him," Calvin said. "After all, it's your life."

"You've just hit one of life's road blocks," Vivian added, pouring coffee in Calvin's mug. "You've been blessed with a wonderful life and you should be grateful."

"I *am* grateful...really I am," Alex said, recalling Desi's accusation. "I just think that my choices would be different if I had to do things all over again."

"You mean, you wouldn't choose to model?" Calvin asked.

"I don't think I really chose it," Alex said with a snort. "I—I really want to get into photography. I'm taking a corre-spondence course right now. I need to start on a market analy-sis, but I have a little time. If I'd gone to live with my broth-er after my Aunt Sarah died, that's probably what I'd be doing."

"Why didn't you?" Calvin asked, a concerned wrinkle creasing his brow. Alex was certain that she saw a hint of intrigue dawn on his face, but she couldn't comprehend why it would be there.

"Uncle Lou said that Zeke had shown that he was irre-sponsible by running away. Then when Aunt Sarah died, his career in law enforcement was still fairly new and Uncle Lou thought that it would be selfish to burden him with a teenage sister."

"Hmph," Calvin loudly grunted. "Living your whole life trying to please other people."

Alex almost laughed out loud when she saw the sour expression on his face. She was getting the distinct impression that he was beginning to dislike her uncle.

"I don't mean to put Uncle Lou in a bad light," she hur-riedly added. "He's been very good to me and extremely pro-tective. I think that I somehow reminded him of a daughter he and his first wife had. Both of them died unexpectedly."

"Well, I guess you *were* much like a daughter to him," Vivian said.

"Anyway, after Uncle Lou talked with Zeke, they decided to send me to school in Paris."

"Oh, how wonderful for you," Vivian said, clasping her hands together. "You've got to tell me all about it."

# Fragment In The Sand

"By the time I returned, I was fully immersed into the industry," she continued. "Uncle Lou has always taken care of the models he agents for. He manages our careers in a way that all we have to do is show up, put on the garb and smile for the cameras."

"You said that you wanted to get into photography. You are pretty handy with that camera," Vivian said. "Maybe you should look into going to school."

Her face flushed with excitement. "My friend, Terri, thinks so, too. I'd like to get out of the fashion industry altogether and focus on photographing people. Real people."

It was the first time she had admitted her thoughts out loud to anyone other than Terri. The verbal acknowledgement had unleashed an unexpected wave of emotion. Sadness was mingled with anger. Now that she'd said it out loud, she felt committed to seeing it through.

"I heard it can be pretty brutal out there for someone as sensitive as you are," Vivian said. "I would've thought you'd have gotten used to it by now."

"I've been very lucky," Alex said, quickly wiping away a run-away tear.

"Luck don't have nothin' to do with it," the woman said with a grunt. "The Lord has been faithfully watching over you. I can tell."

"You can?" Alex asked, intrigued.

Out of the corner of her eye, she caught a glimpse of Calvin giving Vivian an exasperated glare.

"I think she already knows that," Calvin said sulkily. "But I don't think children should feel like they owe parents anything, whether it's a real parent or a guardian. That's emotional blackmail."

"Oh, hush up," Vivian said. "Nobody's blackmailing the child—just watching out for her is all."

"Vivian, you sound so much like my Aunt Sarah," Alex said with an easy chuckle, attempting to make evident to Calvin that she wasn't offended by his friend's assertive nature. "You two would have really liked her."

"I'm sure we would have," Calvin said. "Tell me more about your brother, Zeke. He sounds like an interesting fellow."

"Well, he's tall and handsome and just about the nicest person in the world," Alex said, smiling. "He and his wife, Peg, have the most wonderful three year old little girl named, Tracee. She has more energy than I've ever seen." She laughed aloud as her eyes glistened with delight. "I sure wish I could see her now."

"Why don't you just hop on a plane and go see them?" Vivian asked. "You could probably stand to get away."

"Oh, I don't know...I always feel strange...sort of dark inside when I go back to Oklahoma. But I have been thinking rather seriously about it lately."

"Why don't you like Oklahoma?" Calvin asked. "Isn't that where you were born?"

"Yeah, but I don't remember much about my life there before I came to live out here."

"What do you mean?" he interrupted. "I thought you were six when you moved here."

"I was," she said, a little hesitant to go on. She silently cautioned herself, hoping she hadn't made a mistake in trusting Calvin. The media would love to get hold of this. "I had some emotional problems after I lost Zeke and my parents. I spent several years in therapy."

"Oh, my poor dear. I'm so sorry—I spoke out of turn," Vivian said, her eyes instantly pooling with unshed tears.

"It's okay," Alex said, glancing across at them. "You didn't know." She saw the grief hanging in Calvin's eyes and decided it was safe to go on. Surely, someone with such a compassionate heart wouldn't betray her.

"Where did Zeke run off to?" Vivian asked.

"He ended up in some kind of trouble. The arresting officer, Isaac Oliver, took a liking to him—probably because he had a son the same age. He requested the courts to defer his sentence by releasing him into his custody. They agreed and Zeke was released from the juvenile center and moved in with him and his son, Casey."

"Just look at the faithfulness of God," Vivian said. "He's had his eyes on both of you all your lives. That was so nice of Mr. Oliver to take him in. And he was allowed to stay in touch with you?"

"Yes, of course," Alex said, taking a swallow of her soda. "Mr. Oliver was careful to keep Aunt Sarah updated. He must've been quite a positive influence in both Zeke's and Casey's lives. Zeke is a police detective now and Casey is with the U.S. Marshal Service. I had a chance to meet the Olivers when I was little. Zeke still mentions them from time to time. The guys are still pretty close. I didn't much like Casey when I visited their home with Aunt Sarah. He acted more like Zeke's family than I was."

"You've had a pretty rough go of it for someone so young," Calvin said, reaching back across the table and giving her hand a gentle squeeze.

Her heart sank when she glanced up and saw the stricken expression on his face. She inwardly scolded herself for turning a wonderful evening into something that reminded her friend of his own losses. She wondered what his family had been like and what happened to them.

"I'm sorry, Calvin. I didn't mean to put a cloud over the evening."

"You didn't, dear. I always enjoy your company. I just hate to think of you so sad."

Calvin insisted on hearing more about Alex's little niece. She knew in her heart that his intent was to move the conversation into a less emotional place for her, but talking about the past wasn't affecting her as much as it seemed to be affecting him.

Alex took her leave a short time later. Impelled by the conversation of the evening, she dialed her brother's number the moment she returned to her own apartment.

# CHAPTER 7

## *The Dark*

Alex parked her car and glanced longingly up at her apartment. It was already dark when she left the set and the streetlights did very little to dispel the sense of isolation she felt. She was ready to take a nice long bath and collapse in bed.

In an attempt to dissolve the anguish that darkness summoned forth, she began to hum. Both Star and Desi were out of town on weeklong assignments and it made her realize just how grievously confused she was. All the time alone she'd been craving was now upon her, but she suddenly felt frightened by it. On one hand, she was glad to have the apartment to herself tonight, but apprehension was beginning to paralyze her. The calls she had been receiving late at night weren't helping her disposition either. The caller never said a word—just hovers on the line until she hangs up in frustration. In spite of her attempts to hinder the pervading anxiety they provoked, it was persistent. She only hoped the stress wouldn't incite her subconscious into rebellion.

Shutting off her engine, Alex grabbed her dry cleaning from the back seat and opened her door. Exhausted, she stiffly climbed out of the car. Careful to arm the alarm, she turned to run upstairs to the refuge of her apartment.

She froze dead in her tracks as she tried to determine if she had actually seen movement coming from the trees or if it was just her over-active imagination. Warily eyeing the stairs that led up to her apartment, she blinked in dismay. A shadowy figure moved in her direction, casting multi images against the pavement under the muted lighting of the parking lot. She bit into her lip trying to restrain the scream that rose in her throat.

Calm down, she told herself. It's probably just another tenant out for a stroll or a smoke. She was really letting the dark get to her. But with all the strange occurrences of late, there was no wonder she was a little on edge. She could have been inside already.

Although the logic seemed valid, it did not quell her fear. In a rush to slip back into her car, she dropped her dry cleaning on the pavement and frantically pushed the remote to unlock the door.

"Alex?"

For a moment, she wasn't sure she'd heard her name. Then the massive shadow superimposed itself over her trembling frame and she turned to see him directly behind her. It was Robbie. She remained cautious, despite her relief at seeing a familiar face. It had been two months since she'd broken their engagement, but the sight of him still caused the raw sting of his betrayal to resurface.

"How did you get inside the complex?" she asked.

"You haven't changed your code," he said grinning. "Where have you been?"

The pain was so fierce that she thought she would die. And she found it impossible to stop the tears. "What are you doing here?" she blurted, ignoring his question.

"Alex, please don't cry," he said. "I just had to see you. I knew your roommates were away, and I had to try and talk to you."

"How would you know they—"

"I have my ways," he said with a contrived chuckle.

She lifted her chin, glaring defiantly at the tall, handsome man that she had once planned to marry. Robert Lexington cautiously reached to cradle her face in his hands, his movements as suave as ever.

For one lost moment, she allowed it. Feeling weak and yearning for a warm embrace, Alex had closed her eyes, but then just as quickly, she pushed his hands away and stepped back.

"Why?" she asked. "We surely don't have anything else to talk about." She tried desperately to keep the emotion out of her voice and her gaze unflagging. But there was something about him that was different—unrecognizable. It made her suddenly very uncomfortable.

"One of the partners where I work called me in yesterday after getting a call from an anonymous woman," he said. "She accused me of assaulting her. I think it may delay my promotion."

"I fail to see what that has to do with me, Robbie," Alex said, her heart sinking to a new low. She had known the moment would come when they would have to confront each other, but she wasn't quite prepared for it to come solely because his career was in jeopardy.

"She told my boss that she had placed a restraining order against me, the same as my fiancée. He was surprised to learn that our engagement had been broken."

"I don't know what you're talking about. I haven't—"

"Alex, I'm not accusing you. I know you wouldn't do that, but I think maybe one of your roommates was playing around."

"Don't be ridiculous!"

"I'm only saying that this whole thing made me realize how much I've missed you. I need you back in my life. I love you."

Robbie stepped closer and reached for her a second time, but Alex once again evaded his touch and pushed past him. He grasped her arm in an unbelievably harsh grip and yanked her back. She could smell the alcohol on his breath as he pulled her close. She'd never seen him drink before and was stunned at his behavior. This didn't seem like the Robbie she knew at all. Had she simply not cared before or was she so fanciful that the real Robbie had escaped her notice? Could this really be who he was?

He pressed against her, stumbling over the garment bags on the ground. They both fell against the car, his body smashing her spine against the mirror.

"Robbie, let go of me," she cried. "You're hurting—"

"I love you," he continued, as if she'd said nothing. "I'm sorry about what happened. I still want us to get married. I didn't know that woman. I had no intention for…things just sort of got out of hand."

"What part of, 'I never want to see you again' escapes you?" she asked stiffly, attempting to pull away. "I can't marry

# Fragment In The Sand

someone I don't trust. Now please let go of me." She snatched her arm away from his grasp and stepped past him again.

"You can't expect me to give up on us just like that," he shouted.

"Just like what? It's been two whole months. Why all of a sudden are you showing up on my doorstep? Do you expect me to fix this thing between you and your boss?"

"I thought we could talk—you know, in private. Alex, I know that you still love me and—"

"So you go and guzzle a gallon of courage and stop by to persuade me of that?" Alex interrupted. "You know, Robbie, if I had any doubts before, I certainly don't now. I'm thoroughly convinced that we weren't meant to be. Maybe I didn't really know what love is—I'm sure you don't. Now if you don't mind, I'd like to get inside—alone."

Alex turned away to retrieve her things but was taken aback by his next move. His grim, unsteady form towered over her as he clutched both her wrists down and held them firmly behind her back. A high-pitched gasp escaped her throat as Robbie shoved her back against the car and leaned heavily into her trembling frame.

"Get used to it. I'll never let you go," he whispered as he lowered his mouth to hers. She struggled unsuccessfully to pull away and pondered the possibility of him having something to do with her being followed from Arizona. She closed her eyes. All she wanted to see was the man she had fallen in love with. But he obviously had never existed.

Strenuously contorting her body to escape his grasp, she inhaled deeply and swooned in the mesmerizing effect of his after-shave. She mentally battled with herself, desiring to flee his enraged clutches, but maybe more, wanting him to just hold her, kiss her, just once more.

Glancing into his eyes brought instant recovery to her rambling thoughts and renewed anger surged through her. The vivid memory of him in front of his apartment with another woman only months before their wedding date flooded back. A fresh energy seemed to infiltrate her being. She knew she could never trust him again.

"Let go of me!" she demanded, struggling with renewed

fervor. He surprised her when his grip grew even more brutal.

"You pious little fake," he spat, catching her eyelid with a moist droplet. "You play the little innocent virgin, but everyone knows what you models do to make it. How about me getting in on a little of that, huh?"

His words pricked like slivers of shattered glass, and she recoiled at the sting of his insinuations. There was no point in trying to reason with him. He was beyond reason. Did he really believe the things he was accusing her of? Had her whole relationship with him been a lie? He had been so considerate—so gentle. Had it all been a game? She silently prayed to simply get away from him.

"Hey, what are you doing there?" a voice cried out from across the darkness.

Alex recognized the thick, heavy southwestern inflection of Calvin Prince and breathed a prayer of thanksgiving. She hoped Robbie wouldn't turn and attack him in his inebriated condition. "I advise you to let the lady go, sir, or my dog here just may have to have his way with you."

Alex could hear the fierce snarls coming from Gangster's throat, but she was yet to see either of them. Robbie ceased his assault, sternly pushing her away in disgust. All at once, Gangster appeared, his ears laid back and his tail tucked. His teeth were exhibited menacingly while continuing his low sinister snarl. The atmosphere was charged with fear and tension. She had never seen the animal so fierce and intimidating. Suddenly, he rushed towards Robbie, halting just a couple feet away.

Obviously shaken, Robbie stared at the dog that was poised to attack and abruptly turned on his heels, disappearing in the opposite direction. Just as Gangster was about to give chase, Calvin gave a command and the well-trained animal came to an abrupt halt.

Alex exhaled heavily, sinking to the ground in relief. She was so grateful that Calvin had happened by just then that she reached for his hand to make sure that she wasn't imagining him.

"Honey, are you all right?" Calvin asked. "Let me help you." She was so shaken that she couldn't speak. "Come on, lean on me. I'll help you upstairs." Calvin dropped the folded leather leash from his hand as he helped Alex from the pavement. "Can you stand there for a moment?"

She nodded her head, still trembling fiercely. Calvin retrieved her dry cleaning and took Alex into his comforting clutches. "Come on, boy," he said to Gangster, who reluctantly abandoned his post near where Robbie had vanished. "Get your leash and follow."

Alex glanced back and watched in amazement as Gangster retrieved his leash and followed close behind them. She didn't begin to calm down until safely inside her apartment. For several moments, the two sat side by side on the sofa in complete silence.

"I—I'm," Alex began, trying to tell him that she was all right, but without warning she began to sob. Calvin embraced her, holding her until she'd composed herself again. Feeling that he deserved an explanation, she attempted to explain. "I used—"

"Please don't feel like you owe me an explanation, Alex."

She looked up at her friend sheepishly. "But I don't want you thinking...I want to."

"All right, dear," he said, straightening and clasping his hands together.

"That was Robbie," she said, in barely more than a whisper.

"He's the one you were supposed to marry in June. I'm sorry, Alex."

"Yes." She paused, attempting to quell the rising emotion that stung like bile in her throat. "I had come home early from an assignment. I wanted to surprise him, so I went directly to his apartment. There he was...standing right out front, tangled up with some floozy. I feel so stupid for falling for that louse—"

"I'm sure that was very painful. I'm sorry you had to experience it, but at least you found out before you took your vows...right?"

"Yeah, I guess. It just hurts more than I want it to," she said.

"Things like this are never easy to walk through, but they

usually make us stronger. Everything will work out just fine. You'll see."

"But I feel so—so used. I don't understand why God allowed me to fall in love before intervening."

"Well, there's always the possibility that you were only in love with an opportunity—an idea."

"Given the circumstances, I guess that makes sense."

I believe that God always warns us, honey. But we don't always hear Him. And often we're so wrapped up in the moment that in an instant we ignore the warning...thinking we're imagining it. That's why He wants His children to stay close. So they'll recognize His voice. You're gonna' need to be strong, now."

"What do you mean?" Alex said, wiping her nose with a tissue.

"I mean that you've gotta stop putting your trust in arms of flesh. You rely so much on your uncle—probably without realizing it. It's become a part of your nature almost. And in a sense, you probably relied just as heavily on Robbie."

Alex lowered her head. "I know. My brother says the same thing. He asked me if I was marrying Robbie because I thought it was a rescue from something. But I have been trying to become more self-reliant."

"Darlin', you can't even be self-reliant as a Christian. I meant a God-reliance. Humans can't protect us like He can."

"But I've never had to...maybe Uncle Lou knew what was best for me all along," she said, feeling confused. "Maybe I should stick with modeling."

To her amazement, Calvin began to laugh. Not a harsh laughter, but a gentle one that seemed to reach out and invite her to join in. "Oh, I think you'll be changing your mind when God points you to where you're supposed to go," he said with a warm glimmer in his eyes. "Don't let what that young man said douse your dreams."

"You heard him?"

"Yeah, I did. But I know those things weren't true, and I haven't even known you as long as he has." Calvin paused and once again took her hand in his, and gazed into her eyes. "He wasn't the right one for you. And somebody *is* watching over

**79**

you—somebody a whole lot more sufficient than your Uncle Lou."

"Uncle Lou's really not a bad person," Alex said. "Just over-protective. I didn't mean to make you dislike him."

"You didn't do that," Calvin said, gently touching the new bruise on her arm. "I'd just like to see you doing the things that make you happy. You said yourself that you're not content with the choices you've made so far."

Alex sighed and glanced around uneasily. "You don't think Robbie will come back, do you?"

"Not tonight," he answered. "But I think that it would be wise to report this incident to the police."

"I couldn't do that," she said, rubbing the tender spots on both her arms. "He would certainly come back then."

"I really don't think you have to worry about that, Alex."

Alex glanced down at her arms again. The bruises had already turned purple and blue. She would have to remember to put make-up over the bruises before she showed up on the set tomorrow.

***

Leaning forward in a worn, cracked vinyl chair, Zeke perused through several reports before opening the Curry file. It had taken him most of the day to get his mind settled down enough to focus on his work. He glanced at his watch and swiveled around to peer out his window. It was close to five o'clock. The afternoon sun had begun to soften.

He had to stop worrying so much about his family. He chuckled slightly to himself. Between Alex and Casey, he didn't know where he could find another place on his brow for a frown. Casey had seemed a little despondent lately, and Zeke was more concerned than he had realized. He hated to see his friend so unhappy and wondered what had happened between him and Brenda. He'd known the first time he met her that she wasn't right for him.

Casey had been loaded down with guilt and loneliness since Angie left. Zeke and Peg had both prayed that he would find a wife—someone who would be perfect for him. But Casey didn't seem all that open to remarrying—at least Zeke didn't think so. He knew he shouldn't allow himself to fret so much over his friend. Only God could heal all the hurts that were evident. But Ike worried about him, too. In fact, he had called him a couple of weeks ago to talk about it.

Zeke turned back toward the work at hand and perused the file of fifty-four-year-old Ron Curry, who was the only suspect in the murder of his wife. It looked like an open-and-shut case, but they hadn't been able to locate the weapon. He knew from his investigation that the wife had been involved in an auto accident years earlier that had taken the life of her best friend. On the off chance that a family member might still be holding a grudge, he decided to dig a little deeper. For some reason this case was eating at him.

He glanced up in surprise at the knock on his door and watched as a fellow officer strolled in and laid a stack of papers on his desk. "I still don't have enough evidence to file charges with the DA," Zeke began.

"Now you do," the officer said with a grin. "We have a confession *and* the weapon."

"How did you pull that off?" Zeke asked incredulously, leaning back in his chair.

"Found a twin sister to the girl that got killed in that auto accident. Said she always thought the Curry woman was driving drunk that night—wanted to get even."

"Where is she now?"

"Down in the interrogation room," the officer said. "Good call, Detective. I'll see ya later."

After Zeke had returned from interrogating the woman, he stood at his window and stared at the Oklahoma City streets. She'd been an upstanding citizen in the community, an active church member and a librarian. Why would she do something so out of character, and then confess to it less than forty-eight hours later? Breathing a sigh of relief, he was extremely grateful that God had kept him from committing a terrible injustice against the victim's husband. He silently thanked God, who he knew had been in control by providing just the right insight, just the right details to link the two cases.

He sat back down at his desk and glanced at the photograph of his wife and daughter. Their beautiful faces stared out at him in unreserved devotion. He smiled, thankful that he had them. They were the most beautiful part of himself, he thought.

Moving his eyes toward a second picture, he leaned forward and picked it up. Alex leaned against a tree, and gazed easily toward the camera. Her dark brown eyes were as warm and innocent as Tracee's. He wished more than he could tell her that she would move closer, but there was no point in even going there again.

She had become a successful, well-known icon in the fashion world, but he'd detected something different about her lately. She was more reserved and hesitant to talk things over with him. Maybe he had been a little hard on her. He'd always criticized Lou's controlling manner. He hoped she wasn't letting that New York scare weigh on her.

Blending his worlds into one baffling string of thought, it suddenly occurred to him that the woman who had just confessed to the Curry murder had been entirely too calm about the whole thing. She'd even left the weapon on the front seat of her car—in plain sight. Her confession was too smooth. Quickly, he snatched up his phone and dialed. "Place the McCutcheon woman under suicide watch!"

***

"Desi, what am I doing wrong?" Alex asked, feeling the nervous tension in the base of her neck. "I never would have believed that Robbie was capable of hurting me. He was like an animal. If it hadn't been for Calvin, I'm not sure what he would have done."

"I'd like to go clip his head for this," Desi said, glancing angrily at the bruises on Alex's arms. She lifted her chin resolutely to gaze into her eyes. "Just say the word…better yet, I'll get a couple of guys to go tap on him a little."

Alex watched the fire surge in the redhead's eyes and began to relax in the company of her protective friend. She wondered who in the world Desi thought she could get to rough someone up.

Star gaped at Desi in panic, as if she thought she was living with the Godfather himself. The sight of her widened eyes and ghost white face suddenly struck Alex as funny and she burst into irrepressible laughter. After getting her wind and wiping away the tears of amusement, Alex sighed heavily, feeling a lot more composed than she'd been moments earlier.

"Thanks, you two. I really needed to laugh."

"Have you changed the code on the security gate yet?" Star asked. Star was the designated *fire bell* for their home because she had a knack for verbalizing her misgivings, and there were plenty. She was the epitome of a true alarmist, often jumping to the most outlandish conclusions.

"You bet I did," Alex answered. Star sat glowering in dismay while Desi zealously paced the floor, stubbornly resuming her tirade.

"That sack of slush sure changed his spots," she blurted out. "Star, go call Lou and tell him to get over here. He'll probably wanna put a restraining order on that bum."

"That's exactly what Robbie thought I'd already done," Alex replied curiously. Suddenly, the calm she had started to feel was gone. "No. Please don't do that. I don't wanna' bother Uncle Lou with this. He'll wonder why I didn't tell him when it first happened."

"And why didn't you?" Desi asked. "You know Lou would go bonkers if something happened to you."

"Nothing's going to happen," Alex said skeptically. "Robbie was just drinking and acting out his frustrations."

"I don't know, Alex," Star grumbled. "You can't be too careful. Don't you ever listen to the news? You said yourself you don't think you ever really *knew* him. I think you should at least *tell* Lou about it so he'll know what to expect."

"I thought you two would support me in this," Alex said, her body noticeably slumping.

"We do," Star said. "But don't you think you're taking things to the extreme? This could be dangerous."

"Let me sleep on it," Alex said, slowly standing to her feet. "Promise me you won't say anything to him before I do." She watched as a worried glance passed between her roommates, then back at her.

"Okay," Desi said, "but you've gotta promise me you won't let this go on too long. I want Lou to know about it before the end of the week."

"B—but, Desi…"

"No buts," Desi demanded. "Promise."

"Okay. I promise," Alex said reluctantly.

She was aware that her uncle would be hurt to discover that she'd been concealing so much from him. But she couldn't let anything stand in her way of proving that she could take care of managing her own life. And that meant depending less on him.

She picked up the ringing phone with a brisk "hello." There was no answer. "Hello? Is anyone there?" Again, there was no answer. She was tired of these calls. It couldn't be a wrong number this many times.

"Who was that?" Star asked, staring at her with saucer eyes.

"I don't know. I've gotten several of those where nobody says anything…on my private line, too."

"Probably Robbie," Desi snorted.

Star frowned, looking somewhat pensive. "I wouldn't think he'd be calling like that. What would be the point?"

Alex suddenly felt an icy chill race down her spine.

# CHAPTER 8

## *Presumptions*

Desi, Star and Lou flew to New York for the awards banquet. Although she had been looking forward to the event, Alex chose to stay home to be near Brian. His condition had worsened now to include pneumonia.

Weary from having stayed at the hospital past her shift, she ran a bath and soaked until the water turned cold. Then she retreated to the sofa to relax before going to bed. She wanted to get up early in the morning and get back to the hospital before Mrs. Waters came in. She didn't want her to know that she was still spending so much time with Brian.

She closed her eyes, leaned her head back on the cushion and allowed her mind to roam through the times she had spent with Brian at the hospital. She had watched his dulled innocent eyes grow as bright as the flash from a camera. It was almost frightening how much she'd grown to love him. She had allowed him to coil around her heart dangerously tight, and pondered its unhealthy potential. She really had to get a hold of herself. She knew she had gone way beyond what was proper. But the indulgence had allowed her affections to flow freely, an extremely liberating feeling. It also drained her of energy and clarity.

Her first assignment in the photography course had been sent in late, something she'd promised herself she wouldn't permit. But she'd been very busy with work and spending time with Brian.

Jolted out of her reflections by the ringing of the phone, Alex gasped. Feeling the apprehension bleed through her like iced water, she held her breath and lifted the receiver. After what seemed an enormous amount of time, she cautiously spoke into the mouthpiece. "Hello?"

"May I speak with Alex Webb, please," the low-pitched

voice uttered.

"This is Alex," she said, relieved that it wasn't the breather.

"Hi, this is Casey. Casey Oliver," he stammered. "I know it's been a long time. I hope I'm not disturbing you, but I'm here in the city on business and wondered if you'd care if I dropped by. Have you eaten yet?"

Casey hesitated outside the door as a sudden stab of anxiety hit his gut. He felt a little silly for the way he stammered on the phone, and pondered why he was suddenly so unstrung. After all, he didn't really know her. He hadn't wanted to let Zeke down. He knew he'd expect a full report once he learned that he indeed had come to Los Angeles, so he might as well get it over with.

Casey never claimed to comprehend the depth of Zeke's compulsive preoccupation with his kid sister, but he'd always tried to understand. He thought it had more to do with Zeke's sensitivities than anything. His mother's death, the guilt he felt over leaving Alex, and his animosity toward his father all affected every decision he made.

He had told the cool, indifferent voice on the phone that he was on assignment and had a couple of days before having to report back. She'd shown neither a hint of drama or displeasure at hearing from him. Her voice was friendly enough, he supposed, but clearly detached. As if out-of-town guests were just another day's work. He didn't know what he expected. After all, it had been quite a long time since they had last seen each other, and she was just a kid then. Still, he had felt an elusive sense of disappointment when he hung up, and it struck him as odd. What else could he hope for from the ice princess? Just because Zeke was his friend didn't mean he would be able to expect the same of his sister.

He remembered that as a child, Alex had been quiet and withdrawn. From the earlier tone of her voice, not much had changed. He wondered how she had gone so far in her career with a personality like that.

When the door swung open, Casey lost all sense of deduction. He was, however, keenly aware that he had never knocked. Stunned into silence, he stumbled headfirst into the deep pools of Alex Webb's eyes. Even without all the make-up, her pictures hadn't done her justice. She boldly gazed up into his face with a delightfully impish smile. And his mind raced in search of words, but came up empty.

"Trying to figure out which way to run?" she asked, tilting her head a little. "I'm not psychic or anything. I saw you through the peephole." Her laughter was like water dancing off a welcome breeze.

Casey licked his dry lips and cleared his throat. "N—no, of course not."

Again, she let out a friendly chuckle. It was quite enchanting and seemed to ease his awkwardness.

He found himself staring down at her like an awestruck teenager. Comfortably dressed in blue jeans and an oversized tee, she was the essence of a wildflower in the country. His brow lifted when his eyes traveled past the hem of her jeans to her bare feet. She immediately wiggled her toes and laughed again.

"I don't always look like the magazine covers," she said apologetically. "I get all the way easy when I'm home."

"As you should," he managed, sinking deeper into her overwhelming charm. Casey was stunned to find himself in a place he'd never expected to be—actually finding Alex likable and not the spoiled rich girl he'd envisioned.

"Are you going to stand there all night or would you like to come in?" she said, clutching him by the arm and leading—pulling him through the door.

He sighed heavily with relief as he stepped forward into the bright spacious living room. He immediately noticed the state-of-the-art computer sitting on an antique desk just to the right of the entrance and briefly watched the screensaver randomly splash the faces of children across it.

"I brought enough Chinese for everyone," he said, holding up the bags. "Zeke told me you have a couple of roommates."

"It smells wonderful, but I'm the only one here," Alex said, taking the bags from his hands. "Come on into the kitchen—I'm famished."

While small, the kitchen was quite adequate for three sin-

# Fragment In The Sand

gle women who, from what Zeke told him, were often away. Casey stood by the window overlooking the courtyard where a large swimming pool peered through several ornamental trees. The water reflected the light of the moon in the clear dark night, giving it a sense of charm that surprised him. He turned, then, and watched intrigued as Alex moved with ease around the kitchen. Despite her being a stranger to him, he felt he knew her through Zeke's conversation.

Noisily pulling a step stool from beneath the counter, Alex stood on it to retrieve a platter. "Here, let me do that," Casey said, moving to help her down. As he lightly grasped her wrists, he thought he'd noticed her wince, but dismissed it, assuming it was simply his imagination in light of his own restlessness.

"Thanks," she said, stepping down. She averted her eyes as she took his arm. He was sure then that he had indeed seen her discomfort. "So, how is my brother? Did he send you all this way to check up on me?"

"Not really," Casey said. "He just assumed that I might be coming this way and suggested I give you a call if time allowed."

Alex scrunched up her nose in a funny way, and placed two glasses of iced tea on the table. "He's such a worry wart."

"Does he have reason to worry?" Casey asked, boldly touching the bruise just above her wrist. She promptly responded by drawing back as if she'd touched a hot pan. He noticed the trace of make-up that was still on his fingers where he had touched her arm.

"No, he doesn't," she snapped, handing him a dishtowel. "And I'll thank you to not give him one." Casey was very much aware that her mood had drastically changed. He had obviously touched on a nerve.

"I wouldn't think of it," he said cheerfully, hoping to recover her earlier frame of mind. "But I will expect you to apprise me of the details I exclude from my report." He was stunned by the protective impulse that had surged through him the moment he had seen her arms.

Placing her fists at her waist, she looked up at him defiantly. "It's nothing. Are you always this nosy?"

"Are you always this defensive?" They were at a strange impasse. The silence increased and thickened between the two of them. "Is it all right if someone cares about what happens to you?" When he saw the surprise in her eyes, he immediately wished he hadn't used those exact words. He didn't even know Alex, not Alex the adult. Yet he somehow felt a certain sense of responsibility for her in Zeke's absence.

He studied her expression, noticing that she rather obviously sidestepped his gaze. He thought it strange that he had tossed her so completely off balance, but decided to leave her there for the time being. The table had turned since she first opened the door and now the two of them were engulfed in a little game of cat and mouse.

Alex was bluntly silent as she tautly dished the food onto their plates. He was certain he'd made his point and allowed a wide grin to spread across his face in satisfaction, feeling sure he'd won the first round.

"You look well, Alex," he said, attempting to break the ice again and hopefully, start the evening over. "How have you been?"

Without the slightest response to his comment, she placed her napkin in her lap and obstinately glanced up at him. "You know how to bless the food?"

"Of course," he replied, staring at her blankly.

"Do you mind?" she asked, bowing her head. He felt like an idiot. She had cleverly turned the table again. So much for winning the first round.

"Father, we thank you for the privilege of coming together to break bread. We ask that you would bless our visit and allow our lives to lovingly express your truth. Bless the food we're about to receive for the nourishment of our bodies, causing it to become life for your glory. In Jesus name, Amen."

"I'm doing good," she said, answering his previous question. "So, when did you shave your head?"

Suddenly the ice was warmed and the refreshing water of mirth splashed over them both. Casey let out a robust blast of laughter, which Alex soon joined in on. "You know, Alex, you're all right."

"Well, of course I am," she said. "What did you expect?

## Fragment In The Sand

A witch?"

"Sort of," he said, holding her eyes. She stilled them, challenging him. "Remember, I haven't seen you in several years."

"Casey!" she said, feigning injury. "I'm surprised at you. I'm still Alex."

"Yeah, but if my memory serves me correctly, you weren't very fond of me when you and your aunt visited Gregory Falls."

She slowly laid her fork down and looked up into his eyes. "I—I was a little envious of you back then, that's all. I hope you won't hold the temperament of a child against me."

"Of course not," he said. "But why in the world were you envious of me?"

Just as she was about to answer, the phone rang. Alex hesitated and released a quiet sigh before gracefully standing to answer it. He could tell by the way that her shoulders suddenly sagged when she placed the phone to her ear that she was relieved for the interruption. He couldn't help noticing that she had indeed grown into a beautiful, young woman. And to his delight she could be quite unpredictable.

The biting aroma of the sweet and sour sauce was intense. It yanked at the constraint on his appetite, nudging it into the danger zone. Casey took another swallow of iced tea and was just about to bite into a piece of garlic chicken when he saw Alex collapse heavily against the wall. He watched curiously as the light in her eyes dulled and tears began to pool.

"Oh, God, no," she whispered, sinking to the stool beneath the phone. Not sure what else to do, Casey wiped his hands clean and stood to his feet in a state of alert. After a few moments of not speaking, Alex hung up and turned her back to him for several long seconds. Alarm gripped him as he watched her shoulders began to shake.

"Alex?" He whispered her name, as if afraid to disturb her. "Alex, what is it?"

He never took his eyes from her face. He could tell that she was silently fighting to maintain a degree of dignity, but she was losing the battle. This is how he most remembered her—appearing lost and alone, and just on the brink of some emotional outburst.

Right before him, her widened eyes became two watery black seas that gradually progressed into a gushing river. The tears were flowing so heavily now that he instinctively rushed to her side with a handful of napkins. Awkwardly gathering her into his arms, Casey was stunned by the gulping sobs that ensued and the way she helplessly clung to him.

"What is it, Alex?" He repeated the question, his voice barely a whisper. He couldn't make sense out of the guttural noises that she made and leaned closer, trying to hear her response. He was certain that she had mentioned something about her son. Zeke hadn't told him that Alex had any children and wondered if he was even aware of it.

The mournful sobbing was almost more than he could stand, but he had no real recourse. He thought he had been prepared for just about anything from her, but this was something he hadn't bargained for. He didn't have the slightest idea how to comfort her without making her uncomfortable, nor was he prepared to offer words of solace. She was strangely like a friend, but distinctively not. At a loss, he just stood there holding her for the longest time, letting her cry. He, of course, should do whatever Zeke would do if he were there himself.

Alex finally pulled away and walked into the living room, lowering herself into the corner of the sofa. He followed and sat next to her. "I'm sorry," she said at last. "I should've been more prepared. I've gotta learn to handle life better than this."

"What's got you so upset?"

"A little boy…Brian. He just passed away."

The tears pooled in her eyes quicker than she could wipe them with the already saturated napkin.

"Do you need me to take you some place?" he asked, instinctively reaching for her hand.

As the conflicting emotions came in waves across her face, she began to tremble and protectively wrapped her arms around herself again. Casey felt incompetent and clumsy as he linked himself to the outskirts of her grief.

"Alex, I'm very sorry. I can leave if you'd rather be alone."

"No, please," she said abruptly, wiping her eyes with a

fresh tissue she'd pulled from the box on the lamp table. "I'll be okay. If you don't mind, would you stay for a little while longer?"

"I won't leave until you're all right then," he said, reaching to embrace her trembling shoulders. After a few moments, Casey felt the tenseness flow from her taunt frame. She finally relaxed, resting her head in the curve of his shoulder, almost as if it were an everyday occurrence.

He was surprised when she suddenly began to talk. "I volunteer at the children's hospital. They warn us not to get too attached, but Brian was special. He's been there so long…and I'm…I was the *only* one he responded to. We had grown so close. I'm away so often that I—"

Casey tightened his clasp around her shoulders. "He was four. His eyes were sometimes as haunting as midnight," she said. Her voice trembled, but was as soft as a breeze and he had to strain to hear her. "He'd been badly burned…by his own mother." She stopped and hiccupped as another wave of grief rose in her throat.

"Oh, God," Casey said, intuitively pulling her closer. "I'm so sorry, Alex."

"Thanks for being here, Casey." Her voice was thick and clogged with emotion as waves of grief continued to push through her.

"You're welcome," he said, settling back comfortably onto the sofa. *What a horrible tragedy,* he thought.

It seemed as though an eternity passed. He knew the timing would probably be all wrong but he could hold back his question no longer. "Alex?"

"Yeah?" she answered, still sniffling.

"What happened to your arms?"

He was surprised when, with only slight hesitation, she began to tell him about Robbie's assault and how a friend and his dog had walked up just in time. He was glad that the initial distance between them had dissipated enough that she could talk to him like a friend. Casey sat and listened intently as the anger swelled inside him like thunder. When she stopped her discourse, he didn't quite know what to say. He couldn't stand men who brutalized women to get their own way with them. But he was hesitant to say exactly what he thought, because he'd seen women go right back to their abusers.

"Did you report this attack to the police?"

"It wasn't necessary," she said. "He'd just had too much to drink—and after having been engaged to him, the police would just chalk it up to a domestic disturbance."

"Alex, you can't think to lightly of this. I think it would be a good idea to report it anyway."

"Maybe so," she said with an absent shrug. He knew that she was lost in her thoughts of Brian and probably had no intention of reporting the incident.

Casey kept his word and didn't leave until he felt that Alex was calmer. She had recovered herself quite remarkably, but understandably, her lighthearted posture didn't make its way back into their evening. This little boy had obviously meant a lot to her. He wondered if this crisis was enough to cause her to withdraw again. He hoped not. He knew just by being in her company for a couple of hours that she had too much life to offer the world for him to sit by and let her retreat. Scribbling his cell number on a small pad, he ripped the sheet out.

"Alex, I want you to keep my cell number," he said, pushing the slip of paper into her hand. "Any time you need to talk, or even if you just want to say hello—please feel free to dial it."

"I will," she said, closing her hands over the paper. "Thanks for stopping by to see me. I'm sorry it didn't turn out to be a more pleasant evening." For a moment, her eyes regained their original mirth and she gave him a quick, friendly peck on the cheek. But it was obvious that just underneath the fragile calm lay a somber cloud of grief.

Casey returned a comforting smile and squeezed her hand one last time before leaving. He could almost understand now why Zeke worried about her the way he did. She seemed so vulnerable. He forced himself to halt his thoughts. He couldn't get involved in Alex's personal affairs.

\*\*\*

# Fragment In The Sand

A few days later, Alex and Star sat across from one another at the coffee table playing a game of Scrabble while Desi dressed for an evening out. Alex was a little concerned because Desi was particularly tight lipped about the guy she'd been seeing. She'd never even brought him home for them to meet. Alex's imagination led her into wondering if the reluctance was due to an undisclosed marital status, but she didn't risk asking. Desi could get real testy when pressed for information she wasn't ready to give.

Still sensitive from attending Brian's funeral, Alex could feel a strange tension in the air as she watched Star pretend to be absorbed in their game. She couldn't have been paying attention because she had passed twice without opting to change her letters. Alex wondered if the two girls had quarreled on their trip to New York.

She was relieved when a knock at the door interrupted them. Quickly answering it, she was delighted to find Calvin with Gangster on the other side of the threshold. "Hi," she said, bending down to give Gangster a friendly greeting.

"We were out walking and thought we'd drop in and check on you ladies," Calvin said. "I got your message, Alex. I'm sorry to hear about Brian. You okay?"

"Thanks. I'll be fine," Alex said, gently tugging him through the entrance. She was so relieved to have a break in the tension that filled the air and began chattering before Calvin was even seated. "Zeke asked me if I wanted to have you checked out the other day when I mentioned you."

"He what?" Calvin asked, obviously insulted.

"He was only joking," she said, her smile suddenly waning. "He had just heard me mention you a couple of times and was trying to be nosy."

"Oh," Calvin said, his smile brightening. "I wanted to let you know that I'll be out of town for a few days, Alex...with my job."

"Oh?"

"They're sending a bunch of us to a conference back east," he said, noticing the frown on her forehead. Instinctively, he leaned forward to run his thumbs in opposite directions across her brow, as if wiping away her anguish. "Don't look so con-

94

cerned, my young friend. I'll be back before you know it."
Alex hadn't admitted to herself until then just how much comfort she had taken in knowing that Calvin was only moments
away, should she ever need him. She supposed the bond had
intensified when he and Gangster spared her from Robbie.

Calvin offered to walk Desi to her car as she pranced
through the room after having made herself beautiful for the
evening. "I'll see you when you return, Calvin," Alex said,
feeling a little hurt that he'd taken offense to her teasing
remark about Zeke. She noticed he hadn't stayed very long
either.

After they left, Star seemed to relax and began to play the
game more seriously—obviously playing to win this time.
"So, tell me more about Casey's visit," she asked conspiratorially.

"There's really nothing to tell," Alex said coolly. "He's
nothing like I remembered, though. It's funny how many
crazy notions I had about him."

"Is he anything like Robbie?" Star asked, leaning closer to
Alex. "What's he look like?"

"He's *very* handsome and has this marvelous shaved
head," Alex said, smiling. "He's sensitive and very much the
gentleman—well, when he's not being nosy."

"Sounds good," Star said, nodding her head profoundly.

"He was just here to play "big brother" for Zeke," Alex
said. "He may have some real issues behind those tender
brown eyes of his, though."

"Issues? What kind of issues?" Star urged. "Come on.
Let's have it."

"I don't know exactly," Alex said, laughing at her curious
friend. "He seems sort of lonely in an odd sort of way." Alex
rubbed the nectarine she'd gotten from the fridge on her T-shirt
and bit into it. "I'm really glad he was here when I got the call
from the hospital. That was a rough evening. I'd grown so
attached to Brian—too attached. Casey even called the next
day to check on me before he left town."

"I'm glad he was here, too," Star said. "Lou was really
worried after he'd gotten off the phone with you. He said that
you talked him out of coming back to LA."

# Fragment In The Sand

"Yeah. He's very sweet, isn't he?" Alex muttered.

"Hmph!" Star grunted. "If you say so. He's a big grump if you ask me—your uncle or not. Did you tell Casey about the calls?"

"Nah. I don't want Zeke to know about that. Sometimes, I wish I could turn back time and be a little girl all over again," Alex said thoughtfully. "I can't even let myself think that way. I've got to face the big bad world without my uncle to defend me. You know what I mean?"

"Yeah, I know. But you've had a few heavy blows in the last few months. All of us want to protect you from the pain," Star said. "I admire your resolve to take charge of your own life, but I think that all of us could stand loving support."

"I know. But in moderation."

"You know, I can understand why you let yourself get so close to a patient after canceling your wedding plans. But didn't the hospital warn you about that?"

"What?" Alex had let her mind wonder off about Casey. He had evidently impressed her more than she was willing to admit. She could envision the gentle radiance of his eyes and hadn't been able to stop thinking about his kindness since the night he visited.

"Your patients," Star said. "Didn't they warn you about getting too close to them?"

"Yeah, they did," she said flatly. "But who can turn off their feelings when it comes to children? Terri has worked with them for years and it's getting more and more difficult for her everyday."

"What did Casey do when he heard about Brian?"

"I made a complete fool of myself in front of an almost total stranger," Alex said, feeling embarrassed all over again. "I blubbered like a ninny. I guess everything—the flowers, the calls, Robbie, that nut on the highway, and then Brian—it all caught up with me at the same time."

"Has the caller ever said anything?"

"Nothing. He just sits there and breathes like a dummy," Alex said, barely catching the juice running down her chin from the nectarine. "You know, it could possibly be Robbie, but I have to agree with you. It's wouldn't be like him to play around on the phone."

"Well, he'll give up after a while. I'm sure Casey didn't mind consoling a damsel in distress," Star said, glancing out of the corner of her eye. "In fact, it probably gave him a reason to look deeply into your eyes and declare his undying affection."

"You've really been watching way too many of those old black and whites," Alex said with a playful laugh. "Actually, he was very kind—not at all like I remembered. But it was probably all an act."

"What makes you say that?"

"Men pretend all the time to be something they're not," Alex said. "Though it really doesn't matter with Casey. He's simply a close family friend. He was here on a mission—not because he wanted to know me. I don't ever plan to be gullible with men again. I *am* surprised that Casey's not married, though."

"Well, we could work on that," Star said, perking up. "Where do you wanna start?"

"Star!" Alex shrieked, shaking with waves of laughter. "You're terrible. Casey's not my type. He's too much like Zeke."

"I don't have a life of my own, so I have to live vicariously through yours and Desi's," Star quipped. "Well, more yours...Desi's is a little much. You do want to get married someday, don't you?"

"I'm not sure that I do," Alex said, thinking of Robbie's betrayal. "I know I want children, though. Maybe I'll adopt."

"Nah. You'll get married. And we might as well get some practice in."

"What are we going to do with you?" Alex said, holding her stomach as she continued to laugh.

"Why do you think you made so many assumptions about Casey? How old is this guy, anyway?"

"He's the same age as Zeke. You're right, though. It was foolish to retain so many childhood assumptions. I guess they lingered from my not really knowing him and his dad the way Zeke did. He's really very—"

"Now that's the part I want to hear about," Star said, anxiously getting up and plopping onto the sofa next to Alex. "Do you think that the Lord sent him back into your life?"

"Star, you're really parking on the wrong street. I told you that I don't plan to get involved—" Alex paused and looked up at her friend curiously. "It was quite timely, though—him showing up like that and all."

"It sure was," Star said, allowing her eyes to wander out into space like a hopeless romantic. "Pastor Frank told you to take into account the timing of God. And every man isn't like Robbie. You can't just shut yourself off. You never know, Alex—this might very well be God doing one of those appointed things."

"I almost wish I could believe that," Alex said, lying back against the sofa and closing her eyes. "He probably couldn't even think of me in that way. After all, I'm nine years younger than he is. Why am I even thinking like this? Star, you have me all tangled up."

"Older guys are better," Star said purposefully. "They've already gotten past the whine stage."

"You'd better watch out. You're beginning to sound like Desi," Alex said, peeking from beneath her closed lashes.

"Did he kiss you?"

"Star!" Alex gasped. "Would you please stop all this nonsense!"

"Don't be acting all shocked with me," Star said. "Why didn't he? Is something wrong with him?"

"Of course not. Casey is a gentleman—I think. And he's a friend of Zeke's...and he's a cop, for goodness sake."

"So is Zeke," Star said. "I think you have this invisible charisma that attracts men in uniform. Remember how the postman always tries to give you a little play? I'd venture to say that you'll probably end up marrying one."

"A postman? Or will any male in uniform do?"

The girls went on to enjoy a couple of more games and shared a bowl of popcorn before finally just relaxing in front of the television. Star absently leafed through a magazine while Alex channel-surfed with the remote.

"I think I'll email Zeke before I get too sleepy," Alex said, jumping up and flicking on the computer. "Then you can tell me what you meant by saying that Desi's life was a little much."

After she'd sent the email, she dragged back over to the sofa and flopped down. She was taken aback when Star suddenly turned to her and voiced the very question she'd considered earlier.

"Alex, do you think Desi's seeing a married man?"

"I hope not," Alex said, turning to face her. "Why? Do you think she is?"

Star flipped a stray wisp of hair behind her ears. Her eyes seemed to probe inside Alex's own thoughts. "I think *something* strange is going on," she said, her voice sounding high and panicked.

"Why do you say that?" Alex whispered, intrigued by Star's sudden change of mood. Her face had grown chalky.

Star coiled up in the chair opposite Alex and began her dissertation. "Remember when we were out a couple of weeks ago? She left me sitting at a table full of strangers to make a phone call. She was gone so long that I went looking for her."

"Is that all?" She was probably in the restroom or something."

"That's what I'm trying to tell you. I never found her. She wasn't at the phones or in the restroom. When she *did* finally come back, she was agitated and in a hurry to get home. Then when we got here, she dropped me off and drove off without a word."

"Hmm, I've gotta admit, that *is* odd. You know, Star, I've been thinking for a while that Desi may be beginning to feel insecure because of her age."

"Desi's only thirty something, Alex. It's not like she's over the hill."

"I know, but we don't really know how she thinks of it. I saw her looking at one of those advertisements on surgical procedures for a youthful appearance."

"You know, I came across a page in this magazine. It was dog-eared. She doesn't need anything like that. I think she's very attractive and young looking."

"I know, but in this business, when you're over thirty and

your calls start slowing down, you're bound to start feeling uncertain of your future. And you know how she feels about being financially strapped. We'll just have to support and encourage her as much as she'll let us."

"I guess I never thought of that," Star said. "Do you think that the man she's seeing might be a plastic surgeon?"

"What I think is that we'd better stop jumping to conclusions. Desi doesn't need our wild imagination."

"Yeah, you're right," Star replied, turning to look at the television. "But I just hope she doesn't do anything stupid. She might be in some kind of trouble. She's been awfully nervous lately. And you know that mouth of hers."

"I'm sure she'll tell us when she's ready," Alex said, feeling just as alarmed as Star. "Let's just give her a little space. And try not to build something monstrous out of innocent random events."

Alex realized with a shock that Star might be more in tune with problems concerning Desi than she was. After all, she had been absorbed in her own set of circumstances of late.

"All right," Star said, casually flipping her magazine back open. "You'll see."

"Star? There you go sounding the distress call again—and as usual, it's before you have all the facts."

"You just wait and see if something bad doesn't come of all of this sneaking around she's doing."

"You're hopeless, Star."

"I am not," she retorted, forging a playful pout. "I'm just concerned about a friend."

Alex began to giggle. "Concerned, or nosy? Look, I've known Desi a little longer than you have and she's unquestionably street smart. She will be just fine."

Alex slowly shook her head at her roommate's overactive imagination. Still, for some reason, her stomach crawled with apprehension.

# CHAPTER 9

## *Rings in the Night*

The next day held its usual routine for Alex, ending it with her daily dose of aerobics. She climbed off the riser and grabbed the remote to pause her exercise video, hurrying to answer the phone that was already on its fourth ring. She cradled it between her shoulder and ear while dabbing perspiration from her face with a towel, and breathlessly answered, "Hello."

His voice was smoother than polished satin, yet its bite pierced like the fangs of a peeved rattler.

"Hello, my beautiful, Tabitha."

His speech swept over her—through her, making her so afraid that she lost all force to speak. "I'm sorry the roses I sent lived such a short life. But I wanted you to know that I'm with you…no matter where you go…I'm right there. By the way, I love the way your eyelashes flutter while you're dreaming. Before too much longer, I'll be able to watch them all the time."

"Who is this?" she demanded, finally finding her voice. She felt an icy chill finger its way down her spine. Beads of perspiration sprang back out over her entire body. She involuntarily clasped the phone closer to her ear, glancing around frantically for help.

In that instant, she remembered that Star and Desi had already left for the evening, and incomprehensible panic began to spread through her. Although she had received several calls on her personal line in the middle of the night, the caller had simply remained quiet before she finally hung up. She had assumed it was Robbie or some creep he'd put up to harassing her.

"This is your…" He paused. And in that moment time seemed eternal, ushering in a weightless dread that displaced her normally rational mind with unsound thoughts. "No, my sweet. I think I'll let you guess."

"Did Robbie put you up to this?" she demanded. "Stop this insanity."

"No, sweet, Tabitha," the voice murmured. "I'm a much better man than, Robbie—much better than your new cop friend, too. I didn't like what Robbie did to you. I made sure he would pay for it, too. I promise that you won't be hurt like that again and you won't be disappointed when this is all over, either. I'm the only one who can really take care of you."

"When *what* is all over? Who is this?"

"Let's see if you can guess, sweet, Tabitha. What has no substance other than what light gives it?"

Alex slammed the phone down and stared at it in horror. Her heart raced savagely in her chest as she placed the towel to her brow and sat down. She pondered calling her uncle, but quickly decided against it. She began pacing frantically through the apartment trying to figure out what she should do, but her thoughts were so scrambled that she couldn't come up with anything. The windows—he must be watching her through the windows. She immediately went through every room of the apartment, closing the blinds in each one.

"He" had sent her the yellow roses. So all of this was somehow tied together. What could he possibly want? Why was he calling her?

Alex began to talk aloud to herself—hoping to allay any emotional shift that might come as a result of terror. She glanced down at her hands to see if they were trembling as much as she thought. They were. She was probably overreacting. Nevertheless, she began to quote passages from the Bible to calm herself.

"God did not give me a spirit of fear, but of love, power and a sound mind," she said aloud. "And no weapon formed against me shall prosper." She spoke imposingly, as if trying to convince whoever might be listening that God would protect her from them.

She showered and dressed for bed quickly. Nauseating spurts of adrenaline coursed through her veins, but there seemed to be nothing she could do to relieve it. Her worries continued to mount, even after curling up in bed, and she forced herself to thumb through a magazine. Unable to distract herself from her racing thoughts, she gave up and flung the magazine onto the bed, dislodging a slip of paper from its pages. She picked it up curiously and smiled with sudden relief. It was Casey's cell phone number.

She could talk to him. He told her she could call just to talk, and she simply needed someone to talk to—maybe it would calm her down. His image still stood sharp and clear in her mind—a tall, well-built, bald man with gentle brown eyes and a warm smile. His rugged good looks were polished, but comfortable as smooth confidence flowed from each of his words. Her brother's best friend had grown into a very kind man.

She recalled thinking that she would fall from her chair when she heard the blessing pass so easily from his lips. That didn't mean a lot, though. She knew that well after dealing with Robbie. Anyone could pretend to be a Christian. But what should that matter to her. He was the perfect one to call. He wouldn't lecture her like Zeke, he wouldn't coddle her, and he wouldn't be afraid either.

She glanced around her room nervously. Despite her having turned on a light in every room in the apartment, she still felt apprehensive. It was worse that Calvin hadn't yet returned from his trip. She jumped, certain that she'd heard something at her window, but she wasn't about to check. Deciding to leave the light on beside her bed, she flipped the hourglass and fixed her eyes on the smooth oak spindles that spun gracefully down into its base, compelling her to loosen up.

She couldn't keep her mind from returning to the troublesome call. She thought of his hinting that he'd seen her when she was asleep. How long had this guy been watching her? Could he possibly be the one who had followed her on the highway?

Based on his words, it obviously wasn't Robbie. She could tell it was a man's voice, but very little else. She realized that it was far fetched to think that Omar, an arrogant photographer, would be trying to frighten her like this. He had no real motive.

**103**

## Fragment In The Sand

Alex grasped desperately at every thought that floated through her mind, examining it with the thoroughness of a surgeon. She could be imagining things, but she felt that from the instant she'd broken-up with Robbie, her life had begun spiraling out of control. Could it have started before that? How long *had* this in fact been going on? Who was this man?

By the time all the sand had slipped through the center to the bottom, Alex had decided to call Casey. The very sound of his voice did much to ease her tension. "Well, hello there," he said.

"I didn't wake you, did I?" she asked, drawing in a shaky breath. "I don't have any idea where you might be. I just—I just wanted…"

"There's no need to explain, Alex. I'm glad you called. I've been wondering how you were?"

"Casey?"

"What's wrong?" he asked almost instantly.

Her words rushed out as she began to bombard him with the stories of the yellow roses, Omar, the Arizona highway, the terrifying phone calls, and ended with the call she'd just received.

"My God, Alex!" he blurted out. "Why in the world didn't you tell me about this? Does Zeke know? What is your uncle doing about it?"

"I—I didn't really think it was anything to worry about…I mean, I've been trying to handle things on my own. And I needed to make sure there was a real problem and this wasn't just my imagination running wild, or just some weirdo fan. And no, I haven't told Zeke. I don't want to get him started. He'll just lecture me."

"Remember what fear can do to you, now," Casey warned. "You've gotta stand up to your phobias, and that includes the ones some idiot is trying to push on you. You're safe, Alex."

"But, Casey, he knew about Robbie—and he knew about your visit, too."

"How long have you been getting these calls?"

"A few weeks, maybe. He usually calls at night after I've gone to sleep. He's never said anything until tonight. He implied he's watched me sleeping."

"He may have said that just to frighten you, but he's obviously been watching you. Tell me what Lou is doing about this?"

"I haven't told him. I'm probably just overreacting. Oh, never mind...I'm sorry, Casey. I just ran across your number and maybe used tonight as an excuse to call."

"I'm glad you did, but you don't ever have to find an excuse, Alex. You're so much like your brother. You're so busy protecting everyone else that you lose sight of the real issues."

She smiled slightly and pondered what else they might talk about that would keep him on the phone for a while. She didn't know whether she was settling down from the call or if it was her sudden awareness of the soothing effect of Casey's voice. Whatever it was, she was definitely calmer.

"Alex, I think its time to get the authorities involved. I could fly out there if you want. We can put you under protective surveillance."

"You're very sweet to offer," Alex said with an empty chuckle. "But no—you're right. I'm safe and I have to stand up to my fears. I'll be fine."

"Alex, this is serious," Casey said, his voice suddenly shrill. "I didn't mean for you to pretend that this isn't real."

"Casey, I know it's serious, and I'm not pretending. I don't want to give this guy the satisfaction of knowing that he's scaring me. I'm trying to trust the Lord for my safety. Where are you, anyway?"

"That doesn't mean that you have to throw good-sense out the window," Casey said. "I'm on the east coast tonight. I was planning to go back home tomorrow morning, but..."

"I'm okay, Casey," she said. "I just wanted to hear a friendly voice."

"Try not to let this stress you out," Casey said. "Remember that God is always there. If you remember that, fear can't open a door for hysteria."

"I know," she said. "I'm a little jittery because the girls aren't home, that's all. I generally get that way toward night."

"Zeke *did* mention something about your fear of the dark."

# Fragment In The Sand

"Zeke has apparently mentioned a lot," Alex said with a light chuckle. "Anyway, I really appreciate you taking the time to talk with me. I feel much better."

"Anytime," Casey said. And she knew that he meant it. "You know, Zeke is just very proud of his sister. And don't forget I lived with the guy at the same time you were going through all of that. Why don't you hang up and call him. He'll want to know about this. I'll call and check on you tomorrow, if that's okay."

"I'd like that," she said, hoping she didn't sound too eager.

"Now, call your brother," he demanded playfully. "I'll talk with him and make sure you did."

***

"What do you mean?" Zeke roared, sitting up in bed. "What phone calls? And why am I just now hearing about you being followed? What's going on out there, Alex?"

"Let me…" Alex began.

"Does Lou know about this?" Zeke continued, trying to keep from disturbing Peg. "Do you think Robbie has something to do with it?"

"Zeke, if you're gonna' pitch all these questions at me, at least give me a minute to answer them. I didn't think a whole lot about it until now," she said. "This is the first time he's spoken. And no, I haven't called Uncle Lou."

"Why not?"

"Because…I just haven't, that's all."

"I worry about you, Alex," Zeke said. "Lou is supposed to be taking care of this sort of thing."

"He usually does," Alex said. "And there's nothing to worry about. I'm not going to let this guy push me over the edge."

"But Lou—"

"You've hinted often enough that I should be more independent," she interrupted. "You should let me. Besides, the more I think about it, the more I feel like I'm blowing this whole thing out of proportion. Models have to expect this type of thing, you know."

"I never meant to imply that you should not let Lou do his

job, Sis…"

"Stop it, Zeke. You two don't have any idea of the kind of pressure you place on me just to keep peace between you. I love you both."

"I'm know. And I'm sorry," he said, sheepishly. "But I don't want you worrying about me and Lou."

"How can I not?" she retorted. "I'll think twice about calling next time."

"I guess I deserved that. But please don't leave me out."

Alex sighed heavily. "I won't," she said more gently. "Anyway, this nut knows my given name. It was also on the note he left with some flowers he sent. Zeke, I don't publish my first name."

"I'm not surprised that a fan knows so much with all that's printed. I even have a couple of magazines here that printed your full name, so it's no real secret."

"I guess you're right," she said, haltingly. "I forgot that Calvin told me that he'd read my full name in one of them, too. I'm probably not thinking very clearly right now."

"Tell me more about this *Calvin*?" Zeke asked protectively. "Is it getting serious?"

"Oh, he's just a neighbor," she said casually. "Zeke?"

"Yeah?"

"Is Casey okay? I mean…well…he looks so sad."

"Casey? Casey's fine, Alex," Zeke said. "Why? Have you seen him?"

"A while back. He's on the east coast at the moment. He said he'd be home tomorrow."

"Oh-h-h!" Zeke exclaimed. "What's this, little sister?"

"Don't be ridiculous, Ezekiel Webb. You sent him out here to spy on me in the first place. And he's been very helpful. I was just asking a simple question?"

"Casey is not for you to worry about right now," Zeke said. "Just to be on the safe side, I want you to hang up and report these calls to the police."

"I'll think about it," she said.

"He's a great guy," Zeke said. "I *have* been a little worried about him lately. I'm glad you two got along well."

"Why hasn't he settled down? Is something wrong with

# Fragment In The Sand

him?"

"Nothing's wrong with him—it's just his job.  Most women are insecure and can't deal with the frequent travel and the usual hazards."

"Oh, that's right.  He's been married before."

"Yeah.  You should see him and Tracee together, Sis," Zeke said, instinctively smiling.  "He's a good lawman and loves what he does, but sometimes, that's like being between a rock and a hard place."

"Zeke?  There's something in the way the caller talks that makes me feel like he's standing right outside my window.  It's weird…it sort of makes me feel…naked."

"I tell you what.  I'll give a friend of mine out there a call.  You remember me telling you about Adriel Payne, don't you?"

"I think so," Alex said, feeling a little like she'd backslidden from her resolve to stand on her own.

"He's on the force.  I'll ask him to help you pick out a handgun—something you can handle.  Okay?"

"Zeke, no.  I don't like guns…I don't believe in them," she complained.  "And Uncle Lou would have a stroke if he found out."

"Alex, you called *me*," Zeke snapped.  "And Lou doesn't have to know about this."

"All right, Zeke," she said, resigning to the fact that she was going to be looked after, one way or the other.  "I'll give it a try."

"I'm sorry I snapped," he said.  "I just want you to get Lou off that pedestal."

"I know."

"This caller could just be a prankster, but keep your eyes and ears open.  It could also be a psycho on the loose."

"Zeke, I'm already scared enough," she whispered.

"I just want you to be alert," Zeke said.  "But don't let this pull you down.  And you might as well know I intend to have a little talk with Lou.  He promised me that he would keep this type of thing from happening."

"There's really nothing he could have done to prevent it, Zeke.  I wish you wouldn't.  I'm not a kid anymore.  And you just told me to stand on my own two feet, didn't you?"

**108**

"Well, Lou is still your agent and manager," Zeke said. "And while I do think you need to break away him, you also need to let him do his job—within reason, of course."

"I know. I just…never mind. Go on and do what you think best."

Zeke hung up the phone and gently eased the covers back to slip out of bed without waking Peg. By the time he'd tip-toed across the bedroom, he was stunned by the sound of Peg's voice. "Alex okay?"

"Sorry, baby," he whispered. "Didn't mean to wake you. Yeah. Looks like she's got a fan that's carrying his admiration for her a bit too far. I wanna have Adriel keep an eye on her just in case."

The room was dimly lit by the glow from the lone yard lamp coming through the window. Peg rose up on her elbow and glanced toward her husband. "Don't you think maybe *you're* the one overreacting? You should let Lou handle this?"

"No, I don't, Peg," he snapped with immediate regret. "I'm sorry, sweetheart. I'm just a little edgy. It seems this guy means business. He's actually been stalking her. And I don't want her getting too anxious. Dr. Gleason gave her a clean bill of health, but he warned her that the possibility of a relapse would always exist—any excessive trauma could push her back."

"Does she realize that?" Peg asked. "She must be scared half out of her mind."

"Yeah, she does. It doesn't look to me like Lou is doing such a great job or this guy wouldn't have gotten so close. I don't want to just leave it to him anymore. My sister has been so busy worrying about his happiness that she doesn't realize she's sacrificing her own."

"Then why don't you ask her to move closer to us? You know she cherishes you. I'm sure she'd consider it."

"I think it would mean more if the invitation came from you, honey."

"Why?"

"Because Lou would do anything to keep her out there making him money. As soon as he finds out I broached the subject, he'll convince her she'd be imposing or something.

# Fragment In The Sand

And if it comes from you, maybe you can nip that in the bud. Besides, if I ask, it's going to make me sound like an over-protective brother. And Alex really wants to be independent."

"Ah," Peg murmured with a laugh. "Now we have the truth. Let the wife ask so that the sister won't get the impression you're just as domineering as Lou."

"No. It's just that she's got enough on her hands trying to please him. She's successful in her modeling career and he has the connections to keep her busy, but…"

"But you wish she would give up the business," Peg finished.

Zeke turned and strolled through the dimly lit house to the kitchen and put on a pot of coffee. His wife knew him too well, he thought. The clock on the wall seemed to scream an early one-thirty in the morning, but he knew he wouldn't be able to get back to sleep anytime soon. He pushed a clawed hand through his hair and settled on the couch in the living room to watch television. Maybe he would be able to get sleepy and stop trying to fix Alex's problems in one night.

***

Alex dutifully visited Adriel Payne's office to file a report. She was stunned by all the detailed questions he asked—everything from the sound of the caller's voice to background noises.

By the time she left the precinct, she was more on edge than she'd been when she arrived. She hadn't realized until Adriel talked to her that this person could have been stalking her for months before she got her first call. She was relieved when he decided to put an electronic device on her phone, but he had warned her that for it to do any good, she would have to keep him on the line for almost a full minute. That was longer than she thought she wanted to endure his words, but if it meant catching him, she was willing to try.

For the next couple of weeks, Alex received annoying calls that left her worn out and ill humored. The fact that it was June and coming up on the date she'd originally planned for her wedding was also a source of chafing. Her feelings swung from a plane of levity to one of frustration in a matter of min-

**110**

utes, which kept her nerves on constant alert.

Alex tried to note as many details as she could after the calls, as Adriel had instructed her. But she was never able to keep him on the line for very long. By the time the calls turned more frightening, she had gathered two more riddles and one chilling declaration.

*What has no substance other than what light gives it?* She had already reported that first to Adriel. The other two confirmed her answer. *What's dark, thick and dreaded more than death? What is separate from darkness, yet a part of it?* Mindful that the answer to each riddle was *a shadow,* the LAPD named him as such for their investigation.

She drew in an unsteady breath, paralyzed by his last comment to her. "Bad things happen in the dark, sweet, Tabitha." The words had poured through the line like molten cement. It was as if he was aware of her every thought and discomfort. Was he someone she knew? Maybe it *was* Robbie after all, and he had said those things to throw her off. Alex shuddered as she thought of the fury she'd seen in his eyes the night of his attack. He had been fierce when he told her that he would never let her go.

Adriel agreed to pose as an interested admirer when he picked her up to take her to the shooting range. She had to learn all she could about handling her weapon, but she didn't want Desi and Star becoming nervous because she had a loaded gun in the house. Even though Adriel was a serious investigator, he was intrigued by her request and played along wonderfully as her new romantic interest. This of course, enchanted Star to no end. "See, I told you," she said, matter-of-factly. "He's a policeman—also a man in uniform."

Adriel was tall and stout without being overweight, and his light green eyes came as a shock against his thick dark hair. She had to look twice the first time she met him. He was a no-nonsense kind of a detective with a stiff New-York style of speaking—friendly, but restrained, making it initially difficult to relax around him, especially in a room filled with blasting guns.

He helped her choose an easily concealed, semi-automatic handgun, insisting that she sleep with it unloaded for the

## Fragment In The Sand

first couple of weeks. Alex had been so fidgety about handling it that Adriel initiated their sessions with her recitation of the three prime directives he'd insisted she memorize. Align your sight, maintain a firm grip, and then smoothly squeeze the trigger.

She had giggled the first time she heard them, thinking how much they reminded her of using a camera. She hadn't mentioned this to Adriel, because he probably wouldn't see the humor.

She was thankful when she finally found herself relaxing and feeling more comfortable around him after their third session. She had been startled by an over-enthusiastic patron discharging his weapon. So much so that she humiliated herself by grabbing onto Adriel and clinging like a frightened child. He had calmly leaned down and whispered in her ear, "you want I should kick his butt?"

Instantly, her eyes widened and her jaw fell open. Her expression must have broadcast her shock, because Adriel burst into an unexpected peel of laughter that had the whole room turning. She had never heard him laugh at all, or even smile, for that matter. He was so amused by her discomfort that he flung a heavy arm around her shoulder in an attempt at settling her. "Just kidding, little sister."

True to his word, Casey began calling her every night. If she were away, she'd call him. She'd grown to enjoy his easy way of getting her to talk, and talk she did. It helped that he already knew her past, so she didn't have to watch her words or hold back. In due time, she even disclosed that she'd had hopes of adopting Brian.

Casey invariably encouraged her to avoid letting the calls drain her of grit. And she actually began to feel more confident.

Her ease was short lived, however, when her uncle demanded the apartment complex tighten up their security. She realized that Zeke had gotten to him. He had been very angry with her and made her promise never to keep threats and harassment from him again. He'd even lit into Star and Desi for allowing her to convince them to keep quiet. She was elated when Star didn't crack under the pressure of his reprimand

and disclose her friendship with Calvin or Adriel. Although her roommates weren't aware that Adriel was teaching her to use a gun, they did know that he was a police officer. Her uncle's fury would probably go off the charts if he found out they were all friendly with a cop as well as someone working for the media.

She didn't really know why she felt it necessary to keep so much from him, but she was conscious that her reliance on Calvin was growing. She was also gaining a lot more self-confidence. She was even thinking of signing with a new agent— that is if photography didn't work out for her. A new agent wouldn't be hard to find. There were several bucking for her attention.

Between all the other men in her life—Zeke, Casey, Adriel and Calvin, Alex was learning the importance of not letting fear control her. "I'm very proud of the way you've seized command over your own life," Zeke told her. She felt a little thrilled that she was finally beginning to convince her big brother that she was quite capable of that command.

# CHAPTER 10

## *Fragment*

The season had already become too hot to enjoy. June had brought not only warm and humid days, but also a deeper realization that she had to stay on top of her life and emotions. She felt she was doing pretty well, though, because the dreams had let up a little. She tried to do what her pastor had suggested and write in her journal often, so that she could discover a pattern—something that could give her a clue to the direction of God.

She hadn't seen anything that even slightly resembled the pieces of a puzzle. Nothing that she could understand anyway, but then she wasn't sure that her mind was actually on her journaling. Much less what God might be trying to show her.

Casey had thought the concept was a good one, when she told him about it. But she barely had time to do anything outside of work and studying her assignments. She already knew what she wanted to name her business, if she ever got the nerve to take the leap. Exceptional Expressions. It had come to her when she was talking to Calvin and Vivian about the children.

Casey had pleasantly surprised her when he dropped by the studio on his way back home. He didn't have much time, so he only stayed a few minutes. It had been all she needed to feel as if she was on top of the world. After chatting briefly, he had embraced her and kissed her cheek before leaving. They'd been talking on the phone so much that it seemed natural. It was so strange to her that he wasn't allowed to tell anyone where he was going to be. Not even Zeke was aware until it was all over.

Thinking she'd heard something, Alex glanced around nervously. She had come home to find that someone had gone through her things. Although she couldn't find anything missing, the invasion gave her an eerie sensation of violation. She knew Star or Desi wouldn't go through her things without ask-ing her first. She was glad that she had called and mentioned it to Adriel. Right now, she had to maintain a positive per-spective and believe that it would all end soon.

Star noisily went through the kitchen looking for some-thing to eat. "Maybe we should just call Desi on her cell and ask her to bring something home," Alex said.

"You know she doesn't like running errands after work," Star said, peering around the doorway, "Not unless it's for her-self."

Alex leapt up from the sofa and went into the kitchen to get a glass of water. "We should probably eat more home-cooked meals anyway. Fast food will ruin our figures if we're not more careful." Alex absently began to rinse the sink, and was suddenly seized with an upsurge of frivolity. Quickly turning toward her engrossed roomie, Alex aimed the spray nozzle and reviewed her prime directives.

*Align sight, firm grip, smoothly squeeze trigger.*

Star let out an indignant yelp as the torrent struck her back. She instantly grabbed Alex's half-filled glass and ran after her towards the bedroom. All at once, she changed direc-tions in mid-stride and rushed to answer the doorbell. But Alex turned and tackled her to the floor, causing the water to splash over them both. The girls erupted in a blustering array of shrieks and giggles.

When the door abruptly flew open, they both blinked up into the concerned eyes of Casey Oliver. Annoyed with the picture she felt herself presenting, Alex scrambled up and nervously uttered an unlady-like snort when Star grabbed her ankle.

Casey stared blankly at the two entangled women, his jaw having dropped open in amazement. His expression quickly changed from one of shock to one of amusement.

"I—I thought I heard a scream," he said in explanation of opening their door without invitation.

Alex made her way to the door with Star in tow. Casey cocked his head and peered far too deeply into her eyes, caus-ing her to shudder within.

"Are you in the habit of leaving your door wide open with

the problems you've been having?" he asked, laying the momentary humor aside.

"We were expecting Desi," Alex said, feebly glancing up into his gaze. His mustache and beard were trimmed to perfection, and his smile was inviting. Her heart leapt within her as she glanced around, grateful that Star couldn't actually see it twitter. "I was just thinking about you."

"Good, I hope."

"Of course," Alex said playfully.

"I'm in town for a few hours," Casey said. "I'm sorry—I should have called first. But I was hoping we could go out to dinner?"

Trying to avoid appearing too eager, Alex instantly declined, secretly hoping he wouldn't take it seriously and give up. "Star and I were just talking about preparing something here."

"You know you want to go, Alex" Star said. "Besides, the man said he only had a couple of hours. Don't worry about me. You two go on." Star reached to shake Casey's hand. "Hi. I'm Star. And I gather that you're Casey."

"Yes," he said. "You're welcome to join us."

"Gosh no. I'll wait for Desi," Star said. "It sure is good to finally meet *you*." Her emphasis didn't go unnoticed. Casey was puzzled by how good it made him feel. He couldn't help wondering what Alex had told her roommates about him.

"Come on, Alex," he whined, batting his eyelashes in a playful attempt at persuasion.

"I don't know," she said, glancing at Star.

"Stop cartooning," Star quipped. "There's nothing here, anyway. So Desi and I will probably go out." Alex shot Star a fiery glare of indignation that made Casey want to laugh out loud, but instead he cleared his throat to stifle the urge.

"Besides," Casey said, glancing at his watch for effect. "Time is a wasting."

"Okay, okay," she said, her hands lifted in surrender. "It'll only take me a moment to change." She scurried off down the hall leaving Casey and Star standing in the middle of the living room.

"She's not always so hard to convince," Star said, wiping droplets of water from her face. "Only when she wishes to impress someone with her exceptional control. Come sit down."

Casey followed the friendly blonde to the sofa and sat, feeling remarkably comfortable with her.

"Thanks."

"You know, you're as handsome as Alex said you were."

"Well, thank you," he said, feeling a little flustered.

The two chattered back and forth in small talk and after a few minutes, Star surprised him with her next comment.

"Tell me what the mysterious Zeke is like?" she asked, her eyes seeming to glitter with conspiracy.

"You've never met him?"

"No. Each time he's dropped in, both Desi and I have been away. We've started calling him Phantom Zee."

"Phantom Zee?" Casey's laughter rang out in a resounding rumble. "That will do much to heighten his ego."

"Don't let Star's paranoid delusions get you going," Alex murmured, strolling into the living room. "We call her our little fire bell."

Casey glanced around to find Alex standing in the entry, having changed into a simple navy dress with low matching pumps. The dress took all its elegance from the body it draped, rendering him speechless. He quickly shifted his eyes in embarrassment, hoping his gawking hadn't been obvious.

"I wasn't sure where we were going so I opted for an in-between," Alex said. "Is it okay?"

"Perfect," he said, unaware of the zeal in his inflection. That is, until Star giggled excitedly.

"I wasn't through playing twenty questions, but it looks like you two are itching to get out of here, so go and have a good time," Star said parentally.

Casey noticed the simple smile Alex gave the friendly woman—one that seemed to playfully say; "I'll deal with you later."

The drive was uncommonly quiet, the atmosphere stilted. This was his third visit, and he was as nervous as a cat in a dog pound. They talked each night about everything from pleasant dreams to nightmares, so Casey couldn't figure out why he was so tense all of a sudden. With some alarm, he realized the sentiment was contagious. Alex's lighthearted posture that was so ardently displayed just moments earlier, was now strained and awkward.

After they were seated at a table for two in a cozy out-of-the-way dining room, Casey was disturbed to find his mind empty of insightful, casual conversation. Despite his usual confidence at making small talk, he was totally at a loss and breathed a sigh of relief when the waiter brought the wine list.

"Would you like something to drink before dinner?" he asked.

"No, thank you," she said, shaking her head. "I don't drink."

He closed the list and handed it back to the waiter. "I don't either," he said. "Looks like we'll have to find something to talk about over bread and water."

After ordering two waters with lemon, Casey settled back and glanced around the quiet, dimly lit room. He listened to the delicate clink of flatware hitting china and the ting of glass against glass. Alex's gentle gaze subtly consumed him as he struggled for something witty to say.

"Can we start the evening over?" he finally asked sheepishly. "I don't know what's wrong with me. I'm usually very charming."

Alex offered a shy smile, then an openly inviting chuckle. Casey studied her carefully. He loved the way her lips curved gracefully upward, compelling her cheeks to turn her eyes to little more than slits. Alex was unquestionably a one-of-a-kind—a passionate woman who made no pretenses—a rare breed. She could be funny, plainspoken, and even brash. He knew instinctively that if he weren't careful, the protective affinity he felt towards her could easily change into something more serious—a complication neither of them needed.

Between spontaneous friendly chatter about Zeke and his family, they ordered and were served their dinner. "You know, you're enchanting when you're free," he said, staring at her pensively.

"What do you mean?"

"You're as free as the air when you laugh. Your laughter seems to be your gateway to freedom."

"Very poetic, Mr. Oliver," Alex said, carefully forking a piece of salmon. "So…are you dating anyone?"

Casey looked at her in surprise then took a swallow of water from his glass. "My, you're one for impromptu queries. If I didn't know better, I would say you enjoy trying to shock me."

"I do," she said mischievously, placing a small portion of bread in her mouth.

"You don't always say what's on your mind, though, do you?" Casey challenged.

"That's called diplomacy. But I'm guessing you meant something else."

"Nothing bad. I just don't quite know what to make of you."

Alex looked amused and raised an eyebrow. "Oh? But you know quite a bit about me. Why don't you tell me more about you?"

"No. I'm not currently seeing anyone. My job the way it is, women are a complication I can't afford." A sly smile seeped forth as he tried to prepare for her response.

"Oh," she said with a triumphant little smile. She glanced around, obviously uncomfortable under the boldness of his gaze. He silently scolded himself, but had to admit he enjoyed seeing her squirm a little.

Casey leaned back in his chair and looked reflectively at the dishes on the table. "My life growing up in Gregory Falls is really uneventful—same old small town story, with the exception of reaching a long-time goal of working with the marshals service. As you know, my dad is a retired cop who lives on the same plot of ground that his grandfather grew up on. My mother died when I was nine and Zeke came to live with us when I was fifteen."

"Did you know your great-grandfather?" Alex asked.

"No. I'm told that I'm much like him. I knew my grand-father, though," Casey said, resting his arms on the table. "He died just before Zeke came to live with us. He was a wonder-

**119**

ful old character. He used to sit on his porch under the trees and play checkers with me. We didn't have real checkers, so we used the caps from soda bottles."

"Very creative."

"I remember that I used to feel as if he were always thinking of something funny because his eyes seemed to twinkle with a smile even if he wasn't. I now know that he was simply at peace and content with his simple life."

"I Wish I could feel that."

"You will," Casey said, looking much too deep into her eyes. "And I did. He taught me that the simple pleasures of life are really the stepping stones that take you to the top of your mountains."

"Very profound," she said, admiringly. "I think family and tradition is so important."

"I think so, too. My family tree looks like a perplexing puzzle, but I'm very proud of it."

"That's the second parallel I've been presented with using a puzzle," Alex said, remembering the objective for her journaling."

"That's right. I'd forgotten about your journaling. Have you seen anything yet?"

"I tried to get caught up on it last night," she said. "But if you don't keep it up, you forget too much for it to be effective. Anyway, we were talking about family. Mine is probably just a fragment compared to yours."

"A fragment is a piece broken away from something bigger. As believers, we're all a part of Jesus. You are a puzzle piece. Placed with all us other Christians, we make a beautiful picture."

"Funny how all of this seems to fit together," she uttered, a wrinkle creasing her brow."

"So you probably need to go home and pull that journal out."

"Casey, how did Gregory Falls get its name? It sounds like it may be very interesting."

"It is," Casey said, leaning even closer. "Gregory Falls was established by a Texas Ranger many years ago. Originally, it was called…." He hesitated. "It's a Native

American word that means a maiden's tears."

"A maiden's tears?"

"The legend goes that a handsome French soldier rescued a beautiful maiden from a fall down a rocky bluff. They soon fell in love and became engaged and remained very happy for a few months." Casey took a gulp of the freshly poured coffee, noting the dancing enthusiasm in Alex's eyes. She reminded him of Tracee when she listened to her dad telling her a story. They had the same depth of intrigue that seemed to absorb every detail.

"One day, the young man was unexpectedly called to action. He promised to return to the bluff in thirty days where they first met. Every evening after the thirty days were up, she went out looking for him, weeping, calling his name, convinced that he was there hiding in the cracks of the rocks. After a year of never hearing from him, she could stand it no longer. One moonlit night, she went to the bluff and wept loudly all night, creating a waterfall. When the morning dawned, she threw herself into the canyon below."

"How sad. What happened to the French soldier?" Alex asked, fully mesmerized by now.

"No one knows."

"Oh, that's so tragic," she said, her face reflecting the inner clutter of her thoughts. "It must have been interesting to grow up in a town like that." Her eyes danced again with intrigue.

"Maybe. I guess we treat many of life's wonders as nothing more than trinkets." Casey broke off as a waiter approached to remove their plates and offer desserts. Alex shook her head and mouthed a voiceless no. "We wouldn't care for dessert," he said. "May I have the check?"

"Gregory Falls?" she reminded him. "It must be a home for lawmen. Did your dad influence your decision to become one, or was it the town?"

Casey shook his head. "I'd much rather hear about you. But yes, I'm sure his love for the badge played a part in my choice. That's why I had such a time with it. I prayed a lot about it."

"Why? That's the dream of lots of boys."

**121**

# Fragment In The Sand

"For one thing, I didn't want to get into law enforcement for the wrong reason," Casey said, gazing at her candidly. "For another, I wanted to be sure that this was what God intended for me."

"Did He answer you?"

"Yes, as a matter of fact, He did. You know, it's amazing how God reminds me that He's always there." Casey chuckled. "I've become much more conscious of our loving heavenly father since I've been with the service."

"What about Zeke?"

"I think Zeke's reasons for being in law enforcement are a little more involved. But for the most part, he's very conscious of God's protection. We attend the same church, you know. He and Peg are very serious about their faith."

"I'm glad," she said, lowering her head. "My aunt had this wonderful way of talking to God that always sort of fascinated me. I remember I used to hide and listen to her carry on conversations with someone I couldn't see."

"Did it frighten you?"

"At first it did. Then after I came to know Him for myself, I strove to reach a level of communing with Him the way she had."

"What do you mean?"

"I just wish I were more in tune—more sensitive. Maybe then I wouldn't have to use a journal to try and hear Him," Alex answered. "Most men don't even talk about their relationship with God. But you're different. It's a nice change."

Casey enjoyed watching her eyes light up when she talked. He was glad that she was able to discuss such personal things with him, including her aunt's pet phrase. "A steady rock won't sink or slide, huh?" Casey repeated. "I like that. You know, you're probably more perceptive about these things than you realize." He reached across the table and took her hand in his.

"I'm not as perceptive as my aunt was," she said. "She was the kind of uncompromising Christian that I always wanted to be like."

"Are you really so sure that you're not?"

"I've got too many fears to conquer. I think they get in the way."

"They can be dealt with, Alex," Casey said tenderly. "I think we try to place too many stipulations on how God is supposed to teach us. He's with us all along. We just have to make ourselves be still and listen." Casey recalled her phobia of the dark and pondered how she was really handling it. "If I didn't believe that, I wouldn't be alive."

"I know," she said, needing to change the subject. "I'm learning."

"Casey, how long have you been with the Marshals Service?"

"Almost thirteen years. I transferred from D.C. to Oklahoma City four years ago…just after the Oklahoma City bombing."

"Any regrets?" she asked, resting her chin on the palm of her hand.

"Not about career choices," Casey said. "I think more than anything, I missed not having a mother around growing up." Alex looked at him somberly. It struck him then that at that moment, Alex had the saddest, most complicated expression he had ever seen. He knew that within moments, she could be her playful self again. She had a habit of twirling a stray tuft of hair at the nape of her neck whenever she was restless. She had started the evening doing it—she'd repeatedly done it on his first visit. He found it endearing for some reason and watched her with concern.

"I only remember a few things about my mother. She used to read the Bible to Zeke and me every night. I think that she must have been as much in command of her faith as Aunt Sarah was." Alex closed her eyes for a moment. Her voice softened then. "I remember that her voice was like music in the wind—until the night I heard her scream."

Her last words took Casey completely by surprise. His questioning abruptly halted when, without warning, the waiter reappeared with their check. "Will you be needing anything further, sir?"

"No. Thank you. We'll be leaving now."

\*\*\*

# Fragment In The Sand

Zeke closed the door to the bedroom and hurried to take the call. He had paged Adriel earlier and had been concerned when he didn't call him back right away.

"Webb."

"Zeke, this is Adriel. How's it going?"

"Pretty good," Zeke said, carefully sitting on the edge of the bed. "Did you find anything on the Shadow yet?"

"Everything's fine. Stop worrying so much."

"That's not an answer."

"Nah," Adriel said with a heavy sigh. "He's very evasive. He knows just how long to stay on the line with Alex and he's always a couple of steps ahead of us."

"I appreciate all your attention on this, buddy. But I was sure hoping that this would be a short one. I'm really concerned about how much more Alex can deal with emotionally. I take it she's not aware that you have a unit patrolling the area regularly?"

"Nah. I figured the less she knows about details, the less nervous she'll be. I just hope we catch him soon."

Zeke tapped his fingers anxiously against the nightstand, sensing that Adriel wasn't being completely open with him. "So what is it that you're not telling me? Are you sure she's safe?"

"Alex told me that some of her personal things had been moved around. She tried to sound indifferent, but I think it's pretty evident to both of us that he's been inside her apartment. Especially considering what he said about the way she looked when she's asleep."

"Oh, my God," Zeke cried out. "This has gotten way more serious than I realized."

"I'll keep my eyes open, Zeke. I have someone on the premises. Let's stay calm so that we can be more effective keeping her calm."

"You're right. And she does have her roommates," Zeke said, rubbing his hand grimly over his brow. "I have half a mind to fly out there and force her to come back with me."

"Not Alex," Adriel said, chuckling. "She's a little naïve, but as you know, she can be real stubborn."

"So can I," Zeke said. "I'm not feeling real good about

**124**

this at all. Call me as soon as you have something."

# CHAPTER 11

## *A Maiden's Tears*

Alex stole several side-glances at Casey's pensive expression during the quiet drive back to her apartment. She was taken aback when he abruptly turned and caught her in the act. "Find anything you like?"

She was so embarrassed at being caught that she couldn't think of a clever comeback. Then thankfully, her mischievous nature kicked in. "I like everything I see." She watched him carefully, perplexed as his smile faded into a serious expression.

"Alex?" He paused, as if warning her to prepare herself. "When did you hear her scream?"

"What?" she asked, confused by his question.

"Your mother...you said she screamed."

Alex turned pained eyes on his, inhaled deeply and answered. "The night she died."

"I—I'm sorry," he stammered. "I'm not trying to intrude."

"It's okay," she said, smiling. "It took a long time for the therapists to pull that buried bit of drama out of my memory bank. Maybe that's why I feel I'm at a sort of standstill in my relationship with God. It does me good to talk about it. You're easy to talk to."

"I'm glad you feel that way," he said, reaching for her hand. His reassuring touch almost made her feel more attached to him than she had a right to. She decided to stop being so analytical and enjoy the time with him—if only for the night.

"I couldn't get out of the cellar—it was so dark, and she kept calling my name, begging me to pray." Alex realized in horror that she had a death grip on Casey's hand and abruptly released it, looking for a mental escape through the car window. The anguish she felt rising up within her was unexpected. It coursed through her like a stream of incense coiling it's way into the deep, dark recesses of her soul. At one moment she thought it would ease. Then just as quickly, it was making her struggle to restrain the tears. "I did, but God couldn't hear me."

"I can see why you think you have a reason to be sluggish in your intimacy with the Lord. It also partly explains why you stopped talking for a while," he said tenderly. "The rest…well, obviously the whole scenario was tragic for a six-year-old. You were just a baby really. And being locked in the cellar is probably a type of grave to a child, which explains your dreams and fear of the dark."

"You picked up on that rather easily," she said, breaking into a smile. "And I didn't have to pay you for it."

"Did the doctors tell you that?"

"Something like that. Many hours and lots of dollars later."

"Alex, God didn't turn a deaf ear to your prayer."

She turned to him then, her eyes flashing with sparks of fire. "Then why did he let her die? Is that my fault? Didn't I pray right?"

The angry tone in her voice was apparent as an internal explosion rose to the surface. She felt almost as if she were another person entirely. Why did she feel that strongly now, after so many years of coping?

"I don't understand everything that happens in light of prayer, but I know that He's still there to listen and give you peace when you're ready to ask Him."

"I'm sorry about the outburst. Sometimes I think the therapists did more harm than good when they dug out that memory. I'd really like to understand and be closer to Him."

Her voice broke and after a few moments when she didn't continue, Casey asked, "Remember the puzzle scenario?"

"Yeah," she said, wiping away a lone tear.

"I believe that you can use it in regard to your dreams as well as other things—anything that you think is significant. I'm sure He's always talking to us in one way or another."

"That's what my pastor says, too," Alex whispered.

**127**

# Fragment In The Sand

"Casey?"

"Yeah."

"Why did she have to die? My whole world literally fell apart when she died. I lost her, my dad and my brother at the same time. I just don't understand."

"I don't know the answer to that, Alex. But I don't believe that it was God that busted up your world. I've asked the same questions you have about my own mother too many times to count. I haven't gotten an answer yet that I understand. But I know that God has given me peace and hope. And based on your questions, that's exactly what you need. God didn't *do* this. But He knew it was going to happen and He promised to be there for you as you went through it."

By the time Casey parked his rental car in front of her apartment, Alex was crumbling with the intense urge to weep. She felt as if she would explode. She didn't understand why she'd gotten so emotional all of a sudden. She sat trembling as he came around to open her door.

When he helped her from the car, she walked stiffly toward the street rather than her apartment. Casey caught up with her under a dimmed parking lamp near the security gate. "Alex? You okay?"

Her face was barely visible, but he could see a mixture of emotions play across her well-defined features. He watched as sadness, longing and uncertainty each made an appearance. She swallowed and attempted to speak, but closed her mouth again, slightly turning away. He longed to reach out and touch her, but shoved his hands into his pockets instead.

Although Zeke had only wanted him to check in on his sister, Casey found himself becoming more and more fascinated by her. He wished he hadn't brought back so many painful memories. Why had he pressed her like that?

She was so full of intrigue, moods and memories, but he wanted her to always feel safe in talking with him. Maybe he had taken more liberty than he should with her fragile emotions. But after talking to her every night, he wasn't convinced that she had ever felt safe and totally relaxed with the therapist. Not that he thought of himself as an expert, but he did know he

**128**

cared about her. And that had to be worth something. He wanted to know much more about her—what she thought, how she felt, what inspired her. He supposed that's why his heart moved him to try to help her deal with her past. He wanted her to know emotional and spiritual freedom.

After several moments of watching her struggle, he instinctively gathered her into a brotherly embrace. "I'm sorry. I shouldn't have awakened so many painful memories."

"I wasn't expecting such a flurry," she stammered. "I hope I didn't sound like I was blaming God. I'm too afraid to be angry with Him, but it sort of spills out sometimes." She giggled in spite of herself. "You must think I'm a nut."

"The Bible says that words of despair belong to the wind," he said. "I think you're a remarkable Christian. And it's refreshing to see a woman as beautiful as you represent the light of Christ on the inside. You're honest, intelligent, you love God and you're not afraid to get involved. Like with little Brian. And in spite of my opinion that his situation wasn't good for you, I love the way you poured yourself into him."

Casey was stunned by his words. He could only assume by her abrupt withdrawal that she was, too. "I'm sorry," he began.

"Thank you," she said, abruptly cutting him off. "That's one of the nicest things anyone has ever said to me."

A broad grin slowly spread across his face. "Well, I'm glad I could be of help."

Alex stood on her tiptoes then and planted a kiss on Casey's cheek. She laid her face against his chest and gently squeezed his waist. He didn't know how long they stood there holding each other beneath the lamp, but when his watch alarm went off, he wanted to rip it off and throw it into the street.

"I'm sorry," he said. "But I've gotta get to the airport."

"I know," she said. "I wish you didn't."

"That, my dear, is the story of my life," he said, gently lifting her chin. Without a word, he lowered his mouth to hers. At that moment, he found himself in the midst of a kiss far purer and more passionate than any he had dreamt of. It had certainly been unplanned, but felt so right.

**129**

# Fragment In The Sand

Time became eternal for Alex as an unexpected gasp escaped her lips. Casey abruptly pulled away and without words, escorted her to the door of her apartment before leaving. The only thing left to say now was the simple exchange of farewell pleasantries—and then he was gone.

He had kissed her. Though she couldn't deny that she had wanted him to, it had caught her completely off guard.

*** 

Rosell grimaced as he tossed the camera on the seat beside him. He had carefully hidden in the shadows and watched them kiss. He loved her, and he didn't like the way she let this cop touch her. She had been promised to him and he certainly had no intentions of giving her up now. He would have to punish her when the time was right.

He scowled; wondering who this cop was that had moved in on what belonged to him. He could tell he was a cop—he was packing fire. She must like the type because he was the second one who came around. He knew, of course, that she had been training with the other one, because he'd followed them, too. He knew that this one must be a little more serious because he'd even visited her at the studio. He wasn't sure why, but he hadn't bothered to tell the boss that little bit of news.

He couldn't get anything out of Miss Starch mouth when he asked about this new guy. His boss probably wouldn't like him going on his own to get a few extra shots of his sweet Tabitha. Sleeping…dressing…and wrapped in the arms of—

He sneered and started the engine of his car. He'd have to think of something special for his sweet Tabitha. She didn't have any pets that he could torture. Death of pets always hit a nerve. She did have a couple of roommates that she was fond of, though—as well as Lou, her uncle.

Lou was such a bossy moron—he'd done a couple of jobs for him a while back. He wondered if he was now his boss—maybe had a thing for his little niece. "Nah," he whispered to himself, shaking his head. "Lou was genuinely paternal and devoted to her. He wouldn't want her frightened like this. He recalled how he had snatched the photograph of her that he kept on his desk from his hand. She was younger then. It was destiny, he thought, a grin spreading across his face. She had grown up into a beauty and she was all his. Maybe he should take care of that new boyfriend of hers.

It didn't matter. He would have her all to himself in the end, but he didn't want anybody else handling her. He would have to call her tonight. He needed to keep her reminded that she belonged to him. Rosell pulled out a cigarette and lit it as he slowly drove away into the darkness.

# CHAPTER 12

## *Fortitude*

Zeke opened the garage door for more light so that he could locate his circular saw. He turned just in time to see Casey climbing out of his car. Immediately, he broke into a wide grin.

"Hey," Casey greeted, looking at Zeke curiously. "You know what to do with one of those?"

Zeke glanced down, having forgotten that he still held several screwdrivers and a cordless drill. "I was just replacing the backdoor."

Casey sauntered towards him, a frown beginning to form on his brow. "What's wrong with the old one?"

"I think some kids may have gotten in Sunday while we were at church. They ransacked the place. Peg was pretty upset."

"Why didn't you tell me? Did they take anything?"

"Not that we can tell," Zeke said, shaking his head somberly. "That's why I think it was only kids."

"Where are Peg and my little buddy?" Casey asked, still studying Zeke's face.

"In the house folding laundry, I think."

"Tell me what's going on," Casey said, conspiratorially and in his usual investigative mode. "This is *me* you're talking to."

"I don't want Peg to hear me," Zeke said, casually guiding Casey back out into the front yard. "Ok, maybe it wasn't just kids. Whoever it was came through like a tractor. The alarm had already been disarmed, so they obviously knew what they were doing. I think that it may just be a warning of some kind, or maybe they were looking for something. They didn't even take my gun, which I thought was strange."

"That *is* strange," Casey said reflectively. "Did you get

any prints?"

"None. This person knew what he was doing," Zeke said, with resigned concern. "I asked some of the boys to patrol the area a little more regularly. I found a note taped to the bathroom mirror, too."

"What did it say?"

Zeke anxiously glanced toward the door then turned back to Casey. "Just three words. *You're dead, detective!*"

"Zeke, this is serious. I think maybe I should ask Earl about putting you and the family under surveillance for a while."

"Nah. It would scare Peg half to death," Zeke said, shaking his head. "By the way, I'd appreciate it if you wouldn't mention this to my sister when you talk with her. I understand you two have become pretty good friends."

"Yeah. She's a pretty nice lady, Zeke. She's understandably jittery about all these phone calls she's getting. I just hope this guy doesn't get bored with just talking."

***

"You want a cup of coffee?" Desi asked, glancing around at Alex as she padded into the kitchen. "You look awful."

Alex yawned and dropped heavily into the kitchen chair. "Thanks. I needed that. I didn't get much sleep last night."

"Hey, what time is the picnic?" Star asked, sauntering in behind Alex. "I'm hungry, and it's about time we got out of this apartment for something other than church and work."

"Have a bowl of cereal," Desi sneered impatiently. "Sit down. I'll be a sport this morning."

"What's wrong with you?" Star asked, looking up in surprise.

Desi playfully tapped Star on the head. "Don't look a gift horse in the mouth." A knowing glance passed between Star and Alex as they both fought to hold back a snicker.

"Did you get any sleep last night?" Star asked, studying Alex's wearied expression.

"Not much. I think he waits until I finally get to sleep before he calls. You're right about getting out, Star. I'm looking forward to it, too. You guys have been great to hang

# Fragment In The Sand

around with me since May, but its August and time for me to stop letting this guy put me in bondage with his words."

Star's eyes filled with compassion. "I hadn't realized it had been that long. But I'm glad you don't let him intimidate you anymore. You seem so much stronger since this all started. By the way, can I borrow your gold kitten earrings?"

"You know, I looked for them yesterday and couldn't find them. I intended to ask you guys if you'd seen them."

"They're probably around here somewhere," Desi said, her brow furrowed. "So what is Adriel doing about this creepy caller?"

"There's a device on my private line, but so far, they haven't been able to track him. It's as if he knows just how long to stay on the line."

"As long as they can't hear *my* conversations," Desi said with an arrogant snort. "I like my privacy too much."

Star abruptly turned to Desi and raised an eyebrow. "Yeah, we know. And we wouldn't want Adriel to die of embarrassment after listening in on one of them."

"Oh, be quiet," Desi said, placing cereal before Star and Alex. "What's the creep talking about now?"

Alex hungrily crunched down on her breakfast. "He's gotten pretty nasty. Apparently, he doesn't like it that Casey took me to dinner a few weeks ago."

"Oh, really?" Desi asked, blinking in surprise. "Why?"

"He seems to think that I *belong* to him," Alex said. "He said that he planned to punish me. And if it happens again, I'll be sorry I ever laid eyes on Casey."

Star gazed wide-eyed up at Alex. "How can you stand to listen to all of that?"

"Adriel told me that I had to keep him on the phone as long as I could so they could try to track him."

"Why don't they have someone follow you like they do in the movies?"

"Don't be ridiculous, Star," Desi said, her eyes narrowing with disdain. "LAPD doesn't have the manpower to watch every woman that reports annoying calls. He has to make a move first."

"Like what?" Star asked, her face growing ashen.

**134**

"She's right," Alex said, indifferently. "He's really just enjoying himself on the phone right now. I don't think there's anything to worry about—at least I hope not. The only reason that I've rated a line tracer is because of Zeke being a police officer."

"The fact that he has become obsessive without being caught is ludicrous," Desi said, shaking her head.

Alex finished her breakfast and returned to her room to shower and dress for the picnic. She had awakened this morning as she had for the last few weeks, with warm thoughts of Casey. She was becoming more and more confused by the way her heart quickened each time she heard his voice. Although the feelings were exhilarating, they also frightened her because she didn't want to get involved romantically with any man—even one as charming as Casey. She shuddered at the thought of being hurt again, but her mind kept returning to the gentle sweetness of his kiss. She pondered how the Shadow could have seen them so clearly.

Casey was the first man she'd ever met that was so sure of his faith and wasn't intimidated or afraid to talk about it. She realized she hadn't seen the same clearness in Robbie. And despite her own love and devotion for God, she had allowed her questions to produce a form of doubt that kept her from becoming more intimate with Him—the very thing she desperately wanted. She stopped making her bed just long enough to grab the Bible from the nightstand and relax in a chair.

Something Casey had said reminded her of Simon Peter. She found the passage in Matthew where Jesus gave Simon the name Peter, which means a small rock, or a fragment of a rock.

*Simon Peter answered. "You are the Christ, the Son of the living God." Jesus replied, "Blessed are you, Simon son of Jonah, for this was not revealed to you by man, but by my Father in heaven. And I tell you that you are Peter, and on this rock I will build my church, and the gates of Hades will not overcome it."*

Alex reflected on what Jesus may have been trying to teach his disciples by changing Simon's name. It seemed to her that He was illustrating God's method of blessing his children. It was as if they could remain in Him, they would be a fragment of Him and have access to all knowledge—and on that knowledge Christ would build His church, capable of withstanding the very gates of hell. She sighed deeply, pressing her Bible close against her breast.

"Even the gates of the Shadow," she whispered aloud, relieved that she wasn't as frightened as she had been. "And God can withstand the walls that can prevent my happiness."

Alex leaned back in the chair positioned comfortably in the corner of her room and hugged her knees to her chest, silently hoping that she wasn't setting herself up for a disappointment. She had, after all, been known to misinterpret things.

***

As soon as they returned home from the picnic, Star disappeared to make a phone call. "Come sit with me while I throw a few things together, Alex," Desi suggested, stomping towards her room. "I'm glad CEF finally finished next spring's catalog. They've gotten so picky."

"I think they have a new person in charge of that," Alex said. "I'm just glad they agreed to shoot the last of it here in LA."

"You really don't like traveling, do you?"

Alex sighed and leaned easily against the headboard. "Not really."

"I guess I knew that, but I was still surprised that Zeke didn't come to LA when all of this stalking business got started."

"Adriel and Uncle Lou convinced him that everything was under control. Why are you leaving so early?"

Desi shrugged and perfunctorily opened the drawer to her dresser. "You know me. I like to have a day or so to get the lay out of the city."

Alex chuckled. "You sound like you're planning to commit a crime."

"Don't be ridiculous. I just have a few things I'd like to do before I have to report to work."

Alex glanced skeptically at her roommate. "If I didn't

**136**

know better, I'd think you were awfully anxious for something. Or *someone*. Anyone I know?"

"No," Desi said, laughing. "I don't need to sneak around to have fun. By the way, who is it that Star is talking to so long?"

"Some guy she met downstairs. He helped her with the groceries and she's worn him down to where he finally gave her his cell number."

"Hmph! Sounds married to me."

"You would know," Alex said, aware that she may be stepping too close to the firing line. "I mean, you don't really seem all that happy with your lifestyle. Is everything all right with you?"

"Sure, why do you ask?"

"You've been a little distant lately. Not so much today, but lately. We were getting a little concerned."

"You two are the only family I have left. And I love you both for worrying about me, but don't."

"We feel the same way about you," Alex said, studying Desi's somber expression.

"Did I ever tell you that my dad was an alcoholic?"

"No," Alex answered, wondering why Desi's mood was so amicable all of a sudden. "I thought he was a minister."

"He was."

"I'm sorry."

"Oh, he was harmless. It just worked my mother into an early grave. My brother and I had to fend pretty much for ourselves. Life just sucks sometimes, my friend."

"But you're successful now," Alex said, remembering Desi's dread of being poor again.

Desi waved away the concern. "Don't mind me. I didn't call you back here to talk about me. I actually wanted to make sure you're doing okay with all that's been going on."

"I'm fine," Alex assured her. "I do okay most of the time, except after dark. But then, that's nothing new."

"I can only imagine. I'm so sorry that this is happening…especially now. But you have your faith to get you through it. It's probably some fan that has allowed his fantasies to get away from him. He'll probably snap out of it before too much longer. Maybe he's growing bored with it."

"Do you really think so?"

Desi shrugged. "I wouldn't be surprised. I know that there are times when all of us do things in the passion of a moment and wake up to. We regret it. Unfortunately, sometimes it's too late."

"That's called temporary insanity," Alex replied with a chuckle. "I just want it to be over."

Desi zipped her luggage shut and moved around to sit next to Alex on the bed. "I still worry that I've done things in my life that are irreversible. I've been angry at the world for much too long. It's too late for me."

"Oh, it's never too late, Desi," Alex said tenderly, watching the tears gather in her friend's eyes. "As long as you're breathing and you want to fix it, there's hope."

The apartment was much too quiet with Desi gone to Minneapolis. Yet Alex and Star were enjoying a rare moment of lounging. All at once, Star remembered that she had to go and meet Lou. Her nervousness was very apparent. "Do you think he wants to drop me?"

"Of course not, silly. Maybe he wants to offer you the Paris trip."

"Do you really think so?" Star asked excitedly.

"I don't know. But I'll keep my fingers crossed for you."

Star quickly showered and dressed in a pair of denims and a pullover, standing for what seemed like an eternity to scrutinize her reflection in the darkened television screen. "I don't understand why he can't just come over here," she complained.

Alex sat with her feet propped up on the sofa, devouring an apple. "He's already told us that each of our contracts is a separate and private legal matter," she said unperturbed.

"Why can't he just mail it then?" Star asked anxiously. "Did you already renew?"

"Actually, I was going to talk to both of you when Desi got back. I didn't renew, Star. I told Uncle Lou that I wanted to take a year off."

"What! Why? Does this have anything to do with Casey or Adriel?"

"No."

"Was Lou mad? What did he say? How long have you—
"

"Slow down," Alex said, holding up a hand. "I just had this feeling that I wasn't supposed to renew. He was pretty mad, but he's my uncle. He's gotta' get over it. He tried to talk me out of it—even offering me the Paris assignment. But I told him I wasn't interested."

Star's eyes widened as she covered her mouth in astonishment. "Oh, Alex. Maybe we shouldn't tell Desi about this. She's so sure that she'll get the trip."

"Why should she?" Alex asked quizzically.

"Because she thinks she has Lou in her pocket," Star said, chuckling.

"Well, I wouldn't want her feelings to be hurt, but they're bound to if he chooses someone else. He has so many to choose from. I don't see what all the fuss is about, anyway."

"Everyone except you has been on pins and needles about this trip. Shucks, having a whole month in Paris without having to work—all expenses paid would be a dream come true for any of us."

"Does Desi really assume she's the one that Uncle Lou has chosen?"

"I don't know. It's just the way she acts sometimes—so confident and smug. But don't mind me, my friend," she said, raising her hand dramatically to her brow. "I suppose I'm just being overly stimulated."

"Well, stop it," Alex said, playfully tossing an apple core at her. "You make me crazy when you do that." They both laughed lightheartedly.

"When did you tell Lou you weren't renewing?"

"Last night."

"Thanks a lot, Alex! That means he's gonna' be in a grumpy mood. You know he was crabby during the whole New York trip. Please go with me? It shouldn't take long. You can wait in the car if you want."

"Star! I'm surprised at you. I didn't know you were so intimidated by Uncle Lou. He's really just a big teddy bear."

"You're the only one not afraid of that big grouch," Star

**139**

exclaimed. "You're his niece and have always had his protection rather than his cagey dominance."

"I think you're wrong about that, Star. It may come out in a different way with me, but Uncle Lou is just as pushy with me sometimes. He's just a little more sly about it."

"Whatever!" Star said. "Go with me?"

"Nah. I just want to stay here, curl up with a good book and wait for Casey's call. You don't need me—this is a business meeting—probably just needs your signature."

"You really like Casey, don't you?"

"I enjoy talking to him," Alex said, attempting to keep her voice flat and unconcerned.

"Does Adriel know about him?" Star asked, her eyes beginning to gleam.

"Star, there is nothing between Adriel and me." Alex said, determining that she should tell her friends the whole truth. She had noticed early on that Adriel had asked a lot of questions about Star and it made her feel even guiltier for having lied to them. "He was just helping me out with something as a favor to Zeke."

"With what?" Star asked, a devious smile beginning to spread across her face.

"You don't believe me!" Alex accused. "Honest, I just didn't want you guys to worr—"

"Save it," Star said in exasperation. "You're not gonna' come clean. Besides, I gotta' run. Don't want to give Lou a reason to be mad if he's not already."

\*\*\*

Rosell burst angrily into the motel room, slamming the door behind him. His narrowed eyes raked the room as adrenaline coursed wildly through his arteries. He could feel the muscles twitching in his face as he paced the span of the small space.

His mind recalled the stout words of the woman he'd talked to earlier, and he instantly wanted to find her and wipe away her face. "I'm sorry, but I've been instructed to tell you that your services will no longer be required. Your final payment will be in your post office box in four hours."

"I thought—" he'd begun.

"Sir, I'm sure that you realize that you have deliberately breached the terms of the agreement. You went beyond your instructions for reasons of your own. Therefore, we've found it necessary to terminate your services."

"I demand to speak to the boss," he had shouted.

"I'm sorry. That just isn't possible." The woman had disconnected the call abruptly. By the time he'd calmed down enough to call the service back, the number was no longer in service.

He turned to stare at the enlarged photograph of Alex Webb. It was taped across the door of the bathroom with a pair of gold kitten earrings taped at her ears.

He thoughtfully ran his fingers across the face of the picture, his lips curling disdainfully.

"You still belong to me, my sweet, Tabitha," he whispered. "And it looks like it's about time for me to bring you home."

# CHAPTER 13

## *The Shadow*

Casey breathed a sigh of relief when Alex picked up the phone on the fourth ring. The sound of her voice had a tranquilizing effect on him. He had grown so accustomed to talking to her each evening that he found himself a little ill-tempered when he was delayed for some reason. Alex had become very important to him and he had to be careful from here on out.

He was taken with her very real honesty and spontaneous sense of humor. She was the sort of woman he'd like to bring home to his dad—the sort he had always imagined himself settling down and building a life with. The sort he would even consider leaving the service to make happy. Already treading on thin ice, he wasn't sure how he would handle it if he allowed himself to get much closer. The last thing he wanted to do was abandon her at a time like this, but he certainly needed to get more control over his emotions.

His mouth suddenly felt dry and he swallowed hard. Was he out of his mind thinking like this? She hadn't given him the slightest indication that she would welcome a romantic relationship with him. And he lived clear across the country with career demands that no woman should have to deal with. Especially after all that she'd been through. She had, however, responded favorably to his kiss.

"Hello," Casey said, after she'd answered the phone.

"Oh, hi," she said, her voice lilting after recognizing him. It secretly thrilled him that she looked forward to hearing from him. "I'm so glad it's you and not—" She paused and cleared her throat. "How was your day?"

"Just regular routine," he said, a little deflated. "And how was yours?"

"Exceptional! I went to a picnic, got a chance to talk to

Desi about the Lord, and quit my job."

He was so stunned that he didn't know what to say. Should he congratulate her or console her? "W—what?"

"I told Uncle Lou last night." Her smile transmitted through the phone line and his heart quickened with understanding.

"I'm surprised. When did you decide that?"

"Oh, I think it started coming together when I read through my journal last week. I know it's sudden, but I just don't believe God would have me be miserable the way I've been. Maybe He's guiding me. I told Uncle Lou that I wanted to take a year off. That'll give me time to get more direction."

"I'm very proud of you," Casey said. "Not many in your position would take such a leap of faith. Are you sure this is what you want to do? The industry may not be as forgiving after a whole year without you."

"Then I'll have my answer, won't I?

Casey was almost at a loss for words. He'd never heard her sound so self-assured and expectant. "I'm surprised...I mean, you sound so confident...so determined."

"Don't let my bold words mislead you," she said with a slight laugh. "I'm scared to death, but I feel good about this decision. And the fact that I made it without anybody else's input makes it more exciting."

He could tell she was struggling to recapture the confidence that had unexpectedly slipped away as she spoke.

"I guess I hadn't realized how much everything has been affecting me until I went to the picnic today. I've been so caged in. Not that I mind being home—I enjoy it. But having to be so watchful puts a real bite on it."

"I'm sure you know better than anyone that extremists make threats all the time, Alex. Everything will be fine."

"I know. I know," she said. "But I've been racking my brain trying to think of who might do this, but—"

He could hear the panic in her voice and tried to play the situation down. "Don't go there," Casey said. "You've been doing great. You just be careful and remember what Adriel taught you."

## Fragment In The Sand

"Casey, I don't want to shoot anyone," she whispered.

He hesitated before he made his next comment. "But I need to know that you can take care of yourself. I wouldn't want anything to happen to you." The moment the words were out of his mouth, the thought crossed his mind that Alex could still be in love with Robbie. He grimaced at having allowed himself to get lost in his emotions like that. He felt like an idiot. There was no reason in the world to think that Alex would consider a life with him anyway—unless, of course, she actually, by some miracle, fell in love with him. A faint glimmer of hope flickered through him.

From the way she was beginning to sound, she was definitely learning to trust God more. Casey set his mouth in a firm, hard line, deciding to focus on that hope and continue to encourage her. But he couldn't seem to stop himself from dreaming of making a life with her. He took a deep breath and tried to change the subject.

"I'm sorry that I didn't get to meet Calvin while I was there. I only had a couple hours."

"He wasn't here anyway," she said, with a short chuckle. "He left town when I told him that Zeke was going to check him out."

Casey jolted as sudden awareness signaled an alert. "What?"

"I'm only joking," she said. "What is it with you men? His job sent him out of town for some training. He just happened to tell me right after I mentioned that Zeke had suggested checking him out. He came back, but left a couple of weeks later. He should have been back by now, though. I'm getting a little worried."

"It's probably nothing to worry about. He may have just taken some extra vacation time," Casey said. "Are you still in love with him?"

"In love?" she asked in surprise. "With who?"

Casey held his breath, almost shocked that he had asked. Maybe some of her methods were rubbing off on him. "With Robbie."

Her deliberation was so drawn out that it alarmed him. He was about to tell her not to answer when she did. "No, I'm not," she said with firm resignation. "I know now that I was in love with who I thought he was and what I thought the marriage could do. I've been doing a lot of soul searching."

Casey expelled a sigh of relief and rushed the conversation to a close before he made a fool of himself.

After hanging up, he leaned against the headboard. He considered rolling over and trying to go to sleep, but his mind was bustling with thoughts of Alex—beautiful, amazing Alex. A frown creased his brow as he pondered if he'd imagined that she wanted to say more. His thoughts had become too fanciful—too irregular, and that made him nervous.

Casey half turned toward the window as the sultry air crept into the room, strangling his thoughts. Moaning dolefully, he closed his eyes and envisioned her smile just before dozing off.

*** 

Alex continued to stare at the phone after she hung up. The feeling was exhilarating. Casey's voice, as expected, had suspended any leftover anxiety she may have felt. But it had also increased her expectancy for something she couldn't quite grasp with her mind.

As usual, his words of encouragement were right on time. In a strange way, it reminded her of her Aunt Sarah. She had really depended on her aunt a lot back then for clarity and direction in the things of God. She had complied with biblical principles primarily because of her aunt's influence, but now she knew the necessity of searching out one's own way with God.

After her aunt's death, her uncle, who knew very little about faith, had become her principal tutor. Even though she already had problems in the area of prayer, she could almost see the broken line of fellowship arise between her and God. It would be so easy to become passive. But she didn't want to depend on men anymore. Calvin had been right. She had done that almost all her life.

Finally removing her hand from the phone, Alex pondered their conversation and shivered with the sudden awareness that Casey most certainly was developing feelings for her. She knew, of course, that she could be imagining things, but his awkward response felt so much like her own. She had wanted to talk to him a little longer, but he seemed to rush the conversation after he had asked her about her feelings for Robbie—almost as if he had said more than he intended.

Maybe she was just full of wishful thinking. After all, she was probably still rebounding. In spite of having talked regularly on the phone, she knew they hadn't really known each other that long. She wondered, nonetheless, if a relationship between them could be possible—a deeper relationship.

Mindful of having to arrive on the set early the next morning, Alex watched television until she felt drowsy and prepared for bed, deciding to forego sending Zeke an email. She hadn't been as regular with her email notes as she generally was. But that's okay since Zeke had taken to calling more.

She was just about to turn in when the phone rang again. She hesitated, letting it ring several times before picking up. It could be Casey again. Maybe he'd decided to finish his conversation—or maybe Star had run out of gas again. Although she had done well in beefing up her grit, the calls still left her feeling fragile and anxious. Taking a deep breath, she cautiously lifted the receiver and breathed a sigh of relief when she heard her sister-in-law's cheerful voice. She really had to stop letting the Shadow frighten her like this.

"Oh, Peg, I'm glad it's you."

"Are you okay, Alex?" Peg asked. "You sound a little out of breath."

"Yeah, I'm fine," she answered, feeling her heart began to return to its normal rhythm. "I was just about to turn in…have an early day tomorrow."

"What's that, eleven o'clock?" Peg teased.

"Nope. I'll have you know I don't sleep in like you'd think," she said jubilantly. "My day will start at five."

"Oops!" Peg exclaimed. "Then I won't keep you, honey. I just wanted to check on you. Why don't you call me tomorrow when you get in—I have something I want to talk to you about."

"Is everything all right?" Alex asked, intrigued by Peg's request.

"Everything's fine. I just have a proposition I want you to

consider. Call me tomorrow."

"Sure thing. Thanks for calling, Peg."

As soon as she'd hung up the phone, it rang again. "Is this Grand Central tonight?" she asked aloud. After letting it ring several more times, she snatched up the phone. The instant she did, she somehow knew that it was the Shadow.

"Hello, Tabitha," he murmured. "It's me." His low, trailing tone was glib but taunting. "I've got you so spooked you have to force yourself to answer the phone, don't you, sweet thing?"

His voice was so syrupy that whenever she hung up the phone, she wanted to wipe it off with disinfectant. It was smooth, but low and deep, and grated fiercely on her nerves. She stood clasping the phone to her ear with her mouth open.

All at once, she remembered that she had decided that she would no longer tolerate his fear tactics. After all, like she'd told Star, they were only calls from an obvious coward. She got mad then. And the long buried fury cut like a razor through the remainder of her apprehension.

"You pathetic excuse for a man," she shrieked acidly. "You make me sick."

"Now…now, my sweet. You don't know what that little outburst might cost you. I already owe you a lesson. After all, you need to know how serious I am."

Alex slammed the phone down before she could hear anything more. She didn't care what Adriel had instructed her to do. She wasn't going to it any longer, trying to hold him on a phone. If they hadn't caught him yet, they probably wouldn't. She'd just change her number first thing tomorrow morning.

Marching into the bathroom, she pulled down her prescription of sleeping tablets and took one. She didn't like the stupor they always left her in, but she had to try and get some sleep. Despite the fact that Adriel had explained that she needed to treat her handgun as if it were a part of her body, Alex felt a little silly when she placed it beneath her pillow.

To settle her nerves, she began to quote scripture until she dropped off into a nod. Blissfully unaware that the moment everything would change was near, Alex dreamt of birds gathering in the trees around the pond. The serenity sped by quick-

# Fragment In The Sand

ly as she heard her mother pleading with her to pray. "Pray, Alex, pray—like you've never prayed before." But not a word came from her mouth. She felt paralyzed and consumed with fear. All at once a musical chime sounded in the background and she sprang up in bed. Alex took a moment to make sure she was at last awake. Panic filled her then, as she became more aware that she was not alone.

Reaching for her gun, she held herself as still as she dared—listening intently. She peered around the room trying to find what had awakened her. It was totally dark. She couldn't see anything. She gasped just as a loud crash came from the living room. Unbearable silence filled the apartment then. Alex had no idea what she should do.

She listened as the sound of cushioned footsteps approached her bedroom. She could feel the blood pulsating through her strained fingers as she gripped the gun even tighter. Calm down, she told herself. Breathe. What was happening? The steps stopped and retreated toward the living room. Surely it wasn't a burglar—the alarm would have been activated. No...no. It was evident that the power was off. Was it the whole complex, or had someone cut the line?

She sat rigid in terror, staring into the thick darkness that settled around her like a cloak. Her heart pounded as a prickling sensation rushed up her spine. She couldn't just sit there waiting to die, she thought. She had to do something.

Easing from beneath the covers, gun in hand, Alex slid to the floor. "Oh, God, help me," she whispered. Her breath was coming now in little pants.

Down on her hunches, Alex crawled towards her window to get to the fire escape. Again, heavy footfalls rushed towards her, and instinctively, she aimed the gun. Suddenly, the darkness around her became as thick and heavy as death.

# CHAPTER 14

## *Fade*

Alex slowly opened her eyes and, for an instant, entertained the notion that she was blind. Immediately, getting a whiff of the familiar caustic odor of gunfire, her mind went directly to the firing range. She felt strangely like she was suspended in mid-air while indistinct sounds bounced off the walls in slow motion and hummed past her ears. Fragmented thoughts flowed sporadically while she lay dazed in the depths of her darkness.

Struggling to get to her feet, she moaned in pain. But she felt as though something was holding her down. Too tired to fight it, she let herself fall back to the floor.

"Alex!"

She searched the darkness, praying that it wasn't someone coming back to hurt her again. She couldn't answer—she couldn't move. Confused, she reached up to brush the hair from her face. She was startled to feel the sticky dampness on her forehead. She knew without a doubt that it was blood.

A fluttering light moved towards her, and terror rose up in her throat. Instinctively, she curled protectively into a ball. The gentle radiance gradually became a blaring light. She squinted against the intrusion of the flashlight shining in her face.

"Alex, darlin'. It's Calvin. Oh, my God, you're bleeding."

She breathed a heavy sigh of relief at the sound of her friend's voice and clutched onto him with all she had as he lifted her to the bed. She stiffened against Calvin when she heard another familiar voice call out through the darkness.

"Freeze! Police!"

Following the shaft of Calvin's flashlight beam, Alex stared into Adriel's rigid face. Horror tore through her like

**149**

lightening when she realized he had drawn his weapon.

"Adriel! No!" she screamed, closing her eyes again as he aimed his own flashlight onto her. "He's my friend."

"Jim, in here," Adriel demanded. "Quickly, I need more light."

By the time Adriel had placed a cool damp towel on her head, Alex was trembling so badly she could hardly keep her teeth from chattering. She shrank sluggishly against Calvin who protectively held her close. Within minutes, the power was restored and Alex was able to look into the baffled faces of Adriel and the other officer he had called Jim.

"Sir, would you mind identifying yourself," Jim said, gazing irritably at Calvin. Already taking out his cuffs, he made a move toward Calvin, who quietly stood to his feet."

"No!" Alex shrieked, grasping at Calvin's hand.

"Hold up, Jim," Adriel said, carefully kicking the handgun aside that had fallen to the floor next to the bed. "She's pretty scared. He can probably help keep her calm."

Calvin sat back down, tightening his embrace around Alex. She grew even more uneasy when Adriel pulled a chair closer to the bed and gazed seriously into her eyes.

"Alex, your gun has been fired. Can you tell me what happened?"

She shook her head, as tears blurred her vision. "It was so dark. I heard something. I remember holding the gun, but I swear—I don't remember firing. I didn't hurt anybody, did I? I'm sorry, Adriel. I was so scared. Someone was in here."

Jim clumsily moved about the room, peering around for evidence. He was short and round and wore his rankled mood smugly. It was obvious he was put out with having to be here. Alex could see the spasms of irritation cross Adriel's face as he turned to glare at his fellow officer.

Without warning a sharp, piercing pain radiated from behind her eyes. "What's happened, Adriel?"

"It'll be all right," Adriel said, gently patting her shoulder. "Just relax now."

"The casing's over here on the window sill," Jim said. "It looks like the perp may have gone out this way." Jim peered out onto the fire escape. "Hey, look at this."

**150**

"What is it, Jim?"

"Someone's been smoking out here—a lot. Miss Webb, do you smoke?"

"No," Alex answered without turning.

"I suppose this guy could have come in this way as well. He must have banged Miss Webb on the head with this thing. It's got blood on it."

The pudgy man held up Alex's hourglass. She immediately withdrew from Calvin and reached for it. But before she could move off the bed, Adriel took the piece from Jim.

"Alex, we'll have to take this and your gun in," he said, placing both items in a bag that Jim handed him. "See if you can get those cigarette butts in a bag as well, Jim."

Alex jolted as she heard another voice call out from the living room. "We've got the round!" Jim immediately rambled past the bed and out toward the front. She could hear several voices that she didn't recognize, and was suddenly grateful that she at least knew Adriel.

Adriel placed the bag of evidence on the nightstand and picked up her robe from the floor. He continued to glance around the room curiously as he handed her robe to Calvin. Calvin in turn assisted Alex in putting it on.

"Officer, can you tell me what happened here?" Calvin asked, clutching Alex protectively against himself.

"Sir, I don't believe I got your name," Adriel said, gazing intently into Calvin's face. "May I ask who *you* are?"

"I'm sorry. My name is Calvin Prince. I live in an apartment on the other side of the complex. I'm a friend of these girls."

"Well, Mr. Prince, I'm Detective Adriel Payne with LAPD. May I ask why you're here?"

"Like I said—I'm a friend. When the power went off, I came by to check on Alex. I knew she'd probably be a little frightened."

To Alex's relief, Adriel finally exhibited an air of acceptance and resolve that relaxed his taut features. "It appears that the ladies had an intruder tonight. Someone shut off the electricity, as well as cut their phone lines."

"Do you have any idea how?" Calvin asked. "We have

**151**

pretty good security."

"Apparently not good enough," Adriel commented, turning back to Alex. "This is the only apartment that has its telephones disconnected. Alex, where is Desi?"

"She flew to Minneapolis," she answered reeling. "Is Star home? Is she all right?"

"She's alive," Adriel said, his eyes shadowing over with concern. He quickly recovered himself, however, and set his jaw firmly, restoring his professional distance.

Alex withdrew from Calvin and tried to get up. "Star? Where is she? Did I shoot her?"

"No, ma'am," Jim said from the doorway. "It looks like the round was lodged in that old desk out there with the computer on it. The other girl was roughed up quite a bit, but she wasn't shot."

Alex felt the tears begin to trail down her face, but she had no inclination or energy to wipe them away. She could smell a sour odor as a wave of nausea enveloped her. Trembling, she sank back against Calvin.

"Star has already been transported to the hospital," Adriel said, gently squeezing her hand. "We'll take you as soon as we're done here."

"I can take her," Calvin interrupted.

"Alex, I've gotta go back out front with the others for a while. I'll need you to stay in here with Mr. Prince. Will you be all right?" Again, Adriel glanced at Calvin skeptically.

"Adriel, where did they take Star?"

He looked into her eyes, placing a steadying hand on her shoulder. "Alex, I want you to calm down, now. Star is going to be fine. I don't want you worrying about that. Try to sit tight for a few minutes."

"But I fired the gun, Adriel," she said, a sickening wave of anguish welling up in her belly. "And I couldn't see anything." Tears continually flowed down her face. She silently prayed that Star would be all right and that she hadn't made a mistake to bring the gun into their home.

"The gun might have discharged when you were hit on the head," he said with a kind smile. "You said yourself that you didn't remember firing it. Don't jump to conclusions, okay?"

"Okay," she said, closing her eyes and letting out an unsteady breath. Her mind raced from one thought to another. Everything was happening so fast and furious. She grew even more anxious as she listened to the strange voices coming from the other room. The noises were loud and foreign, and she peered around worriedly. She felt as if she were being lowered into the dark world of her nightmares, only this time, they were for real. Perplexed, she wondered who the people were in her living room. Or had she already asked that?

She turned to Calvin, who had moved to the chair next to her bed. He had a worried eye on her. "What's going on out there? Did you see anything?"

"No. The power was still off when I came up. I was so intent on finding you all that I obviously walked right past Star," he said, his voice edged with tension. "You'd better lie down and let me take a look at that head."

Calvin immediately disappeared into the bath, returning with first aid items to mend the gash on Alex's forehead. She could barely feel a thing other than the monstrous throbbing behind her eyes. Hoping to relieve the pressure, she closed them tightly and sat still as Calvin placed a bandage on her head. She heard him murmuring something about good as new, but at that moment all she wanted to do was sleep.

"What's taking Adriel so long?" she complained, positioning the pillow more comfortably beneath her head. "Why can't I go see Star?"

Adriel returned to Alex's room, a grim expression on his face. "What's happened, Detective?" Calvin asked, springing to his feet.

"As best as I can tell, the intruder entered through the window in here. He apparently surprised your roommate while she was on the computer in the living room."

"That's odd," Alex said, grimacing. "Star doesn't generally use my computer. She wasn't home when I came to my room. Will she be all right?"

"Alex, we really don't know a lot right now," he said worriedly. "Were you here alone all night?"

"We were here together until she left to meet with Uncle Lou. I came to bed, and talked with Casey on the phone," she rambled on, not quite sure how much she had dreamed or what had been real. "The Shadow called, too—I thought it was Casey again."

"Yeah, we heard him," Adriel said. "He said something about owing you a lesson. Perhaps this is what he meant. What time did Star leave the apartment this evening?"

Alex glanced up in disbelief. "I think it was around seven."

"Did you hear her return?"

Her heart hammered wildly against her chest. "No. When I got the call from *him,* I took something to help me get to sleep. I have an early day tomorrow and I knew if I didn't, I wouldn't get any sleep at all."

"I think we'll need to get someone to watch you on a more regular basis," Adriel said. "Assuming that this is the Shadow, we've gotta move as if he plans to do a lot more than this."

"Can I go see Star now?" Alex asked anxiously. "Maybe I should call Desi. She'd want to know."

"No," Adriel said. "Not yet. I think we need to get that head of yours looked at. How do you feel?"

Alex felt as though she were moving in and out of some confused state of phantasm and closed her eyes against the harsh glare of the lighting in her room. "I want to talk to Casey. Adriel, why...what...my head hurts so bad."

Heavy tears blurred her vision, and for a moment, she turned her face away from the two men so she couldn't see their anxiety. Suddenly, it occurred to her that Adriel wasn't being truthful with her?

Certain that she would be able to detect a misleading response from him, she wiped her face and turned back to make eye contact with him. "Is Star going to be all right?"

"I don't know, Alex. All we can do now is pray."

"Oh, God," she said, covering her face with her hands. "What have I done?"

"Alex, this isn't your fault," Adriel said, crouching beside the bed. "Maybe it's mine." She jolted at a burst of laughter coming from the living room and glanced back at Adriel for reassurance.

"It's all right," he said softly. "They're investigators...finishing up."

"What did you mean when you said that it was your fault?"

"I should have known that you weren't ready to use the gun in a stressful situation. Among other things, I never factored in your fear of the dark. It may have been too soon to discontinue your lessons."

"Adriel, how did you know something was wrong?" she asked, finally becoming more alert.

"I came initially because of a call I got from your brother. On the way over, we got the call that the power was out. And some of your neighbors said that they thought they'd heard gunfire."

"Zeke called you?" she asked. "Why?"

"He was out of his mind with worry," Adriel said, turning toward Calvin. "Is her head okay?"

Calvin silently nodded in response, reminding Alex that he'd been extremely quiet through the whole ordeal. It was also the first time she'd seen him in over two weeks. "You okay, Calvin?"

"I'm fine, darlin'. How do *you* feel?"

"I'm not sure." Turning back to Adriel, she asked, "why did Zeke call you?"

"He said he'd gotten an email from *you*."

Alex frowned, intently probing his eyes. "But I distinctly recall skipping sending one tonight...at least I think I did. What aren't you telling me, Adriel?"

"Detective, I assume from the conversation that you're Zeke's friend?" Calvin said.

"Yes, sir," Adriel said, turning to regard Calvin distrustfully. It was the second time she'd noticed Adriel's misgiving, and she instantly wondered why. "Zeke is already on a plane to Los Angeles. He was pretty upset when he got that email and couldn't get through to you by phone. He's coming to try and talk you into going back to Oklahoma."

"He just might not have much convincing to do now," Alex said, feeling more puzzled than ever.

"By the way, your uncle has been notified as well. He's on his way over here."

# Fragment In The Sand

Alex felt a warm flush move over her face as she began processing Adriel's words. They sounded foreign—like the building of a complicated plot for a movie. "What did you say?"

"If you can do without Alex for a while, I'd like to take her out of here," Calvin said, rising to his feet. "As you can see, her mind is roaming a bit."

"I can't let you do that just yet," Adriel objected. "There's a lot…"

"Look, Detective. If you're really Alex's friend, then you can see she needs some medical attention," Calvin interrupted. "She may be going into shock or something…may I at least call my lady friend? She's a nurse."

"I don't see what harm that would do," Adriel said, running his hand through his thick hair. "I assume that she's nearby?"

"Five minutes. I'll go walk her over. We were watching television at my place when the power went out." Just as Calvin left the room, a uniformed officer appeared in the doorway.

"Sir, we've found a suspect. We have him detained downstairs. Shall we bring him up here?"

"No. I'll come down there in just a moment. Let me finish up here." Adriel turned to Alex and smiled warily. "I want you to just lie there and rest until Mr. Prince gets back. Should I send a female officer in to keep you company?"

"No. I'll relax more if I could just be alone," she whispered, feeling relieved that this nightmare was finally over. "Do you really think the Shadow would have let himself be captured so easily, Adriel?"

"I don't know," he said. "Sooner or later, they all get sloppy. I'll be right outside if you need me. Okay?"

"Okay," she said, already snuggling against her pillow. She watched as Adriel pivoted and strolled out of the room, leaving the door a few inches ajar. Maybe she should call and let Casey know that she'd probably see him in a couple of days. She yawned. She'd call in a moment—when she'd had a chance to close her eyes.

# CHAPTER 15

## *Two Fronts*

\*\*\*

It was five o'clock in the morning when Zeke deplaned at LAX. His neck was stiff and his shoulders ached as if he carried the weight of the whole universe on them. He immediately saw Adriel standing at the gate with a somber expression on his face. His heart sank. *Oh, God, please let Alex be safe.*

It wasn't until Lou Ramsey moved past Adriel that Zeke noticed him. He stopped in his tracks, engulfed with apprehension. Was Lou here to discourage him from convincing his sister to return to Oklahoma? Was something wrong?

Lou's eyes were red and he looked much older—heavier. The last time he'd seen him was the day of his aunt's funeral. Lou had convinced him then to allow him to send Alex to Paris to finish school rather than uproot her to return to Oklahoma. "She's lost enough people that she loves. It would be callous to traumatize her further by insisting that she return with you," he'd said. "She still has nightmares of you leaving her in an open grave with her mother. Zeke, we've got to think of Alex first."

Zeke's expression hardened as he recalled how reluctantly he had succumbed to Lou's persuasive interference. He had skillfully played on his guilt. Lou had assured him that if he allowed Alex to fulfill her dream in fashion, he would make sure that she'd be shielded from anything that Zeke thought him capable of.

"Where's my sister, Adriel?" he demanded, not bothering to acknowledge his uncle.

Zeke turned just in time to see Lou swipe at a lone tear as his lips trembled. "Zeke, I…"

Something was wrong. "Lou, I'm not in the mood to hear bravado. I came to escort my sister back to Oklahoma. Now

# Fragment In The Sand

where is she?"

"Zeke, I'm sorry," Adriel injected. "But right now, that's the least of your worries. Your wife...she's safe now...she's been hurt."

Zeke's jaw dropped open in shock as he quickly eased into the nearest chair. At that moment, he felt as if his whole being was caving in around him. Adriel's disquieting words had taken his breath away, and he struggled to assimilate them. Surely he'd heard wrong...maybe he was just tired. After all, he hadn't had any sleep.

"P—Peg...how?"

"Casey pulled a few strings. He's with her now," Adriel said. "The Marshal's Service is working with Oklahoma City PD on this because of that threat you received a while back. They also found an explosive device planted in your assigned car."

As if hearing his friend for the first time, it dawned on him what Adriel was actually saying. "Explosive? Oh, my God...Peg," he wailed, hoping that it was all some kind of cruel joke. Was God actually punishing him for the bitterness that he was still harboring in his heart? He had only left a few hours before. This was crazy. He had come to get his sister out of this horror. Not drag his wife into it. All at once, a renewed panic raced through him. "Tracee?"

"Tracee is fine, Zeke," Lou said. "You were airborne. We couldn't get a call through to you. They think someone was watching when you left the house. The attacker apparently entered through the kitchen window fifteen minutes after you left. Peg's in Mercy Hospital, but she'll be fine. Casey's with her now and Mr. Oliver was airlifted to stay with Tracee."

Zeke, consumed with more grief than he'd ever known, laid his face in his hands and openly wept. Guilt and sorrow were eating away at his conscience and it occurred to him that he'd felt this before. He'd seen it before. His mother had died the same way. He shook his head resolutely, trying to dispel the image of her body saturated with her own blood. He had to hold it together—he had to. "My God, I've gotta get back to them," he said, bolting up. Zeke was several strides away before he remembered the reason for his trip. Turning to

Adriel, he asked, "Alex?"

"Zeke, I don't know how…God, I feel awful. I know you don't think tonight can get any worse. Buddy, Alex was assaulted tonight. After her attack, I stepped out of the apartment for a few minutes and when I got back, she wasn't there. We haven't been able to locate her."

"What!" Zeke snapped, glaring wildly from one man to the other. Abruptly, his eyes settled on his uncle. "Lou?"

"They believe this stalker must have returned to the fire escape outside her bedroom window," he said. "From what they've already pieced together, when the detective and Calvin Prince stepped out of the room…"

"Who is this Calvin Prince?" Zeke exploded, clasping his hands to his head. "Oh, God, please."

"A neighbor," Lou answered. "She's apparently been keeping the friendship a secret—at least from you and me."

"Lou, she's a grown woman," Zeke bellowed, feeling himself lose control. "I asked you to keep her safe—not lock her down! Have you considered asking yourself why she would feel the need all of a sudden to keep things from you?"

"I don't think this is the time or place for this, gentlemen," Adriel said, placing his hand on Zeke's shoulder. "Zeke, I don't think this is anything romantic. Mr. Prince left to get his lady friend, who he said was a nurse. Alex was extremely confused at the time—she may have had a mild concussion. She was resting when I left her…I probably should have insisted on leaving an officer with her, but I was confident that we had the outside roped off.

"If the outside was sealed, how did this stalker get in to her?" Zeke asked.

"We're looking into that right now," Adriel said. "But we believe that each time he appeared tonight, he came and left through Alex's bedroom window."

"Do you think this Mr. Prince has something to do with all of this?" Zeke asked.

"No, I don't. Prince lives right around the corner in the same complex, and he knows he would be the first suspect should anything like this happen. Besides, I talked to him just after we found Alex missing. He's staying by the phone just in case Alex calls."

"This is a nightmare," Zeke said, feeling as if he were whirling wildly away from reality.

"Zeke, by the time I arrived at Alex's apartment, they'd just gotten the call from Oklahoma City about Peg."

Zeke glanced around at Lou, his face filled with anger. He knew there was nothing Lou could say—no words he could offer him that would make everything all right, so he just stood there staring at him—wanting to blame him somehow. But it wasn't his fault. He had to acknowledge that Lou loved Alex as much as he did.

Just then, he glanced up and recognized Sanger Wynn rushing towards them with two other men in tow. Casey had introduced them a while back. He'd always felt that there was something different about him.

"Sanger? What are you doing here?"

"Zeke, these are Special Agents Loy Perry and Deven Williams. They're with the FBI. Our office is working in cooperation with them to determine if the two cases are related. I've been assigned to escort you back to Oklahoma City immediately."

"What about, Casey?" Zeke asked.

"He's with your wife right now," Sanger said. "I was the only one available."

# CHAPTER 16

## *Dazed*

Even with her eyes closed, Alex could tell that lights were flashing across her face. She was completely befuddled by the way familiar images came and went and how words reverberated off the banks of her mind. She smiled as she breathed in the powerful fragrance that she recognized as Vivian's cologne. It somehow gave her comfort in the middle of all her jumbled thoughts. Alex attempted to will the fierce headache away, but instead of easing, it progressively grew worse.

When she heard Gangster's mournful whimper, she sat up to see what had him so disturbed. Strangely disoriented, she wondered why she was in Calvin's car and found it disquieting that she couldn't remember how she had gotten there. She couldn't seem to grasp the fleeting images that drifted through her mind long enough to make any real sense of them.

She examined herself carefully and noticed that she no longer had on her pajamas and robe. Instead, she was wearing a pair of unfamiliar sweats and tennis shoes. Peering nervously around the car, she spotted the evidence bag on the floor behind Calvin's seat and her heart plunged. Had she taken it?

"Alex, there's a pillow and coverlet back there. Why don't you lie back down and cover up. Let the pain medication do its work," Vivian whispered gently.

She sounded so far away. Alex didn't feel like responding. She simply complied with the woman's instructions and curled up on the back seat. Recognizing the afghan as the one that Calvin kept on his sofa, she snuggled comfortably beneath it.

Alex's pain was agonizing as she squeezed her eyes shut against it. She wasn't at all sure if she should be afraid or comforted with Calvin and Vivian. Waves of nausea washed over her with such force she thought she was tangled in the throes

**161**

# Fragment In The Sand

of death.

In her lethargy, she was dimly aware of the low humming sound of the moving car and hoped that she wouldn't heave in the back seat. She wondered if the pain medication Vivian had mentioned was making her so sick.

"Hot," she said aloud, violently tossing the afghan aside.

"Feeling a little squeamish?" Calvin asked, glancing back at her. "I'll roll the window down a little."

Had she remembered to tell Vivian that she'd already taken something to help her sleep? Why had she and Calvin been whispering? She desperately tried to make sense of the evening's occurrences, wondering why she'd noticed suspicion in Adriel's eyes when he'd looked at Calvin.

His voice had been extremely gentle as he said good-bye to Vivian and started the engine. Alex had sensed a conspiratorial atmosphere in their tempered manner as they tenderly kissed. Vivian had kindly patted her hand. Somehow she knew that something was off, but didn't feel much like thinking about it.

Despite Alex's drugged state, she didn't fall asleep right away. The passing lights and sound of horns were mesmerizing. Her head felt so heavy that all she could do was lie there. Night seemed to float around her like a damp whisper—a gentle crisp darkness that surprisingly didn't frighten her at all, perhaps because Calvin was constantly talking to her.

Intensely aware that she was about to lose consciousness, Alex was suddenly swallowed up in a powerful sense of panic.

*** 

Zeke raced down the corridor of the hospital, frantically searching for Peg's room. Two uniformed officers he recognized were posted at her door. Nodding to them, he took a deep breath to compose himself before pushing the door open. He didn't want to upset her by appearing rattled and distressed.

Casey, loyally sitting at her bedside, stood and tiptoed toward him the moment he moved through the door. Zeke felt as if he would fall if he didn't find his way to a chair, but he had to see her face—touch her.

"Zeke, she's all right," Casey whispered, his hands gesturing for him to stay calm. "It looks much worse than it is. She's still sleeping."

"Thanks for being here, man," he said, embracing him firmly.

"You look like you could stand to get a little shut-eye yourself. Why don't we go down to the visitor's lounge?"

"I shouldn't have left them...not after that break-in," Zeke said, his voice teetering with emotion.

"Zeke, this isn't your fault. And Peg is well aware of the risks you have to take as a policeman."

"How can you say that?" Zeke asked, gazing into his friend's eyes. "Especially after what *you've* been through."

"I have regrets, but it can't dictate my future, man," Casey said lowering his head. "You couldn't have stopped this and you know it."

"I know...you're right," Zeke said, emotion distorting his face. "Give me a minute alone with her."

"Sure. I'll be right outside."

Sunday dawned with dazzling sunshine. Zeke stretched himself awake just in time to see Peg's eyes open for the first time since he'd been back. Even with the broken clavicle, cracked ribs and bruised face, she was the most beautiful sight he could've awakened to. Zeke bolted from the recliner towards his wife, a wide grin spreading across his face. "Hey, baby," he whispered. "How do you feel?"

"Umm."

"You've just made my day," Zeke said, his heart fluttering like a candle in the wind.

"Hi," she said through swollen lips. "Alex?"

"Alex will be fine," he said, trusting that God had heard and answered his prayers. "Did you know that you're the most beautiful thing I've ever seen?"

A weak smile formed on her lips. "O u w e e! That hurts."

"Honey, I'm so sorry—"

Peg reached an unsteady hand up and placed it over her husband's lips. "Don't you go blaming yourself for this, Ezekiel Webb," she whispered. "In fact, I'm glad you weren't home."

## Fragment In The Sand

"Why?" he asked, studying her intently.

"Because they may have killed you," she said.

Zeke leaned down and tenderly kissed her on the forehead, feeling very grateful to have such a loving woman in his life. "You're going to have to take it easy for a while."

"I'll be all right, Zeke. When can I go home?"

"Listen to me. You can't just jump out of here after all that you've been through. Now just lie there, obey your husband, and hold your face real stiff," he whispered, "while I try to find a spot to kiss."

Zeke watched the gleam in her eyes come alive as the distorted smile spread across her face. His heart instantly soared and he leaned in to kiss her again, straightening the moment he heard the swoosh of the door. It was Isaac Oliver.

"Hi, Ike," Zeke said, moving to embrace the older man. "Sorry I didn't get home to relieve you last night. Tracee okay?"

"Tracee's just fine," he said. "She's having a grand ole' time. One of the ladies out of Casey's office is with her now. She's in good hands. How's Peg doing?"

"She's doing great," Zeke said, grinning. "She's awake now."

"Case is in the cafeteria downstairs," Ike said, releasing Zeke from his embrace. "He wants to talk to you when you get a minute."

Zeke left to find Casey and after pouring himself a cup of coffee, strolled towards the table covered with foam cups and newspapers. Casey was absorbed in his own thoughts, sipping absently on his coffee.

"Hey, fella'," Zeke said, coming up behind him.

"Good morning," Casey said, turning towards him. "Peg must be doing well this morning."

Zeke immediately noticed the tight, agitated glower on Casey's face. An undercurrent of anger seemed to lie just beneath the surface. It was obvious it had been a sleepless night for Casey, too.

"Yeah, she's doing great," Zeke answered. "I'm glad that you weren't far away."

"It's family, Zeke."

"Ike said you wanted to talk to me."

Casey turned serious eyes on Zeke, absently twirling the contents of the foam cup around in little circles. "Zeke, do you know of anyone other than Tyson that might want to settle something with you?"

Zeke took a swallow of his coffee. It was weak and he made a face that made Casey smile.

"No, I don't. And I've been raking my brain all night. I should have been more suspicious that something was up after we had that break-in, Case."

"You've done everything that you could, Zeke, even having extra patrols come around. This isn't your fault. You're not superman."

"I know. But why don't we check out Tyson's visitor log," Zeke said, glancing up helplessly.

"We'll do that," Casey said.

"Do you know what's going on with Alex?"

Zeke thought he noticed Casey's eyes fog over with worry. "Nah, we haven't heard anything...no phone calls...no ransom demands. Nothing. I've had my cell phone with me all night."

Casey stood up and shoved his hands down into his pockets. Zeke took one more gulp of his coffee and pushed back from the table. "Let's go for a walk."

"The young man they found running near Alex's apartment admitted to shutting off the power," Casey said. "He said someone paid him fifty bucks to do it—a man."

"Do they believe him?"

"Yeah. No reason not to. They've got a sketch artist working on it now to see if it could be the same guy who followed Alex from Arizona."

"Good. Did they ever come up with anything on the picture Alex took of the car?"

"They found the car abandoned two days later. It had been reported stolen the night that Alex saw it," Casey said, shaking his head. "I can't figure it all out—it doesn't make sense. God, Zeke, why hasn't she called? I had just talked with her. I know that she would call if she could. And if—"

**165**

## Fragment In The Sand

Zeke interrupted Casey's next comment by placing his hand on his shoulder. "We've just got to trust God to keep her safe and try to hold it together."

Peg was released from the hospital three days later on the condition that she got plenty of rest. Casey stood on the patio watching Zeke empty trash into the big, black dumpster that sat near the chain link fence encircling the spacious back yard. He was agitated, he thought.

"Did you get a list of Tyson's visitors?" Zeke asked, stepping back onto the patio.

"Are you sure Tyson is behind this?" Casey asked. "After all, he's on death row and has a lot more on his mind than getting even with you."

"He's the only one I've been able to come up with," Zeke said, shaking his head. "But I can go back through my files."

"I'm a step ahead of you, buddy. We're already checking those," Casey said, feeling quite lost and preoccupied. "What about your neighbors?"

"Case, you know most of them," Zeke said shrugging. "They're mostly retired couples." He paused, a frown creasing his brow. "There was a young couple who was renting the old Banks place about a mile down the road. They kept to themselves a lot, but they seemed nice enough. They moved out a couple months ago."

"We'll check them out," Casey said, making rapid notations on a small pad. "Zeke, FBI has determined that this case and Alex's disappearance may just be coincidental. They can't link them like they first thought."

"What does Earl say?" Zeke asked, gazing carefully into Casey's face.

Casey watched as strain and conflicting emotions moved in waves across Zeke's face. He was carrying a heavy load. "He agrees with them."

"Case, has Robbie been checked out? I wouldn't trust him after his attack on Alex."

"I know," Casey answered stiffly. "Alex had mentioned to me that he had somehow known that her roommates were away the night that he assaulted her—that rang a little strange to me. He was the first one I suspected. But his alibi checks out. In fact, he's in the process of relocating to San Francisco."

"Did they question him extensively?"

"I understand that he was very upset that Alex had been hurt. They didn't have any reason to doubt him, but they are still watching him closely," Casey said, as he stretched lazily in the lawn chair. "Since they think these are two different cases, I sort of need to keep my mind focused on one at a time."

"You're just as worried about her as I am. I can tell." Zeke shook his head slowly, and as if talking to himself asked, "Why haven't we gotten a call?"

"I wish I knew," Casey said, his breath feeling raw in his throat. "Zeke, I know what the FBI says, but I can't get rid of this gut feeling that the two cases are related somehow. I can't put my finger on it, and nothing's coming up in my head to validate my feelings."

"I'd trust your gut against a bunch of halfhearted profilers any day of the week," Zeke said.

Feeling extremely antsy, Casey stood up and began to pace back and forth across the concrete surface of the patio. Frustration mounted with each step he took. He somehow had to keep it together, but it was hard. He had grown very fond of Alex, and his protective posture toward her had become hard to restrain. He didn't want to cause Zeke any more anguish than he already felt, so he tried to think of a way to change the subject.

"I feel as though I'm in the twilight zone," Zeke said absently. "First my sister is threatened, stalked and assaulted, my wife is attacked, and now Alex is kidnapped. How much more can I take?"

"To be more accurate," Casey said, without looking up, "you and Alex were threatened around the same time."

"What?"

"Remember her New York trip? Tyson threatened you around the same time. And Alex's disappearance hasn't been officially ruled a kidnapping. There are no indications that she was taken from her apartment against her will."

"But she was obviously unsteady—probably had a concussion from that blow she caught," Zeke said, horrified. "What are these guys thinking? What if she's out there walking around, unaware of who she is or where she needs to go?"

"They're just trying to do their job. It's pretty unlikely Alex was in the complex when they discovered her missing. They brought in a canine unit and checked pretty good. It's just too strange."

"I can't see Tyson getting a thing like this together in so short a time, Casey. I'm with you. I think the cases are somehow related. Otherwise, the timing is a pretty big coincidence."

"I'm real curious about all of the recent events happening around Alex," Casey mumbled thoughtfully. "I wonder why Robbie all of a sudden decided to keep company with a hooker?"

"I thought you didn't think Robbie had anything to do with this."

"I don't. But in retrospect everything that's happened—it all seems...I don't know—scheduled. Planned."

"Yeah, I know what you mean."

"The intruder apparently came through Alex's bedroom," Casey continued. "I've been wondering why he didn't harm her until he was on his way back out? It almost seems that he wasn't out to harm Alex at all. This may or may not have anything to do with the Shadow. But if not, it sure is another huge coincidence."

"That hadn't occurred to me," Zeke said, his eyes taking on a numbed horror. "Who could it be?"

"Adriel seems to feel that the perpetrator followed Star home. But from the looks of cigarette butts on the landing outside of Alex's bedroom window, somebody has also been out there—recently and often. He must have known that he could get into the apartment through that way instead of following Star up the stairs and risk being seen."

"So what are you saying?" Zeke asked. "Is it the guy that's been harassing her or not?

"I don't know. He did threaten to teach Alex a lesson for going out to dinner with me," Casey said, his voice cracking a little. "I need to think on it a little more before I can offer any definite interpretations."

"Case, Alex told me that she felt like somebody was watching her," Zeke said absently. "She said she even felt him watching her in her bedroom. Could she have really been so sensitive to this guy being right outside her bedroom window?"

"Yeah. I think so," Casey said, struggling to control his quavering. "There's another thing that doesn't add up. Star had never used Alex's computer before, but for some reason, *that* night she emails you with a warning to get Alex out. She obviously learned something that frightened her between the time she left for Lou's and the time she returned."

"Yeah, but Star was a sort of—alarmist," Zeke said. "She's always been suspicious of things that had the least resemblance to those classic suspense movies that she loves to watch. Alex always called her their little fire bell."

"Evidently, she wasn't just overreacting this time."

"So you think Star found out something that led her to believe that Alex was in some kind of danger?"

"That's obvious—wouldn't you say?" Casey asked, looking at Zeke's stricken face. "That would somehow eliminate the Shadow. That is, unless he was someone they knew."

"But who?"

"That's what we've gotta find out," Casey said. "Most victims know their assailants, or at least have been acquainted with them. But something about all this just doesn't feel right. You still haven't found anything missing from your intrusion?"

"Nope. It's all so strange."

"Not to mention the distance between Oklahoma and California. Zeke, have you considered...well, it seems to me that all of these occurrences have one common denominator."

Zeke stared up at Casey, his eyes widened in alarm. "Me. I've been thinking about that."

"Star had just emailed you, Peg is your wife and of course, Alex is your sister."

"But whoever attacked Peg was after me. Remember, you guys found a bomb on my car?"

"I think that could've been meant to throw us," Casey said. "He obviously knew that you weren't home when he entered the house."

"Do you think Lou might know more than he's saying?" Zeke asked. "I really don't think that he would intentionally hurt Alex, but he *does* work with all kinds of people."

"I thought of that," Casey said. "What about you? Do you think he's not being up front with us?"

"Well, I was just remembering…just before I ran away, I walked in on Lou giving the order over the phone to hurt someone."

Are you sure?" Casey asked unsettled.

"I was young, but I know what I heard. I already didn't like him because I'd seen him going through our things when we first arrived—as if searching for something specific."

"You almost sound like you've picked up Star's inclinations," Casey said aghast. "Do you mean to tell me that Lou put a contract out on someone?"

"Not exactly. Just ordered that they be roughed up. I don't think it was clear to me what he had intended until now."

"My God," Casey murmured. "He's really a rascal. Why do you think he was looking through your things?"

"I don't have any idea. I'm probably just allowing my suspicions to overshadow my reasoning, but I'd be willing to bet that he knows more than he's saying."

"Not necessarily," Casey countered, recalling the stiff animosity that remained between Zeke and his uncle. "But I have to admit, something's not adding up."

"Tell me what you're feeling," Zeke asked.

"Well, you're recalling your uncle, who may or may not be associated with organized crime, searching through the belongings of children. And whoever broke into your home was evidently searching for something, too. What could you or Alex still have in your possession—that you're more-than-likely unaware of—that would be of any value?"

"Nothing that I know of," Zeke answered, frowning. "Where are you going with all of this?"

"I'm sorry. I really shouldn't be speculating…it's too soon," Casey said, shaking his head. "It's more likely that it stems from one of your cases—either current or past. Remember the vengeance of the Montana stalker?"

"Oh, yeah.  He terrorized everyone in that cop's family," Zeke said.  "Right down to a second cousin."

"We could continue to dig through the files, but I have a feeling that the answer lies within you.  I think you should talk to Earl."  Casey had to swallow to ease the tightness in his throat, and quickly added, "as soon as possible."

"Why?" Zeke asked, a puzzled expression edging his coarse features.

"Before he connected with the Marshal's Service, Earl spent sixteen years as a clinical psychologist.  He knows how to get at things—suppressed memories and things like that.  It can't hurt, Zeke."

# CHAPTER 17

## *Hidden Truths*

Casey absently ran his fingers over the oak trim of the chair while awaiting the arrival of his boss. Anxiously glancing through the drapes, he searched the drive to see if by chance Earl had pulled into the front yard.

The day was cloudy—an unwelcome but precise simile of his frame of mind. He was exhausted, but eager to hear what Earl would come up with after he'd had a chance to talk with Zeke.

From the beginning, he had considered that Lou Ramsey's business transactions might have had something to do with Alex's dilemma, but he didn't want to mention it to Zeke. He had a tendency to draft some pretty creative scenarios, so he had to press himself to avoid letting his imagination get away from him in this.

"Case, why don't you go try to get some shut eye in the guestroom," Zeke offered, glancing worriedly at his friend. "You haven't gotten much sleep lately."

"I'll be okay," Casey muttered, toying with his chin whiskers. "There'll be plenty of time for that after Earl finishes up."

"Suit yourself. But as soon as he does, *I'm* going to get some sleep. I feel like a walking zombie."

Just as Zeke turned to head for the kitchen, the doorbell rang. Casey watched Earl as he woodenly sauntered into the Webb's home. He extended his hand to Zeke and weakly nodded a greeting in Casey's direction.

Earl Gaines was a tall, lean man with gray hair and a face that looked as though it was carved from stone. Casey thought the seasoned cop's face resembled those featured in a Dick Tracy comic strip. As usual, he had an unlit pipe stuck in his mouth and his stride was slow and sober.

Earl had been with the Marshal's Service for fifteen years and had the unique capacity to step outside his own world and see through another man's eyes. Though he did very little profiling for the service, his unique abilities proved handy on occasion. He was a fair man, insisting his deputies operate in what he called "the neutral zone." He regularly reminded them that objectivity in this job was crucial.

"Good to see you again, Zeke," Earl said, shaking his hand. "I'm sorry that it's not under more pleasant circumstances."

"Thanks, Earl," Zeke said, directing him toward a chair. "Can I get you something to…"

Raising his hand to halt Zeke's gracious pleasantries, he sat in the chair next to the couch and pulled his pipe from between his lips. "I don't need anything, Zeke. Thanks. Where is your family?"

"They're both in the bedroom…probably asleep by now. I appreciate your concern, Earl. I really don't want Peg any more upset than she already is."

"Casey, Zeke and I are going to need to be alone," Earl said, wiping his glasses with a handkerchief.

Casey hesitantly stood up, a little surprised by Earl's request, but obligated to comply.

"I don't mind Casey being here," Zeke said, his eyes widening skeptically. "We don't really have any secrets."

As if not hearing Zeke's comment, Earl replaced his glasses and put his pipe into his shirt pocket. "That not withstanding," Earl began, "Casey is a deputy first in my eyes. You both might as well know that I've decided to leave Sanger on this one. Casey's too close."

"But…"

"I don't know what we're facing here," Earl continued, interrupting Zeke's protest. "I can't risk the life of you or your family because a deputy lost his objectivity in the middle of a situation."

"But doesn't it matter that Casey was the one who pulled you into this?"

"No," Earl said, "it doesn't. Now let's get started."

# Fragment In The Sand

### ***

Alex knew this place. She'd traveled it before. It was cool and damp. She wasn't really frightened by it—probably because she was older and familiar with it. Without warning, the darkness began to thicken and she felt she could barely breath in the gummy air. After being pulled into a tunnel by an unseen intruder, she struggled against his rough—almost brutal handling, but she didn't have the energy to fight back.

"Alex, wake up. Alex, it's all right…wake up!"

She sprang up in the back seat, gasping for breath. Her heart fluttered wildly in her chest as she nervously peered around the car and out the windows. Gradually, she began to realize that she was awake now, and worried that Dr. Gleason's warnings might be evolving.

"Where are we?"

"Alex, are you all right? I thought I'd never get you awake…you were tossing and struggling in your sleep."

"I'm okay," she said, glancing away from the rearview mirror where his inquisitive eyes watched her. The events of the previous evening rang sketchily through her mind, heightening her apprehension with a pungent sting of harsh reality.

"Vivian picked up a few things for you," Calvin said, apparently noticing her discomfiture. "You still had on your pajamas when we left your apartment."

"Have we been driving all night?"

"No. I stopped for a couple of hours. I got a little sleepy."

"Why are we sitting on the side of the road?"

"Because you started screaming," Calvin said. "I had to try and get you awake."

"Oh…I suppose so."

"Was it a bad one?"

"I don't want to talk about it, right now, Calvin."

"Okay, darlin'. If it's all right with you, I'll get back on the road. Think you're okay now?"

"Yes, thank you."

This was the first time that she had felt misgivings about Calvin. The suffocating tightness in her gut began to swell and she shuddered as she glanced back through the windshield.

The sun was a blazing orange ball in the sky as they headed straight for it. "Where are we?" she asked again, rubbing the sleep from her eyes.

"Just outside of Flagstaff," he said. "You hungry?"

"Actually, I feel a little sick to my stomach," she said. "How long have I been asleep?"

"You conked out a few minutes after we got on the road," he answered with a light chuckle. "Vivian gave you something for pain. She said it would also help calm you down. How's your head?"

She touched the bandage on her forehead. "It's throbbing a little." She wavered as segments of the night stumbled into her mind. Star had been hurt—she'd been taken to the hospital. She never did get to see her. And someone—maybe the Shadow had hit her on the head with her hourglass. She felt herself recoil as mounting suspicion expanded in her belly, and she gaped wildly at Calvin by way of the rearview. Why was she in Arizona with *him* when Adriel had said that Zeke was on his way to LA?

Her brow furrowed as she strained to remember. She recalled curling up on her bed after Adriel and Calvin had left her room. Calvin had returned, only this time, he was at her window. He had awakened her and asked her to come with him. She remembered thinking he might take her to see Star, and had been so out of it that she had gone without a thought that it might be dangerous. Could Calvin actually be the Shadow? Was Vivian in on it all?

"Let's stop at this diner up here and get something to eat," Calvin said, returning his glance to the rearview. "We'll stop at a motel in a little while so I can get some real shut eye."

Alex gazed pointedly at his reflection. "Calvin, where are you taking me?"

"To safety, darlin'," he said, pulling onto the gravel path. The place was more of an off the road truck stop than a family bistro, but she would simply be thankful for the chance to get away and call Adriel.

"Where is Zeke?" she asked confused. She watched Calvin carefully pull into a parking spot in front of Dave's Diner and turn off the engine. When he turned around to face her, his eyes looked severe—almost sinister.

# Fragment In The Sand

"Alex, I'm gonna' need you to trust me. I realize that you're a little confused and even leery right now, but you have to believe that I would never harm you or put you in jeopardy. Can you believe that?"

She shuddered involuntarily as dread coursed through her entire being. "I'm not sure. I'm afraid to trust anyone right now. Everything just feels so weird."

"I understand how you must feel," he said, reaching over the seat to pat her hand. "But with all that's been happening to you lately, I just had to get you out of LA—for your own safety. Whoever's been stalking you made his move last night. I don't know what's going on or who's behind it, but I don't like the way the authorities sidestep the issues. If they had done more to protect you, this never would have happened."

"But won't you be in trouble? I heard Adriel say that I had to stay around."

"I'm not worried about myself. My main concern is your safety," he said, finally allowing a smile to warm his face. It somehow gave her comfort. "It's obvious to everyone involved that you were in danger. Zeke, Casey, your room-mates…even your uncle was irritated with the authorities for not doing more sooner."

"You've talked to Uncle Lou?" she asked, growing even more puzzled.

"Not directly. I believe your policeman friend, Adriel, told him you were missing. Your uncle started raising a real stink about it. I decided it was time for you to get to safety while everybody else figured out what they were gonna' do."

"Why didn't you tell him I was with you?"

Calvin shrugged, but the smile never waned or left his face. "I'm an old-fashioned man, darlin'. I don't trust many people. And the very purpose of stealing you through that window was to keep them from knowing where you were. Vivian helped, too. She was at the front door asking for you while I was pulling you out onto the fire escape."

Alex vaguely remembered turning to look for her shoes. Calvin had told her to leave everything, but she had ignored his order and grabbed the bag with the hourglass and her gun.

She was so dazed by the predicament they were in that she

**176**

found it hard to comprehend. "I see."

"That hourglass…it must have some special meaning for you? You flat refused to leave it behind."

She reached for the bag. "It does. It once belonged to my dad. He sent it to me when I was a little girl. Aunt Sarah told me that it has been in our family for a very long time."

"It's a pretty piece. I know where you could get quite a bit for it. That is, if you're willing to part with it. That plate on the end there—it looks like solid gold."

Alex glared at him aghast. "I wouldn't think of selling it, Calvin. It's the only thing that I have left of my dad."

Calvin stared blankly at her. "I've said it before. You should place that kind of trust and devotion in God alone. He's the only one who'll never leave you alone."

Alex absently flipped the hourglass over in her hands. "You don't understand. It just helps me feel connected to someone. You know…this hourglass is very close to accurate? Every little grain of sand is needed." She lost herself then, in the comfort of her treasured heirloom."

"Just like each of us, I guess. We're all a small part of something big."

Alex smiled pensively, recalling the things that she and Casey had talked about. "A small piece of a big puzzle, as well as a piece of the Christ the rock," Alex muttered.

Calvin eyed the glass again and tapped it with his finger. "You must've loved your father very much."

"I think so, but I can't remember him. Aunt Sarah said he looked like Zeke. She didn't have any pictures around or anything because they'd been destroyed in a fire. I've wanted to ask Zeke about him, but I don't want to conjure up unpleasant memories for him. We don't seem to be able to talk much about our dad."

"Why is that?" Calvin asked. "Does Zeke have a problem with your dad?"

She shrugged, still gazing at the spilling grains of sand. "I think it's a matter of how you look at it. A lot of pain and hostility is still there for my brother. He blames him for the two of us not being raised together."

Calvin chuckled under his breath. "Zeke is probably right.

# Fragment In The Sand

You have a real soft way of putting things. You're very protective of your big brother, aren't you?"

"What makes you think I'm so protective of him? He's the one who drives me half out of my mind trying to shelter *me*."

"I think that's because you obviously wanna know more about your dad, but you're risking never knowing to protect Zeke's feelings. You know, after listening to you go on about him and his family, I feel as though I know him. Quite frankly, Alex, the only person I'll feel comfortable leaving you with *is* your brother. And that's where I aim to take you…if that's all right with you."

Grateful tears rose to Alex's eyes as she stared over the seat at Calvin. The anguish immediately began to diminish. Unable to hold back the appreciation, she placed her palms on either side of his face and kissed him on the cheek. "It's perfectly okay with me. Where's Gangster?"

"I left him with Vivian. By the way, I sneaked back into your apartment last night and got one of your cameras out."

Excitement raced through her. "Really?"

"Yeah. I thought you'd want it with you. I couldn't bring the tripod and bag though. Now, why don't you go and freshen up in the restroom while I fill up the gas tank. Then we'll get us a bite to eat."

\*\*\*

Casey stood quietly surveying the men sitting around Earl's office. He was painfully aware that Earl had already noticed him in the doorway.

The early morning sunbeam was a florescent path for weightless dust particles that danced about randomly. Casey scanned the room, noticing files and fresh coffee cups about. He wondered what was being discussed in the huddle of four men.

He remained silent as the agents went over details that he himself found unimportant at this stage in the game. Earl was well respected not only in the Marshal's Service, but also throughout the federal agencies. He had been a great supervisor in the time he had known him, but Casey was certain that he was wrong for not allowing him to be a part of this.

Earl sat behind his desk buried in a mass of scattered papers, explaining his take on the case. The possibilities seemed endless. Casey glanced at the two agents seated in chairs across from him—and a very astute Sanger, who stood looking over his shoulder. He wondered why they were still involved if they'd already determined the cases weren't related.

"Sir, are you certain the two cases *aren't* related?"

That seized Casey's attention.

"I have to admit, the timing is remarkable. But based on the facts we've already gathered, I don't believe they are. There are too many holes," Earl said.

The query had come from Williams. Casey had to restrain himself from bursting forth with his own perception, but he knew Earl would never tolerate that from him.

"I could be wrong, of course," Earl continued, eyeing the men obstinately. "On the chance that I am, I've asked you fellas to hang with us a little while longer. Right now, in order to maintain the integrity of both cases, I suggest we proceed as if they're separate."

"Earl, are you sure that's wise?" Sanger asked. "I mean, what about the possibility of a communication failure between the two groups. One of us may miss something and get somebody hurt?"

"That possibility always exists," Earl said impatiently. "Perry and I will serve at center of operations with both cases. He is flying back to LA immediately after this meeting. You and Williams are to report directly to us with a daily update and any discoveries. Our primary concern is protecting Detective Zeke Webb and his family, as well as finding his missing sister before it's too late. Is that understood?"

"Yes, sir," both men said in unison.

Casey swallowed to ease the pressure from the lump that had risen in his throat the moment Earl referenced the possibility that Alex was in real danger.

"In the meantime," Loy began, "Earl and I will work with LAPD and Oklahoma City PD obtaining as much information as possible. We've already obtained copies of the files that Zeke has been working on. We'll keep you informed."

## Fragment In The Sand

"A—hem." Casey cleared his throat, making his presence known. They all turned toward him in unison—a move that had an aspect of dance routine.

"I was wondering when you'd speak up," Earl said, not bothering to look up. "Come on in. You know Special Agents Deven Williams and Loy Perry, don't you?" Casey nodded to the men and glanced over at Sanger who was browsing through a file that he'd picked up from the desk. "We were just going over the Webb matter."

"That's why I'm here, Earl. I want to be assigned to protect Zeke and his family."

"We've talked about this, Casey. I know you do," Earl said, finally glancing up from the papers in front of him. "But you're aware of my thoughts on that. You're much too close, Case. For goodness sakes, you two are like brothers."

"I know I can remain objective in this. And I have some ideas about the case that I think would be helpful. Earl, I'm a good deputy."

"One of the best I have," Earl said, shaking his head confidently. "But you've never been faced with having to protect a family member. That's why I chose to put Sanger on this. You're welcome to shine any light on this case you may have, but Sanger will be working closely with FBI. It shouldn't take us long to figure things out while keeping Zeke and his family safe."

It ticked him off that Earl seemed to be so casual about the whole thing. He acted as if this was an annoying interruption—a minor deviation—just another case. Sanger glanced at Casey, then averted his eyes guiltily.

"I guess you're right, Earl. I appreciate your taking on the case, and I'm confident that Sanger will do a good job. But I…"

"I'm glad you agree," Earl interrupted.

"Is there anything I can do to change…"

"The subject is non-negotiable, deputy." This time, Earl's voice was impatient and firm. Casey knew there was no use in trying to sway him.

"Would you at least keep me apprised of any developments?"

"That I can do," Sanger said, looking directly at Casey, "as long as it doesn't compromise ethics, of course."

Perry looked up quizzically. "I don't think that would be a good…"

"I think that would be acceptable," Earl interrupted. "After all, Casey is a deputy, and given his proximity to the family, he just might be able to consult with us from that perspective."

"Take good care of them," Casey said, looking directly at Sanger. He pulled the door closed as he left, feeling overwhelmed and even a little scared. His heart swelled with apprehension even more when an image of Alex's face flashed across his mind.

*Please keep her safe, Lord, and wherever she is, let her know that you're with her.*

# CHAPTER 18

## *Turbulence*

Casey watched Zeke glance warily across the patio toward Tracee and Sanger as they played with the puppy. The scowl on his face clearly revealed his inner turmoil. That, along with the hot August heat, did very little to lift his own crumbling spirits.

"Where in the name of God can she be?" The question seemed to tear from the depth of his gut, assaulting even the scrap of composure that Casey had somehow managed to hold on to.

He had known Zeke a long time and had seen him under pressure before, but this was different. He'd never seen the broad shoulders so slumped, the eyes so filled with pain, or the strong face so tightly drawn. He sensed a deep turbulence in his friend and wished desperately that he could be of more help to him.

Casey struggled to keep his mind from asking the same questions that Zeke was asking. He regularly pushed the gentleness of Alex's smile and the musical sound of her voice away to focus on the job at hand. And right now, that was unofficially keeping an eye on Zeke and his family.

He couldn't help thinking about the peculiarities in the cases—the timing, semblance and even relationships. The threat had come to Alex just prior to her breakup with Robbie. And just before she was attacked, she had informed Lou that she was going to quit for a year.

From the recounting that Zeke had given him of Lou's obsessive behavior toward Alex, he doubted if he was a part of this—unless he was in some kind of financial difficulty. Experience had taught him that people sometimes did uncharacteristic things when pressured, and the possibility of Lou being responsible for her disappearance wasn't out of the question. The answer had to be right before his eyes and he had to figure it out.

"Zeke, calm down. Tracee's right over there watching you," he warned, understanding exactly how he felt. "She's already reacting to her mother's appearance."

"I will…I know," Zeke said. "I just thank God that she didn't see the attack. She didn't know anything about it."

"I know," Casey said. "By the time I got here, she was still half asleep, trying to pull that old doll out of her toy box."

"It's just so frustrating…like I'm being burned from both ends," Zeke said annoyed. "Did Earl change his mind about your working the case?"

"I'm sorry, Zeke. But he's not budging on this. I suppose I knew he wouldn't, but I had to give it a try."

"Maybe if I talked to him again," Zeke offered. "It's just weird having someone follow me around…everywhere. And Peg is a nervous wreck. The atmosphere around here is even affecting Tracee. She's got to feel something isn't right. If it were just you, maybe it wouldn't feel so invasive."

Casey struggled to control his own quavering. "Sanger assures me that he'll keep me updated as well as remember Tracee's sensibilities. I'll keep my eye on things, too. Maybe I'll take my vacation, that way…"

"Yeah, right. You know it wouldn't take very long for Earl to see through that ploy."

"You're probably right," Casey said, absently kicking a rock from the patio. "By the way, I've been trying to phone Alex on her cell—on the off chance she'd taken it with her."

Zeke stood and strolled across the patio. "Adriel told me last night that her cell phone was left in the apartment. She doesn't usually go anywhere without it. I really hope that she left on her own free will, Casey, but it doesn't look good. She couldn't have been in any shape to go on her own. Certain aspects of this are very odd."

"What?" Casey asked, noticing the furrows in Zeke's brow.

"Don't you find it strange that the gun and hourglass are missing? Who would grab those at the last minute?"

"That *is* odd. But that reinforces my thinking that the girls might somehow be acquainted with whoever is behind this thing—someone they trust."

"I don't know. Alex didn't recognize the driver of that car...and I thought we were assuming that he and the Shadow were one and the same."

"I'm not sure about that anymore, Zeke. We can't *assume* anything. But something's not ringing true on this. It's not like they had a lot of traffic in and out of their apartment. And after seven, you have to have a code to get through the security gate...I wonder—"

"Maybe the perp is someone that lives in the complex?"

"Either that, or it's someone who has access to their code. I still can't see a stranger bothering with something as useless as an hourglass?"

"That hourglass didn't mean anything to anyone except Alex. Maybe he just took it 'cause it had prints on it or something."

"Or maybe Alex went on her own free will. That would sure be a relief, sort of. Of course, whoever helped her down that fire escape must care about her. She probably would have had a hard time getting down in her condition, not to mention handling that bag. If someone helped her, he obviously knew how much the glass meant to her."

"That would really narrow it down. We have to rule out her roommates," Zeke said. "Desi was out of town and Star wound up in the apartment. Lou? Robbie?"

"Robbie's out...and despite the way things are looking, I'd really be surprised if Lou could bring himself to hurt Alex."

"He called last night to see if I'd heard anything. I guess he *is* pretty torn up about this," Zeke said. "But I still think the man has ice water running through his veins."

"You could be wrong about him. After all, you were just a boy. Maybe you misunderstood what you heard."

"You don't understand. He acknowledged that he worked with people that were into all kinds of things," Zeke said.

"But he never admitted to taking part in illegal activities. Right?"

"So..."

"Even if he wanted to, Lou wouldn't take the chance of

doing anything that would so point to him. It would be suicide."

"Maybe he has a death wish," Zeke said sullenly. "You're right, though. Maybe the Shadow is actually a crazed fan that thinks he's in love with Alex?"

"I've heard stranger things. That would explain him taking the hourglass, as well as why there's been no demand for money. And she never recognized his voice when he called."

"Apparently not."

"I don't know…it may give us a little hope. If he does think he's in love with her, we may have a little time. But—"

Casey stopped short, impelling Zeke to look up. "But what?"

"I hope that he won't try to act out his fantasies in any form on her. Her rejection could set him off. If this is the same guy that sent her the note in New York, it's clear that his mind swings extremely wide. We can't say what kind of mental shape he's in."

"I'd forgotten about that. He would have to be someone that has access to her schedule. Taking into account her physical and mental condition when Adriel left her, I would definitely lean toward her having to know whoever she might have left with."

"That's a fair assessment," Casey said, grateful for the opportunity to talk out his impressions. "We'll check out the complex security, maintenance crew, office staff and the neighbors. Maybe we can come up with something else. Desi should be able to give us some clues as well."

Zeke turned toward the little doghouse and watched Sanger squat down to pet the animal in Tracee's arms. Her high-pitched laughter rang out like a bell and made him smile. "She reminds me so much of her Aunt Alex."

"Zeke, do you have any idea why Alex didn't want her roommates to know about the gun?"

"She thought it would frighten them. And she didn't want to add anything else to their list of things to keep from Lou."

"What's up with that? I thought she and Lou were very close. In fact, I got the notion that she is just as protective of him as she is of you."

# Fragment In The Sand

"She is," Zeke said, his eyes wide with grief. "If something happens to her, it'll be all my fault."

Casey did a double take, uncertain that he had heard right. "Zeke, you know that's not true. Why would you say that?"

"It's true, Case. I've been riding her for some time about standing on her own two feet. I thought she depended on him entirely too much—just like when he was pretending to be her father after we first arrived in California."

"But what does that have to do with your idea that all of this is your fault?"

"This happened because of my hard attitude—because of my lack of tolerance for Lou."

"Zeke, you can't possibly think that. I noticed that she was overly conscious of Lou's particulars, but she seemed to be pulling away effectively. She was obviously beginning to strive to be more independent."

"That's what I mean," Zeke said, his eyes taking on a haunted look. "I've been keeping Lou in check about her safety, but he couldn't do the very thing I needed him to if she stopped communicating with him. My own angry suspicions and jealousies have done this."

"I'm sorry, man," Casey said, his brow furrowed. "But you're forgetting the very thing you reminded Lou of…she *is* an adult. Besides, I think Alex's recent transition goes a little deeper than your carping."

"What do you mean?" Zeke asked, glancing up at Casey.

"I believe her reluctance to disappoint Lou stems from an idea that he's the only man that's been a *constant* in her life. She subconsciously gave him more control over her than what was healthy, but your observations *did* start to wake her up."

"How can you know that?"

"Deposits from my psychology courses, I guess."

Zeke shook his head doubtfully. "But look at where it's gotten her, Case. She picked a lousy time to listen to me."

The wispy hairs on the back of Casey's neck stirred. "Alex was trying to make some pretty huge changes in her life, Zeke. She's been through a lot, but she was dealing with it the only way she knew how without disappointing you or Lou."

Zeke looked at Casey and strolled back to the chair he'd

**186**

vacated earlier. "I don't follow. What was she doing?"

"For one, she agreed to purchase that gun and take lessons from Adriel. She's still not comfortable with it."

"I was really proud of her. I thought I'd have to do a lot more persuading than I did."

"I also think that her desire to marry Robbie had more to do with forcing a change in her life than it had to do with affection for him. She obviously wasn't seeing him very clearly." Casey paused, surprised by his own statement. "And did you know that she had looked into adopting a little boy from the hospital?"

"W—What!" Zeke shot. "What would—"

"Remember the night that I told you I first visited her? That's when she got the phone call that he had died. She took it pretty hard."

"Brian?"

"Yeah."

"Are you saying that she wanted change so badly that she would adopt Brian?"

"Zeke, don't get me wrong. I have no doubt that Alex loved that little boy. But I think, in her mind, it did present a passageway to get out of modeling."

Zeke's mouth dropped open in surprise. "Get out of modeling? Casey, are you sure? I was under the impression that Alex loved her career."

"Not so, big brother. Alex has been trying to keep too many other people satisfied by her choices, including you. In fact, she had just informed Lou that she wasn't signing a new contract. She wanted to take a year off."

"Casey," Zeke said, his eyes widening. "Alex is Lou's highest producing client. She made him a lot of money. That sounds like a perfect motive."

* * *

The next morning, Zeke found himself sitting on a wooden stool among the cobwebs and dust bunnies in the attic. The smell of moist cardboard boxes filled his nostrils as he tackled the chore of cleaning. Apart from the fact that it was the first among many chores on a list that Peg had given him to do, he

**187**

realized it was a device to keep his anxiety at a manageable level. She was very intuitive about such things.

Earlier, he had ridden with Sanger to the courthouse where he had given a deposition. When they returned to his office, his superior had put him on administrative leave with pay, pending the resolution of his case. Several of his follow-up reports and investigations had been boxed up and passed on to other detectives—as if they didn't already have enough on their plates. He understood, of course, but it hadn't done much to encourage his already wounded ego. He found himself skirmishing with feelings of guilt and deficiency regarding the safety of his family, including his sister.

He could tell that Casey was just as worried about Alex as he was. He was a good friend to let him roll all of his chaotic feelings off on him. He appreciated the talk they'd had, but was surprised that Casey knew so much more about Alex than he did. He chuckled softly, thinking how ironic it was that all this time he'd thought that Alex was captivated by her career when in reality she was looking for a way out of it.

Thumbing reflectively through an old photo album, Zeke jolted at the abrupt clanging of pans coming from the kitchen below him. Judy Mahaney was certainly making her presence known, he thought smiling. Unaware that the housekeeper he'd hired was in reality with the Marshal's Service, Peg had opposed her engagement. That is, until he appealed to her zealous devotion to her family. It wasn't an entirely deceptive move, he mused, but effective.

"We can't afford such silly extravagance," she'd whispered close to tears. "I can keep my own house."

"We can afford whatever it takes to help you fully recover, Peg. I have so much on my mind lately…I need to know you're not pushing yourself for Tracee and me. Please let me do this—for us."

"Well, I guess I can tolerate her for a few days," she finally said. "But she needs to stay out of my way."

Ever since high school, Peg had been the one bright constant of his life. He recalled the moment Casey had introduced them. He'd instantly been drawn to her and admired her unwavering strength—her devotion. God, he desperately loved her.

A feeling of protective rage rose up in Zeke, remembering with a pang of alarm how helpless she'd looked lying in the hospital bed. It had broken his heart and taken every ounce of restraint within him to keep from going to the prison and relieving his frustration on Tyson. Despite the fact that he had no proof that Tyson was behind the attack, he had wanted to strike back. He knew it was wrong. He was a Christian, as well as a detective with the police department. He knew he couldn't risk allowing himself to lose control like that. It would clearly place him in the same category with the depraved people who had done all this to his family and Alex.

He ran his fingers gently over the photograph of Peg. She deserved better. How could he have allowed this thing to touch her? What if...

He couldn't even think it. He wouldn't. Zeke's mind moved to his father. What had Charles Webb felt when he had found his wife murdered? Zeke couldn't imagine. Maybe he had been much too harsh in his criticism. He set his mouth in a firm, hard line. He could never again allow himself to become so unfocused that he placed his family in jeopardy.

"Zeke?" It was Sanger. He stuck his head up through the small entry appearing huge and uncomfortable.

"Yeah?"

"You'd better come down. We've got some things to go over."

"Sanger, I don't really want Peg upset by hearing things too..."

Sanger raised a palm toward Zeke to interrupt his discourse. "I'm very aware of that," he said and gingerly climbed backwards down the ladder.

Zeke abruptly closed the album and put it away. "I'll be there in a minute."

Sanger stood solemnly in the garage watching as Zeke climbed down from the attic. "Sorry, I'm a little uneasy in tight places."

"No problem. What's going on?"

"Casey is on his way over," he said, leading the way into the kitchen. "Earl called with some news from LA."

Zeke's heart began to pound wildly. "Is Alex okay,

**189**

# Fragment In The Sand

Sanger?"

Without replying, Sanger rushed to the front door at hearing the sound of a car out front. Casey strolled through the door, murmuring something about appreciating the call.

"Hey, Case," Zeke said, trying to keep his voice level. "What's going on?" The knot in his throat tightened as he swallowed to relieve the pressure. He watched as Casey wearily leaned against the wall near the stove.

He removed his sunglasses. "I'm officially on vacation. I think that I may fly out to LA in the morning."

"Are you gonna' tell me what's going on, or do I have to call Earl?"

"Zeke, LAPD placed an APB on Calvin Prince this morning," Casey said. "Apparently, he disappeared the morning after Alex did. They only discovered it yesterday when they returned to question him further."

"I knew it!" Zeke bellowed. "Adriel told me that he was very helpful in calming Alex down, but I thought something was strange about how much she mentioned him without really saying much. Who is he anyway? And what does he have to do with my sister?"

Zeke's voice was growing explosive. He restrained himself only after noticing Casey silently motion toward the bedrooms. Zeke anxiously turned from the deputies and pushed his clawed fingers through his cropped hair.

"Prince used to work for *The Lamp Lighter*," Sanger said. "That's one of those weekly tabloids."

"What? No wonder she didn't want Lou to know about him. Lou should have been on top of this. By the way, did you check out what we talked about yesterday?"

"Yeah, Earl told me that they'd already checked into Lou's financial status," Casey said. Zeke watched curiously as Casey glanced in Sanger's direction. He was both surprised and amused to see Sanger avert his gaze. "Apparently, Lou has been banking quite a bit as a modeling agent. Although the percentage is uniform, Alex brings him quite a bit more than the others. He represents a total of twelve models."

"I knew it!" Zeke said, his heart hammering against his chest.

"But he's made a lot of people angry, including other casino owners. It seems that he lost quite a bit in a lawsuit several months ago involving an accident at the casino. Apparently, his casino has been newly restored after a very extensive fire."

"Casey, are you saying that someone is after Lou?"

"No," chimed in Sanger. "We were assuming that Lou had the place burned himself. In fact, the insurance company is refusing to pay the claim. The accident could be valid, but it could be a set-up to get back at him for his shady dealings."

"Earl also told me that the FBI can't seem to find a photograph of Prince," Casey said.

"Is this Prince an honest suspect now?" Zeke asked. "What about the chance that Lou is involved?"

"The description that we got from the roommate doesn't match the description that Alex gave to police," Sanger said. "So we know they're two different people."

"But that doesn't exclude the possibility that someone has hired this man to frighten her. And who knows what else," Zeke said. "We all know that this could be anyone."

"The man on the highway sounds a lot like the same person that paid the kid to shut off all the power to the complex. FBI ran both descriptions through the computer. It's not much, but they think he may be a Las Vegas thug-for-hire named Eddie Rosell."

"Eddie Rosell?" Casey asked.

"It's too soon to come to any real conclusions," Sanger said, taking a gulp of his coffee. "But at this point, they only want Prince for questioning."

"I don't know anything about a Rosell," Casey blurted out. "And how long have you known about Lou Ramsey?"

Zeke was stunned into silence to see the anger flash in Casey's eyes as they bore into Sanger.

"I'm sorry, Casey," Sanger said, a defiant smile spreading across his face. "I agreed to keep you informed only as a courtesy. My main objective has been to keep Zeke and his family safe."

"I am well aware of what your main objective should be, Sanger," Casey said, gazing at him intently. "But I can also see you playing a game with their lives that should only be

**191**

between you and me."

"Casey, what's going on?" Zeke asked.

Without even acknowledging Zeke's question, Casey eyes glared angrily at Sanger without flinching. "Do you know if Prince left word of his plans with his employer?" he asked, acidly.

The two men locked gazes and held them until Zeke abruptly cleared his throat. Sanger leaned over the edge of the table, encircling the coffee cup with his hands.

"He apparently went into his office the next morning and quit. He demanded his last check," Sanger said, his face deepening in hue. "They said he was extremely agitated. It was only noticeable because he's usually very quiet and unassuming."

"Any demands yet?" Zeke asked, hoping whatever conflict there was between the two had blown over. "And what about the nurse that Prince was supposedly seeing?"

"They didn't have her name, so they're assuming that she's with him," Judy said, wiping her hands on a towel.

"Alex mentioned her to me a couple of times," Casey said, grimacing. "I think her first name is Vivian, but I don't know anything more."

"I'd better get a call back to Earl," Sanger said, jumping to his feet.

"I'm calling Desi first," Zeke said, sprinting for the phone on the wall. Instantly, Casey stood and placed a hand on Zeke's.

"I can't let you do that," he said. "You've gotta calm down, Zeke, and let us do our job."

"How can you say that, Case?" Zeke protested. "They're obviously not keeping you very informed. And this is my sister we're talking about."

"It'll be all right, Zeke," Casey said. "You know that. I'm on vacation, but I'll keep in touch with Earl myself. FBI is surely keeping Lou under surveillance." He glanced in Sanger's direction. Sanger offered a confirming nod. "Besides, they don't need the added responsibility of dealing with an overwrought brother."

Zeke gazed into his friend's eyes and knew instinctively

that he was telling him he intended to do more than he wanted to say in front of his colleagues. "All right, Case. But what kind of an impasse is this regarding Prince?"

"I'm not quite sure yet, but I'll let you know everything I find out when I get back from California. I promise."

Zeke bent down then to bind the half-filled plastic liner in the trash can. Then hoisting it out, he strode toward the back door and glanced around. "I assume it's okay for me to take out my own garbage."

The sarcasm was uncalled for and he knew it, but he needed to lash out at someone. He felt so useless. Zeke glanced across the large back yard and moved to open the storm door. Sanger hurriedly moved past him and glanced around suspiciously.

On occasion, Zeke had found himself thinking about the vulnerability in the location of his home. He'd even pondered the nightmare it would be if anyone ever wanted to get revenge. His home was situated with the perfect backdrop for a sniper attack—a large wooded area on three sides, very few neighbors and a slightly rustic setting. He didn't know why he'd occasionally thought like that, or why it happened to be on his mind at this moment, but it unsettled him. Maybe all cops had those kind of eerie reflections.

Just as Sanger signaled for Zeke to come ahead, they heard the screeching of tires and gravel being thrown from the road. Without thinking, Zeke rushed past Sanger to look over the chain link toward the front of the house, assuming that someone was about to have an accident.

Three successive shots rang out. They came so close that he could hear them buzz past his ear. Before he could respond, he was thrown to the ground under the weight of Sanger Wynn.

# CHAPTER 19

## *Flight*

Casey was halfway across the yard when he heard an ear-splitting scream that stopped him in his tracks. Quickly swinging around, he caught sight of Judy trying to restrain Peg while holding a kicking, wailing three-year-old in her arms. The pandemonium was so unreal that at first, it stunned him into inaction. He snapped back however, and grabbed Peg before she could rush any farther into the yard. Recklessly anxious for her husband, she fought Casey so fervently that he was afraid she would hurt herself in the effort. Finally, he physically lifted her and returned her to the house.

Peg's voice was mournful but piercing. "Oh, God, please let him be all right!"

After Casey set her down in the kitchen, he moved back towards the door. "I've gotta get to Zeke." He turned quickly to Judy who was trying unsuccessfully to console Tracee. "Peg, I need you to stay calm so Tracee can settle down," he said. "Please, don't move."

Casey reached for the child who was so agitated she almost seemed savage. When he tenderly drew her to him, she immediately reached for his head and shoved her thumb into her mouth. Her face was wet and puffy, and her body quivered like that of a trapped bird.

"Tracee?" he whispered, hoping his anxiety to get back to Zeke wasn't noticed.

"Hmm," she answered, in the midst of shutters and hiccups.

"Uncle Case wants you to be a real big girl and sit here next to your mommy. Okay? I've gotta go help Daddy with something." He easily moved toward the chair next to Peg and placed her down in it. Crouching down beside them, he asked, "Can you do that for me?"

**194**

"Okay, Uncle Case," she said, rubbing her glistening eyes with her fist.

"Can I have my special smile?" Casey urged. Without hesitation, Tracee tilted herself towards him, a dawdling smile on her face.

At that moment the back door sprang open, and Zeke stumbled in, his arms wrapped around Sanger who had obviously been hit. Casey quickly rushed to help him, yelling instructions at Judy. "Get Peg and Tracee back to the bedroom!" he said. "And call Earl—now!"

An eternity seemed to pass while waiting for back-up and an ambulance for Sanger. But when it did, Casey was able to convince Earl to let him stay with the family until he could get someone to take his place. Sanger, having caught a round in the shoulder, would recover. However, they realized, with great sobriety, that the perpetrator was serious. He wanted Zeke dead.

Casey wandered down the hall toward the bedroom pondering how Zeke would take the news that Peg and Tracee would have to be moved to a more secure location for protection. He stood in the doorway, watching Zeke affectionately look upon his resting wife and daughter while Judy looked on from the chair beside the bed. When Zeke turned to see that he was there, he strolled across the room and joined him in the hall, shutting the door behind them.

"You know what we're gonna' have to do, don't you?" Casey asked.

"I know that it would be safer for them if they weren't around me," he said sadly. "It would kill me if anything happened to either one of them, Casey, but…"

"I know it would," Casey said, laying a sympathetic hand on his friend's shoulder. He was taken aback when Zeke floundered blindly against him, weeping unchecked. Casey embraced him supportively and guided him back down the hall into the living room where Earl and Special Agent Perry were waiting.

After Zeke composed himself, Earl began his recommendation. To Casey's relief, it included also getting Zeke out of town in a separate locale from his family. It had been determined that since the perpetrator wasn't after Peg and Tracee, they would be escorted to her parent's home in Houston and kept under protective surveillance.

"Have you heard anything more about Alex?" Zeke asked somberly, sampling the coffee that Earl had handed him.

"No, we haven't, which gives us further evidence that the two cases are probably unrelated. Maybe this Mr. Prince is simply a concerned friend who wanted to get Alex out of the line of fire. She obviously trusts him. I'm finding out they had a good friendship going."

"How can you still reason that the cases are not related after all that's happened?" Casey asked. "The timing and random events in the two cases are extraordinary."

"Well, we've spoken to her roommate—the one who was out-of-town when the invasion occurred. She says that Mr. Prince was a very good friend to all of them—a type of fatherly figure who was especially devoted to Alex. She didn't seem to think that he would hurt her, but of course, there is no way she could be sure."

"What about the fact that he worked for a paper?" Casey asked, "and if everything is okay, why hasn't she contacted us, or at least him?"

"We checked past articles in Mr. Prince's paper. They haven't done an article on Alex and don't have plans for one," replied Agent Perry. "If he were out for a story, there would be plenty in print by now. Don't forget…we aren't certain the two are together. It's just a hunch," replied Agent Perry.

"That could mean any number of things," Zeke said. "He could have been setting this whole thing up."

"Have we heard about the other roommate—Star? How's she doing?" Casey asked, the muscles twitching in his jaw.

"She's still in a coma," Earl said. "Your friend, Detective Payne has been personally staying on top of her surveillance. She was hit on the head several times with a blunt object. What's so curious is that Alex was hit with a lot less force. I can't figure out the extreme shift in emotion. One moment he was lethally brutal. The next…well, I don't know…seems he was just trying to slow her down rather than beat her half to death. It's almost as if there were two different individuals at the scene."

"Do you think that maybe Star was the target?" Zeke asked, recalling Casey's earlier speculation. "The shadow had mentioned that he owed Alex a lesson."

"We're not sure," Agent Perry said. "I understand that you received an email from her."

"Yeah. It troubled me enough to call Adriel."

"I know. We've talked with him on several occasions," Agent Perry said. "Do you still have a copy of that email?"

"Yes, I do. I printed it out."

"Don't bother getting up. I have a copy of it right here," Earl said, opening his attaché case. He pulled the sheet from a file and handed it to Agent Perry and turned his attention back to Zeke.

Agent Perry stared at the sheet he'd been handed and began to read it aloud. "*Zeke, get her out of here quick.* It says it's *from* Alex."

"It's from her computer," Zeke explained. "Adriel told me that Star was apparently sitting at the computer in the living room when she was struck from behind. Alex was in the bedroom asleep."

"I'm beginning to think that the perpetrator was already in the house," Earl said, his brow furrowed in contemplation. "It would make more sense."

"I was thinking that if Star saw or heard something that she wasn't meant to," Zeke explained, "someone could've followed her home, gone through the window and attacked her."

"The apartment security shows that Star arrived home around ten-thirty. Only two others came through the gates prior to the authorities arriving."

"Do you think that he may live in the complex?" Zeke asked. "Alex told me that she felt as if this Shadow was watching her all the time."

"That's a very real possibility," Earl said, biting down on his pipe. "It's odd that they found several cigarette butts on the fire escape outside her bedroom window. None of the girls smoked, and it does appear that whoever the smoker is, he'd camped out there for several evenings. Some of the butts were rather old."

"The words on this email would certainly lead one to believe that Star knew something and was scared about it. It's enough to provoke anyone to move as you did, Detective," Agent Perry said. "So don't beat up on yourself for leaving your family to go to your sister's aid. You had no idea someone was watching you as well."

Casey and Zeke exchanged knowing glances. "Earl, I'd like to call Adriel or Desi to see if they have any other information," Zeke said.

"Right now, Zeke, I'd prefer that you get busy preparing your family for the trip to Houston. We need to get everyone out of here before dark."

"All right," Zeke said, rising mechanically to return to the bedroom.

With Zeke out of the room, Earl took a more serious tone and turned his eyes to Casey. "What are you doing here, deputy?"

"Actually, Sanger had phoned me so that I could be here when he talked to Zeke," Casey said. "I was going to take a flight out of town tomorrow morning."

"To be honest, sir," Judy interjected. "I couldn't have handled the wife and child alone. I'm glad he was here."

"That notwithstanding, deputies, I expect you to follow orders," Earl said. "Casey, I have half a mind to write you up on this. You will not blatantly disregard the directives put in place for the safety of this family, whether you're on vacation or not. Am I making myself clear?"

"Yes, sir," Casey said, shifting uncomfortably on the sofa. He realized that he had done exactly what Earl had warned he would do. Because of family ties, he'd allowed himself to become an encumbrance to the safety of fellow deputies as well as Zeke and his family.

"At this point, I have no other choice but to terminate your leave so you can cover Zeke," Earl said, agitatedly. It was obvious he didn't want to, but there weren't any options left at the moment. "*But*, the moment I get a replacement for Sanger, you're to go somewhere…anywhere. Is that understood?"

"Yes, sir."

\*\*\*

Alex glanced out the window at the "Welcome to Albuquerque" sign. Calvin was stopping to rest a lot along the way, apparently making certain that he moved inconspicuously along the route. She found Calvin's moods rather fickle. One minute, he'd appear excited, as if the two were on a planned vacation. But quickly in the next, he'd appear very sullen. He obviously had a lot on his mind, she thought.

She lightheartedly joined in on the hymn that Calvin sang. When he went up an octave in his harmony, he made a face that reminded Alex of Gangster, and she chuckled. Her merriment instantly turned into sadness and her laughter into sobbing. Without understanding why, misery seemed to pour through her with a vengeance. This frightened her.

The onslaught of submerged feelings caught her so off guard that they escalated into a zenith that peeked over a past of mixed up dreams and disappointments. She felt abandoned. She felt angry.

"Alex, it's going to be all right, darlin'," Calvin said, squeezing her hand. "I think we need to get off this road for a little while. Why don't we both get a little sleep—maybe lay low for a day or two."

Alex nodded in quick jerks, blowing her nose on the tissue she had snatched from the box on the console. "I'm sorry," she said. "I don't know what's wrong with me."

"You've no need to apologize. You've been through a lot."

"I'm so scared, Calvin," Alex said, quietly sniffling. "I've started having those dreams again. And Casey and Zeke are probably half out of their minds with worry."

"What dreams?" Calvin asked frowning. "I know that you've been restless in your sleep and you were a little hard to wake up a couple of times, but I thought it was due to this little unplanned excursion."

"No. My therapist warned me about regression. They don't feel I can be thrown into too much distress without it having some adverse effect. I handle it better than I used to, but there's always the possibility of relapse."

**199**

# Fragment In The Sand

"I don't understand," Calvin said, clearly shocked.

"Well, I was so emotionally bruised by my mother's death and my dad's disappearance that I withdrew—made up a world in my own head," Alex said, taking a deep breath. "I finally came back to the real world after Zeke persistently called me back."

"What do you mean?"

"He worked with the therapists. I didn't really want to leave that place," she said, leaning her head back against the seat, "but I kept hearing his voice. It was a beautiful open field, but the terror that I had to endure to get there was dreadful."

"So if you're subjected to too much stress, it could push you back to that place?"

"I could be emotionally lured past the point of no return," she said with a shudder. "I don't want that to happen, Calvin. Every time I feel myself slipping, I get so scared. I can't let it happen."

"Oh, my God, I didn't know. When…what—"

"When I was six," Alex said, glancing back out of the window. "Right after I got to California."

"You won't go back there," Calvin said, his voice noticeably breaking. "The Lord will take care of you. Maybe we can call Zeke when we get to the motel."

Alex turned back around to face him and attempted a smile. It came and faded simultaneously and she quickly looked back through her window to avoid the emotion that welled up in her throat. She had to hold her self together. She wondered if she could really count on God this time to be there for her.

"When we get Zeke on the line, you must promise me that you won't mention where we are. It's for your own protection, darlin'. I'm certain that by now the feds are expecting us to call."

"I don't understand why you're being so deliberate, Calvin. Nobody is following us."

"We don't know that," he said, glancing into the rearview.

"Do you think this situation is so serious that someone would actually come after us?"

**200**

"There's more going on than meets the eye, darlin'. I just know you can't go back to that apartment until this is figured out. I'm not trying to scare you, but I have a gut feeling someone may not be too far behind us."

# CHAPTER 20

## *Gregory Falls*

Zeke turned the car off the main highway and traveled down the bumpy road to the home he'd grown to love as a teenager. The darkness lay over the countryside like a thick blanket, evoking a sense of peace he couldn't explain. He loved this place. He had grown to feel secure and a part of it, but never quite complete—not without his sister. He inhaled deeply and slowly released the air as the familiar sensing of warmth spread through him.

His thoughts drifted back to the onset of the trip to Gregory Falls. It had taken less than an hour to get Peg and Tracee packed and on their way to Houston. Tracee had been very excited, as if they were going on a field trip or something. He hoped that the presence of the agents traveling with them wouldn't scare her too much, and wished he could be with them. It would probably take the edge off the excursion.

Earl had rushed them so aggressively that in his haste, he had forgotten his cell phone. What if Alex had tried to call? He glanced over at Casey to ask if he had brought his, but his friend was sound asleep. He somehow knew his friend was just as distressed as he was over the situation with Alex. He hadn't asked him about his relationship with her, but he had obviously developed a protective attitude towards her.

Casey had been protective of Zeke, as well. He recalled how he had been there for him as young boys when bullies were teasing that Zeke had to rent a family. Casey hadn't hesitated to get right in the middle of them.

Chuckling aloud to himself, Zeke turned the car into the gate of the Oliver farm, and pulled onto the right leg of a road that approached the front of the house. The other continued around toward the back.

He hoped that Ike had heard from Peg by now. She probably had tried to call, too. Casey jolted awake when the tires pressed into the rocks, making an unbroken jangling sound. "Hey," he said rubbing his eyes. "When did it get dark?"

"A few minutes after you fell asleep," Zeke said grinning.

Just as they both pulled themselves from the car, Isaac Oliver turned the porch light on and opened the front door. "I thought it was about time for you two to be rolling in here," he said.

"Dad, we'll spend the night here in the house," Casey said, pulling the bags out of the trunk. "We'll get moved out to the cottage tomorrow, okay?"

"That's fine," Ike said, giving each of them a hug. "Zeke, Peg called. They were just about to make Houston. Tracee's having a high ole' time. Y'all heard anything from Alex yet?"

"No," Zeke and Casey said in unison.

"Zeke, I think I'd better pull the car around to the back of the house...out of sight." Casey pulled his cell phone from his pocket and blurted out his frustration. "Ah, man! My phone is turned off! How could I have been so irresponsible?"

***

It was midnight when Alex jolted up in bed. Sluggishly rubbing her eyes, she scanned the unfamiliar surroundings. Oh, yeah, she remembered now. It wasn't home—it was a motel room.

She panicked when she discovered that Calvin wasn't in the room. Glancing around the dimly lit room, she was suddenly repulsed by the musty smell that hung in the carpet and drapes. On impulse, she jumped up and dialed Zeke's number. There was still no answer. She hung up and dialed Casey's number again.

Where were they? Why wasn't anyone answering? Uneasiness began to fill her when she realized not only was she alone, but she couldn't even hear a familiar voice on the phone. Could they both be in Los Angeles looking for her?

When the door opened, Alex stiffened and stared wide-eyed as Calvin cautiously stepped into the room. The moment he turned and gazed into her eyes, he stopped in his tracks.

# Fragment In The Sand

"Where have you been? I was worried."

"I had to take a little walk. I'm sorry. I thought you would be sleeping. I didn't want to disturb you," he said, moving to sit next to her. "Alex, what's wrong? You're trembling."

"I tried to phone Zeke and Casey again. They're still not answering—not even their cell phones."

"Well, I know you're anxious to talk to them, but don't worry about it. I'm sure there's a good reason why they aren't using their phones right now. We'll try again in the morning. Right now, we need to stay off the road for a while and get some rest."

Alex clasped her hands together in an effort to stop the trembling. Calvin gently squeezed them. "Did you have anymore nightmares?" he asked, scrutinizing her face. "You're obviously upset about more than not being able to reach Zeke."

Alex nodded her head, wrapping her arms around herself protectively. "It wasn't very bad this time."

"Maybe that means that you're becoming stronger," Calvin said.

Alex swallowed dryly. Her voice was barely more than a whisper. "Dr. Gleason…that's my therapist—he seems to think that my dreams are some type of gauge."

"Surely there's nothing to worry about after all this time. You just went through a sad spell there and you're feeling a little sad again. That's all."

"Actually, Calvin, it was a little bit more serious than that," Alex said, forcing a smile. "I don't talk about it much. Star and Desi know about the dreams, but they think it's because of the Shadow."

"You poor dear," Calvin said, shaking his head incredulously. "So, your dreams determine how you're faring?"

"Supposedly, if I'm confronted with too much stress, the other world will become more appealing. Therein lies the danger of my regressing. Dr. Gleason thinks that I will start having the same nightmares that chased me into that other world."

"Even after so long a time?"

"He said that with a psychosis such as this, there always exists the danger of relapse." Calvin grew quiet. Alex lifted her eyes just in time to see him wipe at his eyes as he sharply turned his head away. "I'll be fine, Calvin," she said. "Please don't worry about me."

"It just hurts me to see you go through so much, Alex. But you're a strong young woman…and you trust in God. With His help, you can get through anything…so you hold on."

"It gets scary sometimes when I can't stop the thoughts—the feelings," she said, gasping for air. "Sometimes they're so sudden."

"Can you tell me about your dreams?"

"Are you sure you want to hear it?" Alex asked. "It probably won't sound very frightening to you."

"If it would help you to talk about it, I'll be more than happy to listen."

Alex felt numb and shivered as another wave of hysteria loomed up within her. "I suppose it's the same for everyone—the terror, death, and a prison of silence—everything nightmares are made of. In mine, I always hear my mother's voice, but I can't see her face. She's telling me about the angels watching over me."

Alex yawned and leaned back against the headboard. "The shadows dance against the window blinds in my room. It's storming and dark." She smiles, but only for an instant. "My dad comes to get me and carries me away."

"What does he look like?"

"I never see his face," Alex said, her brow furrowed. "I can't remember anything about him." Alex glanced around at Calvin and scrunched up her nose. "I hate to be awakened when I'm sleeping good. Anyway, I ask him about Mama, but he says she's still sleeping. He calls me "little one"—I like that. It makes me feel secure somehow. But the next thing I know, I'm in a grave—lying next to my mother. And I can see Zeke running away—leaving me there. But I can't even scream."

Alex's eyes stared at Calvin with fascinated horror. "I can't get out, Calvin. I try and try, but I can't get out of that grave."

"It's all right, darlin'," Calvin said. "It's all right. Why don't you try to go back to sleep now and we'll just pray that your dreams will be much sweeter this time."

# Fragment In The Sand

"Okay," she said, yawning. "Would you sit here for a lit-tle while?"

"As long as you like," Calvin said. Alex was nearly asleep when she heard Calvin begin to whisper a prayer.

\*\*\*

Casey hung up the phone and stared at it, his back to Zeke and Ike. How was he going to tell Zeke that his sister might be in more danger than they had allowed themselves to believe?

"What is it, Case?" Zeke demanded. "Tell me."

Casey walked woodenly toward the kitchen table where Zeke was seated with Ike, drinking a cup of coffee. His eyes were wild with alarm.

"Was that Earl? What did he say?"

Glancing nervously at Ike, Casey sat down in the chair next to Zeke. "They've been running a check on this Calvin Prince, Zeke."

"And?"

"He's not who he says he is."

# CHAPTER 21

## *Tactics*

Casey sat at the kitchen table drinking a cup of coffee, his face etched with desperation. He envisioned Alex's deep brown eyes so filled with enchantment, and he closed his own against the anguish that rushed up in him. She didn't deserve this, he thought. He felt himself stiffen at the thought that she could be somewhere hurt.

He recalled her tears when she learned of Brian's death and how easily she had allowed him to comfort her. It had been somewhat comforting to *him* as well when she snuggled close to him in her grief. In light of his previous perspective of her, he had been dismayed.

Casey was not conscious that his left hand reached up to stroke agitatedly at his beard. From somewhere out in the distance a lone dog howled and his father's old collie set up a chorus in response. He smiled as he recalled how much she'd talked about Gangster, Calvin Prince's dog. *God, please don't let him hurt her.*

His mind quickly moved to the moment he had kissed Alex—he hadn't planned to, but it certainly felt like the right thing to do at the time. He smiled, recalling how her heart had hammered against his chest in time with his own. Momentarily stunned by the unprecedented rise in emotion, Casey rapidly blinked away the pools that were forming in his eyes.

Get a grip, he told himself. He was reacting much too emotionally for a deputy. He had to get control of himself before it was noticed by anyone else, especially Earl.

Scolding himself did no good. He wanted to know that she was alive and well—to see her eyes and touch her smile. She had indeed become much too important to him.

Powerless was only one of the words that described how

he felt. He knew without a doubt that he was in love with her—simple as that. There, he'd finally admitted it.

With reality exploding in him, Casey wondered what he could do about it. Had he waited too long to come in touch with his own feelings? He had no idea where she was.

Even if they weren't in dire circumstances—even if she weren't his friend's sister, he could never let her know how he felt. She wouldn't be able to handle the conflict it might create, much less take on his career. She probably wouldn't want to. He could never put her through what his mother went through—what Angie had gone through.

He'd seen so many of his fellow deputies get married and end up in divorce court because their wives couldn't handle it. He couldn't let himself become vulnerable like that again. He had to be a loner. What was worse, he had to like it.

He never should have kissed her. Earl had been right all along. He was indeed too close and personal for this assignment. He knew that Earl had been referring to his friendship with Zeke, but in his own mind, it was all the same. What would Earl think if he knew that his deputy had let himself fall for Alex?

Casey knew the answer to that question. He would have his hide. His lingering thoughts halted when the phone rang. After listening to the caller for a brief moment, he said, "I'll be sure to tell him."

Zeke was instantly in the doorway, staring anxiously. Casey hung up. "What is it?"

"A woman called the hospital asking about Star. They believe it may have been Alex."

"That means that she's all right if she called, right?" Zeke's voice lifted with excitement. "Thank God."

Casey cleared his throat. "They also found Rosell's motel room, Zeke. It looked like he'd left in a hurry."

"And?" Zeke asked, carefully studying Casey's face.

"It was a literal shrine to Alex...covered with photographs that he'd taken. He was even beginning to dress the photographs with some of her personal items."

"What?"

"Zeke, this guy is obsessed. And he's dangerous. You

know this type of profile. He even had an enlarged photograph of me. He had drawn a target board on it. FBI also found Star's personal number in his room. When they checked her phone records, they found that she'd made several calls to a cell phone that has since been disconnected."

Casey could see the horror on Zeke's face. "Is he a killer? Does Star have something to do with all of this?"

"He's slick—they can't get him on anything. But he is a known hire for the mob. And either Star is an innocent by-stander or an accomplice."

Zeke's countenance was falling fast. "Couldn't the call to the hospital have come from Desi? How can they know for sure it was Alex?"

Casey willed himself to stay calm and help Zeke through the horror of this new information. "It wasn't Desi. She's under surveillance. So is Lou."

"Why?"

"Just a precaution. She could be in danger, too. FBI wants to cover every base," Casey said, taking another swallow from his coffee mug. "Zeke, do you remember Peg's description of her attacker?"

"She couldn't get a good look at him. But she could tell that he was white, tall, bulky…but his face was covered with a ski mask…that's all she remembers."

"That doesn't sound like Eddie Rosell. Do you know anything at all about Prince?"

Zeke moved to sit next to Casey at the table. "No. Alex was careful not to tell me much. Case, what are you getting at?"

A frown creased Casey's brow. "The more I think about it, the more I think that Prince may be on our side. Now that we know about Rosell's obsession, we have little doubt that he indeed is the Shadow. My concern now is where he might be."

"Somebody had to hire him. Do you think that could be Star?"

"I really doubt it. I've met her and she doesn't have a harmful thought in her head. Conceivably Rosell was hired by somebody without moral fiber. He must have grown obsessive while on the job. It happens. Did you know that Star wasn't even dressed for bed when they found her at the computer? She came right in and jumped on to send you a message."

"Yeah. I'd been wondering what she could have seen or heard at Lou's office to prompt her to write me? Maybe she saw the man whom she unknowingly had given access to their apartment."

"Has she ever written you before?" Casey asked, eyeing Zeke intently.

"No. She would tell Alex to say hello periodically, but that's it. I hadn't even met the girls, but knew a lot about them through Alex. Did you know that she and Desi called me Phantom Zee?"

Casey lightly chuckled. "Yeah, I did. Do we even know for sure that Star arrived at Lou's?"

"I don't know. Maybe you'd better call Adriel."

\*\*\*

Alex stared anxiously out the window, feeling detached from anything that felt normal to her. Being on the road again should have been a good thing, but it just magnified the fact that she was "on the run."

She gloomily pondered how things had gotten so crazy in the last few months following the yellow roses in New York. She and Robbie had broken up, Brian had died, someone had frightened her on the highway, and she was getting threatening phone calls. And now this—all possible pieces of another big puzzle that she couldn't understand.

Robbie had certainly not been the man that she thought he was. She didn't know why she had chosen him. Well, maybe she did. It had something to do with the fact that her uncle had introduced them and had liked him a lot—even to the point of awarding his firm the audit on his businesses.

She'd developed a deep emotional bond with Robbie over the years, but she wondered if in some mixed-up sense she had allowed her uncle to choose him for her—just as he had chosen her career.

She had to admit that Zeke had been right about her needing to take charge of her own affairs. She had depended on others so long that she couldn't tell where their desires ended and hers began.

Alex turned a heedless eye on Calvin, who instantly turned towards her and smiled. He had been very kind to her, despite not having known her long. In a lot of ways, she had begun to depend on him. Not as much as on Uncle Lou, though. She had made quite a bit of progress in becoming independent, and she didn't want to undo it all by letting Calvin think for her.

She felt removed and numb as she rubbed a hand over her brow. She almost wished she could go to sleep in spite of having just awakened, but her mind seemed to dart in and out of lucidity—jumping from one thing to another.

"Are you doing okay, darlin'?"

"I'm so mixed up. I can't seem to focus on any one thing very long."

"Why don't you talk it out with me," Calvin suggested. "Maybe that will help."

"I wonder how Star is doing? Hospitals are so guarded in giving out information. They have to be, though."

"I expect those injuries of hers will take a while to mend. All you can do at this point is pray for her."

"I know. Do you think that we can call Uncle Lou?" Alex asked, glancing up at Calvin.

"I think it would be better if we wait until we talk to Zeke."

"It's just that he's always been there for me. I never meant to worry him."

"I'm sure they're all worried about you, darlin'. A lot has happened to you in the last few months. A lot more than meets the eye, I think."

Alex glanced up, her eyes questioning. "You don't think Uncle Lou would have anything to do with all of this, do you?"

"I can't say. I don't really know your uncle. One thing is for sure—it looks like whoever is behind it is somebody you know."

The breath caught in Alex's throat as she glanced up at Calvin stunned. "Why do you say that? I don't know anyone that would want to hurt me."

Calvin looked at her sternly and reached for her arm. "I

don't think any of us can honestly make a statement like that."

"Robbie was just a little—"

"Drunk," Calvin finished. "But his conduct was a big surprise to you. Right?"

"Well. Yes. But are you saying that Robbie may have something to do—"

Calvin gave her hand a gentle squeeze. "I'm only saying that we don't know what another person will do if pushed to a point. Before you go saying that you don't know anyone that could do this, you'd better remember that."

"I guess you're right," she said, looking away dejectedly. "It's scary to think about. But I suppose it's time to stop being afraid of my own reckoning."

"In light of what you've told me about your fear of slipping back, I think that you should prepare yourself for anything. I don't know whose doing this, but it's bound to be a bit of a shock when you find out."

Alex laid her head back and closed her eyes, allowing her mind to move toward her uncle. She knew that he loved her—he was extremely protective. She tried to dismiss the mounting feelings of resentment she'd been feeling for him lately. Her thoughts strained to determine they're inception, but she couldn't narrow it down. Maybe Calvin was right. Maybe she didn't know people like she thought she did.

It occurred to her then, that it might have begun last Thanksgiving when she had returned to what she thought was an empty apartment to find her uncle in her bedroom. She recalled that when she'd questioned him, he simply stated that he had stopped by to make certain the apartment was secure.

Although she had accepted the flimsy excuse, she felt it didn't exactly ring true. It wasn't until later when she was preparing for bed that she discovered several of her drawers were askew. She was very orderly with her belongings and could tell that they had been gone through. It had haunted her for weeks, but she willfully dismissed the possibility that he had gone through her things. She now wondered if her uncle could've repeated this just recently.

Alex thought of Casey. She had tried not to, but just as gently as a cloud moves across the sky, thoughts of him drifted into her mind. She wished she had gotten to know him sooner.

She mentally shook herself and forced her mind back toward LA. She wondered how Desi was dealing with all that had happened. Knowing her, she was probably out searching for the scumbag that had done this awful thing.

"Are you okay, darlin'?" Calvin asked again, pulling her from her musing. She knew that he was frightened for her, especially after she had told him about Dr. Gleason's warnings.

"I was just wondering about Desi. I miss her and Star. Living with them was the closest I've ever come to having sisters. And Star in many ways is so much like a child—she didn't deserve this."

Calvin briefly glanced at her with a note of concentration in his expression. "Nobody deserves this. Alex, have you ever had this type of thing happen to you before?"

"No," she said, alarmed. "When the calls first began, we assumed it was an over-enthused fan, but now, I guess we know it's more than that." She involuntarily shuddered and folded her hands in her lap. Calvin reached over and covered them with his own, silently offering her support.

"It'll be fine," he said. "I feel much better to have you out of LA. When we get to Oklahoma City, I'm sure your brother will know what to do to keep you safe."

"Where could they be, Calvin? Couldn't we try and call them again?"

"I've been thinking about that, honey. I don't know if that's a good idea. I wouldn't want you any more worried than you already are. Besides, the police are probably looking for me by now and I want to make sure you're safely with your brother before they catch up with me. I'm sure that his home phone is tapped. For the safety of Zeke's family as well as your own, I think it would be better if we just get you there."

Alex sat dumbfounded, staring incredulously at Calvin. Her mind suddenly seemed to be as clear as a bell. "Why would the safety of Zeke's family be in question?"

"I hadn't said anything to you about this because I didn't want you to worry. Do you think you can keep yourself calm?"

# Fragment In The Sand

"Of course," Alex answered, bracing herself for what must be a blow.

"Remember Zeke was on his way to LA? When Adriel came back to my apartment that night, he told me that Zeke was forced to turn right around and go back to Oklahoma City."

"Did they tell him I was missing? That's why I wond—"

Calvin held up a hand to silence her. "Yes, Alex. But when he arrived in LA, he was told that his wife had been attacked. She had been taken to the hospital."

Alex stared at Calvin in fascinated horror, beginning to tremble. But it was anger, not fear that fueled it. "Why?" she asked, tears flooding her eyes. "Why does God punish me and Zeke so much?"

"Alex!"

Unable to comprehend anything above the anger and confusion that rushed through her, Alex briskly shook her head. "No! I don't want to hear anymore. I've tried so hard to do things right for God, but it doesn't seem like He's playing fair."

Calvin continued to drive, not saying anything. After a few moments, Alex calmed down and began to feel guilty for biting his head off. "Is Peg okay?" she whispered. "Was Tracee hurt?"

"I'm sure they're both fine."

"I'm sorry I shouted."

"I don't see this as punishment from God, darlin'. This is the work of depraved men. From where I sit, it looks as if God has indeed been on your side a long time."

"Calvin, is the same person after Zeke?"

"Not real sure. According to the detective, Zeke had gotten a threat of some kind several weeks ago. I know that they probably have him and his family under some kind of protection right now—and they certainly know that you're missing. I was thinking that if I could get you into that same protection…"

"Why didn't he tell me?" Alex asked dumbfounded. "He's had all this stuff going on in his own life and he's been worried about me. I shouldn't have told him anything. He probably feels awful for leaving them to come check on me."

**214**

"Alex, Zeke is your brother and he's a police detective. He knows the risks."

"I wonder if any of this could be related," Alex mumbled.

"I don't see how it could be, but I'm not trusting anybody. Do you understand a little better why I'm doing this?"

"I'm trying, but not really." Alex gave Calvin a sidelong glance. "I'm very grateful that you want to help me, but I don't understand…I mean, you've got a job, you're on the run, you're driving clear across the country to deliver me safely to my brother. Why?"

Calvin chuckled a little under his breath. "I suppose because you remind me of someone I used to know."

"Your daughter?"

Calvin turned stunned eyes to Alex and, for a moment, she thought he looked frantic. "Actually, I was thinking of my late wife."

Alex quickly let the matter drop, feeling as if she had treaded on something much too private. She didn't want him getting upset in the middle of what they were going through. She did wonder, however, what had happened to his family. Had they died? Who was left for him?

"Do you think I could call Casey again? Surely they won't be listening in on his phone, since he's a federal deputy."

"Tell me more about this Casey," Calvin said, the lively gleam returning to his eyes.

Alex blew her nose and lowered her head. "He's a Christian. He's sensitive and very, very nice. I guess I still expected him to be the person that I met as a child. I didn't even consider that we had both grown up." She chuckled absently and gazed back out the window.

"He certainly seems to have aroused more than a passing interest in a young woman we both know," Calvin said, returning the chuckle.

She glanced back around at Calvin doubtfully. "Do you think it's weird? I mean…it's only been four months since I broke up with Robbie. And I've only seen Casey a few times." She paused, thinking of his warm smile. "We've been talking on the phone nearly every night, though."

"No. I don't think its weird at all. But I would pray about

**215**

**Fragment In The Sand**

it before it got too serious. You don't need another disappointment."

"I think it may already be too late for that, Calvin. I hope he's not too worried."

"Tell ya' what…does he have one of those answering machines on his home phone?"

"Yeah."

"Good. I don't really want you revealing our whereabouts. Let's try leaving a message now. That way, maybe we can alleviate some worry. But remember, say nothing about our plans or where we are."

"I don't have my cell phone with me, Calvin," she said frustrated.

"Look in the glove box," he said. "Mine should be in there." Alex opened the glove box and pulled out the phone and immediately started dialing Casey's number.

*** 

"Zeke, this is Lou," the strained voice said. "I got your message. I understand that Eddie Rosell is the one behind stalking Alex."

"Yeah," Zeke said cautiously. "Do you know him?"

"I'm acquainted with him. He hires out to do anything, but he's a sort of loose cannon. Have you heard anything from Alex?"

"No," Zeke answered. "I was wondering if you had. They won't let me call anyone." Zeke cringed at the fact that he was helping to set Lou up. Their suspicions had grown after he and Casey had confronted Earl about the probability of Alex knowing the person who hired the Shadow.

"Zeke, I don't want you to think that I had anything to do with this. If you think it's okay, I'd like to come to wait for news with you," Lou said. "I tried every way that I know to keep this type of thing from touching her."

Zeke could hear the agony in the man's voice and couldn't help softening toward him. "So you think it has something to do with your business affairs?"

"We all know it's a possibility…even a probability."

Zeke's nostrils contracted reflexively. "Yeah. I guess

**216**

you're right. I'm in Gregory Falls right now, Lou. And I am very much aware how much you love Alex."

After a few more minutes on the phone, Zeke hung up. He turned and nodded to Earl and Casey who were seated on the couch, listening intently.

Earl was convinced that Zeke was indeed suppressing things with regard to Lou. Because of the suspicious nature of Lou's business, he had instructed Zeke to call him and leave Casey's cell number on the answering machine.

Lou had taken the bite, but Zeke couldn't help wondering if he was doing the right thing.

# CHAPTER 22

## *Tracks in the sun*

By the time Calvin and Alex pulled into Amarillo, Alex was famished. "How 'bout pizza, Calvin?"

Calvin surveyed the many eatery signs along the perimeter of the highway. "That sounds good."

"I'd like to call and check on Star again. Is that okay?"

"Sure. But just call the hospital. I'm going to pull into the next service station up there and freshen up a bit," he said, taking the exit. He stepped out and stretched his legs before moving toward the attendant to retrieve the key.

Alex sat anxiously and watched as Calvin disappeared behind the building before dialing the hospital's number. When they wouldn't tell her anything, she immediately panicked and dialed Desi's cell phone.

"Alex! We've been worried sick about you. Where are you?"

Feeling horrid for defying Calvin's request, Alex tried to get to the point and quickly get off the phone without divulging their whereabouts. "Desi, I just called to check on Star. Is she okay?" She was sure that something was wrong when the hospital refused to answer her questions. The moment she realized they were trying to keep her on the line, she'd hung up.

"Star is still unconscious, but she's alive. Alex, the police are looking for Calvin," Desi blurted out. "They say his name isn't really Calvin Prince. Where are you?"

A cold chill raced up her spine as Desi's words penetrated her mind. "What?" Her thoughts ran rampant with questions. She thought of how she had joked about Calvin leaving town when she had teasingly told him that Zeke had wanted to check him out. She knew now why he'd become so annoyed.

"Honey, he could be dangerous. Is he there with you? Can you talk?"

"Yes."

"Oh, Alex, tell me where you are," Desi pressed.

Alex hesitated, considering what her betrayal would mean for Calvin. She was so frightened and confused, not knowing who she should trust anymore.

Tears ran down her cheeks. "We're in Amarillo. Just off I-40 at the Binco service station. We're getting ready to go have pizza."

"Are you heading for Oklahoma City?" Desi asked. "Zeke isn't there, Alex! Lou told me that he was in Gregory Falls. Don't trust Calvin. Stay at the restaurant as long as you can. Pretend to be sick…anything. Lou will send someone to get you."

Desi's agitation produced renewed fear in Alex. Now what was she supposed to do? She looked around anxiously at her surroundings, giving Desi her exact location.

The phone was suddenly ripped from Alex's hand through the open window. Startled, she turned to stare into Calvin's angry face. He instantly disconnected the call and tossed the phone into the back seat, then rushed around to the driver's side. Alex sat paralyzed with alarm.

Calvin turned the key in the ignition and turned to her. She instantly drew back, not knowing what to expect next. "Why in the world would you do that, Alex? I told you we can't trust *anyone*."

As if she hadn't heard his questions, Alex's anger surged forth. "Why did you lie to me? What are you going to do to me?"

"Listen to me," he snapped. "You don't have any idea what you've done." Alex moved closer to her door, reaching for its handle. Instantly, Calvin reached across her and slammed it shut again. Her jaw dropped open as she stared at him in disbelief. "You *are* going to listen to me. After that, you can go wherever you want."

"Desi said you're not who you claim to be. Who are you?" she demanded, her voice near hysterics. "Zeke is in Gregory Falls. You're not taking me to him at all!"

"Alex, calm down. I know you don't understand what's going on. You couldn't."

# Fragment In The Sand

"Who are you?" she demanded, catching the attention of several of the station's customers.

"Keep your voice down," he snapped through clenched teeth. "I said I was taking you to safety and I am. If Zeke is in Gregory Falls, he's probably there under protection. That's where Casey is from, I believe."

"Yes."

"Alex, if you don't feel you can trust me to take you to your brother, then I'll give you the keys and get out right here. You can take the car and return to LA if you like. But for your own safety, I suggest you go to Zeke."

Something broke in her when he said that. She recalled the day they had met, when Gangster had run up to her in the park. He had been so open with her from the very start that she'd been peculiarly drawn to him. She wanted to believe with all her heart that he wouldn't hurt her now, but Desi was her friend. She had known her longer. Still, Calvin *had* let her make those phone calls. If he intended to harm her, he wouldn't have permitted that.

The two sat quietly for several long minutes while Alex agonized over her own thoughts. Maybe changing his identity had something to do with his own family. Maybe he had changed his name for professional reasons—people do that all the time. There had to be a logical explanation to this and everyone was simply overreacting.

"I'm sorry, Calvin. But why would Desi lie to me?"

"She didn't," he said in a strained voice. Calvin frantically began clutching his chest and gasping for air. His eyes rolled upwards and he instantly looked terribly flushed. He threw open his door and struggled with his collar.

Alex reached across the seat to grasp his shoulder. "Calvin! What is it?"

"I'll be okay in a few minutes," he said, turning off the engine. Alex stared in horror as Calvin reached trembling hands into his shirt pocket. He became frustrated when he couldn't stop the shaking long enough to obtain whatever he was reaching for. She quickly opened the pocket for him and pulled out a prescription bottle.

"How many?"

"One. Under...tongue." Calvin spoke through labored breaths. Alex sat for a long time, waiting for a sign that his pain was subsiding. Without warning, she began to sob.

"I'm so sorry I upset you."

"I've had a ticker problem for several years now," he said, finally beginning to breathe normally. "It's not your fault. But I'm going to need to rest for a while. Can I have your word that you won't make anymore calls until we've had a chance to talk this out?"

***

Zeke's nerves were as taut as wire. His expectation level was peaked, but he felt stiff and exhausted. Cleaning the cottage would keep his mind off all the things that were whirling around in his head. He pondered the likelihood that Lou was actually behind hiring Rosell. It didn't make sense. In spite of Lou's questionable character, Zeke knew that he loved Alex and wouldn't do anything to hurt her. On the other hand, Zeke had no problem believing that Lou would hurt him. If it wasn't so absurd, he would be a perfect suspect.

The breeze felt good coming through the trees that surrounded the little cottage. He stood on the landing just opposite the porch, and glanced up into the limbs. It had been a long time since he'd allowed himself the luxury of enjoying the outdoors like this.

The cottage was overrun with dust, cobwebs and junk. It had no doubt seen better years. Zeke and Casey had busied themselves carting boxes of items to the small shed in the back. The grounds were still quite pleasing to the eye and soothing to the soul.

The flowers, trees and even the little spring—though it was presently dry due to the lack of rain, were beautiful. It would make a nice scene for a post card, something he was sure Alex would enjoy photographing. Though rustic and worn, the property had a distinction that he knew she could appreciate.

He wondered why he hadn't figured out that she wasn't happy with her modeling career any earlier. It all seemed so clear now—her love for photography, her throwing herself into the hospital work, and God knows what else. Puzzles, he thought.

After several hours, Zeke and Casey stopped cleaning and took a break on the porch. They had spruced up the little place as much as they could and it wasn't looking half-bad. Sylvia had brought down a load of towels, linens and a couple of throws to drape over the antediluvian furniture. Zeke smiled at the drab color, but had to admit that it gave the place more of a lift than just brushing out the dust alone had done.

"You know, this really is a nice place," Casey said, seeming to read Zeke's thoughts. "Maybe we didn't quite appreciate it when we were younger."

"Yeah, we did. Just in a different way. We thought we were rich, remember?"

"We were—where it mattered."

"I was just thinking that Alex would be out here taking hundreds of pictures."

"I was thinking of her, too," Casey said. "Zeke, I need to tell you something. I've been wondering how to tell you this without getting your hopes up. But Earl told me just a while ago that Desi got a call from Alex on her cell phone. He didn't know any details. He was going to check it out and see if he could ascertain the number she called from."

"Just in case Alex has tried to call one of us—I think we should check our answering machines again," Zeke said.

***

Alex anxiously flipped the remote while she listened to Calvin's deafening snore in the next bed. She had been extremely relieved that the pain in his chest had lessened, but wondered how long he'd been in agony. She had initially thought that all the stops they made along the way were due to his wanting to keep a low profile, but apparently he had needed the rest. She was sick with remorse for having betrayed his trust. Here he was trying to help her escape the same fate that had come to Star, and all she was doing was fighting him every step of the way.

Despite her previous vacillating, she did trust him. She knew that now. She wasn't sure why with all the unanswered questions plaguing her thoughts, but she did. He had said that Desi hadn't lied about saying he wasn't who he said he was, but he hadn't elaborated. What could he have meant?

Clearly, there was something about him that was unthreatening and sincere. And even after knowing him only a few months, she had trusted him with her life.

What had he reminded her of earlier? Something about her trust having to be in the one who would never leave her. She knew he'd been referring to God. And she knew that he was sincere in his faith. How could she have let her frustration overrun good sense and accuse him? She'd even made the mistake of accusing God—like Job's wife. "Forgive me, Lord," she whispered.

*A steady rock won't sink or slide.*

Her aunt's adage floated into her thoughts and made her smile. God *is* a steady rock; she reminded herself. She pondered the depth of her aunt's pet phrase and hungered to understand its fullness. Maybe He would make it clear to her soon.

For as long as Alex could remember, most of the men in her world hadn't been very consistent. Even her uncle, who she was sure loved her, hadn't been consistent—available, but not consistent. She had trusted so willingly—so foolishly. It was no wonder she had become suspicious of Calvin.

Though the change in objective might be a noble aim, she had to admit that it had its drawbacks. She had maybe become far too unstable—suspicious. Her uncle, who had given her no reason to doubt his love, had even fallen victim to her skepticism.

She thought about the hedge of protection that God had placed around her. And despite His obvious use of mere men to protect her, she was to look only to Him. She knew God would never change or forsake her. She had to keep that in her mind, even when it looked the other way around.

She silently craved the same kind of happiness that Zeke seemed to have with Peg and Tracee, and wondered if she would ever experience it. That should be the last thing on her mind right now, she thought, glancing over at Calvin.

She was very happy that Zeke had a beautiful family. She admired their devotion to each other. Theirs was a special bond—one that God was an intricate part of. But maybe that wasn't even a part of His plan for her. Her heart sank at the thought, but soared when she remembered that He had placed the desires in her heart that would come to fruition if she allowed them. Perhaps marriage was one of them. She hoped so anyway.

Alex impatiently flicked the television off and lay back against the headboard. By the dim lighting in the room, she watched a daddy-long-leg saunter across the flowery plain of wallpaper.

She was so tired of looking at motel rooms and highway lines that she could scream. All at once, the door in the room next to theirs slammed shut, jarring the wall and literally knocking the vermin to the floor. Instinctively, Alex leapt to her feet in the middle of the bed.

"What are you doing?" Calvin asked sleepily, having been jarred awake by the door.

"T—There's a daddy-long-leg," Alex said, pointing and prancing from one foot to the other. Calvin chuckled lightly and got up.

He quickly slammed his shoe against the leggy creature. "How long have I been asleep?"

"A couple of hours," Alex said, dropping back down onto the bed. "How do you feel?"

"Good as new. Did you get any sleep at all?"

"Not really," she answered, not wanting to tell him that his snoring had disallowed it.

"Well, I'm good to go. You can sleep in the car. We have to keep moving."

"You want me to drive for a while?"

"Get some sleep first."

Alex was jarred awake when she felt the engine stop. She opened her eyes to find them at a service station and glanced at Calvin doubtfully as he glanced at the darkening sky over head.

"Why don't you go freshen up? We've been driving while. It looks like we may be in for a little rain. I'll just run next door and pick us up something to eat. Will you be al right?"

"Sure," she said muddled. "But something a little health-
ier than we've been eating."

"Yes, ma'am."

She watched Calvin drive to the pump to gas up, while she
casually strolled to the attendant for the key. By the time she
stepped around the corner, he was pulling into the parking lot
next door. She waved and entered the rest room.

Alex found herself wondering when Calvin would explain
his identity, but she wasn't worried about it. Tossing the paper
towel into the trash, she combed through her hair and grabbed
her bag from the sink. She was abruptly jolted by the familiar
sound of a musical chime. She had heard it that night in the
dark—the night that she and Star were hurt.

Quickly swinging around, she was stunned to find herself
facing the man she recognized as the driver who had followed
her from Arizona. She gasped and tried to back away as he
toyed with the braided cord in his hands. All at once, the
description that Star had given her of the grocery man came to
mind. This was Star's new friend, Ed.

Alex watched his face, horrified, as the fine lines around
his eyes tightened in laughter.

"Hello, sweet Tabitha." There was no mistaking it. This
was indeed the Shadow. The low gravelly tone of his voice
and the sneer were repulsive to her. She turned her face away,
hoping he would just disappear.

Moving closer, the stranger took her chin between his fingers, forcing her to face him again. She shrank back and drew
in a sharp breath as terror gripped her all over again. This guy
was obviously mentally unstable, so she determined that she
had to calm down and keep her expression carefully passive—
lest the slightest quiver push him over the edge.

She felt her strength gradually abandoning her as she
shrank back even more against the wall. *A steady rock wont
sink or slide.*

"What do you want?" she shouted. "Why have you been
following me?"

"Don't you know?" He moved close enough that Alex
could smell the pungent combination of cigarettes and a foul

# Fragment In The Sand

breath. "Because you belong to me, my sweet. No one else can have you."

"Get away from me!" she demanded, attempting to push him away. "I belong to God alone."

"Ahh," he crooned, "the illustrious sound of piety. I'm impressed." His wicked laugh was raspy and devious. "I've been following you ever since you left California, you know. Been waiting to get you alone. I'll have you cursing your God before too long."

Alex opened her mouth to scream, but he quickly shoved something in it that made her retch. Roughly spinning her around, he placed tape across it and began to bind her hands behind her back with the cord. Alex struggled violently against him, weaving in and out of coherence. *Oh, God. Please help me.*

He grabbed her by the collar, yanking her face up close to his. She stiffened, feeling the abrasive stubble scraping against her skin. The gag along with the scent of this evil brute was nauseating.

"I've been fired," he said through clenched teeth. "I'm on my own now. You were promised to me from the beginning and I intend to collect." He began to snicker again, winding his fingers tightly through her hair. "Your roommate had a little crush on me. Did you know that? But it was you that I wanted. You're so pretty. I can hardly wait to finally get you home." His eyes were bloodshot and his teeth were ragged.

Finally, after all this time, she was face to face with her stalker, a moment she had dreaded for weeks. Only she had hoped that her first encounter with him would be from behind a locked cage. Now that the moment was here, she could hardly keep her eyes open, yet she wanted desperately to figure out who he was and why he was so obsessed with her. Star obviously had no idea that she had been interested in a psychopath.

*I'm going to die in a gas station bathroom.* Her breathing suddenly sped up and her heart felt as if it would pound her in two. As the moments passed, she grew totally numb. The sensation was familiar. She had experienced it as a child when she'd slipped into her inner world.

Nearly slipping from his arms, she shrank back as he low-

226

ered his mouth to her neck. She could feel his hot, sticky breath against her skin and involuntarily gagged. All strength was draining from her, and he caught her just as her knees gave way. His hands were rough. She hoped keeping her eyes closed would squelch the nausea.

"Open your eyes, sweet Tabitha. I want you to watch what I'm about to do."

She ignored him, closing them even tighter.

He angrily yanked her up by her collar again. "Open them, I said!" He predatorily began to tear at her blouse with his free hand. She felt nothing.

Though bound and gagged, she felt as though she was floating upwards. Even through her closed eyes, she saw flashing lights—almost like lightening streaks. *Oh, God! Where are my angels?*

He ripped away her blouse like a mad man, but she felt nothing. What was wrong with her? Why wasn't she fighting back? Why was she so tired?

With a distinct sound of fury, the door burst open. Without effort, her eyes sprang open to find that Calvin had rushed in and clipped the man on the head with the handgun. Alex fell to the floor as his grip loosened.

Watching him lie next to her, her burning eyes gave way to heavy tears. She tried to huddle close to the wall.

"We've gotta get out of here," Calvin bellowed as he worked frantically to untie her.

Calvin stood by Alex's side patiently as she vomited profusely into the toilet. Handing her a wet towel for her face, he embraced her gently. "The car is just outside the door. I saw him when I was coming out of the restaurant next door."

"Oh, Calvin," she sobbed, falling into his arms.

"Alex, I've got to get you a change of clothes from the car." Calvin glanced around at Rosell and saw that he was still motionless. "Don't be afraid. I'll hurry."

Returning within seconds, he handed her a fresh folded pull over. Alex burst into tears again as she pulled on the shirt.

"Let's get out of here," Calvin said. "That monster will be up soon."

Alex blinked in surprise at how dark the clouds seemed to

# Fragment In The Sand

have gotten. Her eyelids felt as heavy as steel. She craved for sleep—a long sleep—long enough to forget.

*A steady rock won't sink or slide.*

Calvin's voice sounded like it was moving farther and farther away—almost as if he were in a tunnel. "You're safe now, but we'd better take some detours. I don't want him to get too close to us on the highway. It could get ugly."

Alex tried to remember the list she had started in constructing her puzzle. *The desires of her heart, appointed correction, the timing of God, and a stable rock don't sink or slide.*

Several miles later, Calvin turned to her. "Alex, did you happen to see what kind of car this guy got out of? There were a few cars parked right there and I wasn't sure which was his."

She tried to answer, but couldn't seem to move her mouth. Tears welled up in her eyes. She fought off closing them for fear she might not open them again. And if she did, would she have wanted to. She felt as if she were drifting away.

"Alex, stay with me," Calvin shouted. "Oh, God, help us. She's going into shock."

She could hear him praying and slapping her on the face, but she didn't feel anything. She simply stared at him and tried to make her lips tell him that she was okay.

The words to her aunt's hymn wandered into her mind. *My hope is built on nothing less than Jesus' blood and righteousness; I dare not trust the sweetest frame, but wholly lean on Jesus name. On Christ, the solid rock I stand—all other ground is sinking sand, all other ground is sinking sand.*

Calvin pulled off to the side of the road and reached into the back seat. Punching a couple of numbers on the panel, he shouted into the phone.

\*\*\*

Rosell's eyes tightened in anger. He was too good for this. That old man had spoiled his plans and he wouldn't forget it. He had rushed in just at the wrong time, but he'd show him—yeah, he would show him.

Pleasure and eagerness surged through him as he caught sight of their car just ahead of him. He smiled as large drops of rain began to spatter against his windshield. Switching on

**228**

the wipers, he watched them draw a muddy streak across his view.

All of a sudden the smile faded from his face as it occurred to him that his queen had allowed him to be attacked by the old man. She had betrayed him, he thought appalled, just like his mother—his queen had betrayed him. Tears pooled in his eyes as he woefully realized he would have to kill her—his beautiful Tabitha.

Abandoning good sense, Rosell slammed on the brakes to avoid a car pulling out in front of him. "Get out of my way, you idiot!"

His heart pounded furiously as his fists convulsed against the steering wheel. Swerving dangerously to avoid a head-on collision, he straightened, accelerated and surged ahead. As the breath came raw in his throat, he wove in and out of traffic in order to catch up with his quarry. He'd been wrong. He thought his queen loved him. And that old man would pay.

Rosell's lips curled wickedly as his mind drifted toward his untimely discharge. He would have to find out exactly who had hired and fired him. He was too good to be used like a patsy at the whims of an obvious coward. He laughed arrogantly as the vein in his neck quickened its rhythm.

He'd show them his gratitude…after he took care of his deceptive queen.

# CHAPTER 23
## *Longing*

Casey swallowed dryly as he dialed his home number from his cell phone. His heart beat fast as he punched in the code to retrieve his messages. Zeke sat on the sofa, drumming his fingers against the makeshift coffee table, his eyes watching with numbed horror. Casey was aware that he was distraught to have learned that Star never showed up at Lou's office—that is, according to Lou. They had to rethink their initial conclusions.

"Zeke, you really think that Lou could be behind all this, don't you?"

"Not intentionally," Zeke said absently. "You said yourself that he's made a lot of enemies. We know the type of people he sometimes associates with won't stop at anything to get even."

Casey blinked, trying to subdue the rush of emotion as he glanced up at Zeke. "Thank God," he whispered. "It's Alex." Casey hit the pause and replay code so Zeke could hear his sister's voice.

"Casey, I'm all right. Tell Zeke. I'll see you soon."

Tears were already traveling down Zeke's cheeks.

"Zeke, that means she's safe. She doesn't sound scared. I was right—Prince *is* on our side. They must be on their way to Oklahoma City." The relief he felt was jarring. If he weren't careful, he'd reveal his feelings. He knew that he should phone Earl, but he wasn't sure he wanted to tip his hand yet. Alex had called *him*. That meant the authorities weren't aware of her whereabouts yet. He didn't want FBI getting in the middle of this and placing her life in danger.

"Thank God," Zeke repeated, falling back against the sofa. "Thank you, God."

"I've gotta find a way to divert them to Gregory Falls,"

Casey said, listening for the next message. He fast-forwarded through a call from a telemarketer and anxiously went on to the next. A combination of gloom and alarm warmed his face as he listened to a voice he didn't recognize.

"Mr. Oliver, my name is Calvin Prince. We've had a little trouble. Alex is safe now, but she's been assaulted by the Shadow, and he's hot on our trail. I'm going to give you my cell phone number. We've been trying to reach you and Zeke, but can't get an answer. I understand Zeke is in Gregory Falls, but I need to know what to do. Just in case we don't make it out of this, tell Zeke that Alex's twenty-fifth birthday is coming up."

When Zeke heard the second message, he exploded. "What does that mean? Who in the name of God *is* Calvin Prince, and what—"

"Zeke, hold up," Casey said, grabbing his friend's shoulder in an effort to get his attention. "Could he be trying to tell us something else? He seems to be a smart man who doesn't mind taking chances."

"What do you mean?"

"Well, if Alex is with him and she's all right, he's with us. But he's apparently evading the authorities for some reason. He doesn't trust them, Zeke."

Agitated, Zeke paced back and forth through the scanty living room. The silence was maddening, but somehow Casey couldn't bring himself to rush him.

"I guess we've got no other choice but to trust him," Zeke finally said. "He obviously knows something that we don't."

When the cell phone rang, Casey answered it. "Oliver."

"Casey, this is Earl. There's been a change of plans. I'm sending Sanger down to stay with Zeke. I need you on another case."

"What do you mean?" Casey demanded, his temper edging toward the point of no return. "Isn't he still on medical leave?"

"No. We have a dignitary coming into Austin tonight. They need someone on him immediately."

"Earl, what is this? If I'm not on Zeke, then I'm on vacation."

# Fragment In The Sand

"You know better than that, deputy," Earl said. "This job requires being on call twenty-four seven—vacation or not."

"Put Sanger on the dignitary, Earl," Casey snapped, and with more force than he intended, he hurled the cell phone onto the sofa.

"Case, do you know what you're doing?" Zeke asked, alarmed. "Why didn't you tell him about Alex's call? That may have had a bearing on his decision."

"Not with him so certain that the cases are unrelated." Casey looked away notably shaken, then spun back around to face Zeke. "I can't let him pull me off of this right now, Zeke."

"Case, we've first got to find her. I wrote down the number," Zeke said, his eyes pleading. "Please. This is my sister, and I'd feel a lot better if we let Earl know about this. We'll need his help."

"Zeke, can you interpret any hidden meaning behind Alex's birthday?" Does the twenty-fifth mean anything—anything at all?" Casey asked while dialing the number. He listened anxiously as the call failed to connect.

Before Casey had time to redial, Zeke was on his feet again, his eyes widened in horror. "Case, I know that voice."

Casey stared at his friend as tears began to flood his eyes and the muscles twitched in his jaw.

"Zeke?" Casey licked dry lips as he felt sweat trickling from his armpits. "Who is it? Will he hurt her?"

"You'd better get Earl back on the phone. I need to talk to him."

***

The dull drone of the car lulled Alex into a pleasant easy sleep. She floated carelessly away—to another place—another time. She was in her bedroom with her new dolly. . "Can I sleep a little while longer?" she asked.

"Yes, little one. The storm is starting up again. It would be safer if you slept in the cellar tonight?"

"Where's Mama?"

Alex jolted awake when the cell phone rang. Calvin picked it up quickly, giving her a cursory glance as she settled back against the door. Her heart thumped so loudly that it sounded like a bass drum in her ears.

Calvin's voice was weary and strained, but soothing. "Hello. This is Calvin Prince." She watched as he began to bat his eyes in an obvious attempt to dismiss the tears that welled up. He cleared his throat and glanced away from her. She hoped that everything was all right. Who could he be talking to? She thought she might reach for the phone, but decided she didn't have the energy.

"I don't have time to talk about that now," he said sternly. "It's raining and we may be in for a little trouble. We need some help—and fast."

Alex's heart continued it's pounding as she watched Calvin turn to her and smile. Somehow it relieved the intense apprehension that had risen with the dream. "I'm sorry, but it seems she's not all the way with us," Calvin said, choking on emotion. "I never knew all she'd gone through until recently."

The car lunged forward, causing a shrill scream to erupt from Alex's throat. "We've been hit from behind!" Calvin yelled into the phone. "This guy is right on us! He's in a late model white SUV. I don't have a choice but to exit onto 27 outside Amarillo."

Calvin grunted as he listened intently, then disconnected the call.

"Daddy!" Alex screamed. "Where is she…where's Mama?"

*** 

"Zeke, I've gotta go after them. Rosell is right on their tail," Casey bellowed, pulling on his shoes.

Zeke sprang to his feet. "I'm going with you. Earl will have your job if—"

"I'll need you here in case Sanger shows up. You have my cell number. Call me if you hear anything. Besides, you need to stay concealed, remember?"

"Don't you think we need to get some choppers out there? They said this guy was on them. Come on, Case. Calm down and use your head. You can't run out the door without a plan."

"Maybe you're right. He let his head fall into his hands in exasperation. Then he picked up the phone and dialed Earl.

# Fragment In The Sand

They had to move fast. He couldn't shake Alex's scream from his mind. *Keep her safe, Lord.*

***

Totally out of her head, Alex struggled to a sitting position and glanced through the rear window. The next impact came just as suddenly as the first, slamming Calvin's head into the steering wheel. Blood surged from an open gash. Instinctively, she began searching the car for the tissues.

"Daddy?"

"Don't worry, darlin'," he said with a warm smile. "I can't give up now."

She knew he was trying to make light of the situation to relieve her terror, but she felt herself slipping towards detachment again. "Sing to me," she said, hoping it would bring clarity to her deep swings from reality. "Please."

Calvin burst into song as they both allowed the tears to flow from their eyes. She watched his face intently as he sang the hymn that her aunt had liked so well. She couldn't lose herself now, she thought. She could hardly comprehend it, but she had found her father. Or maybe she was hallucinating. Could this really be him?

Suddenly, a jovial euphoria bubbled up from her feet and sprang to life in the midst of her belly. The rush felt exhilarating.

*"...All other ground is sinking sand."*

"Is it true?" she asked, skeptically touching his face like a blind woman. "Are you—"

Calvin glanced toward her with a smile on his face, and slowly nodded. Suddenly, the Shadow pulled alongside them and with an angry glower, rammed the front of his vehicle into theirs. "Brace yourself, darlin'. Put that seatbelt back on. This guy isn't giving up."

The rain was coming down in sheets now, making it difficult to see. Just as she adjusted her seatbelt, she heard the tires skid on the wet highway. All of a sudden, the car flipped and slid on the slippery pavement. Instinctively she screamed out the name of Jesus as loud as she could.

*A steady rock won't sink or slide.*

Everything seemed to move in slow motion. For one long instant, she held her breath. She thought she felt the car being lifted and carefully lowered to the earth. The sound of breaking glass and crushing metal was a dull echo as they skidded into the trench below the highway.

"Alex! You all right?

She heard the voice as if it came from outside the car. She reached out her arm to grab hold of Calvin to make sure she could feel him next to her. She wasn't sure if she was still alive or not. Everything hurt.

"Alex?"

"Huh?"

"I want you to listen to me now," Calvin pleaded. "Can you move?"

Alex sluggishly lifted her legs and arms, making very slow motions until she could tell if she were all right or not. She could see blood and shattered glass all over her. Calvin looked worse. His face was covered with blood.

"Daddy!" she screamed as she clumsily unbuckled her belt and flung herself towards him. Her heart raced in panic as she surveyed the dazed man lying so still. "Your heart."

"I'm pinned in, darlin'. You've gotta leave me."

"No," she shrieked, shaking her head wildly. "I'm so sorry. This is all my fault." Choking on her sobs, she wrapped her arms around him as best she could and placed her head on his chest. "I can't leave you."

"Alex, please don't be afraid. I wouldn't have changed these few days for all the time in the world. I want you to listen to me very carefully now."

She vigorously shook her head, sobbing and gasping for air. "Daddy, please don't leave me again."

"I don't intend to," he said, his voice just above a whisper. "You've gotta do exactly what I tell you. Okay?"

She nodded, hoping to take the edge off any anxiety he felt. How could she leave him? Her head continued to pound as she tried desperately to hear and understand everything he was trying to say. She sensed her mind vacillating away from awareness and back again in a matter of seconds. "Lord, please hold me steady," she prayed. "Keep me in my right

# Fragment In The Sand

mind."

"He's at the top of that embankment. It will take him a few minutes to get down here, so you've gotta get out of here. Don't look back. Reach in my pocket and get the gun. Take it with you. Go!"

Alex complied, glancing down at the white shirt she'd pulled on at the service station. It was now heavily soiled with blood. She couldn't leave him lying there hurt. "But—"

"Open that door now, and climb out," he snapped. "Run like the devil himself was behind you. This guy is after *you*."

"Calvin—Daddy, I don't want to—"

"It won't be for long. I promise. Listen," he pleaded. "Lose yourself in those woods and don't come out for anyone but Zeke or Casey. Now go!"

Calvin forcefully pushed her away from him. Alex used all the strength she could muster to shove open the door and run in blind panic toward the heavily wooded area a hundred yards west of the interstate. The tall, wet grass seemed to wrap around her ankles like wiry straps. Not only did they slow her down, they offered very little traction for her socked feet.

She stumbled and fell as she made her way through a densely tangled web of darkness that felt damp and dismal. When her wet socks became entangled in something, she pulled her feet free of them and kept on running.

Stumbling hard against a tree stump, she screamed out again still holding onto the gun. Then she lay as still as she dared, certain that she could hear the sound of sirens. Clinging half-cognizant onto the base of the stump, she wondered if she were dying. It felt so easy—so peaceful.

Then she slipped painlessly into blackness.

# CHAPTER 24

## *Evasion*

With more hope than he had felt in over a week, Casey gripped the steering wheel and drove north as fast as he dared. Mr. Webb had given him his approximate location on highway 27, which he had conveyed to Earl just as Zeke had asked.

Earl had gotten a few minutes head start, but had assured him that he would notify the local authorities as soon as possible. Casey knew that he had to be within fifteen miles of the location.

"Oh, God, please let Alex be safe."

As he approached the area, the highway swarmed with flashing lights, piling traffic and curious onlookers. Police cars, helicopters, a fire engine and ambulances littered the southbound lanes. Although all traffic had been blocked, Casey quickly maneuvered his car across the median and badged his way through.

His rapid heartbeat reminded him of how sickened he had felt at the possibility that Alex could be hurt. He could only hope that all these emergency vehicles didn't mean the worst.

Leaping from his car, he rushed toward the paramedics. His heart sank when he realized it wasn't Alex. It was a bloodied man who looked vaguely familiar. It had to be Zeke's father who lay on the stretcher.

Where was Alex? He looked around the site in a state of total frustration. He had to find her. Glancing back at the man, he bent down close to his ear and softly spoke.

"Mr. Webb?"

"Casey? Is that you?" he whispered, hardly able to speak. He extended a trembling hand.

"It's my pleasure to meet you, sir."

Casey quickly took hold of his hand, glancing into eyes that were filled with concern. "She's in those woods over there," he whispered, pointing toward the west. "She's in shock and real scared. Call out to her…she's got her handgun. Please take care of her."

Casey gave his hand a reassuring squeeze, and quickly scaled the steep embankment and rushed toward the trees. The ground was extremely slippery, but he had to find her. She had to still be alive. The heavy drops of rain felt like small pebbles pelting his scalp, and his eyes darted wildly about as his mind reeled with visions of her battered body.

"Casey? Over here!"

Casey swung around to face Earl. "I've gotta find her, Earl."

"Go ahead," he said, waving his hand. "I've already been over there. I'm right behind you."

"Right!" he yelled over the roar of the thunder and continued running toward the trees, following the path of flattened grass. The rapid flicker of lightening made the whole scene appear rather ghostly.

"Alex!" he called. "It's Case, where are you?"

The only answer came from the sound of raindrops thumping against the leaves and the wind gusting through the thick stand of trees. A flash of lightening illuminated the entire stand of trees. Then he saw it. A soggy white sock caught on a stump branch.

***

Zeke glanced around at all the flashing lights and panicked. "Oh, God, where is she?" he shouted impatiently. "Hurry up, Sanger."

"Will you please calm down?" Sanger answered, pulling in behind Casey's car. "Look at that. Oliver left his engine running."

Zeke jumped from the car before Sanger had come to a complete stop, searching wildly for any sign of Casey. On impulse, he rushed toward the paramedics preparing someone for Mediflight.

"Hold it!"

He felt like he'd collided with a brick wall. His halt was so abrupt that everyone, even the paramedics, stood in total silence. No one dared move. Zeke stood rigid, at the sight of his father for the first time in almost twenty years.

Their eyes met and clung together like magnets. Zeke's heart pounded against his chest as he gazed, unable to speak. He wanted desperately to move—to say something, but he was frozen in his tracks, overwhelmed. Then the pilot yelled out and the paramedics resumed loading.

Zeke stared in amazement as the chopper lifted his father into the sky.

*** 

Casey shouted her name as he moved blindly through the thick mass of trees. Feeling extremely grateful that Zeke had talked him into calling Earl, Casey began to silently pray that they would find her soon. Why hadn't he thought to bring his flashlight?

"I think we'll have more of a chance if I go in the opposite direction," Earl called out to him from several yards away. At least he had a flashlight.

"Good idea," Casey said, maintaining his anxious stride.

Small crystal pellets beat angrily against the dense vegetation, covering the sounds beyond them. Casey stopped, hoping that he would hear something.

"Alex!" he shouted. "It's Casey. Please tell me where you are. Everything is all right now."

He knew she wouldn't be able to hear him over the roar, but he had to keep calling her name. Suddenly, another bolt of lightning illuminated something only about four yards away. His heart leapt when he saw the strip of white caught on the brush just to the left of him. Moving cautiously, Casey strained to see as he rushed toward the object.

# CHAPTER 25
## *Gregory Falls General*

Alex opened her eyes slowly and winced as pain shot through her entire body. Was she dreaming again? It was getting more and more difficult for her to tell whether she was asleep or awake. She shuddered at the thought that she might be losing her grasp. Who was carrying her?

Her questions faded to the background when she heard Casey's voice. "Alex, you're going be all right."

She attempted to lift her head, but it felt so heavy that she immediately laid it back against his shoulder.

Thoughts drifted in and out of her mind. She felt afraid, though she wasn't sure why. She could be hallucinating again. She had earlier been so sure that she had seen her father. This may not really be Casey, either. Maybe it was the Shadow carrying her away from the safety of her grave. What was he going to do to her? She had to get away before it was too late.

Alex suddenly whipped an unsteady hand toward Casey's face and struggled to get away.

"Alex. It's all right. It's Casey. You're safe now."

"Casey?" she murmured, confused.

"Yeah," he said, as a gigantic smile spread across his face.

"Calvin?"

"Your father is fine. He's on his way to the hospital."

He had said *father*. Was she right in thinking she had seen him? She clung tightly to Casey's neck. Her head was still throbbing angrily and her eyes were extremely heavy. She tried to curl tighter into a ball. That position had always helped her sleep. She was leaving again.

"Sing to me," she said, fighting to stay conscious. "I'm scared."

"Everything's all right now," he soothed. "I've got you." Using those exact words, Casey began to carol them softly.

**240**

Alex could feel every part of her body vibrating with unmanageable trembles. Casey felt them to—she could tell. He drew her even closer and gently kissed her forehead.

"Where are your shoes?" he asked, grinning. She felt herself stiffen in his arms when he approached the flashing lights. "It's okay, Alex. It's all over."

"I wasn't afraid of the dark," she whispered, as once again she gave way to the comfort of an enfolding black void.

*** 

Zeke stood listening to the raindrops thrash against the window in Alex's private hospital room. He was worried about her. She had been unconscious when Casey placed her on the stretcher for the paramedics to take her. She hadn't awakened.

Glancing down into his sister's peaceful face, he blinked in awkward turmoil. It disturbed him a little to see her face looking so ashen—her eyes so tightly closed. In spite of it all, he was happy that she was near him. How many times had he prayed for the opportunity to make up for leaving her behind? He knew that he was just as bad—maybe even worse than Lou in his haunting anxiety over her, but they both had cause. And now their worst fears may have come true.

"Zeke? How's she doing?" Casey cautiously moved through the door. "Have you seen that crowd?"

Zeke glanced up. "Still the same. I know. There's gotta be hundreds of reporters out there. How in the world did they get wind of this?"

Casey shrugged. "The Regal Nubian is big news. Especially in these parts." He moved to the side of Alex's bed and gently lifted her hand. Zeke was stunned by the tenderness he saw on his friend's face as he watched her closed eyes. "Come back," he whispered. "Come back to us."

Leaving his sister's side he began to prowl back and forth across the floor. "It seems to me they should have more respect for the sick and their family members," he complained to Casey. "It's been five days. I'm trying not to think the worst, but…"

"What did the doctor say?"

# Fragment In The Sand

"Physically she's fine. A few cuts and bruises, but there are no nasty bumps to explain her unconsciousness," Zeke said, feeling a dull ache gnawing at his gut. "I have to admit that I almost wished there were, considering the alternative."

"She seemed so sound when I found her...it's hard to believe she could've slipped away just that fast." Casey dropped wearily into the chair next to the bed, his eyes riveted with distress. "Please God, bring her back to us."

Zeke shook his head. "I've been praying all night. I don't know if we'll get her back this time, Case." Zeke began to tear up as he watched his sister helplessly.

"We've got to believe that she's grown strong enough to fight the lure—that something as small as seeing Tracee or getting into photography might've given her enough hope to fight her way back."

"It's no wonder," Zeke said. "Just when she begins to gain a little self-confidence, she's plummeted with a batch of shocks. I imagine it's been like a roller coaster ride—her emotions being yanked around in every direction." Zeke gestured with his head toward the hospital lobby. "I know the media will lose interest eventually, but I really wish you could do something to get them out of here."

Zeke glanced up when he heard the door open. A tall, slender woman with a white coat strolled in and looked incredulously at him and Casey.

"Detective Webb?"

Zeke stepped forward, his hand outstretched. "I'm Zeke Webb."

"I'm Dr. Doris Ervin," she said. "I've spoken with Dr. Gleason. He's already apprised me of Alex's history."

Casey moved aside as she pulled a small light from her pocket and stepped toward the bed. She held each of Alex's eyes open—one at a time, making a path in them with the light. Then she stared kindly down into her face before turning back to Zeke.

"Don't get many cases like this around here. But I've worked with a lot of similar ones in Chicago. I have to be honest—it doesn't look promising, but it's different with each individual. Based on her vitals, it looks like she's drifted even deeper since last night."

"Have we lost her?" Zeke asked.

"It's been several years since she's been in this state. Hopefully, she's got enough grit to fight her way back. How old was she when she suffered the first episode?"

"About six."

"It's all up to her, I'm afraid. What kind of person is she? Withdrawn…aggressive…arrogant?"

"Naïve and stubborn," Zeke said, feeling the strain of the slight smile he wore.

"When will we know any more?" Casey asked anxiously.

"I believe she's already passed through decompensation. That's the early stage of a relapse. It was probably triggered by the long-term stress she's been under. Mr. Prince stated to me that she seemed to become more incoherent after she was attacked at the gas station. It could be hours. Quite honestly, it could be years, or maybe never."

Casey's eyes widened in horror as he turned wordlessly toward Zeke, each looking as if they'd lost the largest battle they'd ever fought.

"Oh, my God," Zeke said, collapsing against the wall. "We've lost her."

"Detective, I won't lie to you. If Alex feels that it's safer in that other place, she may choose to continue in that direction. From what I've gathered from Mr. Prince, she interfaced quite a bit before the accident. He said that she was very deliberate in her struggle to stay on this side—so *that* in itself gives us hope. Keep talking to her. Keep encouraging her. She may just hear you."

Casey walked toward the window, his hands shoved deep into his pockets. When he swung around, his lips trembled and his eyes were glazed over. "I don't understand. She was a little confused, but she seemed fine when we found her. What can we do to help her?"

"Let her know that she's loved. Let her know there is something for her to return to—something that she was hopeful about. Did I understand that you were helpful in bringing her back when she was a child?" she asked, turning to Zeke.

"Yeah. I just talked about things I knew were important to

her—her doll, books and whatever I could think of."

"The same thing applies now," she said, moving toward the door. "That's all I can tell you now. I'll look in on her later."

Both men gaped helplessly at the closed door for a long time after Dr. Ervin had left, and both men had tears rolling down their faces.

The media swarmed Lou the moment he stepped off the elevator. Peering out into the hall to apprise the new disturbance, Zeke watched curiously as he avoided them with professional tact and toughness. He then made his way through the throng with the help of hospital security.

The head nurse frowned as she stared over Lou's head at the crowd of reporters being held back. "We can't tolerate this disruption," she said. "We've had enough trouble keeping the media away from Miss Webb. She's a sick woman."

"I'm sorry. Someone must have alerted them that she was here." Lou continued on past the nurse and made his way to Alex's room. "Hello, Zeke. Do you think I can see her now?"

"Yeah, sure. Come on in."

\*\*\*

Casey hoped that what the doctor said was true—that Alex could hear him. He opened the Bible to Psalm 46 and began to read.

*"God is our refuge and strength, and ever-present help in trouble. Therefore we will not fear, though the earth give way and the mountains fall into the heart of the sea, though its waters roar and foam and the mountains quake with their surging."*

When he heard the muted monotone voice of the PA, he glanced up into the face of a bearded, white male he assumed was Lou Ramsey. The officer who escorted him in looked as if unsure what to do next.

"Mr. Oliver, I'm Lou Ramsey. I saw Zeke just outside the door. He said it was all right if I came in to see Alex."

"I'm sorry, Mr. Ramsey, but we're not permitted to leave anyone alone with her," Casey said, nodding toward the officer.

"I understand."

"The doctor has asked us to caution any visitors to keep their speaking positive, even though she's...asleep."

"I know," he said, his eyes notably misty.

Lou looked as though he hadn't slept in weeks. He walked to the bed and carefully lifted her hand to his lips.

"Little one," he said, his voice cracking. "We love you and need you back with us. I finally figured out what your aunt was trying to say in that little slogan of hers. *A steady rock won't sink or slide.* I'm sure that you probably have, too, by now. Come on back, Alex."

Both Lou and Casey's eyes moved toward the door when they heard it open. Zeke ambled into the room while Sanger peeked in and backed out, closing the door. When Lou turned around to face Zeke, Casey noticed that his expression hardened. It was only there for a fleeting second, but he was sure he'd seen it and felt a sudden stab of anxiety in his gut. Could this man hate Zeke so much?

"Zeke, I never wanted anything like this to touch her," Lou stuttered. "She's been like a daughter to me for eighteen years."

"I know that," Zeke said, his face a stony mask.

"Are Peg and Tracee doing all right?"

"They're fine, Lou. Thanks for asking."

The frigid atmosphere was awkward.

"Lou, what can you tell us about Eddie Rosell?" Casey asked in a low voice, trying to move the men away from the bed. "I believe you indicated that you had worked with him before?"

"Did they get him?" Lou asked.

"He got away," Zeke answered. "Probably when he heard the sirens at the accident."

"Someone obviously hired him," Lou said, glancing toward the bed. "He's a rebel and hard to control...likes to do things his own way. Most of the people he works for don't care. They just want a job done. But Rosell usually comes up with his own agenda."

"Do you have any idea who may have hired him?"

## Fragment In The Sand

"Anybody could have," Lou answered, clearing his throat. "Perhaps even some of my competitors. I think that I need to get back to the hotel. If it's all right, I'll come back and see her tomorrow."

Lou turned toward the door and stopped. Turning back, he gazed hard into Zeke's face. "Rosell will have to be found. He will come after her again."

Casey's heart skipped. He watched Zeke's face exhibit his own anguish, knowing that what he had to do next was difficult.

"Lou, are you aware that our dad…Charles Webb is still alive?"

The ploy hit home—Casey could tell. He watched as Lou's face grew pale and his lip began to twitch. Zeke and Casey glanced at each other knowingly.

"No. I wasn't," he said, slowly moving toward the door. His eyes took on a look of pain and his shoulders sagged as if he'd finally surrendered to a fierce inner battle. "I need to get back and make some phone calls."

"Is someone monitoring his phone?" Zeke asked, after the door had closed.

"He's covered."

\*\*\*

Two days later, Alex still hadn't awakened. Earl took a formal statement from Calvin in an attempt to clear him of any wrongdoing.

A team of FBI agents swarmed into Gregory Falls and cleared the hospital of media. Local officers were placed at the hospital around the clock and monitoring equipment was set up. The basement of Isaac Oliver's home became a temporary command post for both agencies.

"Do you think Tyson could have hired Rosell?" Zeke asked.

"I wouldn't think so," Casey said. "He doesn't fit the profile. This is obviously someone with the connections to get things done. He didn't really have any. The only one that fits right now, Zeke, is—well, Lou."

"I wish I'd gone to LA when I first thought about it," Zeke

said, glancing at his friend guiltily. "If I could've convinced Alex to come back with me then, she would be all right."

Casey peered down into Alex's face. "You can't really be sure of that. What are you planning to do when they discharge her?"

"Peg and I are bringing her home with us," Zeke said solemnly.

"That's putting a lot on the two of you, don't you think?"

"I want her with me, Casey," Zeke said firmly. "This is all my fault."

"Your dad has suggested that she live with him. He's agreed to take care of her."

"No!" Zeke bellowed. "Absolutely not. And I don't understand how you can even suggest—"

Casey held up his hands in surrender. "Zeke, you've got to make some decisions pretty quick. I just wanted you to be aware of his proposition. I've been thinking. I know it might sound silly, but I've been wondering why Alex was carefully placed in the cellar the night your mother was killed."

"What?"

"Well, when we were discussing who may have cared enough for her to take the hourglass, my mind thought back to the scenario of what happened when she was a child. It was just a hunch, but I've been thinking about it a lot."

"Casey, what are you trying to say?"

"Well, nobody ever solved the case of your mother's murder, right?"

"No."

"Remember when you said that you found Lou going through your things? He's obviously been searching for something. Who's to say he hasn't gone through Alex's belongings? He certainly has had the access. I wish I could put my finger on this uncertainty I feel, but I can't."

"Oh, come on, Case. You mean to tell me that you think that Lou has something to do with my mother's death, too?"

"I'm not sure."

\*\*\*

Alex felt herself sliding downward and there was nothing

**247**

# Fragment In The Sand

to grab onto to slow her descent. The darkness was as dense as granite, yet she passed through it as smoothly as if it were a mist.

The intense foreboding she felt rise up within her was suffocating, and she instinctively reached out in desperation.

All at once, she saw four men ahead of her and she began to move toward them, feeling a cool dankness against her skin. Her approach seemed methodical—as if she knew she was supposed to go to them.

Although they all had their backs turned, she knew who they were—Calvin, Zeke, Uncle Lou and Casey. They were calling for her—searching for her, but in the wrong direction.

"Here I am," she tried to say, but the words froze in her throat. Without warning, she came to a grinding halt and found herself struggling to move. She was trapped—wedged between paralysis and a large rock.

Then she saw the beautiful face of her mother and was instantly released from the strange confinement. Rushing towards her, Alex sensed agitation, as she drew closer. Her mother turned then, but beckoned her daughter to follow. The closer Alex came to her, the farther her mother moved away.

Suddenly, she turned back and saw her uncle staring straight through her—as if he couldn't see her there, but knew somehow that she was. "A steady rock won't sink or slide," he said into the darkness. His voice trembled and sounded more like an echo filled with sadness. Then suddenly, they all vanished before her eyes.

Without warning, Alex jolted awake, drenched with perspiration. Gasping frantically for air, she stared wildly about the room.

Her scream was blood curdling and mournful. "Daddy!"

# CHAPTER 26

## *First Turn*

Casey pushed the wheelchair through the double glass doors that opened automatically as they approached. When they arrived at Charles Webb's room, Alex got out of the chair and leaned drunkenly against the railing of her father's bed.

Rolling the chair to the side, Casey moved to stand next to her in case she needed more support. When he opened his eyes, Casey clearly saw the genuine love the man felt for his daughter. And by the way she clutched his hand, she obviously felt the same way about him.

"Why aren't you in bed?" he asked weakly. "You've only been awake a couple of days."

"Don't get started," she said in that brassy manner that he'd come to expect. "You're not going to get rid of me that easily."

"Zeke?" he asked softly, seeming to pull strength from Alex's presence. She shook her head, making no comment.

Her father nodded solemnly. "Don't fault him—"

He seemed to choke up, unable to go on as his gaze dropped. Casey noticed that his hands were trembling and watched as Alex tenderly closed hers around them. He was deeply moved by the demonstration and quickly turned away to give them a moment of privacy.

"Daddy, can I ask you a question?"

"Anything."

"Did you ever have a pet name for me…when I was a little girl?"

"No," he said, smiling. "We all just called you Alex. Why?"

"In the dream you called me 'little one'."

"Maybe it's just a dream, darlin'. I'm getting a little tired. Would you come back later?"

# Fragment In The Sand

She leaned closer to kiss him on the cheek. "Sure. There's one more thing. I haven't had a chance to tell you thanks. You promised to get me to Zeke and you have."

She offered her father another kiss on his cheek, but this time she held her face to his for several moments.

"Zeke will come around," Casey said, retrieving the chair and pushing it closer to Alex.

"I wish you'd let me walk," Alex complained, placing her feet on the pads.

"This is painful for Zeke, but he's a strong man—a good man," Casey continued. "We just need to back off and let God do his work."

Charles Webb smiled weakly. "You're not so bad your-self, Casey. Thank you, son." Casey extended his hand to grasp his.

Alex leaned over and kissed her father on the hand then. "I called Vivian. I hope that's okay. She and Gangster are on their way."

He smiled contentedly and closed his eyes.

\*\*\*

Alex watched in bewilderment as Zeke pulled the car through the large boarded gate of his former home. She winced at a passing impression of emotional distance, but it quickly vanished when she studied the scene unfolding before her.

Dr. Ervin had told her that flashes of incoherence could occur, but she would be able to dispel them by instantly focus-ing on something positive in the present.

*A steady rock won't sink or slide.*

That phrase had rolled around in her head often in the last couple of days—the last few months, actually. She lay back on the headrest and continued to survey her surroundings. Although it looked vaguely familiar, she had remembered the property as being bigger. It somehow seemed smaller today.

She supposed that as a child, most things would appear rather large. It was still very charming, though. While she hadn't been able to remember much about the place, she felt now as if she was stepping into the portrait that Casey's words

**250**

had created in her mind.

"Fortunately, the last few days have been wet," Casey said, jolting her out of her reverie. She glanced toward the back seat and smiled as he absently flipped the hourglass. "Dad says that it's been so dry that most of the green burned up."

"It's still so lovely," she said sincerely, glancing around with child-like intrigue. "It looks just perfect."

Zeke pulled onto the left fork of the road, leading them around to the rear. The farmhouse seemed to emit an air of loneliness that tugged at her heart. Several evergreens bordered the sides of the two-story frame structure while two large columns stood at each end of the wide front porch. The grass had browned in the front yard and there was indeed a decided absence of color. Yet the scene seemed to whisper out a welcome to her.

"Why are we going to the back?" she asked, turning toward her brother's solemn face. He had spoken very little on the ride from the hospital—even when she'd told him about Star's relationship with Eddie Rosell. All he'd said was, "we know."

He was probably stewing over his own stubbornness, she thought. She didn't understand why he wasn't as thrilled as she was to learn that their father was alive.

"We're ordered to the cottage," Zeke said. "We've gotta think of Ike's safety. Casey and Judy Mahaney will be out here keeping an eye on us."

"Why? I thought it was all over."

"Alex, Eddie Rosell was never captured. He's still on the loose. And they still can't seem to figure out if our two cases are related, so we're both still under the protection of the federal government. I'm just thankful to have you right here with me. Maybe our being together will help alleviate a little of my homesickness for Peg and Tracee."

"Someone obviously hired Rosell and you're in danger until we find out who it was," Casey added.

"Oh," she said, glancing over her shoulder. "I'm sure you'll catch him soon."

"I wish I were that sure."

# Fragment In The Sand

When he brought the car to a halt in the rear of the house at yet another gate, Casey jumped out of the back seat. Alex turned a questioning gaze toward her brother.

"The cottage is back behind those trees," Zeke said, pointing through the windshield. "Sylvia will bring us our dinner in a little while. She's Ike's housekeeper. She's actually more like a member of the family."

"You really love them, don't you?"

"They're my family, Alex."

Alex couldn't help feeling a little chided by his words. With a notable measure of contrition, she purposefully reached for Casey's hand when he opened her car door.

"Its quite a little ways through these trees," Casey said, his face oddly vacant of expression. "Think you can hike a little?"

"Hey," Ike called, approaching them from behind. "You *are* going to let me get a look at her before you hide her off behind those trees, aren't you?"

"Hello, Mr. Oliver," Alex said, swinging around eagerly. "It's been a long time. How have you been?" The same genuine warmth she had seen in Casey's eyes was also present in the older man's.

"Call me Ike," he said, sweeping her into an embrace. "I'm a lot better now that you kids are home. And you're still as pretty as ever, Alex."

"After these last few days, I imagine I look like a sour clam," she said, smiling jauntily. "But it's nice of you to say that."

"Casey, Earl said that you need to go on and get Alex settled in and come back up to the house," Ike said, still glancing down into her eyes. "Now if these two give you any trouble at all, you just let me know."

"It's a deal," she said, beaming up at him.

Zeke immediately led the way through a thick stand of cedars to a wide metal gate a few feet away. Alex glanced around, intrigued by the large wooded area that instantly reminded her of the moments just after the accident.

She stiffened when they sauntered beneath the thick canopy of evergreens and turned. Casey placed a steadying hand on her elbow as she watched Ike and the car disappear

**252**

into the background. Then she saw the abundance of green that lay just beyond the gate and gasped in astonishment. It was as different as walking from one world into another—a rustic oasis in the middle of a forest. It would be a perfect setting for a photography shoot, she thought. There were flowers of every kind just strewn about in no particular order. Blooming bushes were scattered along a mound a few feet away.

The scene took her breath away. She glanced down, startled by the sound their steps made against the slabs on an old redwood bridge. She remembered that this had once been Casey's grandparent's home. It was truly no more than a large shed—unsophisticated and crude, but it had a serenity that held her spellbound.

"Sorry about the humble accommodations, but—"

"It's beautiful!" she interrupted, absently patting his hand as she took in the quiet setting. "Did either of you get my camera from the trunk?"

Casey chuckled. "Yeah. It's already inside."

\*\*\*

Earl was talking on the phone when Casey and Zeke wandered down into the basement of the main house. After he hung up, he gave Casey a long admonishing glance and shook his head in frustration. "Well, how is she?"

"She's doing great," Zeke said, impatiently. "Did Lou make any calls?"

Earl bit down on his pipe. "Yeah. Looks like he made one to Desiree' Sparks. He advised her that Alex was still out. But that's it. He's probably aware we're watching him."

"Anything else significant about their conversation?" Casey asked, puzzled.

"Not on the top. But he was pretty anxious. We'll see if your decision to tell him about your father pays off, Zeke. It's just a waiting game right now."

"A waiting game," Zeke repeated somberly. "I thought he would have done more by now than just call Desi."

Earl crossed his long, lean legs. "He's understandably distressed about Alex. Did you notice anything different about him when he came to the hospital?"

"He was notably shaken," Casey said. "When Zeke mentioned that Charles Webb was alive, he seemed—well, almost frightened."

"We need something else to shake him up," Earl said with a firm puzzled look. "I'm just not sure what it could be. We've gotta be ready to move in an instant."

"Lou told us that Rosell was probably hired by one of his competitors," Zeke said. "He also alluded to Rosell tending to take matters into his own hands."

"You mean that he would disobey instructions?" Earl asked.

"Sort of," Casey said, toying with his beard. "I got the impression that he would go outside his orders if it suited him."

"But what is his connection with Lou Ramsey, now?" Earl asked.

"Something's not pulling together," Zeke said, turning his back on the two men. "I want this to be over. We keep going over the same thing and still don't have a clue."

"Zeke, calm down," Casey said. "We all want it to be over. You know how this works."

"I really want to keep you here for your own safety, Zeke," Earl said, "but your father has information that he refuses to give FBI without your presence. He doesn't trust anyone. I need you and Casey to go to the hospital."

"Are you sure Alex won't be hurt?" Zeke asked. "I just—"

"She'll be fine," Earl said.

Casey noticed that Zeke grew quieter and grimmer with each mile that drew them closer to the hospital. He wondered what light Mr. Webb would be able to shine on the situation and why Zeke had to be present. Maybe it was just a ploy to get to see his son.

Charles Webb was sitting up and waved them over when they entered the room. "You grew up fine," the older man said, his smile brightening. His voice was much stronger than it had been the day before, Casey thought.

Zeke's face looked drawn and distant as he stood with his hands in his pockets. He nodded without comment, but Casey knew that he was at the threshold of possibly his greatest emotional outburst yet.

He silently prayed that he would hold it together and was relieved that he didn't see the former rage he'd come to expect whenever Zeke spoke of his father.

"Casey, I didn't want to share everything without Zeke hearing it from me first hand. I know you both must have a lot of questions. I'll answer them before too long, but I believe Alex's life is still very much in jeopardy."

Casey wet his lips, moving closer to the bed. "Mr. Webb?"

"Call me Calvin," he said. "My name was changed legally many years ago."

"Why?"

Zeke's sudden compulsion to speak brought Casey's head up in surprise. A dubious expression had settled on his face. It was somehow softer, but drawn and anxious. Calvin ignored the question and went on to say what he'd apparently been waiting to talk to him about.

"Zeke, did you understand the message I sent about Alex's twenty-fifth birthday?"

"No, sir."

"Many years ago, I set up a trust for her," Calvin began. "Made my sister, Sarah the trustee. I deposited money into it for years until I learned that Sarah had appointed her husband as co-trustee against my will. He was investing it at his own whim. When I confronted her, she assured me that everything was all right and that she had placed you as a joint co-trustee. If something happened to her, Lou would become trustee and you would be co-trustee."

"Maybe Aunt Sarah *did* mention something about a trust, but that was a long time ago and she didn't act like it was very much. What does that have to do with any of this now?"

"Well, it was considerably more than she ever let on. The problem is, Lou could get to the money without you or Sarah even knowing about it. I found out several months ago that he's been embezzling Alex's money. He ran into a little trouble a while back. The trust is practically empty."

"Does she know?" Casey asked.

"No," Calvin said. "Alex wasn't supposed to know about it because I didn't want her living her life expecting it. The articles of the trust stipulate that it is to be turned over to her in its entirety when she reaches the age of twenty-five. That's in a few weeks."

Casey watched as realization washed over Zeke's austere expression, shaking him to the core. He feebly reached back to grasp a chair and sit down, never taking his widened eyes from his father's face.

"Are you saying that Lou was trying to kill Alex for her money."

"It's a little bit more complicated than that, son. I believe that in his own warped way, Lou loves Alex. He probably thought he'd be able to replace it. But he's simply a greedy hustler—an uncircumcised Philistine. Hmph. I never understood what Sarah saw in him, but that was her affair. He's always been corrupt. I just didn't know how much until it was too late."

Casey sneered at Calvin's comparison of Lou to the Philistines and glanced over just in time to see Zeke attempt to stifle his own urge to smile. He sat rigid beside the bed, stunned and attentive.

"I never knew that Alex had gone through so much until we took this little road trip. Sarah must have kept it from me because she knew I would have taken her."

Casey watched as Calvin's chin began to tremble while tears flooded his eyes.

"But how did you know that she wouldn't have recognized you when you befriended her back in the spring?" Zeke asked.

"I'd lived in the complex for some time—made sure I inadvertently ran into her from time to time. I figured that since she'd seen me in the park and around the complex—if she got any inkling that I could be her father, she would have approached me already."

"So you simulated a chance meeting?"

"Yeah. Gangster helped a lot with that."

"How did this situation with Lou Ramsey get started?" Casey asked, attempting to stir the conversation back around to the issue at hand.

"A couple of years before my wife died, I bought 5,000 shares of the company that I worked for. We had talked about it a lot, even sought Lou's advice since he seemed to know about that type of thing."

"My God," Zeke said. "Do you realize what Max-Stem is worth now?"

"Yeah." Calvin turned his head toward the window. "We stripped our savings and bought in. Afterwards, I found out that one of the owners was connected in some way to Lou and a group of other dishonest investors."

"What does all this boil down to?" Zeke asked.

"Lou knew the company's potential for prominence, in fact, I understand that his group somehow influenced the market. There was a lot of illegal activity—drugs, imports—"

"How could it still be doing so well?" Casey asked puzzled.

"I blew the whistle," Calvin said. "Ever since, Lou has been operating a lot cleaner. He knows the feds are keeping an eye on him. He's still been looking for an opportunity to get his hands on those certificates."

"That was a very dangerous move—blowing the whistle," Zeke said.

"I know right well. When I gave the FBI information into Lou's dark involvement, it made me a target."

"Why didn't the FBI know who you were?" Zeke asked. "We've been trying to dig up information on you ever since you disappeared."

"The witness protection program is very successful. It's separate from the others," Casey answered. "Once a person is in it, records are pretty much sealed."

"That's why Lou was so upset to hear that you were still alive," Zeke said, his eyes taking on a look of horror. "What's he planning?"

"I don't know," Casey said, "but we'd better keep a pretty sharp eye on him. You'll be safe here, Mr. Webb—Calvin. Guards are posted."

# Fragment In The Sand

"The certificate," Zeke said, lifting an eyebrow. "Could that be the reason he was searching through our things when we arrived in California?"

"Probably. Sarah never would have agreed to take you kids if she'd known about Lou. Back then, I didn't know for sure, either. I started my own investigation after I found out that you'd run away."

"Did Aunt Sarah know where you were?"

"No, she didn't. I'd call her when Lou wasn't there—sometimes from right across the street. Before I went into hiding, I would send packages to Alex through a friend in another state. Afterward it was leaked that I was killed...I was just so afraid that Lou would find a way to hurt Alex if he knew that I was alive—use her as a pawn to manipulate me."

"And you've been in Los Angeles all along?" Casey asked.

"The last fifteen years anyway. Sometimes the safest place to hide is in plain sight," Calvin said with a chuckle. "That's why I sent Alex that old hourglass that used to sit on our mantle." He paused, his head lowered with a gentle smile of recollection.

"She loves that thing," Casey said, smiling. "But I don't understand why you didn't just take her away?"

"I moved to LA when she was ten years old. I wanted to...God knows I did. Many times I'd gone to the schoolyard to do just that. But like I said, I couldn't let him know I was still alive. Alex has a very fragile heart. She'd lost everything and had become very attached to Lou. I could tell that he had grown very fond of her, too. I couldn't bring myself to take that away from her, and I never believed he would hurt her...until now. She was safer with him than me, especially with Zeke keeping him in check."

"You knew about that?" Zeke asked, sheepishly.

"I know quite a bit, son. I'm very proud of the way you've looked after your sister."

Zeke lifted his eyes and stared awkwardly out the window. After a few moments, Calvin continued. "Zeke, I purposely made my acquaintance with Alex when I learned that there was a group of business owners that had it in for Lou."

"What about Lou's old friends at Max-Stem?"

"The former owners have already been sent to prison. A couple of weeks ago, I went with an attorney to make sure everything was all right with my stock since my name has changed. They still know me there." Calvin smiled, his eyes pooling with tears. "I have a safe deposit box located in an Oklahoma City bank. The key is inside a small envelope in the base of that glass—just under the gold plate."

"Why are you telling me this?" Zeke asked gruffly.

"I want the two of you to have it."

Casey stepped aside to answer his cell phone. His smile vanished the instant he heard his boss's voice. Earl was panting with news and Casey silently prayed that it was good.

"We've just linked Lou Ramsey to a nine-year-old murder case. He's also been tied to several occurrences of extortion, blackmail, illegal stock-and-bond trading, and money laundering," Earl declared, breathlessly.

"Any real proof?" Casey asked. "We're still with Calvin at the hospital. We were just learning a great deal about Mr. Ramsey ourselves."

"I'm sure he can fill in some of the details later," Earl said. "I need you to get Zeke back out here as soon as possible. I don't feel comfortable with him out in the open."

"Do we know anything about where Rosell might have disappeared to?"

"No, but we've checked phone records and found that Rosell has worked with Lou within the last six months. It looks like this one may be coming to a close—one way or another."

"Are you sure Ramsey doesn't know that he's a suspect?" Casey asked. "Calvin seems to feel that Alex is still in danger."

"If he doesn't, he's a lot more dense than we thought," Earl said. "He's being extremely cooperative."

Casey shook his head. "It doesn't feel right," he said. He paused and then added, "So that's it? You're going to just close her case?"

"It's just about over, Casey. Face it," Earl said. "There's other evidence, of course, but as I understand it, Sanger didn't

# Fragment In The Sand

share what he had collected against Ramsey with you."

"You knew?"

"Your friend, Brenda called me the other day at the office. She was afraid that someone would be hurt by Sanger's determination to make you look bad. He apparently bragged to her about being top dog."

"He gave her confidential information?" Casey asked, trying to ignore the anger he felt rising in his chest. "He could have jeopardized—"

"I know," Earl said. "Listen. We still have to figure out the situation with Zeke."

"Earl, there's still something sticking in my gut. Something's not right. I didn't like the feeling I got the other day when I saw Ramsey look at Zeke."

"Are you still trying to make me think that these two cases are the same?"

"I believe they are," Casey said. He rubbed the back of his neck and immediately thought of Alex. "Are Sanger and Judy still with Alex?"

"Judy and Special Agent Williams are with her. Sanger has been relieved of duty."

Casey was tired and frustrated. "I don't know, Earl. My instincts are telling me that this is all wrong. I don't think Lou would move on Alex that way. Maybe I'm losing it."

"Your objectivity?"

"Yeah, I guess. I really did figure it all wrong. Tell me something. Is Star still in a coma?"

"I'm not sure."

"We could certainly use whatever information she may have. Especially since she talked with Rosell."

Casey was filled with self-doubt. Maybe he just didn't want to believe what was staring him in the face. From the very beginning, Sanger had put him in the position of presuming several aspects of the case in the dark. The evidence they had should clinch the whole matter. Yet he still wasn't convinced.

"Why are you fighting this?" Earl asked. "We *do* have results."

Casey sighed. "I know. I guess I do need that time off.

You were right," he finally admitted. "I am too personally involved."

"With Alex?"

Casey remained silent for a moment, not sure how to respond. "It doesn't matter. I can't really do anything about it."

"She's charming."

"We should be back at the farm in a little while."

"Good. I'll feel easier with Zeke back here."

Casey disconnected the call and turned back into the room to find the two men anxiously waiting for him. He was trying to work it out in his mind to go with Earl's assumptions—to simply believe that it was all over. But he just kept feeling that the case was more complicated.

# CHAPTER 27

## *Showers of Silver*

Alex tried to suppress a sneeze while Gangster lay with his head between his paws at her feet. He hadn't left her side since Casey brought him from the airport. Vivian had popped in to check on her but then insisted on being given a ride into town to a motel near the hospital.

According to Casey's description, she had lashed out at the nurses for their lack of commitment and immediately taken over some of their responsibilities.

Alex leaned forward and stroked Gangster on the head, grateful that Vivian was so devoted to her dad. *Her dad*—it still sounded so foreign, even in her thoughts. She wasn't at all sure how to think in relation to having a real dad and despite Zeke's resistance, she was also thrilled to finally have him in her life. In her wildest dreams, she never thought she would actually know how it felt.

She wondered what was going to happen to him. For that matter, what was going to happen to her? Remarkably relaxed, she surveyed the room and sneezed three times in succession, grabbing a tissue from the coffee table.

"Bless you," Zeke said, peering worriedly at her from the couch.

"I guess we stirred up the dust more than cleaned," Casey said with a sheepish grin.

Alex glanced up and smiled as Gangster sat up and raised his ears. Casey had said very little to her when they were alone. She was amazed at how neglected it made her feel. She knew he was on duty, but it was as though the warm friendliness had all but disappeared.

Perhaps her recent bout had frightened him—nobody wanted to be burdened with a person who might lapse into a state of silence at the slightest bit of stress. She glanced around again, trying to avoid looking at him.

She had fallen in love with the little cottage that was constructed of gray-brown wood and logs. She smiled as she peered through the gap in the boards of the living room wall. She could see Judy resting on the top bunk in the small bedroom.

Judy and Casey took turns staying awake during the night. Now she was tired and had decided to take a mid-day nap. She and Judy shared the only bedroom and Casey and Zeke bunked in the living room. It was crowded and not very comfortable. She didn't mind, though, especially now that they were all together. The inconvenience and limitations almost felt like an adventure of some sort—not nearly as scary as the drive from California.

She still had a lot of questions regarding her dad. Everything was so perplexing that she almost wanted to stop the wild merry-go-round so that she could get off.

Zeke and Casey were so intense as they went over several elements of the case that they didn't even notice when she and Gangster moved toward the screen door. She could hardly believe that they suspected her uncle of such atrocities. He couldn't have done this. At least, she didn't think so.

"Zeke, why did you and Uncle Lou believe that Daddy was dead?"

The question was direct and had obviously come as a shock to both men, but she refused to be kept in the dark any longer.

"I think that he'll want to tell you about that himself, Alex," Zeke said, glancing over at Casey.

"Do you really believe that Uncle Lou could do these things to me…after all he's—"

"Alex, there is a lot that you don't understand," Zeke began, his face growing more serious. "Lou was involved in things that weren't right."

"How's your head?" Casey asked in an obvious attempt to distract her. But she didn't want to be diverted from her question. Her uncle hadn't given them any real reason to suspect him. She wasn't so naïve that she didn't know he had business acquaintances that weren't very nice. And despite her recent

# Fragment In The Sand

withdrawal from him, he had been like a father to her.

Instantly, Alex's mind returned to the day she found her uncle in her bedroom and she unconsciously gasped.

"What was he looking for?"

She hadn't realized that she had spoken aloud until she noticed the conspiratorial glances pass between the two men.

***

Casey stood within the shadows of the small kitchen, watching Alex stroke the dog while she gazed off into the distance. A camera lay on the ground, less than a foot away. Her slender figure was slumped against the trunk of a tree, as if she was grieving for the childhood that had been taken from her. She slowly sank to the ground, having selected the large root system of one of the oldest trees on the property.

She had asked them to give her a moment of privacy and taken Gangster out back after she had told them about finding her uncle in her apartment. Casey knew she had gone there to be alone with her thoughts. What was she thinking, he wondered?

She looked so vulnerable, but it was a mistake to think that she was. He knew this determined young woman possessed the stubborn resolve to get through the curves she'd been thrown. Even so, he'd noticed that there were moments like this one when stillness gathered about her like a fog. She was hurting. Her features were as serious and abstruse as Zeke's had been for the last few days.

He felt a little guilty for spying on her, but he didn't want her wandering off too far on her own. Although Gangster would probably chase away any approaching threat, he'd been acting a little nervous and despondent.

Alex suddenly looked up and caught sight of him in the window. All at once the forlorn expression was transformed into a bright smile as she waved him out to join her.

"I thought you were going to give me a minute," she said, her eyes crinkling with mirth.

"I still have to keep an eye on you," Casey said a little embarrassed. "Care for a walk?"

She jumped to her feet and dusted herself off while

**264**

Gangster playfully pranced around the two of them. He squatted down beside the dog and playfully rubbed him behind his ears. "What's the matter, fella—you missing your master?"

"I'm sure he is. He and Calvin are extremely close and he hasn't seen him in over a week."

"How 'bout if I go saddle a couple of horses?" Casey asked. "Would you like that?"

He watched in stunned silence as her face lit up as bright as the noonday sun. "Oh, yeah," she yelped. "Can we?"

"Sure. I'll just go let Earl know and bring them back." Suddenly, as if a dark cloud had moved over the sky, Alex's face soured. "What is it?"

"I—I've never been on a horse. Her voice was so musical that he felt as if he should be able to reach out and touch it.

"I thought for sure with all the modeling you've done…"

"I mostly do runway and catalog," she said. "We've never used a horse."

After seeing the excitement on her face, he hated to disappoint her. "Tell you what. I'll get one horse and you can ride with me. Stay here with Gangster. Judy is right over there," he said, pointing toward the chair on the little porch.

Judy waved as she rested her head on the high back of the rattan chair, and Zeke sat swinging his legs over the edge of the porch.

Her heart leapt as she watched Casey sprint across the bridge to the path that led to the big house. While Alex loved the fresh atmosphere and was particularly excited that Casey's mood had lightened, she had to remember that this wasn't a friendly vacation.

Something was definitely going on with her uncle that they were keeping from her. She was determined to find out what it was. For now, she would just enjoy her time with Casey.

Already having discussed moving to Oklahoma City with Zeke, she wondered if she would be able to keep her dad in her life. She hoped that she wouldn't have to run interference between him and Zeke like she had for years with Lou.

She was curious what her uncle's reaction was going to be

## Fragment In The Sand

when he learned that Calvin was actually her father. Zeke had told her that he had visited the hospital and was staying in town at the Sunset Motel.

She questioned whether he would be allowed to come out to the farm, since he was under suspicion. She would be glad to get everything cleared up and hoped beyond hope that he'd had nothing to do with the awful things that had happened to her.

***

Casey smiled, as he strapped the camera onto the saddle. He noted how jittery Alex was as he lifted her to the back of the gentlest horse on the farm.

"This is Starbrite," he said, placing his feet into the stirrup. Once he had mounted, he caught her wiping away a tear. He assumed that the horse's name had reminded her of her roommate.

Casey watched admiringly as Alex promptly regained a gallant façade. Tenderly stroking the blond gelding's mane, she whispered gentle words to him.

"He's so tall," she whispered, glancing back at him. "I didn't know that they danced around so much."

Casey reached around her to retrieve the reins. His heart seemed to swell with elation at her nearness. He listened in amusement to her enthusiastic clamor, and wondered how long the simple distractions would entertain her before her mind returned to the present circumstances.

As if prompted by his worry, she began to speak as if to herself. "I wonder if it was this peaceful back in the days of wagons. I could stay here forever."

"You'd change your mind after a couple of weeks without running water, fragrant soap and no washer and dryer."

"I don't think I need those types of things to keep me happy."

"What would keep you happy, Alex?" he asked, leaning closer to hear her reply.

She bit into her lower lip. "My family...together again. And dreams fulfilled...photography for one."

266

Settling back comfortably against Casey, Alex took pleasure in the feel of his strength encompassing her waist. She shivered a little when she caught the fresh scent of his aftershave.

His arms were strangely comfortable—protective, and she found herself wanting the moment to last forever. Almost giddy at the possibilities, she giggled as Casey urged Starbrite into a slow gait. She blinked against the stream of sunlight glistening through the trees as they moved steadily down a narrow dirt path. The intense blueness of the sky, the rich fragrance of her surroundings and Casey's nearness was mesmerizing.

"Where are we going?"

"It's a surprise," Casey whispered against her ear.

Ascending several inclines, they moved out into the open pasture, then back beneath a canopy of trees much different from the ones that surrounded the cottage. The dirt path was constantly weaving up and down, but Starbrite moved as if he knew exactly where he was going. Despite the recent rain, his hooves made loud clanking sounds against the hardened ground.

"Are we on someone else's property?"

"Yeah."

"We won't get into any trouble, will we?"

"I won't tell if you don't," he said with a light chuckle. "There's an understanding between property owners around here regarding passage. They don't put up fences if they don't have livestock."

After moving across several borders, Casey reined Starbrite into a clearing that led behind red clay hills. Alex saw several signs now that stated they were on property owned by the U.S. government.

She shuddered with excitement when she heard the roar of rushing water. "The falls!" she blurted out. "You're taking me to see the falls."

She had, of course, seen many waterfalls, but something about the way Casey had described this one excited her. Perhaps the legend of the Indian maiden had fascinated her to the point of conveying some romantic notions.

# Fragment In The Sand

They slowly moved over rough terrain that gradually ascended and looped around the rocky hills. It almost drove her mad with expectation. Casey chuckled and attempted to reiterate some of the history of the region.

Long before she could see them, the thunderous tumult of the falls resounded in her ears, and the soaring mist filled her nostrils.

Casey reined Starbrite to a stop atop a steep, rocky bluff that overlooked a miniature river valley.

"This looks so remote," she said glancing around eagerly. "I can hear them, but I don't see them."

"You will," he said, grinning widely. "I promise." He carefully helped her down and carefully removed the camera. After handing it to her, he led her toward a large, spiked rock. It was positioned just to the north of where he tied the horse and had a gash just large enough to squeeze through. She was so excited that she used extra caution with the camera as she inched through the rocks.

They emerged on the other side on a ledge surmounting the valley. She squealed with rapture the moment she looked up. The beautiful silvery water skirted the rocks in an untamed effort to join the river. She was frozen in awe. Her voice was as hushed as if she were praying. "It's breathtaking."

"I thought you'd like it."

"My goodness," she said. "Is that the only way to get to such a beautiful display of God's conception?"

"Oh, no," he said, never taking his eyes off of her. "I just thought it would be more suspenseful coming the back way. Besides, Earl wouldn't let me bring you out in the open."

Alex glanced up at the top of the bluff, looking for the place from which the sorrowful maiden had leapt. "Can we just sit here and watch it for a while?"

Sliding to the ground, she snuggled comfortably against a rock and immediately began snapping the shutter of the medium format camera. "I wish I had my tripod."

In defiance of the sultry heat, the secluded enclosure was cool and enchanting. It also evoked fanciful thoughts that made her quiver in quandary.

Out of the corner of her eye, she stole a glance at Casey who squatted close to the ground just ahead of her. He stared stoically at the falls, seemingly unaware that she was even there. She couldn't resist snapping several shots of him with the serene but vigorous backdrop.

Overwhelmed with intrusive thoughts, Alex placed the camera by her side and gazed at the man she'd fallen in love with. She suddenly felt very lonely, and realized that she was being silly. She obviously expected him to feel the same enchantment as she did, and that simply wasn't being fair. He hadn't made her any promises, nor had they discussed their feelings. He hadn't even tried to kiss her again. That had to tell her something.

She had grown. She could tell. Like adjusting the lens of her camera, she had perfected tactics to refocus when she felt the other world closing in around her. She had to use the same trust in God to stabilize her affections.

*A steady rock won't sink or slide.*

The sound and the movement of the water over the face of such an unmoving, steep, bluff suddenly overwhelmed her. In spite of how small it made her feel it also sparked a sense of awareness in her. She shuddered as her aunt's pet phrase and the hymn she now found herself humming came together in her mind.

She recalled the puzzle list she had started. She knew that the desires of her heart were photography and a family of her own. The appointed correction of her marriage to Robbie had come just after she recognized her true desires. Then there was the timing of God that Pastor Frank had mentioned. And the strange way that she'd met Calvin, only to learn later that he was her father. She'd actually gotten the answer to her child-hood quest.

Alex frowned as she silently worked to put the puzzle together. She knew that God had awakened her to the desires of her heart so that she would recognize them when He brought them to her. She thought of her aunt's hymn and adage, and suddenly realized that they were one and the same. She didn't know how, but she knew that He had been showing her that she must depend only on Him for everything, including her fulfill-

# Fragment In The Sand

ment.

No matter how many people there were around her—no matter how many of them she trusted—she had to trust God more. The Holy Spirit was actually showing her something—offering her comfort, hope and strength. Overcome with delight, her eyes began to pool with tears.

"What's that tune?" Casey asked, still looking ahead. Her silence prompted him to turn around, and she abruptly tried to glance away before he saw her tears. He instantly moved to her side and turned her face back toward him.

"You've been crying."

"Not really," she said, swallowing dryly. She watched his solemn expression grow tender as he traced the damp trail down her cheeks with his finger. Her heart pounded savagely against her chest as she watched the beads of perspiration form on his head. His mustache twitched a little as the natural curve of his lips began to melt.

"Christ the solid Rock," she managed.

"Your aunt's hymn?"

"Yeah."

"Your uncle mentioned something about figuring out its meaning when he came to the hospital."

"He did?" she asked, puzzled. "How bizarre."

Casey absently picked up a blade of grass and placed it between his teeth as he turned back towards the falls.

She felt something stir inside her—a rush of longing and affection welling up. He was handsome—wonderful—and his quiet attitude was mocking her like the illusive images of a dream.

Without conscious thought, Alex extended a hand toward him as if she could pull him back from the miles he'd abruptly placed between them. But he never saw it. What was he thinking about, she wondered. Why was he so distant? She had allowed him to become much too important to her, she realized. She also recognized that she was in love with him. But she knew that she would be all right if he couldn't feel the same way. She actually knew.

"Casey?"

No response.

"Casey!" This time her voice was stronger, louder and more certain. He turned.

"Yeah?"

"Are you all right?"

It was a simple question—one that should bring him back within her reach. But when their eyes met, his gaze was filled with an expression that made her shudder. Suddenly, he glanced away again and stood up, removing the grass from his lips. "We'd better be getting back," he said coolly. "It'll be dark soon and Earl will have my hide if we're not back."

Disappointment and agony washed over her. Why was she putting herself through this? She had to give it up. Now.

Alex stiffened and straightened her back as she grabbed her camera. Reaching for the hand that he offered her, she stood and following him through the split in the rock. She silently winced at the feeling of rejection easing over her.

"We'll come back another time," he whispered.

Alex looked up into his brawny face, and without warning, Casey drew her closer. His gaze seemed to permeate the very depths of her soul. Instantly, she longed to feel his lips against hers. She shivered as a tingle danced down her spine in anticipation.

When he abruptly released her, the disappointment was so overwhelming she wanted to slap his face. Why was he toying with her feelings like this?

Before she could utter the question, she halted at the hardness in his expression. Clasping a dispassionate hand on her elbow, Casey steered her toward the horse. The warmth and daring she'd seen a moment earlier was gone.

# CHAPTER 28

## *Struggles*

"You look about as low as a flat tire," Ike said. "What's wrong, Zeke?"

Ike Oliver poured coffee into Zeke's half empty cup while Sylvia noisily went about doing her cleaning.

They had always spent more time in the kitchen than any other room in the house. It was large, warm, and homey.

"Guess I'm missing my family."

"Peg and Tracee doing all right?"

"Yeah. They're great," Zeke answered, gulping a sample of the hot coffee. "I don't know…I just feel so out of place with everything that's going on—Alex and, well, you know."

"Having trouble knowing how to respond to your dad?" Ike asked, sitting down at the table across from Zeke. Ike had always had an uncanny ability to see through things and state it as if it were a fact from his note pad. Zeke had grown accustomed to his straightforward way and actually appreciated it. Even as a boy, he didn't feel awkward talking over personal things with the older man because he'd always treated situations like they were all a normal part of life.

"More than I expected," Zeke answered, wrapping both hands around the coffee cup. He chuckled. "I think my little sister is just about ready to lance my head."

"I imagine so," Ike said, smiling. The crinkles at the sides of his eyes tightened as he took a swill of his own coffee. "She's probably as excited at finding her dad as Tracee is over that new puppy. She's lived her entire life craving for what she lost as a small child…a real family. And now, a semblance of it has come into view." Zeke glanced up at Ike with tormented eyes. "She simply wants her family back, son. She needs it and God knows she deserves it."

"I know," Zeke muttered somberly. "He tried to explain—

"

"He's proven that he's a good man by getting Alex to you, Zeke. He's made mistakes like all of us. I think God gave you an idea of what he must have gone through back then—when Peg was hurt."

"Yeah. He sure did. But I'm still having a little trouble putting it all together. Maybe I'll be able to once this is all over."

"I'm sure you will."

"I sort of—well, I wish it were as easy for me as it is for Alex to shove the past aside."

"You've had something Alex didn't," Ike said. "You had a family that had the same values as your own parents—not a perfect one, mind you, but a family just the same. It may have given you something to hide your true feelings behind."

"Alex loved Lou and Aunt Sarah," Zeke said. "She thought of *them* as her family."

"It's not the same," Ike said. "I think you know that. You were older and didn't need as much nurturing as Alex. You had Casey to bounce things off of. I suppose that after she grew to a place where she didn't crave the attention, she somehow felt imprisoned by it. And every little girl needs a mother, Zeke. She not only lost her own, but lost her Aunt Sarah, too. Her needs were just different from yours."

"But even though I understand…a little, the anger is still so obvious."

"Give him a chance to explain everything to you, Zeke."

Zeke lowered his head and absently swiveled the cup in his hands. "I want to. It's hard. He owes me a whole lifetime."

"There's no way that he can pay the debt," Ike said. "So you might as well forgive it." The older man paused and placed a hand over Zeke's on the table. "Everything will be fine."

"How can you be so sure?"

"It's always a bigger picture than what we can see. God was always in control, son," Ike said. "You know that you'll always be like a son to me. That won't ever change. But your father needs your forgiveness…and so do you."

# Fragment In The Sand

***

Casey didn't like the look in Alex's eyes when she jumped from the horse without waiting for his help. It was as if she had all of a sudden become a different person—not the gentle Alex that he'd come to love.

He'd been so close to kissing her again and asking her to become his wife, but had backed off for fear of it being another impulsive mistake that would end up hurting them both.

It occurred to him then that his struggle at the falls might have something to do with her shift in mood. She had instantly responded when he had taken her into his arms. But he'd had to stop himself.

She probably thought he was toying with her emotions, but he couldn't allow himself to do anything that would hurt her later. It would be cruel. Especially after all she's been through.

Her eyes briefly scanned his face as she bolted for the backdoor of the main house.

"Alex?" Casey called her name after having caught up with her in the kitchen. But she turned and swooped down the basement stairs. He followed closely, taking two steps at a time.

Earl was talking to a couple of agents while sitting behind a desk made of a door slung across a couple of crates. Casey instantly saw the look of agitated surprise when he shot up from his chair.

"Miss Webb," he said, a floundering smile beginning to break.

"I want to see Uncle Lou," Alex demanded, her hands obstinately settled at her waist. Earl raised questioning eyes in Casey's direction. "I want a car so that I can drive myself and I don't need a bodyguard."

"Miss Webb, I can't let you—"

"You guys aren't doing anything but sitting around waiting on a very intelligent man to make a move in a town that right now has more security than citizens," she interrupted. "I need to talk to my uncle."

Casey felt a rush of heat on his face as he moved up next

**274**

to her. "Alex, what's gotten into you? You can't place your-self in the middle of this like that."

Her eyes seemed to beam fire when she turned to him. "I'm already in the middle of it. The only way to catch a fish is by using bait. I think Mr. Gaines would agree with me."

"She does have a point," Earl said. "But I can't say that I agree with allowing you to go anywhere unescorted. Do you have some ideas about the situation that we're not aware of?"

"No," she said, her features becoming more composed. "But we all need this little drama to be over with. You can put one of those wires on me."

"Miss Webb, there are a lot of things about your uncle that you don't know."

"So I'm told."

"What I'm trying to say is that you don't realize just how dangerous he is right now."

"The only reason that I don't know is because I didn't ask," Alex said. "I've lived my whole life with him and other people taking care of all the details. I've got to face this, Mr. Gaines. I don't want to be sheltered from life anymore. And whatever happens…happens."

Casey grasped her arm and swung her around before he realized what he was doing. "You can't do this. Zeke will blow his top."

"I'm probably the only one thinking clearly," she retorted, abruptly yanking away from him. "And Zeke can't stop me if Mr. Gaines agrees."

"I can't stop what?" Zeke said, glaring at them from the foot of the stairs.

# CHAPTER 29

## *Encounter*

The men stood gaping at each other long after Alex had stormed back up the basement stairs. "She'll cool down after a while," Zeke said. "What's gotten into her, Case?"

"I'm not sure," Casey said reflectively. "She was fine when we were out at the falls."

Both men turned when the phone rang. Earl quickly grabbed it up.

"Gaines." Casey's heart leapt as he watched Earl rise methodically from his chair, his face crimson with anger. "Why didn't you stop her?"

"Earl?" Casey moved toward the desk, stopping only when Earl held up his hand.

"No," Earl said into the phone. "Casey's right here. I'll send him. I know where she's going." After hanging up, Earl glanced ruefully at Zeke. "I'm sorry, Zeke. She got away from us."

"What?" Zeke roared, his hands having bald into fists.

"Casey, go after her," Earl said. "She's probably gone to the hotel to see Ramsey. I'll alert the others that she's coming."

"I'm going with you," Zeke said, following Casey up the stairs.

"No," Earl said. "I can't let both of you go trotting around in the open. Go back to the cottage, Zeke. Mahaney's waiting outside for you."

\*\*\*

Alex was annoyed with herself for getting so mad, especially after such a noteworthy revelation at the falls. Maybe she was still half-way living in a dream world, but she didn't understand why Casey was toying with her feelings?

After her anger had subsided, she realized she was due a harsh reprimand for running away in a deputy's car. She anxiously pulled into the small parking lot and glanced around warily. She had been impulsive, she realized, but the drive had cleared her head a little. Nevertheless, she intended to confront her uncle.

Forcing a dry swallow, Alex got out of the car and moved toward the room that she knew her uncle occupied. She was surprised that she didn't see any deputies or agents around. She hoped he hadn't gone out. Maybe Earl had decided that she was right about this after all. But she had to admit that she was a little frightened. What if the things they were saying about her uncle were true? What if he'd hired someone to hurt her?

Thoughts raced through her head with a vengeance as she rapped on his door. The things that she'd recently heard from Zeke about her uncle's questionable practices far surpassed anything she could have imagined. Her heart pounded as she waited for him to answer the door.

"Alex?" he said, pulling her into an enthusiastic embrace. "I'm so glad to see you up and around. Where's…"

"Why haven't you come out to the farm to see me?" she asked abruptly. "I had to sneak off to get here."

"Sneak off?" Lou asked alarmed. "Alex, you shouldn't have done that. Honey, they're only trying to keep you safe."

"Uncle Lou, what's going on? Do you have anything to do with all of this?"

"Alex…"

"Tell me," she shrieked. "Why would you want to hurt me?"

Just then the door burst open and she spun around to look into the enraged eyes of Casey Oliver. She glared up at him impudently, feeling a little embarrassed for her foolhardy exploit.

"Are you always in the habit of entering a room without being invited?" she asked icily.

"Alex, have you lost your mind?" Casey thundered, moving across the room in only two steps. "Don't you realize someone's still after you?"

# Fragment In The Sand

The scorching look began to wither as she shrank from his touch and opened her mouth to protest. "What are you doing? Casey…"

Without letting her finish, Casey pulled out his handcuffs and closed them around her wrists in one flowing move. She gaped at him in disbelief as he began pulling her from the room.

"I simply wanted to talk to my uncle." She knew it was no use resisting. He wasn't going to let her go.

He silently pushed her head down and carefully nudged her into the front seat of his car while tossing the keys he'd taken from her hand to another deputy.

\*\*\*

Rosell grinned triumphantly as he slowly drove through the small town of Gregory Falls. He parked across the street from the Sunset Motel where he knew Lou would be. He'd followed him from the hospital the day he visited. Rolling down the window, he emptied his ashtray onto the gravel.

Almost an hour later, he watched Lou saunter out and get into his rental car. He waited until the feds followed him before he moved to take a look inside. Maybe something in there would give him the location of his Sweet Tabitha. He regretted having to execute her, but she had proven to be like all the others—she wasn't as unsullied as he'd thought. She would have to die, but not before he punished her.

A wicked grin tightened his face. He would find her and there was nothing dull-witted cops could do to stop him. He chuckled aloud and took a long drag on the cigarette before tossing it away.

\*\*\*

Alex shook her head in disgust as she paced the length of the small rectangular kitchen. She'd been stupid to do such an irrational thing. Casey was right—she wasn't only rejecting sound judgment, but she was compromising the protection of her brother.

Relieved, Zeke had approached his sister, but she could clearly see the irritation in his eyes. He refrained from giving

**278**

her the reprimand she deserved, however, when he saw her in cuffs.

Convulsing with anxious frustration, she wondered when this whole situation would finally be over. She had exhausted enough of her mental energy hoping for the impossible and wanted to hurry and get on with the rest of her life. She began to dip water from a pail to make coffee on the wood-burning stove.

Alex flinched as Gangster whimpered at the back door, pulling her from her thoughts. Unlatching the hook, she opened it for him to go out. "Don't go wandering off," she warned, tenderly stroking his coat.

Leaning against the old wooden door, she found herself hoping that she could still have a private moment with her uncle. She knew that she could probably get to the bottom of this whole thing in no time, removing the need for Casey to be stuck with her any longer.

Alex began to recount all the times she'd had doubts about her uncle, but had dismissed them as elements of an over-active imagination. The calls she'd overheard, meetings she'd walked in on, occasions where accidents seemed a little too coincidental for her comfort, and of course, the moment she'd suspected him of going through her things. Not only had the latter incident made her feel invaded, but betrayed as well.

She shuddered, absently listening to the nebulous groan of voices in the front room. Zeke and Casey talked endlessly about the details of the case, but she was wearied of all the talk. When Casey's cell phone rang, she silently hoped that it was Earl giving his okay for her to finish her meeting with her uncle. Her heart quickened when the next room grew strangely quiet. She stood silently in the small kitchen, trying to hear something—anything.

After a few moments, Zeke meandered into the kitchen and embraced her from behind. Her heart hastened in panic.

"Is it Daddy?"

"No. Alex, Lou is up at the house."

"Good," she said, moving to leave. "I can go right up…"

"He refuses to see you again."

She felt the warmth drain from her face at the same

moment that the strength left her legs. Instinctively, she seized her brother's arm for support.

"Why?" she whispered in disbelief. "Why would he refuse to see me?"

"I'm not sure yet," Zeke answered, his brows deeply furrowed. "Did he tell you anything when you saw him earlier?"

"No. He never got a chance."

"We'll know more after he gives his statement."

After a moment of regaining control over her emotions, she asked, "Zeke, do you think Uncle Lou hired that guy to hurt me?"

"I don't know, honey. He alleges that the only reason he is going to cooperate now is to protect you from any further danger."

"What about *your* case? Who hurt Peg?

"Casey still thinks the cases are related. And I'm not very objective right now. Lou has admitted using Rosell's services from time to time."

"Zeke, I just can't believe he would hurt me. He loves me. Maybe he knows something. Maybe he just couldn't go through with it."

"With these new developments, we've gotta rethink some things," Zeke said, tenderly gazing down at her. "Maybe your running off the way you did forced Lou's hand. Do you think you'll be able to handle whatever the outcome is?"

Alex straightened and withdrew from her brother's embrace. "I have to. I've made up my mind that nothing will drive me back into that prison. In God's strength, I'll face whatever comes."

"I'm proud of you, Sis," Zeke said, kissing her forehead. After a few more moments, he left her to her thoughts. She moved back to the wash pan sitting on the wooden counter and began to finish washing the few dishes.

Her mind returned to thoughts of her uncle. She couldn't deny the fact that she had recently begun to pull away from him. She turned his covetous attitudes and Zeke's constant complaints about him over in her mind. Shaking her head, Alex rejected the explanations that rose up in her.

She reached into the window and pulled back the dusty

curtains to look for Gangster. She caught a glimpse of something—a fleeting shadow. Adrenaline instantly coursed through her veins and she quickly allowed the curtain to drop back to a close. A split second later, she felt the aftermath—a quickened pulse and a coat of sweat on her brow. Her imagination was probably working overtime, she thought. She bit into her lip, hoping the men wouldn't notice her shaking hands when she took them their coffee.

Judy had gone into town for more sodas. Alex found herself wishing she hadn't. She'd feel a lot better with an additional person around. She would feel real silly though, if she sounded an alarm only to find that agents were simply securing the property for the evening.

Alex slowly moved into the front room carrying two mugs of coffee. She glanced around thankful that they had lit the oil lamps. When Casey glanced up and saw her, he leapt from the couch. "I would've helped."

"I'm okay," she said, waving a wobbly hand. She tried to smile, but then she couldn't. She was having a difficult time looking into Casey's gaze.

"Are you sure?"

"I will be."

Zeke was staring at the two with a saddened look on his face. He tapped on the couch beside him for her to join him. "I'm sorry, Sis. I know all this information about Lou must have caught you off guard."

"At least we know that it's almost over," Casey said, taking a swallow of his coffee. "FBI is trying to get him to admit that he hired Eddie Rosell. Once that's done, you can get on with your life."

She glanced down at her trembling hands. Get on with her life, she thought. Her life would never be the same. How could it be? Everything was so distorted and twisted and she felt as if she had lost all sense of reality.

"Have you heard from Peg and Tracee?" she asked Zeke, attempting to quell the apprehension she felt rising in her belly.

"They're doing great. Peg's looking forward to your staying near the family when this is all over."

"We'll see."

# Fragment In The Sand

"What do you mean?" Zeke asked, regarding her curiously. "You already promised."

"I want to see what Daddy is going to do. And you haven't said much about him. What do you think of him?"

"Now Alex, don't go starting in on me. I don't think you need to be getting your hopes on any notion of—"

"Zeke, he's our father," she said, disappointed that he hadn't softened. "Can't you find it in your heart to forgive him?"

Without warning, Alex found herself wrestling with a barrage of emotions. Tears began to run down her cheeks.

"Alex, why don't you go and get some rest," Casey said. "You're probably too tired to get into anything like this right now. It's been a long day."

"I just want things to be right," she said, her face growing warm. "Why can't Zeke just do the right thing?"

Zeke abruptly jumped up and moved towards the front door, then spun around angrily. "And how can you be so willing, Alex? He walked out on both of us."

Before she could respond, Zeke had reeled around and pushed through the door. She hadn't expected such an angry response. He obviously was just as tormented as she was about all that was happening to them. She glanced around at Casey who sat speechless, watching Zeke standing rigid on the porch.

Without warning, her fury rose to match Zeke's. Everything she had trusted was tumbling down around her feet and there was nothing she could do about it. "You hypocrite!" she snapped. "You walked, too. I've forgiven you."

Alex could see that she'd hit a nerve. Zeke turned to face her, shock clouding his expression. Without a word, he turned on his heels and stalked down the steps and across the yard.

Alex instantly scrambled up to go after him. "Zeke!"

"Let him go," Casey said, grasping her hand. "He's got a lot to think about."

"What's wrong with me? I'm being so—"

"You're both hurting," Casey said, pulling her towards the door.

"But I shouldn't have lashed out at him—not now."

"Come out on the porch with me. I still need to keep an

eye on him."

She studied the grim expression on Casey's face. She could read nothing in the blank stare, but she was sure that he was holding something back. Zeke had told her that Casey felt that the two cases were related, despite what FBI believed.

Once they were seated in the rattan chairs on the porch, she glanced out at the trees and shuddered. Something seemed awfully wrong. The evening was soft and hushed and Alex noticed Casey skeptically glancing around too. He felt it, too. She could tell.

"I'm sorry about earlier," she said.

"It's okay. It worked out. It *did* prod Lou into acting."

"Is something going on that I don't know about?" she asked, wondering if she had imagined seeing someone in the woods.

Casey pulled the other chair closer to hers. "Alex, I need to tell you something else,"

"What?"

"When your brother ran away at fifteen leaving you with your Aunt Sarah, he was involved in something that he's not too proud of."

"I know. He got in some kind of trouble. That's when your dad brought him to live with you."

"Yeah. But do you know *why* he got in trouble?"

"No."

"Zeke got caught trying to steal enough money to get back to you. He certainly wasn't going to live in the same house with Lou. I think he'd planned to kidnap you."

Alex felt her face grow hot at the sudden realization that Zeke wasn't just angry with his father, but also angry with himself. He was guilt ridden. "Oh, Casey. What have I done?"

"You had no idea. He's very much ashamed of it and did-n't want you to know."

Alex held her breath, trying to will back the tears that were much too easily incited. She'd taken a chance in being so blunt with Zeke, but she had promised herself that she was going to stop being so careful and start reaching for what she wanted. Even with Casey. And whether she liked the outcome or not, she had to find a way to accept them.

To her great satisfaction, she could. She spent the next several minutes trying to produce the words that she wanted to say to Casey. She couldn't help wondering what his deafening silence meant. Out of the side of her eye, she tracked every breath he took. Closing her eyes tightly, she plunged ahead.

"Casey," she began softly. "I don't expect anything from you—from anybody. I've learned where to place my trust. B—but I need to tell you that I love you. I realize that you may not feel the same way, but I wanted you to know. I wanted to start my new beginning not being afraid to speak up."

Unable to bring herself to look at him, she shivered when she heard his gentle reply. "I love you, too, Alex."

Time slowed to a crawl. For an instant it seemed as though her heart had stopped. "I mean that I'm in love with you."

"That's what I mean, too."

Despite the relief she felt at hearing him say the words, she wondered why they sounded like dry cardboard. "Is this possible?" she asked, breathlessly. "I mean—it's so fast."

"Alex, I *am* very much in love with you," he said, standing to his feet. She drew in a sharp breath and struggled to stay seated, not knowing exactly how to respond.

"Casey, I'm scared."

"So am I. I'm not sure—I don't know what to do about it right now—what I can do about it."

"Everything I love disappears," she said, overwhelmed with panic. "Maybe this isn't right. Maybe…"

"Alex, I *do* love you."

She gasped again, not sure if she should have said anything or not—not sure how to react to the words she had longed to hear. "Oh, Case, what if—"

He pulled her to her feet and gathered her into his arms. "We've really gotta do something about all those confused ideas you have." Drawing her ever closer, he tenderly brought his mouth down on hers.

# CHAPTER 30

## *Directives*

The sun was rapidly descending behind the trees as Zeke hurried back down the path toward the cottage. Just as he approached the miniature bridge, he heard the sound of movement behind him. He whirled around and chuckled at himself for being so restless. It was only a squirrel racing up the trunk of a tree. Maybe Casey's misgivings were rubbing off on him, he thought.

Alex had been right. He was behaving like a hypocrite. He knew his dad loved them. He'd always known it. But in spite of the things he had revealed from his hospital bed, he just couldn't come to terms with his leaving them the way he did.

Zeke recalled how his heart had melted the moment he'd looked into his father's eyes at the scene of the accident. He had wanted to go to him, but he was a coward in the worst way. He held on to his anger in order to keep from making a fool of himself. Somehow he knew it was pride.

"Help me, Lord," Zeke prayed softly. "Help me allow the love that I feel for my dad to flow forth."

He scolded himself for overreacting with his sister. Ike was right about Alex. He realized that now. He hated being so touchy about everything. Well, not everything, he countered, just his family and the ghosts of Wade Sparkman.

Zeke's mind inadvertently drifted back to the Ron Curry case. It was the last case he'd worked before all of this started. He had been stunned to discover how long the twin sister of an accident victim had held a grudge. And how God had directed him by a minor misgiving—like the one he felt wrapping around his gut now.

He supposed he could understand. Pain or anger didn't necessarily diminish with time. Before he'd had time to document her confession, God had led him to place Tina McCutcheon under suicide watch. That was also a good call. She had somehow managed to smuggle powerful tranquilizers into the cell with her.

Ten years of holding a grudge was a long time, Zeke thought. But then who was he to question it, considering the way he felt about his dad. And it was kind of ironic the way Sparkman continued to haunt him. Despite his desire to be more like Alex, he realized that there was no way that she could understand how he felt. After all, she, and her roommates had been seeing life through rose-colored glasses. Zeke stopped in his tracks as apprehension crawled through his chest like hundreds of ants.

*Desi—Desiree Sparks.* He quickly pulled the cell phone from his pocket that Judy had given him and dialed Casey's number.

"Case, I just thought of something. Have Earl run a check on any relatives that may have survived Wade Sparkman."

"Come on, Zeke," Casey said. "You're becoming as paranoid about this as I am. Aren't you grabbing at straws?"

"It's just a feeling, Case. But it's paid off for me before. Do it now. Please?"

Zeke picked up his pace until he was running toward the cottage. A sense of dread urged his steps. As he drew closer he could see Casey opening the screen door for Alex while he simultaneously talked on his cell. Zeke hoped he was talking to Earl.

Just as he stepped up onto the porch, he heard it—the crushing of a twig. Pulling open the screen door, he held Casey's eyes as he disconnected from the call. Casey nodded wide-eyed and glanced sideways at Alex.

"His father died in May and he has one sister," Casey said. "What do you intend to do with that?

"What are you two going on about, now?" Alex asked moving toward the couch.

"Alex, I want you to quietly get into the bedroom and lie flat on the floor beneath the bed," Zeke demanded. "Don' come out until one of us comes for you."

"Zeke, what's wrong?" she asked, her eyes widening in

rror.

"Do it, Alex," Casey said, pressing her toward the door to e bedroom. "Lie on the floor."

"Okay," she said, glancing worriedly at her brother.

Zeke turned to Casey. "The surveillance equipment still ing?"

"Yeah. What's up?"

"Someone's out there. I heard him following along the th."

A loud pop erupted, followed immediately by the sound of attering glass. Alex had been at the gun range enough to rec- nize the sound of a discharged weapon. She had just posi- ned herself beneath the lower bunk and was about to rush ck toward the front when her blouse caught on a protruding ring. She instantly recalled her brother's warning about only ming out when he or Casey came for her. It was the exact me thing that Calvin had asked of her.

Her whole body became rigid as every muscle and tendon ained and quivered with fear. The sun had already sunk neath the trees when Zeke returned, so it was pitch-black side the room. She could, however, see a beam of light rough the hole in the wall.

Forcing herself to move from her position, Alex fought the ring that had snagged her blouse and scooted toward the uthwest wall, careful not to make the slightest sound. eering through the hole, she noted the warm glow created by e oil lamps.

Her initial response at seeing one of her roommates was ne of elation. She had missed them so much. But something as strange. Who had fired their weapon? And why was Desi oving so strangely?

Alex gasped in dismay when she saw her friend aiming a nall semi-automatic handgun toward Zeke and Casey. Her d hair was pulled back into a ponytail and she wore all black. Vhat was she doing? The realization intensified the guilt she lt at not mentioning what she thought she'd seen earlier. Vhat on earth had gotten into Desi? Did she think that Zeke r Casey had harmed her in some way?

**287**

## Fragment In The Sand

"Well, we finally meet face to face, Phantom Zee," De spat. "Where is your sister?"

"Desi," Zeke answered with a nod. "What do you wa with Alex?"

Alex blinked in disbelief as Desi moved farther into t room, motioning with the gun for the men to sit on the couc As they complied, she noticed a knowing glance pass betwee the two. This must have been what Casey had asked Earl check on, she thought. So they hadn't been totally surpris after all. She remembered Casey asking Earl about Wa Sparkman. But Desi's name was Sparks. Alex felt too mue disbelief to make reason out of any of it.

"I tried to stop all of this, but it was too late." she said.

Zeke's eyes widened in alarm. "What do you mean?"

"I wanted you to watch me kill your precious little siste like I watched you kill my brother," she said acidly. "I need see both of your weapons on the table. Now."

"Desi?" Casey pleaded, placing his gun on the coffee tab beside Zeke's. "Zeke had no other option. Don't you kno that? Your brother had his weapon shoved in the mouth of police officer."

"My brother wasn't as lucky as you, was he, Zeke?" De said, ignoring Casey. "You had an understanding arrestin officer—one who gave you a new lease on life." She pause and surveyed the room, then glanced back at Zeke. "I se you're surprised that I know that. Yeah, I did my homewor I know more about you than sweet little Alex does."

"Desi, you said that you tried to stop this?" Zeke aske "What did you mean?"

"I'm sure that you've figured out that I hired Rosell," sh said. Her laughter reverberated through the wall like thunde causing Alex to shrink back. "Believe it or not, Zeke...I gre to love Alex. She has a way of growing on a person." Des lowered her gaze—just a fraction of a moment, then lifted he chin defiantly. "But some things can't be taken back once pu in motion. I really wanted you to come to Los Angeles so w could do this on my turf."

"But why hurt Alex?" Zeke asked, his voice cracking.

"Because you need to hurt like I do! I don't have a brotl

**288**

er anymore," she said, her eyes narrowing with disdain. "I guess I'm what Alex calls 'unforgiving'. I've been envious, too. Confession is good for the soul, right? Alex and Star had a hook-up with each other that was deeper than the one she had with me. I didn't like that."

"So you hurt Star because you envied her relationship with Alex?" Zeke asked in horror.

"No. Rosell became obsessed with Alex. I fired him after she started having nightmares. But he broke into the apartment anyway. Everyone thought I was out of town."

"But why would Rosell hurt Star?" Casey asked.

"Probably just a warning to Alex. He's crazy," Desi said, with an impassive shrug. "It worked out for me, though. It kept her quiet. I was at Lou's office, not realizing that he had an appointment with Star. I saw her after I stormed out. I knew she had heard too much."

"Why are you telling us this now, Desi?" Casey asked.

"Because I think the Shadow is somewhere close. He'll hurt Alex because he thinks she belongs to him. By now he'll want revenge against her for betraying him."

"This doesn't make sense," Zeke said. "If you want to help her, why did you come here to hurt her?"

"I don't really know," she said, frowning. Her voice broke then. "It's too late for me."

"It's never too late," Casey said tenderly. "Why don't you give me the gun? We'll talk this whole thing out. You'll see it's not too late."

Alex shuddered and backed away from the wall, pausing to allow her eyes a moment to adjust to the darkness. She had to do something—but what?

Her eyes darted around her darkened surroundings, and located her bag hanging on the makeshift door latch. She scooted across the floor and lifted it from its place.

Alex's hands shook violently as she pulled out her handgun. She had known and loved Desi like a sister for years, and never had any inkling that she'd harbored such hatred for Zeke. The impact of the situation was infuriating, yet it was finally becoming clear.

A surge of emotion rose to her throat, but she suppressed

it. She didn't have time for that. She knew that she couldn't allow Desi to hurt the men she loved. "God, I need your wisdom in this situation," she whispered. "I don't want to hurt anyone. Please be my refuge. I hide myself in You right now, and expect your Spirit of grace to guide me."

Alex glanced at the gun in her hands and blinked incredulously. Could she do this? Could she shoot someone that had been her friend? Standing upright, she knew full well that she had to get outside.

All at once, she glimpsed her camera on the top bunk. The standing strobe stood out like a giant eye atop an alien, but she instantly knew that this was what she was to use instead of the handgun. If she timed it just right, the flash would distract and confuse Desi long enough for Casey and Zeke to get control.

Slowly raising the window in the room, she secured it with the stick left on the windowsill. It was a lot heavier than she'd expected, but it wasn't squeaky.

Rehearsing the three prime directives, she steadied herself on the edge of the lower bunk and eased herself through the window.

*Align my sights—maintain a firm grip—smoothly squeeze on the shutter.*

\*\*\*

Casey watched as the crazed gleam in Desi's eye abruptly turned toward him. He had to think of a way to retrieve his hide-away weapon from his leg strap.

"So, Mr. Casey Oliver, I can certainly see why Alex was so taken with you. You strike me as the protective type. But I'm afraid you won't be able to protect sweet Alex now."

Casey forced himself to think professionally, as he would on any other case. He knew he had to get her to admit as much as possible on tape. "I suppose that Robbie and Lou were working with you on this all along?"

Desi laughed. "Robbie was a grimy cheat. I knew it when he approached me at a club one night. I didn't have the heart to tell Alex, but I couldn't let her marry the creep."

Without warning, Desi's eyes began to well up with tears. Casey was surprised to see her shift so quickly from anger to compassion. She really did have a soft spot for Alex, but it was obvious that she was unstable. The core of her plan was incredibly volatile. He couldn't understand how such an obviously intelligent woman thought it could work. Perhaps the hatred and inability to forgive had crippled her somehow.

"It was the first time in a long time I had actually tried to pray," Desi said. "I had decided by then to just let everything go."

"What changed your mind?" Casey asked, intrigued.

"Lou. He was ruthless in the way he told me that he wasn't going to renew my contract." She let out a dispassionate laugh. "I was too offensive, he said—too rude. And he wasn't gonna' pay me anymore. So I figured I could kill two birds with one shot."

"Why was Lou paying you?"

"I've been siphoning that dope dry for months," Desi raved. "He deserved it. He set fire to his own casino, you know—for the insurance money. But that backfired. After all I've done for him, he throws me aside like a used tire. I'd kept my mouth shut for months about Alex's trust."

"Ah," Casey said. "Blackmail." He glanced in shock past Desi. Alex stood at the foot of the steps in the dim reflection of the lamps, taking careful aim...with a camera. What in the world was she doing? He noticed the flash on the camera then, and surmised that she was probably intent on creating a diversion. Good, he thought. He'd be ready.

Noisily clearing his throat, he began to question Desi again. He feared she had noticed the momentary shift in his focus.

"But why would that change your mind about Alex? She's done nothing to deserve this," Casey said. "Besides, you don't want to allow your anger at Lou to force you to do something like this. He won't pay for this—you will. Come on. Think about it."

"Zeke and Lou can't stand each other," she said with a chuckle. "But they both loved perfect little Alex. I can't wait to see their faces when this was all over. Besides, the Bible says an eye for an eye."

"It also says turn the other cheek and love your neighbor,"

# Fragment In The Sand

Casey countered. "You're young and beautiful. You have your whole life ahead of you. You don't need to do this."

"I told you it's too late," she said, angrily. "I already know I won't get out of this alive. But you're going with me. It took me three years to get myself into the fashion world—I enjoyed every bit of it. Now it's over."

Casey could see that Desi had a lot of emotional issues, but he had to keep her talking. "It doesn't have to be over, Desi. Lou isn't the only agent."

"They don't want me. I've been put out to pasture."

"Why did you get into modeling in the first place?" Zeke asked.

"I had to find a way to get next to Alex."

"This is all so peculiar. Where did you find Rosell?"

"From Lou. But he didn't know what I was up to. He kept a personal book in his desk. It was easy to snoop through it. Calling him the shadow was my idea. Alex is so afraid of the dark that I thought it would be fitting. That's pretty good, don't you think?"

"Yeah—real ingenious. Did you also send someone to attack Zeke's wife?" Casey asked, finally attempting to tie the two cases together.

She threw her head back and laughed. "Don't be ridiculous. Nah, that was Lou. He wanted Zeke out of the picture so he couldn't raise a stink about Alex's trust. He was bound to find out on her twenty fifth birthday."

"So are you saying that you never wanted to kill Zeke?"

"That's right. I wanted him to see his only sibling shot down in cold blood like I saw mine. But Lou wanted him dead."

Casey noticed Desi's hands trembling. "Did Lou know about your engaging scheme to kill Alex?"

"Of course not," she said. "He probably would have had *me* killed."

Casey watched anxiously as Alex wiped the tears from her eyes and focused the camera again. She was upset. He prayed she knew what she was doing while deliberately moving to scratch his ankle. It was a ploy to get in position to pull the Derringer from his leg strap.

**292**

"I kept Lou so busy trying to keep me happy that it was easy to get around his watchful eye. Now I've had enough talk. Since Alex isn't here, Casey, you can stand in for her. And Zeke, you can just know that your good buddy here took a bullet because of you."

It must have shown in his face when he saw Alex losing her balance because Desi swung around, giving Casey a chance to bring out the gun.

# CHAPTER 31

## *Gangster*

Just as Alex began to squeeze down on the button, she heard the familiar musical chime. Suddenly, she was seized from behind with the crude possessive clasp of a man's arms. She knew before she turned that it was Rosell.

"Hello, Sweet Tabitha," he whispered against her ear.

Alex could feel the harsh stubble on his chin as it brushed against her face, and she instantly went rigid with terror.

All of a sudden, Gangster charged out of the darkness propelling the two of them to the ground. The canine snarled viciously as he tore into the leg of her captor.

After Rosell lay still on the ground, Gangster stood triumphantly atop his bloody frame. It seemed to take only seconds for Earl to swarm in with several other agents and deputies. Zeke ran to Alex and pulled her to her feet, away from Rosell.

In the commotion, Casey managed to grab Desi and cuff her without a fight. She buckled into a sobbing child, while Alex looked on in disbelief.

"Poor Desi," she whispered. She watched as Casey held her up and gently turned her over to Judy. When his eyes met Alex's, she smiled at him to let him know she was okay. This time, the tears she felt were not out of fear, but relief that maybe, finally, the whole nightmare was over.

"Zeke, I didn't have to shoot anyone. The camera…He showed me the camera," she rambled. "Did you see him? Did you see Gangster?"

"I saw him, honey," Zeke said, embracing his sister. "I've seen a lot tonight. I saw what happens when you won't forgive. I saw it in Desi—all the anger, all the jealousy. It turned her into a monster."

With Rosell and Desi safely tucked away in a police cruiser

er, Gangster bounded toward the Alex, wagging his tail like an oversized puppy, obviously proud of himself.

"God is still watching over us," Zeke said, gently making room between them for the dog.

"Good boy, Gangster," Alex said, squeezing the dog's neck.

\*\*\*

Following the removal of the prisoners from the premises, they all returned to the front room of the cottage. Earl leaned back in the chair across from Casey and lit his pipe. It was the first time he'd ever seen him actually smoke it. "Earl, your pipe," Casey said with a smile.

"I stopped smoking the day the Murrah building came down...said I wouldn't light it again until I felt better about the condition of human nature," Earl said with a chuckle. "You've done it for me, Casey. I guess your instincts were right. I think you're in line for a commendation. But we need to talk about some things."

"It's not necessary, Earl," Casey said, his toes curling in his shoes. "You were right. Even though it turned out all right, I did get too close."

"Yeah, you did. I know your story deputy. I might have some alternatives for you to consider."

"Alternatives?" Casey repeated. "You're not going to write me up?"

"Nah. In spite of getting too personally involved, you read the circumstances precisely," Earl said. "That's a mark of a good investigator. You didn't even have all the information, but you had instinct. You deserve this, Casey."

"Did you get everything on tape?" Zeke interrupted.

"Yeah. We got it."

"What about Uncle Lou?" Alex asked anxiously.

"Miss Webb, your uncle confessed to placing a contract on Zeke. We picked up some calls he made after you left him at the hotel yesterday."

"Who did he call?" Alex asked.

"He called his accountant, his stock broker, and finally his attorney. It sounds like he gave instructions to liquidate all of his assets. He instructed his attorney to offer his casino to a

# Fragment In The Sand

competitor as soon as possible and place the funds into your trust." Earl hesitated, glancing toward Zeke. He slowly proceeded. "Among other things, he also confessed to accidentally killing your mother eighteen years ago."

Suddenly, everyone's eyes were on Zeke and Alex. Zeke squeezed his sister into his embrace, while tears flowed from both their eyes. Then she gracefully composed herself and gently pulled away from her brother, offering him a quiet smile. She brushed Zeke's face with her trembling hands, hoping to ease the pain.

"Alex, did you already know?" Casey asked.

"I think somewhere deep down, I suspected," she said, her voice now a sluggish monotone. "I guess it was another piece of the puzzle that I couldn't bring myself to log. I didn't want to mistrust him—not until lately."

"Lately?"

"I had started resenting him without understanding why," she said. "And when I found him in my apartment, I started remembering what Zeke had been trying to tell me all along."

"I believe Lou does love you, Alex," Casey interrupted. "But people who aren't yielded to God, no matter how good you think they are, are depraved. God is the only one who can see into a man's heart."

Alex lowered her head, ashamed. "The dreams. The man who carried me to the cellar wasn't my dad. It was the only man that ever called me 'little one.' Zeke never liked Uncle Lou. He didn't trust him. I guess his judgment was far better than mine. If I'd only kept a journal or a diary when I was teenager. Maybe—"

Zeke gave his sister's hand a gentle squeeze. "Don't beat up on yourself, Sis. I've been trained to be suspicious? But I promise to fix things where my family is concerned."

"Zeke, you were very close to your father at one time, weren't you?" Earl asked.

"Yeah. The last time we were together, I fell into the lake. Dad came in after me and fell against a rock, gashing his shoulder open."

"The Christmas tree!" Alex exclaimed.

"What?"

"Daddy has a scar on his shoulder that's shaped like a Christmas tree," Alex said. "I'd forgotten all about that."

"Well, I'm sure you could stand to hear some good news," Earl muttered, placing the pipe on the coffee table. "Star is doing fine. She woke up a couple of hours ago and the prognosis looks good. She gave a very enlightening statement to FBI agents."

"Thank God," Alex said, with a soft snivel. "Thank God."

# CHAPTER 32
## *Letting Go*

Alex and Casey sat comfortably in the swing on the porch of the big house. It was all over. Everyone had packed up and moved on. Vivian was at the hospital and Gangster was sniffing eagerly around the front yard.

She was still giddy from the tenderness which God had used to show her a way out of using her weapon against Desi, as well as the truth He'd revealed at the falls. She indeed felt very loved and cared for.

She, Casey and Zeke were scheduled to head back to Oklahoma City tomorrow. She was excited about starting her new life.

Resting her head against Casey's shoulder, she sighed contentedly as he held her tight against him. Every place on her body hurt. Every inch seemed to be throbbing in pain. She couldn't make up her mind what was worse—her head or her legs. She would love to just lie down for several long days and sleep.

Her thoughts drifted toward Star and how excited she had been to hear from her. "Your nurse friend, Terri, is here with me," she had said. "She transferred to this hospital."

"Why?"

"The children were getting to her," Star answered, sounding surprised that she should ask. "Anyway, she talked to a relative of hers about you and showed them your pictures. They want to talk to you about an assignment when you get back."

"Star, I'm not sure what I'm going to do," Alex said, reluctantly. "I may not be coming back to Los Angeles to stay."

"Call him anyway," Star said amidst a yawn. "Hey, I assume you're done with Adriel."

"What?"

Star chuckled lightly. "He explained what your relationship was all about. He asked me out when I get out of here. Can you believe it?"

"That's great," Alex said, feeling a surge of elation. "He's a very nice guy."

"Cute, too," Star said, yawning again. "I'm getting tired, now."

"Then I'll let you go," Alex said. "I'm glad that the Lord has been watching over you, too, Star."

\*\*\*

"Thank God it's all over," Calvin said, looking at Zeke. "And you say Gangster saved the day?"

Unexpected emotion surged through Zeke's sober stance as he struggled to keep a collected demeanor. "Yes, sir."

He had been infantile and selfish. There were obviously many reasons why his dad had to leave—reasons that couldn't be explained to a fifteen-year-old boy. He had only considered his own anger and hurt. He hadn't given any thought to how his dad felt leaving two children behind that he obviously adored.

Peg had told him for years that he needed to forgive and let it go—and now he was just about to do it. It was the first time that Zeke had fully accepted *his* need for God's forgiveness for carrying the offense.

Zeke dropped his head. "Dad. I—I need to tell you that I forgive you."

Shimmering tears instantly appeared in Calvin's eyes as he lifted his arms and opened them to his son. The tension in the room was suddenly very dry and awkward, but as Zeke fell against his father's shoulder and sobbed, he felt it dissipate. "I'm so sorry," he said. "Would you forgive me for…"

"There's nothing to forgive, son. But if you need me to say it…yes, I do forgive you."

"Thank you," Zeke muttered, smiling through his tears.

"Zeke, I never wanted you to grow up thinking I didn't love you. But sometimes—if it's safer—if it'll make you stronger—"

"I know." Zeke said, noticing Vivian quietly tiptoe from the room. "This may come as a shock, but your doctors gave

**299**

me permission to tell you something else."

"Now that I have the two of you back in my life, I can hear anything," Calvin said, beaming through his tears. "What is it?"

"Lou confessed to murdering Mom?"

Zeke watched as his father's eyes flooded over again. "I had a feeling he knew something about that."

"I'm sorry, Dad," Zeke said. "He said he hadn't meant for it to happen. She fell against the fireplace."

"I'll be all right, son. It's all over now."

"You gave me and Alex all your money," Zeke said. "What about you? What are you going to do?"

"Not quite all of it," he said grinning. "I'm getting married. When I was in Oklahoma a couple of weeks ago, I also looked into buying a house. It's down the road from a certain police detective that I know. I understand that Alex plans to stick around Oklahoma as well."

"I'd like that," Zeke said, suppressing the emotion that rose up in him. "We've got a lot to catch up on."

\*\*\*

Alex wept when Zeke told her that he had made amends with their father, but her elation was short lived.

Casey had come down stairs just before breakfast and found her helping Sylvia in the kitchen. "Can I speak with you a moment?" he asked, looking as if he hadn't slept in a week.

"Sure," Alex said, stepping out on the enclosed back porch. "What is it?"

"Alex, I won't be returning to the city with you and Zeke this morning. I've got a lot of things to work through."

Her mouth had dropped open in shock. The pain must have registered on her face because he instantly turned away from her. "Have I done—"

"Alex, I've got to clear my head," Casey interrupted. "I can't ask you to be a part of my life until I know for sure that I won't be hurting you. Most of what I've gotta work through has nothing to do with you."

The shock of his change of heart was almost more than she could bear. She couldn't have stopped the tears if she had wanted to. "I see," she said weakly. What a senseless phrase, she thought. But she had said it—mainly because she couldn't think of anything else.

The kitchen door had been left slightly ajar and the warm fragrance of biscuits in the oven drifted through it. The agony was so vicious in her that she didn't have the energy to try to understand. Without a word, she had walked back through the kitchen and gone directly up to her brother's room.

Assuring her that everything would work out for her good, Zeke had eagerly agreed to leave before they'd had breakfast. "I love both of you, Alex," he said. "And I know Casey would never intentionally do anything to hurt you. His timing is lousy—but he's got to allow God to untangle things he's been wrestling with for years. And you've got to trust Him to do it in a way that would benefit you both."

"I know," she whispered, her eyes transfixed with grief. "I'm just afraid that the Lord never intended for me and Casey to be a couple. I suppose it was too much to hope for. He's given me so much already."

"Think of this as an opportunity for a new start," Zeke said. "You have your restored trust account, as well as the stock certificates that Dad gave us. You can start your own photography business."

"I don't know, Zeke." Although Alex desperately wanted her life to include Casey, she had learned enough to know that she had to yield to God's will. Whatever it was. Obviously her thinking that He had directed Casey into her life was just wishful thinking. She just hoped that Casey would find the peace he sought in the God he was already so intimate with.

Two weeks later, Alex celebrated her twenty-fifth birthday at the home of Calvin and Vivian Prince. She had chosen to stay with them until she had to fly back to LA to complete all the paperwork from Lou's businesses.

The birthday dinner party had been wonderful. Even Ike had come up. She was lavished with warmth, love and family in a way she had never known. But she couldn't deny the emptiness she felt at Casey's absence. It was agonizing. Despite the inner turmoil, Gangster, Chuck and little Tracee, kept her busy enough to keep the tears at bay.

She had been sure he would come, but he hadn't. She hadn't seen or spoken to him since she had waved good-bye in Gregory Falls.

After the festivities, Alex lay quietly in the dim glow of the nightlight that warmed her room with peace. In that moment, she knew without a doubt that she would be fine. She soberly fluffed her pillow, closed her eyes and willed herself to go to sleep.

# EPILOGUE
## *Letting God*

Casey paused at the door, his throat closing to the rhythm of his hammering heart. He had rushed to the home of the Prince's from the airport, hoping that he hadn't waited too late.

His father had been right. He had been trying to be so careful to avoid the same mistakes that he was making another. "You simply need to let go of the past, son," Ike Oliver had said. "Let go and let God repair the mistakes that you've made."

"I just don't want to hurt her, Dad."

"I know," Ike had said. "And as long as you stay connected to God you won't. But if you keep running from the very things God can use to mend your own pain, you'll wind up hurting everyone around you. Live free, son."

"Casey?" Vivian said, struggling to keep Gangster from pushing her aside. "Come on in."

As soon as she had opened the storm door, Gangster excitedly bounded toward him. "Hello, boy," Casey said, stroking the dog's head. "I hope it's not too early in the morning."

"Hey!" Calvin said, rushing towards him. "What on earth are you doing here? And so early?"

"I was hoping to talk to Alex," Casey said, his nostrils flaring with anticipation. "Is she up yet?"

Casey's breath caught in his throat as he watched an agonizing glance pass between the couple. Casey moved skeptically to the recliner that Calvin silently indicated.

"Alex isn't here, son. She flew back to Los Angeles."

The words fell like stones against clay. Casey's body sank deeper into the chair as the empty ache gnawed through his heart. "Oh, my God!" he said, a hitch snaring his voice.

\*\*\*

## Fragment In The Sand

Calvin and Vivian stood in the shadow of the door and watched Casey stumble aimlessly back towards his car. After a few seconds, Calvin returned to his newspaper on the sofa, but Vivian continued standing at the door watching Casey sit for several long moments before starting the car.

Calvin instinctively glanced up when Vivian snapped the lock on the storm door. Conspiratorially wagging her finger at him, she chuckled without reserve.

"You're a meddling old romantic, Calvin Prince," she said. "Why didn't you tell him that she would be back in a few days?"

Calvin's eyes glistened with amusement, as the smile on his face grew wider. "Hmph! He didn't ask."

***

It hadn't been an easy afternoon. The time of letting go of the past several months had surrounded Alex with surprising force. She had found herself totally unprepared for all the emotions that had confronted her when she had come back to LA.

When she had seen Star, all the joy and anguish had come pouring out—Uncle Lou's deception, Desi's betrayal, and Casey's rejection. They'd both cried and laughed and made promises to always trust God to keep them safe.

As the evening had worn on, God had shown her that much of her disappointment had been of her own making. In her attempt at reaching to Him for comfort, she had inadvertently closed Him out by being so fixed on how she thought God should correct things. She still didn't have all the answers, but she had peace. She should have realized—should have understood that she'd be required to give up everything else she'd learned to trust. Including Casey.

She was free for the very first time. Liberated to live and laugh—and make her own choices about her future. Alex threw back the covers on her bed and was climbing in just as Star padded through the door. "You going to bed already?"

"It's been a long day," Alex said, yawning. "Adriel and I have got a long drive ahead of me tomorrow. I really should have gotten Zeke to come with me, but I didn't want to take

**304**

him away from his family again."

"That's okay," Star said, glancing around sadly. "He's looking forward to the trip."

"I just hate to take him away from you when things seem to be developing."

"It'll only be for a few days," Star said. "You sure you want to leave?"

"I want to be near my family," Alex said, shoving her hands beneath her head.

"Man!" Star blurted out. "I had everything figured all wrong. I was so sure that God was working one of those appointed corrections in your life through Casey."

"Me, too. But I guess we can't place Him in a box. We've gotta trust Him enough to know just how to bring correction into our lives."

"I suppose in a way, all of this was an appointed correction for Desi, too," Star said. "Will she be all right?"

"I think so. Pastor Frank told me that she called and asked him to come talk with her."

"That's great," Star said, her voice quavering. "You know, I'm going to miss both of you."

"You'll come visit me, won't you?" Alex asked, trying to swallow past the lump in her throat. "I'm so sorry that Uncle Lou left everyone in a bind."

"That's not your fault," Star said, moving to stretch herself across the foot of the bed. "Besides, I've already found a smaller place. I found a job as a receptionist and the others have already signed with other agents."

Alex was a little surprised to hear the doorbell ring. "You expecting company?"

"Yeah," Star said rushing for the door. "Adriel is dropping by for a few minutes. What time are you guys leaving?"

"I'd like to be gone by ten," Alex said, groggily. "Why don't you close my door."

After turning out the light, Alex closed her eyes and envisioned Casey's smile. She wasn't sure what she would do when she inevitably ran into him in Oklahoma City, but she knew she would be okay. Right now, she just wanted to push him from her mind, just as she had done with Robbie. She could do it. With God's help, she didn't have to hurt like this.

She was finally about to dose off when a light tap on the door caused her eyes to spring open. Star peered in. "You still awake?" she whispered.

Alex managed a nod. The door opened wider and to her surprise, Casey moved his broad shoulders through the narrow crack. Her breath caught in her throat as their eyes found each other's through the dimness. She didn't know what he would say—what he *could* say.

Silently, he knelt by her bed and took her hand in his, but not without an audience. Star and Adriel huddled quietly in the hallway. Wordlessly he caressed the slender fingers with one thumb. Alex felt her heart would pound right out of her chest. She couldn't imagine why he hadn't said anything, but she didn't dare break the silence. As he raised his eyes to meet hers, the nightlight revealed that they were filled with tears.

"Happy Birthday," he whispered hoarsely. "Sorry that I'm a little—a lot late."

Alex nodded, unable to speak.

"Would you like to open your present now?" he asked.

She nodded her head again and turned on the lamp beside her bed. "Casey," she whispered. "I—I don't really—"

She broke off the moment she saw the royal blue velvet box. When she opened it, the glimmer of the diamond caught her eye. All she could do was sit there, frozen, with her mouth hanging open. She finally let out her breath when she heard Star squeal from the doorway.

"This was my mother's," Casey said. "Alex, I would like it—I would be honored if you would agree to be my wife." He smiled softly and lifted her hand to press it to his lips. "I've accepted a position with our investigative services division. There's not near the travel involved."

Happy tears rolled unchecked down her cheeks as Casey tried to wipe them away. She wasn't sure exactly when it was that she leapt from the bed to the floor, but she found comfort in Casey's arms, scarcely taking her eyes off the ring.

"I'm so sorry that I let fear cut my step, Alex. I forgot to put the pieces of my puzzle together to come up with the picture for my life. You're in that picture, baby. You and as many

Annetta P. Lee

kids as we want to have. Will you forgive my hesitance?"

"I will," she whispered through tears. "I'm still reeling myself—from how a simple puzzle came together to show me true fulfillment. I can look back and see how He's led me around so many pitfalls—how He even tried to show me that Calvin was really my father. So much that I can't even tell it all. Everything that fear stole from me has been restored in perfect time." Alex realized that she was babbling and began to softly chuckle as tears of joy rolled down her face. "You've just given me a wonderful start…hope of love and family. I love you so much, Case."

**THE END**

307

# Excerpts from future publications

One Day At A Time by Bella McFarland
Release Date March 2003

"Why Montana, Angela? Why not go on a Caribbean cruise or visit an island resort?" Nikki asked as she tilted her head to stare at Angela McGee's pensive face.

Angela shrugged. Nikki Taylor was her childhood friend and legal advisor but at times she was so damn nosey. Angela wasn't about to disclose her reasons for going to Montana, not to Nikki anyway. "Hmm-mm, I want to go to a place that's different, a place where I can breathe fresh air and just relax. I doubt that I can do that on a cruise or at a resort. Such places usually have meddlesome people and the last thing I want to do is socialize." Her smile disappeared when her glance shifted to her five-year-old nephew, Reggie.

Reggie was lying on a hospital bed, stiff and silent, his mind locked in some place where no one could reach him. Even with the best experts at his disposal, Reggie had not awakened from the coma caused by the accident that had killed his father and mother—Angela's sister, Savannah. "Oh, Nikki, when I look at him I wish I didn't have to go."

"Don't start on that, Angela. You need a break or you'll make yourself sick," Nikki protested.

"What if he wakes up while I'm gone? What if he gets worse? It has been hard enough for me to see him lying there so still when he was once full of life. But now I have this nightmare that something might happen while I'm gone."

"You've been by his side every day for the last six months, Angela. You've become a recluse, you don't date any more; you even stopped writing music except for those you compose for him."

Angela shrugged indifferently.  She once aspired to become a professional singer, but circumstances forced her to forget that dream.  Well, not exactly circumstances, just her parents and her innate will to please them.  One unemployed artist in the family was enough; her parents had said when Savannah had insisted on being a professional painter.  And like the dutiful daughter that Angela was, she had pushed aside her personal dream and gone into nursing.

"Things never go as we plan, Nikki.  Sav didn't foresee the accident that killed her and Bernard or the traumatic effect it would have on her only child.  But it happened.  And in her will, she entrusted me with the care of Reggie.  Yet here I am, leaving him with strangers."  Angela's voice shook as she finished the last sentence.  She blinked rapidly to stop the sudden rush of tears.  It had been a year but she still couldn't deal with her sister's death.  Reggie's coma made it hard to let go.  Every time Angela saw how still and unreachable her nephew was, she was reminded of those last moments when she'd held her sister in her arms.  Angela was a registered nurse but she'd been helpless to save her sister.  And now she couldn't help her nephew, either.

But her helplessness was easily transformed to anger at the thought of the person responsible for the entire tragedy getting off lightly and living his life to the fullest just because he was rich and famous.  Baseball legend Jerry Tyrell Taylor a.k.a. JT, the marble man, hadn't cared enough to check on the victims of his wife's carelessness—a woman whose state of mind had been entirely his fault.

Even now, a year after the incident, Angela could recall the headline...L. A. ANGELS' PITCHER, JERRY TAYLOR, EXONERATED OF WIFE'S DEATH.

How could he be blameless when bystanders had said otherwise?  According to the papers, an eyewitness had seen Carmen Taylor trying to get away from her husband, Jerry, before she drove her Porsche into the highway.  Another witness claimed that Carmen had been meeting another man at the time and that Jerry had caught them together.  Whatever the outcome of the police investigation, Jerry Taylor bore some responsibility for his wife's untimely death.  Wasn't he seen

running after her, jumping into her car, and trying to wrestl
the wheel from her hands? Hadn't she been busy shouting a
him instead of watching where she was going? The justic
system may have exonerated him but Angela hadn't. In he
book, Jerry Taylor killed her sister, Sav. The fact that he ha
never bothered to apologize to her family or visited Reggi
only made him more guilty in her eyes. And he should b
made to pay.

"Hey!"

Angela blinked and turned apologetically toward Nikki
"Sorry."

"Do you know you do that a lot?" Nikki asked.

"Do what?" Angela asked defensively.

"Space out. One minute you are here and the next gone
And the expression on your face is usually very peculiar—
mixture of anger, pain, and regret. There was nothing yo
could have done for Sav, Angela. And, Reggie...well...he'
come back to us when he's ready. None of this is your faul
you know."

"Don't analyze me, girl. Of course I know it isn't m
fault. I just regret not spending enough time with Sav whil
she was alive," Angela finished wistfully.

"With the demands of those art exhibitions, you're luck
to have seen her at all. But at least you often babysat Reggi
while she was gone."

Angela knew that if it weren't for the fact that she ran he
Website design business from home and that she had flexibl
hours at the private hospital where she worked part-time, sh
would never have been there for her only sister or nephew
"She had so much talent, Nikki. She didn't deserve to die tha
young."

Nikki nodded. "Wasn't it spooky the way that museum i
San Francisco called and offered to exhibit her work? Now he
paintings are the in thing for most African American art col
lectors."

"And worth every dollar they pay." The cheapest of Sav'
paintings had been sold for five hundred dollars. She hadn'
been gone six months when everyone was talking about own
ing an original Hanna Vas—Sav signed her name backward o

**310**

every painting she did. She even used the pseudonym when she exhibited her work. "I just hate how the art world makes money off dead artists, Nikki. I'd rather have her alive and selling her work for pittance than renowned and dead," Angela murmured.

"So would I." Nikki got up and glanced down at Angela. "Now, unless you intend to miss your flight, we better get moving."

Angela nodded then glanced briefly at Reggie. "Do you think they'll take good care of him?"

"Yes, they will, Angela. Look at this place." Nikki spread her arms for emphasis. Reggie had a room in a private hospital and nothing was spared for his comfort. The hospital was only a few blocks from Charles Maitland's mansion—his paternal grandfather. The millionaire car-dealer had even donated funds towards the hospital's new wing so that his grandson would be given the best treatment. "Does this look like a typical hospital room to you? The room is done with Power Ranger paraphernalia—Reggie's favorite TV-series. He's under watch by private nurses—paid for by Maitland. And he has state-of-the-art instruments monitoring his vitals twenty-four-seven. Let's not forget Marjorie Maitland, his larger than life grandmother. She is in here every other day, reading to him. In fact, I'd bet he's had more stories read to him than any five-year-old child under the sun. Everything around here indicates he is cared for. What more proof do you need, huh?"

## About Annetta P. Lee

Annetta P. Lee grew up on the farm of her maternal grandparents in Starkville, Mississippi. She moved temporarily with her mother in Ohio, during her high school years, but returned to Mississippi prior to graduating.

Although she started writing early in grade school, she did not get serious about it until 1990. Her poetry, articles and stories were always filled with an inspirational quality, which is still found in her writing. After graduating from *The Institute of Children's Literature* in 1997, Annetta pursued a life long dream of becoming a published writer. Her first work, A Bitter Rose, was published in 2000.

She later moved to Oklahoma, where she now lives with her husband, Kenneth. Annetta has worked as an Administrative Assistant for a Worldwide Accounting Firm for seventeen years and is currently a Chiropractic Assistant.

# ORDER FORM

**Mail to: Genesis Press, Inc.**
**315 3rd Avenue North**
**Columbus, MS 39701**

Name _____

Address _____

City/State _____ Zip _____

Telephone _____

*Ship to (if different from above)*

Name _____

Address _____

City/State _____ Zip _____

Telephone _____

| Qty. | Author | Title | Price | Total |
|------|--------|-------|-------|-------|
|      |        |       |       |       |
|      |        |       |       |       |
|      |        |       |       |       |
|      |        |       |       |       |
|      |        |       |       |       |
|      |        |       |       |       |
|      |        |       |       |       |
|      |        |       |       |       |
|      |        |       |       |       |
|      |        |       |       |       |
|      |        |       |       |       |
|      |        |       |       |       |

|  |  |
|---|---|
| Use this order form, or call 1-888-INDIGO-1 | **Total for books** _____ |
| | **Shipping and handling:** |
| | **$5 first two books, $1 each additional book** _____ |
| | **Total S & H** _____ |
| | **Total amount enclosed** _____ |
| | *Mississippi residents add 7% sales tax* |

## 2003 Publications

January
Twist of Fate
Beverly Clark
1-58571-084-9

Ebony Butterfly II
Delilah Dawson
1-58571-086-5

February
Fragment in the Sand
Annetta P. Lee
1-58571-097-0

Fate
Pamela Leigh Starr
1-58571-115-2

March
One Day At A Time
Bella McFarland
1-58571-099-7

Unbreak my Heart
Dar Tomlinson
1-58571-101-2

April
At Last   Brown
Lisa Riley
1-58571-093-8

Sugar Diaries
Delores Bundy
1-58571-091-1

May
Three Wishes
Seressia Glass
1-58571-092-X

Acquisitions
Kimberley White
1-58571-095-4

June
Taken By You
Dorothy Love
1-58571-104-7

Revelations
Cheris F. Hodges
1-58571-085-7

July
The Color of Trouble
Dyanne Davis
1-58571-096-2

Someone To Love
Alicia Wiggins
1-58571-098-9

August
Object Of His Desire
Artiste C Arthur
1-58571-094-6

A Lark on the Wing
Phyliss Hamilton
1-58571-105-5

September
Relentless Pursuit
Charlyne Dickerson
1-58571-113-6

Hart & Soul
Angie Daniels
1-58571-087-3